Charge!
A Story Of Briton And Boer

by

George Manville Fenn

Double9
BOOKS

Charge!
A Story Of Briton And Boer
by George Manville Fenn

ISBN: 978-93-59957-28-9

Published by

DOUBLE 9 BOOKS
2/13-B, Ansari Road
Daryaganj, New Delhi – 110002
info@double9books.com
www.double9books.com
Tel. 011-40042856

ABOUT THE AUTHOR

George Manville Fenn was a very productive author of novels, a writer, an editor, and an educator from England. He was born on January 3, 1831, in Pimlico, London. He mostly learned on his own; he taught himself Italian, French, and German. During the years 1851-1854, he went to Battersea Training College for Teachers and then became the head of a state school in Alford, Lincolnshire. In the early 1850s, Fenn started to write short stories and pieces for newspapers and magazines. The Old Forest Ranger, his first book, came out in 1856. Afterward, he wrote more than 100 books, many of them for teenagers and young adults. He was one of the most famous writers of his time, and his books were well-liked and read by many people. I also worked as a reporter and writer for Fenn. Among the newspapers and magazines, he worked for was The Boy's Own Paper, which he ran from 1866 to 1874. He worked hard to make children's books better and was a strong supporter of education and reading. The Englishman Fenn passed away on August 26, 1909, in Isleworth.

CONTENTS

Chapter One
Home, Sweet Home

"Hi! Val! Come, quick!"

"What's the matter?" I said excitedly, for my brother Bob came tearing down to the enclosure, sending the long-legged young ostriches scampering away towards the other side; and I knew directly that something unusual must be on the way, or, after the warnings he had received about not startling the wild young coveys, he would not have dashed up like that.

"I dunno. Father sent me to fetch you while he got the guns ready. He said something about mounted men on the other side of the kopje, so it can't be Kaffirs. I say, do back me up, Val, and get father to let me have a gun."

"Ugh! you bloodthirsty young wretch!" I cried as I started with him for our place, now partly hidden by the orchard—apple and pear trees—I had helped to plant seven years before, when father really pitched his tent by the kopje, and he, Bob—a little, round-headed tot of a fellow then—Aunt Jenny, and I lived in the canvas construction till we had built a house of stone.

The orchard was planted long before the tent was given up—all trees that father had ordered to be sent to us from a famous nursery in Hertfordshire. How well I remember it all!—the arrival of the four big bundles wrapped in matting, and tied behind a great Cape wagon drawn by twenty oxen, whose foreloper was a big, shiny black fellow, who wore a tremendous straw hat, and seemed to think that was all he needed in the way of clothes, as it was big enough to keep off the sun (of which there was a great deal) and the rain (of which there was little). In fact, he wore scarcely anything else—only part of a very old pair of canvas trousers, which he made comfortable and according to his taste by cutting down at the top, so as to get rid of the waist, and tearing close in the fork till the legs were about three inches long.

I remember it all so well: seeing the foreloper come striding along by the foremost pair of oxen, holding one of them by its horn, and carrying a long, thin pole like a very big fishing-rod over his shoulder, for use instead of a whip to guide the oxen. Yes, I recollect it as if it were only yesterday. I looked at him, and he looked at me. My eyes were fixed upon those trousers;

and I burst out, boy-like, into the heartiest fit of laughter I ever had. As I laughed his eyes opened wider and wider, and the corners of his mouth began to creep back farther and farther till they nearly disappeared. Then, suddenly, his mouth flew open, showing a wonderfully white set of teeth, and he gave vent to "Yer-her! Yawk, yawk, yawk, yawk! Yor-hor!" Then he helped to outspan the oxen, and I showed him and the man with the wagon where to find water. At every order I gave he opened his mouth and laughed at me; but he eagerly did all I bade, and followed me back to the wagon to help in unloading the bundles of trees, taking the greatest interest in everything, and lifting the boxes and packages of stores which had come with the trees, no matter what their weight, as if he enjoyed putting forth his tremendous strength.

"Well, Val," said my father as he took out his big knife to cut the string, and then carefully unlaced it—for string was precious out in the desert—"I thought I'd chance a few; but it's quite a spec, and I'm afraid they'll be all dried up. However, we'll try them; and now they are here we must get them in at once. Mind, I shall look to you to make them grow if they are still alive."

"How am I to make them grow, father?" I said.

"With water, my boy. You must bring down buckets from the spring till we have time to dig a channel; and then they'll shift for themselves. I hope they'll grow, for it will be pleasant for you and Bob to sit under them sometimes and eat apples and pears such as your father used to have in his old orchard at home."

"Yes, father," I said; "and for you too."

"Perhaps, my boy; perhaps," he said, with a sigh. "We shall see.—Here, Jenny!"

My aunt was already at the door, in her print sun-bonnet, and looking very cross, I thought.

"Yes," she said.

"Give these two men a good hearty meal; I dare say they're pretty hungry."

"It's all ready, John," she said.

"That's right, my dear," said my father; and then, as if to himself, "I might have known." Turning to the short, thick-set Dutch Boer in charge of the wagon, father told him to go to the big wagon-sheet supported on poles, which we used for a dining-room, and then clapped the big black on the shoulder, bidding him go too.

"Get two spades, Val," he said as soon as the men were gone; "and you, Bob, come off that bundle of trees. It wasn't sent all these thousands of miles by ship and wagon to make you a horse."

I fetched the spades while my father went on unpacking the little trees, Bob being set to help by unlacing the string from the pleasant-smelling Russian mats. Before the new arrivals were cast loose, the big black, with a tremendous sandwich of bread and bacon, had joined us, and showed at once that he meant to help. After taking a big bite, he put his sandwich down while he carried trees to the places where they were to be planted, and after putting them down, returned for another bite, giving me a grin every time.

Then the spades were taken up; and by that time the Boer had eaten and drunk as much as he could, and gone to sit on the big chest in front of the wagon, where he filled his pipe and began to smoke, never offering to help, but watching us with his eyes half-closed.

"Here, steady, nigger!" said my father, smiling; "we're not going to bury bullocks. Little holes like this just where I put in these pegs. — You keep him in hand, Val. I never saw such a strong fellow before."

The great black fellow grinned and dug away, making the rich and soft dry earth fly as he turned it out; while he laughed with delight every time I checked him, and followed me to another place.

By that time he had finished his sandwich, and a thought occurred to me.

"Here, Bob," I said; "put down those pegs" — for he was marching about with us, looking very serious, with the bundle of pegs under his arm. "Go and ask Aunt Jenny to cut another big bit of bread and a very large slice of bacon, and bring 'em here."

Bob ran off, and the big black looked at me, threw back his head, and laughed, and laughed again, as he drove the spade deeply into the rich loamy soil; and when the bread and bacon came he laughed, and bit with those great white teeth of his, and munched and chewed like the lying-down oxen, and dug and dug, till my father said, "No more to-night," and bade me carry in the spades.

That night, before going to bed, tired, but happy with the thoughts of our orchard to come, I walked with father beneath the great stars, going round the place—father with his rifle over his shoulder—to see if all was safe.

We went straight to the wagon, to find the oxen all lying down chewing their cud, and from under the tilt there came a deep, heavy snore; but there was also a rustling sound, a big black head popped out, and the man said, in a deep, thick voice:

"Boss, hear lion?"

"No," said my father sharply. "Did you, boy?"

"Iss. *Oom! Wawk, wawk, wawk.* Boss, lissum."

We stood there in the silence, and for a full minute I could hear nothing but the deep snore of the Boer and chewing of the oxen. Then, distinctly heard, but evidently at a great distance, there was the tremendous barking roar of a lion, and my father uttered a deep "Ha!"

"Boss shoot lion," said the black in a quiet, contented way; and from out of the darkness beneath the great wagon came the sound of the foreloper settling himself down once more to sleep. I remember wondering whether he had anything to cover himself, for the night was fresh and cold. I asked my father.

"Yes; I saw him with a sheepskin over his shoulders. He won't hurt."

We were interrupted by no lion that night, and at the first dawn of day we were out with the spades again; our black visitor, under my direction, digging the holes for the trees, while father planted, and Bob held the stems straight upright till their roots were all nicely spread out, and soil carefully placed amongst them, and trampled firmly in.

This went on till breakfast-time, when Aunt Jenny called us, and the Dutchman came and sat with us, while the great Kaffir carried his portion away, and sat under the wagon to munch.

After the meal the Boer lit his pipe, sat down on a piece of rock, and smoked and looked on till midday, by which time the fruit-trees were all planted, and the big Kaffir had trotted to and fro with a couple of buckets, bringing water to fill up the saucer-like depressions placed about each tree. Then Aunt Jenny called us to dinner, and after that the Boer said it was time to inspan and begin the journey back.

Oh, how well I remember it all!—seeing my father opening a wash-leather bag and paying the Boer the sum that had been agreed upon, and that he wasn't satisfied, but asked for another dollar for the work done by his man. Then father laughed and said he ought to charge for the meals that had been eaten; but he gave the Boer the money all the same; and Aunt Jenny uttered a deep grunt, and said afterwards in her old-fashioned way, "Oh John, what a foolish boy you are!" Then he kissed her and said, "Yes, Jen. I always was. You didn't half-teach me when I was young."

This was after we had watched the wagon grow smaller and smaller in the distance on its way back, and after the great black had stood and looked down at me and laughed in his big, noisy way.

Then once more we were alone in the great desert, father looking proudly down at his little orchard, and Bob walking up and down touching every tree, and counting them over again.

"Begins to look homely now, Val," he said; "but we must work, boy—work."

We did work hard to make that place the home it grew to.

"It's for you, boys," he said, "when I'm dead and gone;" and it was about that time I began to think and understand more fully how father was doing it all for the sake of us boys, and to try and ease his heart-ache. Aunt Jenny set me thinking by her words, and at last I fully grasped how it all was.

"I believe he'd have died broken-hearted, Val," she said to me, "if I hadn't come to him. It was after your poor dear mother passed away. I told him he was not acting like a man and a father to give up like that, and it roused him; and one day—you remember, it was when I had come to keep house for him—he turned to me and said, 'I shall never be happy in England again; and I've been thinking it would be a good thing to take those boys out to the Cape and settle there. They'll grow up well and strong in the new land, and I shall try to make a home for them yonder.' 'Yes, John,' I said, 'that's the very thing you ought to do.' 'Ah,' he said, 'but it means leaving you behind, Jenny, dear, and you'll perhaps never set eyes upon them again.' 'Oh, yes, I shall, John,' I said, 'for I've come to stay.' 'What!' he cried; 'would you go with us, sis?' 'Yes,' I said, 'to the very end of the world.' So we came here, Val, where there's plenty of room, and no neighbours to find fault with our ways."

That's how it was; and now I can admire and think of how Aunt Jenny, the prim maiden lady, gave up all her own old ways to set to and work and drudge for us all, living in a wagon and then in a tent, and smiling pleasantly at the trees we planted, and bringing us lunch where we were working away, dragging down stones for the house which progressed so slowly, though father's ideas wore modest.

"For," said he, "we'll build one big stone room, Val, and make it into two with part of the tent. Then by-and-by we'll build another room against it, and then another and another till we get it into a house."

Yes, it was hard work getting the stones, and we were busy enough one day in the hot sunshine, about a month after the wagon had been with the trees and stores, when Bob suddenly stood shading his eyes, and cried:

"Some one's coming!"

We looked up, and there, far in the distance, I saw a black figure striding along under a great, broad matting-hat.

"Why, it looks like that great Kaffir, father," I said.

"Nonsense, boy," he replied; "the Kaffirs all look alike at a distance."

"But it is, father," I cried excitedly. "Look; he's waving his big hat because he sees us." I waved mine in answer; and directly after he began to run, coming up laughing merrily, and ending by throwing down three assagais and the bundle he carried, as he cried:

"Come back, boss."

We gave him something to eat, and the next minute he was lifting and carrying stones, working like a slave; and at night he told me in his way that he was going to stop along with old boss and young boss and little boss and old gal, and never go away no more.

Chapter Two
Our Ugly Visitor

The black fellow's arrival at such a time was most welcome; but my father put no faith in his declaration.

"They're all alike, Val," he said. "He's a quick worker, and as willing and good-tempered as a man can be; but he'll only stay with us till he has earned wages enough to buy himself some bright-coloured blankets and handkerchiefs, and then he'll be off back to his tribe."

"Think so, father?" I said. "He seems to like us all here. He says it's better than being with the Boers. He always says he means to stay."

"He does mean it, of course," said my father; "but these black fellows are like big children, and are easily led away by some new attraction. We shall wake up some morning and find him gone."

But seven years glided away, during which apprenticeshiplike time Joeboy, as we called him—for he would not be content with Joe when he had heard the "boy" after it once or twice, "Joeboy" quite taking his fancy—worked for us constantly, and became the most useful of fellows upon our farm, ready to do anything and do it well, as his strength became tempered with education. In fact, it grew to be a favourite saying with my father, "I don't know what we should have done without Joeboy."

One of the first persons I saw that morning, when I trotted towards the house after being called by my brother, was the great black hurrying out to meet us; and as we got closer it was to see his face puckered up and his eyes flashing, as he said to me hoarsely:

"Won't go, Boss Val; won't go. You tell the Boss I've run up into the hills. Won't go."

"Here, what do you mean?" I said.

"Boss Boers come to fetch up go and fight. Won't go."

"Nonsense," I said. "I dare say they've only come to buy bullocks."

"No," said the black, shaking his head fiercely. "Come to fetch Joeboy."

"Here, don't run away."

"On'y go up in kopje," he said. "Hide dar."

He rushed away, and I was sure I knew where he would hide himself. Then I walked on with my brother, to find my father and Aunt Jenny by the door.

"What's it all about, father?" I asked.

"I don't know yet, my boy; but we soon shall. There's about a score of the Boers, well mounted and armed. Yonder they are, coming at a walk. There were only twelve; but another party have caught up to them, and maybe there are more."

"Joeboy has run off in a fright," I said. "He thinks they've come to fetch him."

"Oh no; it isn't that, my boy," said my father. "I fear it's something worse."

"What?" I said wonderingly.

Chapter Three
My First Real Trouble

Before my father could reply a body of horsemen cantered up, every man well mounted, rifle in hand, and carrying a cross-belt over his left shoulder fitted with cartridges, bandolier fashion. Their leader, a big, heavily-bearded, fierce-looking fellow, dropped from his saddle, threw the rein to one of his companions, and then swaggered up to us, scanning us with his eyes half-closed, and with a haughty, contemptuous expression in his countenance.

"Ye're John Moray, I suppose?" he said, turning to my father, after looking me up and down in a way I, a hot-blooded and independent lad of eighteen, did not at all like.

"Yes," said my father quietly, "I'm John Moray. Do you want some refreshment for your men and horses?"

"Yes, of course," said our visitor; and I wondered why such a big-bearded, broad-shouldered fellow should speak in so high-pitched a tone. That he was Irish he proved directly; but that excited no surprise, for we were accustomed to offer hospitality to men of various nationalities from time to time—Scots, Finns, Germans, Swedes, and Norwegians—trekking up-country in search of a place to settle on.

"Will you dismount and tie up, then?" said my father; "and we'll see what we can do.—Val, my lad, you will see to the horses having a feed?"

"Yes, father," was on my lips, when the Irish leader turned upon me sharply with:

"Oh, ye're Val—are ye?"

"Yes," I said, rather sharply, for the man's aggressive manner nettled me; "my name is Valentine."

"And is it, now?" he said, with a mocking laugh. "Ye're a penny plain and tuppence coloured, I suppose? Coloured, bedad! Look at his face!"

"I don't see the joke," I said sharply.

"Don't ye, now? Then ye soon will, my fine chap. Let's see, now; how old are ye?"

I made no reply, and my father replied gravely:

"My son is eighteen."

"Is he, now? And ye're forty, I suppose?"

"I am sorry to say I am over fifty," replied my father, as I stood chafing at the man's insolent, bullying tone.

"Then ye don't look it, sor. But there, we'll leave ye alone for a bit. I dare say we can do without ye this time, and take the bhoy."

"What for—where?" said my father quickly.

"What for—where?" cried the man. "For the commando, of course."

"The commando?" said my father, while I felt staggered, only half-grasping the import of his words.

"Yes, sor, the commando. D'ye suppose ye are to have the protection of the State, and do nothing again' your counthry's inimies? If ye do ye're greatly mistaken. Every man must take his turn to difind the counthry, and ye may feel preciously contented that ye don't have to join yerself."

"But I have heard of no rising," said my father, looking at me anxiously. "The blacks all about here are peaceable and friendly."

"Not the blackest blacks, sor," said the man, drawing himself up and raising one hand and his voice in an oratorical way; "the blacks I mane are white-skinned, but black in the heart through and through; the blacks who are the dispisers of progress, the foes of freedom, the inimies of the counthry, sor—the despicable, insolent Saxons."

"Do you mean the English?" said my father coolly.

"I do that, sor," said the man defiantly; "and the day has dawned at last when the down-thrampled Boers are goin' to give them a lesson that shall make the British lion snaik out of this counthry with his tail between his legs like a beaten dog."

"You are a British subject, sir," said my father.

"Mahn, I scorrun it," cried our visitor. "I have thrown off all fealty years ago, and am a free Irishman, and captain of the body of brave men who are going to dhrive the tyranny of England out of this colony for ever."

"This is all news to me, sir," said my father coldly.

"Is it, sor?" said our visitor mockingly. "Then I'm proud to be the bearer of the great news."

"Do you mean to tell me, then," said my father, "that there is war declared by England against the Boers?"

"No, sor," cried the fellow insolently; "but I tell you that we have declared war again' the brutal Saxon."

"We, sir?" said my father gravely. "But you are one of the Queen's servants—an Irishman."

"Nothing of the sort, sor. I disown England; I disowned her when I came out here to throw meself into the arrums of the brave, suffering, pathriotic race around me, and placed my sword at their service."

"Then you are a soldier, I presume?" said my father.

"I was tin years in the arrmy, sor," said our visitor, drawing himself up and clapping his hand upon his chest. "Look at thim," he continued, pointing to his followers drawn up in line. "A part of my following, and as fine irrigular cavalry as ever threw leg over saddle.—Look here, young man, ye're in luck, for ye'll have the honour of serving in Captain Eustace Moriarty's troop."

"You are Captain Eustace Moriarty?" said my father.

"I am, sor."

"Then I must tell you, sir," said my father, "that though I have taken up land here and made it my home, I claim my rights as an Englishman not to make myself a traitor by taking up arms against my Queen."

"A thraitor!" cried the captain. "Bah! That for the Queen;" and he snapped his fingers. "But ye're not asked to serve now. That can wait till ye're wanted. It's the bhoy we want, and maybe after a bit it'll be you."

"My son thinks as I do," said my father sternly.

"Does he, now?" said the captain mockingly. "Then I shall have to tache him to think as I do, and it won't take long. D'ye hear me, bhoy?"

"I hear what you say, sir," I replied. "Of course I think as my father does, and I refuse to serve against England."

"I expected it," said the man, with cool insolence. "It's what I expected from a young Saxon. But look here, me bhoy; ye've got to serrve whether ye like it or whether ye don't. What's more, ye've got to come at once. So get yer horse, and clap the saddle on. Fetch him his rifle and his cartridge-bolt, and let there be no more nonsense."

"You heard what my son said, sir," said my father haughtily. "If it were against a black enemy of the country we should both be willing."

"Didn't I tell ye it was again' a black inimy?" said the man mockingly.

"I heard you insult the Queen and her Government, sir," said my father; "and, once more, my son refuses to serve."

Charge! A Story Of Briton And Boer | 19

"The coward!—the white-livered cub!" cried the captain contemptuously.

"What!" I cried, springing forward; but my father flung his hand across my chest, and Bob rushed in past Aunt Jenny, as if to take refuge from the scene.

"Quite right, old man," said the captain, coolly stroking his beard. "And look here, bhoy whether ye like it or not, ye're a sojer now; I'm yer shuperior officer, and it's time of war. If a man strikes his shuperior officer, he's stood up with a handkerchief tied across his eyes to prevent him from winking and spoiling the men's aim, and then the firing-party does the rest."

As he spoke he made a sign, and half-a-dozen of the mounted Boers rode up.

"Sargint," he said, "the young colt's a bit fractious. Ye'll take him in hand. Fasten his hands behind him ready. Two of ye go round to the pen there and pick out the most likely horse, saddle and bridle him, and bring him here. Ye've got some green-leather thongs. Then put him upon the horse with his face to the tail, and tie his ankles underneath. It'll be a fine lesson for the bhoy in rough-riding."

The men were quick enough. Before I had even thought of trying to make my escape, two of the Boers were off their horses and made me their prisoner, while the rest of the little troop rode closer up and surrounded us.

Then other two of the men rode off behind the house, and I stood breathing hard, biting my lips, and feeling as if something hot was burning my chest as I tried hard to catch my father's averted eyes.

Just then the Irish renegade captain burst into a hearty laugh, and I wrenched myself round to look, and felt better. A minute before, I had seen Bob disappear into the house, and had mentally denounced him as a miserable little coward; but my eyes flashed now as I saw him hurry out with three rifles over his right shoulder, a bandolier belt across his left, and two more, well filled with cartridges, hanging to the barrels of the rifles.

"Bedad!" said the captain, "and he's worth fifty of his big, hulking brother! But ye're too shmall, darlint. Wait a year or two longer, and ye shall fight under me like a man."

Bob made a rush for father; but one of the Boers leaned down and caught him by the shoulder, while another snatched the rifles from his hands, and laid them across the pommel of the saddle in which he sat.

"Give up, Bob; give up," cried father sternly, as my brother began to struggle with all his might. "It is no use to fight against fate."

"Hear him now," said the captain. "He can talk sinse at times."

"Yes," said my father, "at times;" and he gave the captain a look which made him turn away his eyes.—"Val, my boy, I cannot have you exposed to the ignominy of being bound."

"Sure, no," cried the captain. "I forgot to say a wurrud about stirrup-leathers across his back if he didn't behave himself."

"Fate is against us for the present, my boy," continued my father, "and you must ride with this party till I have applied to the proper quarters to get the matter righted."

"Now, man, be aloive," said the captain, and I winced and looked vainly round for a way of escape; but I was seized by the wrist by another dismounted Boer, who slipped a raw-hide noose over my wrist, just as two more came riding back, leading my own horse, Sandho, between them. The poor beast, who followed me like a dog, uttered a shrill neigh as soon as he caught sight of me, springing forward to reach my side.

"Stop!" cried my father loudly; "there is no need for that. My son will ride with you, sir."

"Indade, sir, I'm obleeged to ye for the inforrmation," said the captain mockingly; "but sure it's a work of shupererrogation, me dear friend, for I knew it, and that he was going to ride backward. If, however, he gives up sinsibly, he may ride with his back to the horse's tail, and ye needn't tie his ankles togither. Have ye ever ridden that horse before?"

"He has ridden it hundreds of times, ever since it was a foal," said my father quickly, for I felt choked.—"Stop, man," he added angrily; "your captain said my son was not to be bound."

"Sure I didn't say a wurrud about his wrists, old man," cried the captain contemptuously. "Ye want too much. I've let him off about the ankles, and let him ride face forward, so be contint. Make his wrists fast behind him."

I was compelled to resign myself to my fate, and stood fighting hard to keep down all emotion while my wrists were secured firmly behind my back, the thin raw-hide cutting painfully into the flesh.

By this time Sandho was bridled and saddled, and just then my father turned to Bob.

"Take in those rifles, my boy," he said.

The captain turned sharply and gave my father a searching look; but he contented himself with nodding, and my brother snatched the rifles from where they lay across the Boer's knees, and rushed indoors with them.

I knew well enough why, poor fellow: it was to hide the tears struggling to rise, and of which he was ashamed.

Just then I had harder work than ever to control my own feelings, for Aunt Jenny hurried towards me, but was kept back by my captors; and I saw her go to my father and throw her arms about his neck, while he bent over her and seemed to be trying to whisper comfort.

"There, up with ye, me bhoy," cried the captain. "Ye can't mount, though, with yer hands behind yer like a prishner.—Lift him on, two of ye, like a sack."

"That they shan't," I said between my teeth; and feeling now that what was to como was inevitable, I took a couple of steps to my horse's side.

"Stand!" I said aloud as I raised one foot to the stirrup; and Sandho stood as rigid as if of bronze, while I made a spring, raised myself up, and threw my leg over.

"Well done, bhoy!" cried the captain as I sank into the saddle.—"You, Hooger, take his rein. Unfasten one end from the bit so as to give ye double length, and ye'd better buckle it to your saddle-bow.—Now look here, me fine fellow," he continued, addressing me, "ye'll give me none of your nawnsense; for, look ye, my bhoys are all practised shots with the rifle. They can bring down a spring-bok going at full speed, so they can easily bring ye down and yer nag too. There's twenty of them, and I'm a good shot meself, so ye know what to expect if ye thry to escape."

I said nothing, for I was thinking with agony about poor Aunt Jenny, who was now coming up to me, and the captain laughed as he saw her pain-wrung countenance.

"Good-bye, Val, my boy," said my father slowly; "and bear up like a man."

That was all, and he turned away.

The next moment Bob was clinging to my arm.

"O Val! O Val! O Val!" he cried in a choking voice, and then he dropped back, poor boy, for he could say no more.

"Be sharp there and get it done, me bhoy," said the captain. "Ye can say good-bye to the owld woman; but lave the cat and the dogs till ye come back."

"Are you going to march at once?" said my father as Aunt Jenny came to my side, and I gripped my saddle and bent down for her to put her arms round my neck.

"Sor, ye see that I am," said the captain.

"But you and your men will take something to eat and drink?"

"Something to send them asleep?" said the captain suspiciously. "I'm thinkin' they can last till we get back to Drak Pass, where there's a shtore. I'm obleeged to ye all the same.—There, that'll do, owld lady. I'll make a man of the bhoy, and send him back safe and sound, if some of the raw recruits of the brutal Saxons don't shoot him."

"Good-bye, then. God bless you and protect you, Val!" said Aunt Jenny, with a sob, as she loosened her grip of my neck, and I straightened myself up, feeling my heart swell and the blood bound in my veins, for while my father kept the captain in converse, she, with quivering lips, had breathed words of hope into my ear.

"Listen, Val," she said. "Your father bids me say that you are to watch for your chance, and then make a dash for your liberty. Gallop to Echo Nek, and you will find Joeboy waiting there with a rifle and cartridges. But you must not come back here. Joeboy will bring a letter."

My heart was bounding with hope, and I felt ready for anything just then, as the captain gave the orders "Mount!" and then "Forward!" But the next minute my spirits sank into the darkness of misery. For what had Aunt Jenny said? Joeboy would be waiting at Echo Nek with a rifle and cartridges. Yes; but poor Joeboy had taken flight at the appearance of the Boers, and fled for his liberty, in the belief that they had come for him.

Chapter Four
Waiting for my Chance

I rode on painfully as regarded my wrists; for above them my arms throbbed and burned as if the veins were distended almost to bursting-point, while my hands grew gradually cold and numb, and then became insensible as so much lead. The physical pain, however, was nothing to what I felt mentally. Only an hour or two before I was leading that calm, happy home-life, without a trouble beyond some petty disappointment in the garden or farm or during one of the hunting or shooting expeditions with Joeboy to carry my game; and now a lightning-like stroke seemed to have descended to end my idyllic boy-life and make me a man full of suffering, and with a future which I abhorred.

"No," I argued, "I must escape, even if they do send a shower of bullets to bring me down." I did not believe much in the vaunted powers of the Boers with the rifle. I knew that they could shoot well, but no better than my father and his two pupils, meaning Bob and myself; and I felt that we should have been very doubtful about bringing down a man going at full gallop, even in the brightest daylight; and I meant to make my venture in the dusk of the evening or after dark if only my captors would continue their journey then. Once well started, and my rein free of the man who held it buckled to his saddle-bow, I had no fear at all, for I was sure that in a straight race there was not a Boer amongst them who could overtake me, they being heavy, middle-aged men, while I was young and light, quite at home in the saddle, and Sandho as much at home with me, upon his back. Arms? I could do without them. Reins? I needed none, if only free of the one which held me to my left-hand guard; for an extra pressure of either leg would send my beautiful little Australian horse in the direction I wished to turn, while a word of encouragement would send him on like the wind, and an order sharply uttered check him even if at full speed.

I had had Sandho four years, mounting him as soon as he was strong enough to bear me, and ever since we seemed to have been companions more than master and servant. We had played together; I had hunted him, and he had hunted me—finding me, too, when I hid from him; and he answered when out grazing on the veldt with a cheery neigh before galloping to meet me. Why, there had been times when we had both lain down to sleep together on the distant plains, my head resting on his glossy neck; so, now that he was bearing me along, comparatively helpless, and I felt his elastic, springy form beneath me, I was ashamed of my despair, convinced that if I gave the word he would snap that rein at the first bound, and bear me safely away.

I made up my mind that if I could defer my attempt till it was dark I should be safe. If, however, I were obliged to venture in daylight, I would make my dash by some rocky pass or kopje on the way, where Sandho would easily leave the Boers' horses behind, he being almost as sure-footed as a goat.

The captain drew rein a little, so that I came alongside during the first part of our ride, and he cast his eye over my bonds and gave the Boer who had the leading-rein a sharp order or two about keeping a good lookout. To this the dull, heavy fellow responded with a surly growl. After this the Irishman banteringly asked me if I was comfortable.

My answer was an angry glare—at least, I meant it to be—but the only effect was to make him laugh.

"Ye've got a bad seat in the saddle, and it will be a good lesson to ye in riding, bhoy. Make ye sit up. I hate to see a military man with his showlders up and his nose down close to his charrger's mane. Faith, I'm half-disposed to make ye throw the stirrups over the nag's neck, and I would if we'd toime. But we've none to spare for picking ye up when ye came off.—Here," he cried to the two men next behind, for we now rode two and two; "why are your carbines not full-cocked—rifles, I mane? That's right. Fire at wanst if he tries to bowlt; don't wait for ordhers."

I listened to the sharp clicking of the rifle-locks as the men cocked their pieces; but somehow I did not feel scared, for a feeling of desperation was upon me, and I was strung-up to dare anything to get my liberty; and, besides, my father's orders were that I should make a dash.

"They can't hit me," I said to myself; and wherever the track was fair going we went on at a canter, drawing rein wherever the ground grew bad. At these latter times the captain began talking loudly in a highly-pitched and half-contemptuous way to the leading men; and when his words reached my ears I made out that his subject was either about military evolutions and a man's bearing in the saddle, or else, in a harsh and bitter tone, about the brutal Saxon who was at last going to receive his dues for his long years of evil-doing and tyranny towards the oppressed. Hearing such talk, I rode on half-wondering what England had been doing towards the Irish at home and the Boers abroad, for this was all news to me, and I had never noticed among the Dutch settlers on the veldt anything but a stolid kind of contentment with their prosperous lot; there not being a single case of poverty, as far as I knew, within a hundred miles of our pleasant home.

At the thought of home a strange swelling came in my throat, and the wide, open veldt before me looked dim as I pictured all I had left behind; for, happy as had been the life I led, and lovely as everything around had always seemed, home had never seemed so beautiful as now. However, I set my teeth hard, knit my brows, and with an effort seemed to swallow down that swelling lump in my throat, at the same time nipping Sandho's sides so sharply that he gathered himself up to bound off; but he was checked by a savage snatch at the rein, and received a blow with the barrel of my escort's rifle, as the surly and scowling brute beside me growled out a fierce oath in Dutch.

The plunge Sandho gave nearly unseated me, and in another moment he would have been rearing and kicking to get free; but a few gentle words from my lips soothed the poor beast down, and he settled into his canter once more, while I fell to wondering whether my poor horse could think and would understand that the brutal treatment did not come from his master.

On and on we rode over ground familiar to me, for many a long journey from home had I been in every direction—hunting, shooting, or with our wagon and oxen and Joeboy as foreloper, on journeys of many days through the wilderness, to fetch stores for home use or to dispose of game or stock. So beautiful it all seemed; now it was so wretched for me to leave it all, and to be forced to go and fight against my brothers, so to speak, in a cause that I felt I must hate. As I rode on, thinking thus, I could see that there was no such oppression and tyranny as the Irish captain spoke of; nothing but a bitter and contemptible race-hatred, fostered by idle and discontented men.

"But I shan't have to fight," I said to myself. "They talk about freedom, and drag me away as a slave; but I too mean to be free."

From that moment the gloomy lookout ahead seemed to pass away, the veldt seeming glorious in the afternoon sunshine; and, cantering through the invigorating air, I could have enjoyed my ride but for the constrained position in which I sat, and the dull pain in my arms and shoulders. I tried to forget this, and listened to the captain's words, for he grew more and more loquacious. I gathered that he reckoned upon picking up other two young fellows of my own stamp at the farm twenty miles from ours; and I noted that, no matter what he said, his words were listened to in gloomy silence or received with grunting monosyllables, while the Boers talked among themselves only about home and farming work or the sale of stock. More than once, too, I heard one of the men near me wonder how the housewife would be getting on with the beasts and sheep. The words were spoken in Boer Dutch; but in the course of years I had become pretty well acquainted with the expressions of ordinary life. Thus it seemed as if the men were anything but contented followers of their noisy, vapouring leader.

At last the farm was reached, and we halted for refreshment, spending about half-an-hour to water and feed the horses, during which time I was carefully guarded. There was no opposition here. The two recruits to the commando, as they termed it, had been duly served with notice, and within the time named they were ready with their horses, and armed; but when we made our start I could see with what surly unwillingness they took their places in the rank, and noticed too that they were nearly as strictly watched as I was. In fact, I saw them exchange glances after receiving a bullying order from Moriarty, and felt that it would not have taken much to cause a display of temper on the part of the recruits.

That, however, by the way: my thoughts were too much taken up with my own position to pay much heed to the two young Boers; for when we were once more on our route for our next stopping-place, where we were to halt for the night, I felt that the time was rapidly approaching when I must make my escape. I did not say to myself *try* to make my escape, but to make it; for I had no fear of being unsuccessful. The night was coming on fast, and I knew that there was no moon, which was all in my favour; and, once free, all I had to do was to make straight for home—a ride of perhaps thirty miles through the wild country, keeping away from the track, and with nothing to fear. Yes, there wore the lions, plentiful enough in the wilder parts; but the thought of them did not damp me, for Sandho would soon give me warning if any were near, and carry me well out of danger.

Then there was the next day. I was to make for Echo Nek, and there, meet Joeboy, who would bear my father's instructions; but would Joeboy be there? My heart sank a little at the thought of how doubtful this was; but I soon cheered up again. At the worst it meant waiting a day or two, for I should not venture, home. The Boers would ride back—of that I felt sure; then, thinking I should certainly seek for refuge with my people, they would scour the country in search of me, and they might search Echo Nek, though it was ten miles away.

"Never mind," I said to myself cheerily enough; "that all belongs to what *may be*: let's think only of *will be*;" and I rode on, scanning the track and keeping a good lookout from side to side for the likeliest spot for my attempt. I was still keenly watching when the shades of evening darkened into night, and the right place had not yet come; there were even moments when doubts began to creep in, for my arms grew acutely painful, and this thought worried me terribly: "Helpless as I am now, and growing weary, shall I have the strength to carry out my plan?" I still had strength enough to drive out the doubting thought, and forced myself into watching eagerly for my chance, having pretty well determined what I would do first, trusting to the sudden surprise to give me a few moments' start.

In vain I looked for such a sanctuary as a rocky pile of scattered granite would afford, for it had at last grown dark—a clear, semi-transparent darkness, through which I could see twenty or thirty yards in any direction; beyond that distance everything rapidly grew black. If I could at once get fifty yards away, there was apparently clear galloping ground, and distance would at any moment furnish me with a dark hiding-place. All I wanted was the start; but how to get it?

I had my big knife in my pocket; but I might as well have been without it, fastened as I was. So, though I thought and thought, I could see no way of dividing that rein; the idea of raising it to my teeth being dismissed as an impossibility, as also of Sandho cutting it with his own powerful nip, for I knew the idea of communicating my desire to the horse was absurd. "How to manage? How to manage?" I kept on saying to myself. The idea would not come; and as it grew darker our canter gave place to a round trot, and soon after we steadied down to a walk.

Suppose I suddenly made Sandho rear up? That would be easy, for I could make him rise on his hind-legs and fight with his fore. But what good would that do? No more than making him kick violently in all directions, as he turned his fore-feet into a pivot upon which he turned, bringing his heels round to all points of the compass, and delivering smashing blows with them. Splendid practice this when a litter of half-grown lions were trying to pull him down, but now not likely to do more than bring down punishment upon the poor beast.

Again and again I made up my mind to make him give a sudden bound; but the chances were that it would not snap the rein, only cruelly drag the poor fellow's mouth. And the minutes glided by, and the position grew more and more hopeless. Then, suddenly, I seemed to see the only possible way of getting clear. We rode with long reins, my father and I, and I began to wonder why I had not thought of putting my plan in action before.

Chapter Five
A Dash for Liberty

As I have said, one of my reins was unbuckled, passed over the horse's neck, and buckled to the Boer's saddle-bow; and in consequence of the length of the strap, it hung down in a long curve when we were riding a fair distance apart, so I felt I had only to press my horse close alongside that of my companion to slacken the leather strap still further. My plan was almost a forlorn hope; but I could think of no other, and determined to try it, even if, as would probably be the case, it meant no more than dragging me suddenly from the saddle, to fall and be trampled among the horses' heels. Still, I was determined, and only waited now for the thrilling moment when I would try.

We rode on for what seemed to me another mile, and still one moment seemed as good as another. I was ready to despair. Then the time came. The Boer at my side, having slung his cocked rifle over his shoulder, fumbled in the darkness for something. Guessing what my companion was about to do, with a slight pressure of my right leg I made Sandho edge gradually closer. I was quite right. He took out a big Dutch pipe and a pouch, proceeding to fill the bowl and press down the tobacco; and as he worked so did I. Edging Sandho nearer and nearer, with my heart beginning to beat with big, heavy throbs, I withdrew my left foot from the stirrup, lowered it down in front of the loosely-hanging rein, and, as soon as that was level with my ankle, twisted my foot again and again, till the rein was three times round. Then I felt the drag upon the Boer's saddle-bow, just as the man was getting a light; and at that moment my leg came in contact with his so suddenly that it jerked him, and the match he had struck went out.

"Thunder and lightning!" he growled, kicking out to drive Sandho farther away, but missing him, for I had just thrust my toe back into the stirrup-iron and was pressing my horse away.

The next minute scratch went another match, the bright light shining out for a moment between us so that I could see the man's face plainly as he held the burning splint between his hands on a level with his chin. Then it was out again, for with a loud, shrill cry I was urging Sandho to make his great effort—one which, as I have said, meant either freedom—if the escape of one bound as I was could be so regarded—or the horse galloping away and leaving me to be trampled under foot.

"*Ri—ri—ri—ri—ri—ri!*" I half-shrieked, and Sandho made a tremendous bound. There was a jerk at my left leg which nearly dragged me from the saddle, and then we were off and away, the horse tearing over the level plain out into the darkness; while close behind, after a momentary pause, I heard the trampling of horses and the high-pitched voice of the Irish leader yelling out orders. Then flash after flash cut the darkness, and *crack, crack, crack* came the reports of the rifles, as the men fired in what they believed to be my direction; but I heard no whistling bullet, and the firing ceased as quickly as it had begun, for there was the risk of my pursuers inflicting injury upon their fellows who led, and whom I could hear thundering along behind me, while with voice and knee I urged Sandho on at his greatest speed.

A wild feeling of elation sent the blood dancing through my veins as we raced along, and I was ready to burst out into shout after shout of triumph, for I was free! free! And away we went, I almost perfectly helpless, and knowing I must trust to my brave horse to carry me beyond the reach of pursuit.

Throb, throb, throb went his hoofs on the soft earth, and *throb, throb, throb* went my heart, during what seemed now like some wild, feverish dream in which I was careering onward through the semi-transparent darkness, fully expecting every moment to see some great patch of brush or pile of loose granite loom up before us, to be followed by a tremendous leap, a crash as we came to horrible grief, and then insensibility; but nothing of the kind occurred, for I had chosen the happiest moment for my attempt, and we were galloping over the almost level veldt. But evidently guided by the beat of my horse's hoofs, the Boers were still in full chase, the deep thudding of their troopers sounding loud and clear.

For a few minutes, in the wild excitement, I could think of nothing but whispering words of encouragement to Sandho, as I lay right forward now and pressed and caressed him with my legs; while, as I reached towards his head, I could just make out the delicate ears, and see them laid back to listen to my words every time I spoke.

Then a strange pain brought me more consciousness of my position. It was not the aching above my crippled wrists, but in my left leg, which felt strained and stretched as if on the rack, and for a few moments I fancied my foot had been torn off at the ankle; but the next moment I knew this was absurd, for I could rise in my stirrups. Still, I knew my leg was badly hurt, and that I must now endeavour to do something to free my hands.

All this time we were tearing along at racing pace, while with dogged obstinacy the Boers—ten or a dozen of them, I judged by the beating of the hoofs—had settled themselves to the pursuit, meaning to hunt me down as they would track some wounded eland trying its best for life.

"This won't do," I thought as I began to grow calmer, and listened.

There they were, tearing along, far enough behind, but well on my track; and there was I, almost helpless, struggling to get my bonds undone, but only giving myself more pain.

The darkness was my only friend and refuge, and after a few moments' consideration I made up my mind what to do. At any moment the chase might be at an end. Seven years on the veldt had taught me well the risks of a horseman, and I knew only too well what would happen if Sandho did not rise in time, or failed to clear some one of the thousands of scattered rocks; or he might plunge his foot in a hole made by some burrowing animal, and come down crippled for life, while I was flung over his head. Yes, the chase might come to an end at any moment, and all hope of reaching Echo Nek be gone; so, drawing a deep breath, I steadied myself. Then I strained forward as far as I could reach, and spoke to Sandho, who uttered a whinnying snort and began to check himself. As soon as he had eased down into a canter I brought my left leg to bear upon him, and an agonising pain shot up to my hip, turning me so faint that for a minute I was giddy and nearly lost my seat; but my pressure upon his flank had caused him to amble on at right angles to our former course. As my head grew clearer I brought him down to a walk, and directly after stopped him short. I saw his ears twitching, and his head turned in the direction from whence came the heavy beat of hoofs. This sound came closer and closer, and then swept past, as I sat with beating heart, mental distress being added to my bodily pain, for at any moment I knew Sandho might utter a neighing challenge to the passing horses; but he was silent, and they passed at a swinging gallop, the sound soon growing fainter. I was beginning to breathe more freely when my agony was renewed; for the beating of hoofs was resumed, and I could tell that the little troop of Boers was divided into two, and the risk had again to be encountered.

I dared not whisper to Sandho for fear he should answer me in his own way and reach round his soft, velvety muzzle to touch my expected hand, now so painfully held back. These seemed the worst, the most agonising, moments of my flight; and I felt sick with pain, too. If the horse whinnied, all my desperate struggle would have been in vain; and I was ready in my anguish to ask whether it was worth while to go on with the desperate attempt.

All this time the horsemen came nearer and nearer. In my agitation it seemed they were not following the departing hoof-sounds in a direct line, but riding in a curve which would bring them right over the spot where we stood.

How long the moments are in such an emergency! The time seemed to me stretched out to an agonising length; but this second strain came to an end, and Sandho stood motionless, with his flanks heaving beneath me. I could hear his breath come hard as the Boers galloped on abreast, closer and closer; and then the *thud, thud, thud* grew less and less plain, till the sounds gradually became faint in the distance. I now felt ready to spring from my saddle and go down in thankfulness upon my knees; but I dared not stir, for if I managed to throw myself down, I knew perfectly well I could never get into the saddle again.

Chapter Six
Night on the Veldt

I sat there in the chilly darkness, listening till the last sounds of the beating hoofs died out—began again—grew fainter—finally ceased altogether. Sandho stood perfectly still, with the painful heaving of his flanks gradually easing down. At last he uttered a low whinnying sound, as if asking me why we did not go on; but I made no movement, spoke no word, only sat and listened for the return of the Boers.

There was no sound, for my ruse had succeeded; and I was just beginning to try to rouse myself from a faint, half-swooning state, when my nerves received a fillip; for there in the distance rose the deep, barking roar of a lion, followed by a pause, and then from a different direction came the horrible wailing howl of the unclean prowlers who follow the monarch of the desert to finish the remains of his feasts.

Sandho stirred uneasily and drew a deep breath, which was followed by something strangely resembling a sigh. I knew it was time to move; and, shaking off a sensation of fast-approaching lethargy, I tried to get rid of the feeling of faintness, and only roused the sharp pain afresh. Still, that spurred me into effort; and as I pressed Sandho's sides lightly, he began to amble gently along, while I raised my eyes to the stars, and endeavoured to make out which way we were travelling. There was a soft mistiness in the great arch above me, and it was some minutes before I could pick out a few of the familiar stars; but at last I was certain, and made out that the Boers had galloped on nearly due north, while Sandho's nose was pointed east.

North meant home; and without doubt they would keep on in that direction, feeling sure that I should make for the farm. East meant going in the right direction for Echo Nek and the mountains, though I should have to bear off after a time towards the north-east. Anyhow, matters were so far in my favour, and I tried to sit firm in the saddle as I let the horse amble on at the pace which I had often compared to swinging in an easy-chair; but the movement was agony now, and my great dread was lest I should faint and fall, for the suffering seemed greater than I could bear.

In times of emergency—as I have often learned since—we are very poor judges, whether as boys or men, of how much the human frame can bear. Thus, in spite of all I suffered, I kept in the saddle, while, in what gradually seemed to grow into a horrible, fevered dream, my brave little horse ambled on and on, and later settled into a walk. He seemed always to be aiming for one great dim star, which gave me encouragement; then the dread came over me that, from his steady pursuance of our journey, he must be making for home, and taking me right into the midst of my enemies.

After a time he stopped short, and from the steady *crop, crop, crop,* I knew he was amongst grass; and he grazed away long enough before moving on again at his old amble. Again he pulled up for another good long feed, while I managed to find words to talk to him—foolishly, no doubt; but it helped me and kept off the feeling of pain and loneliness, seeming to give me strength, too, as I called him "Poor fellow," and told him how sorry I was I could not get down to rest him, and make his meal pleasanter by unfastening the curb and taking out his bit.

It was all folly perhaps; but my words were very earnest and true, and I believe the poor, faithful slave liked to hear my voice, for every now and then when I spoke he would cease cropping the rich grass, whose moist odour rose pleasantly to my nostrils, and utter one of his low whinnying calls.

"He is happy enough," I thought, in my dull misery; "while I, suffering as I do, would give anything for a mouthful of water. Oh!" I sighed aloud at last, "if this long night would only come to an end, and I could reach a spruit. Just to get down and have one long drink, before trying to sleep and rest!"

As I said these words I felt that no sleep could possibly come to one suffering such pain, and in desperation I once more made an effort to free my hands, but only to set my teeth hard and utter a faint groan, for the pain I suffered in the act seemed to increase tenfold.

I felt half-delirious and strange after that, or at least it seems so now; but I have some recollection of Sandho going on, stopping to crop the grass, and then going on again and again, till I found myself gazing straight before me at a faint, dull light in the distance—a light which increased more and more, bringing with it a kind of feeling of hope that the long night of agony was coming to an end, for I knew I was gazing eastward, and that it would soon be day.

Shortly afterwards I could see we were getting to the termination of the plain, for there were scattered blocks of stone, with mountains beyond; and something seemed to flash through me at the sight. "Stones," I said aloud;

"of course! Why not some rough edge against which I can saw the raw-hide straps which bind my hands?"

There was a faint speck of orange light high up in the sky just then, and it seemed to be reflected somehow into my brain, making me see my way at last to a better state of things. Hope was coming with the new day, and the blackness of despair slowly dying out.

With the sun rapidly brightening the sky, I urged Sandho forward, but only at a walk, for he was weary and sluggish, and the slightest movement beyond that pace brought back the sickening pain so intensely that I believe if he had broken into a trot I should have fainted and fallen to the ground. By going gently, however, we gradually neared the wild and rocky portion beyond which the huge masses of stone towered up into a mighty heap, forming one of the rough hills with precipitous sides known to the Dutch settlers as "kopjes" or "heads."

I now began to revive more and more in the fresh, invigorating morning air, and carefully examined the open veldt away to the north and east in search of the enemy; but not a living thing was visible. Then I turned my attention towards the rough ground in front and the kopje beyond, as I knew full well these were likely to be the home of other enemies, which on an ordinary occasion would retreat before an armed and mounted man; how they would behave towards one so completely helpless I shuddered to think. Sandho, however, made no sign beyond raising his muzzle again to sniff at the breeze we encountered; and when I called upon him to halt, he lowered his head directly and began to crop the rich grass growing amongst the stones.

My intention now was to dismount; but I sat still, hesitating, and looking away over the open veldt, fearing to alight, being fully aware how helpless I should be and unequal to the task of remounting.

However, it had to be done; so, pulling myself together, I drew my feet from the stirrups, and called upon Sandho to stand fast. Then, lying forward till my face touched my steed's neck, I made a desperate effort—quickly, for I could not trust my strength—drew my injured left leg right up on to the horse's back, and lay there perfectly still for a few moments, suffering horribly from the pain of my overstrained muscles, before making another effort, and then dropped down on my right foot, dismounting on the wrong side of the horse, feeling, as I did so, everything give way. I had completely collapsed, and all was blank. It may have been an hour, or it may have been only a few minutes—possibly only seconds—passed before I opened my eyes and gazed up, wondering what was the meaning of the soft, warm puffs of moist air, and what it was that kept on snuffing at my face.

"Sandho, old boy!" I said, gazing up in his great, soft eyes, and the wondering horse whinnied and then turned away to begin grazing once more; while I waited for the sick feeling from which I suffered to pass off, before trying to get up and find some sharp-edged stone against which I could rub the raw-hide thong which bound my wrists.

It was terrible work, and I had to make a severe call upon my courage before I made the first effort. For it was like this: I was quite exhausted and in a state of semi-stupor, combined with drowsiness. So long as I lay quite still my injuries felt dull and numbed; but at the slightest movement my arms and shoulders gave a burning, fiery pain, while my left leg and ankle shot out pangs almost unbearable.

The effort had to be made, though; and, setting my teeth hard, I called up all my powers of endurance, and after a severe struggle managed to get upon my knees.

The pain now was excruciating; and, realising that my left leg must be badly hurt, I made another effort before I was overcome again, getting upon my feet and reeling towards a big upright mass of granite; but before I had taken half-a-dozen limping steps the whole scene began to glide round me, and I fell heavily, insensible once more.

It is no easy task to rise to one's feet when lying with arms tightly bound behind the back. Think, then, what it must have been to one suffering as I was—arms swollen and cut into by the leather thong, utterly exhausted, and with one leg rendered completely useless.

Again I passed through that sickening phase of recovery from a swoon; and then it was some time before my senses would act, and I could fully grasp the situation and understand I must once more make that same effort to rise.

I was thoroughly desperate now; and as soon as I fully grasped my position I made another attempt, turning over from my back, where I lay in agony upon my swollen hands and wrists, on to my face. It was impossible to keep it back, and I uttered a low cry, which brought Sandho trotting towards me from where he was making a hearty meal. Then I lay quite still, with the deathly sickness passing off once more, my heart beating heavily all the time and a feeling of thankfulness making me glow; for there, as I lay face downwards, I knew that my helpless and swollen arms and hands were lying on either side, perfectly numb, but free. In that last heavy fall, in trying to reach the stone, the thong must have snapped, the dew-soaked raw leather falling loose; and now I had only to wait till the circulation and sense of feeling returned.

The pain I suffered was still bad enough, but it seemed to be softened by the feeling of joy which pervaded me; and soon after, Sandho having wandered off again to graze, I heard a sound which nerved me to renewed efforts—the peculiar plashing made by a horse wading into a pebbly stream. That was enough. A minute later I was struggling to reach the stone I had fought to gain before; and by its help I got upon my feet, when I saw Sandho some twenty yards away, standing in a depression by the side of a perpendicular mass of rock, down whose side a spring of water gushed and ran off below the rock, to sink out of sight some distance off.

It was hard work, and the pain excessive; but I limped and shuffled along till I was close to the stream, and then sank down again, to lie and drink and drink again of the sweet, pure water, every mouthful giving me renewed energy.

I must have fallen asleep after dragging myself from the pool—a swoon-like sleep, from which I awoke in a confused, muddled state—only gradually grasping my position and realising how long I must have been insensible, for the kopje above me was glowing as if on fire, bathed in the glory which suffused the west. My horse was lying down a dozen yards away, with his head just raised; and in front, forming a charming picture, was a little herd of about a dozen graceful antelopes, some drinking, some standing in the water, and another upon the top of a low flat stone, with head erect and long horns gracefully curving over its back as it kept a lookout for danger; a slight movement upon my part a few moments later making the beautiful animal utter a snort, and then the whole party were off like the wind.

Their rush made Sandho spring to his feet with a neigh of alarm, and then, as I made an effort and rose to a sitting position, he bounded up to me, whinnying with pleasure, and thrust his muzzle over my shoulder.

To my delight, I found that, though painful and tender, the swelling of my arms and wrists had gone down; while much of the pain had left my leg, which was, however, stiff and helpless from the terrible wrench.

My first movement was to get to the spring above where the little stream had been trampled and discoloured by the antelopes; and after a good draught I stood up once more, feeling ready to attempt mounting again, and see if I could reach the spot my father had appointed for the meeting with Joeboy. I knew, too, from sundry symptoms, that I must be better—far better than I could have expected, for I was ravenously hungry; and as I realised this I could not keep back a laugh. A capital sign this, though painful, for there was no chance of obtaining food till I could reach some farm; but I could recall no likely place on my way to the Nek, and so the hunger-pains had to be borne.

Leaving Sandho browsing upon the rich grass near the spring in a dainty way, which, in combination with his appearance, suggested that he had been feeding to his heart's content, I climbed over the rocks till I reached the highest point of the kopje. There, lying down, I set myself to carefully scan the open veldt in search of mounted men; till, satisfied there were none to be seen, I descended, mounted my horse, and rode gently away, not suffering more than was to be expected after what I had gone through.

The country where I now was seemed fairly familiar, and I soon made out mountain-tops in the distance, which served as guides. One peak in particular I marked down as lying to the left of Echo Nek, or at all events near the gap in the mountains I was to reach; and towards this Sandho ambled for another hour, when the night began to close in fast. After marking down the direction of the peak as well as I could before the light died out on the misty horizon, I waited till it was quite dark, then I selected a star which I calculated was just over where I had last seen the peak, and once more rode on for what must have been three hours; but then, concluding that to ride farther might possibly mean going astray, I walked my horse till a tolerably suitable spot offered itself for a halting-place till daylight, where I off-saddled Sandho, turned him loose to graze, and settled myself down in a patch of thorny bush to pass the night as I could.

I longed to light a fire to keep off lions; but in avoiding one enemy I felt I might be attracting another; for if there were Boers anywhere in the neighbourhood they would be certain to ride up, and then all my efforts would prove to have been in vain. Hence there was nothing for it but to take the risk.

The night was glorious though cold, for I had been imperceptibly rising into high ground. The stars sparkled as if there was frost; but I had no eyes for the beauty of the scene, hemmed in as I was by enemies. Twice over I shivered as to the fate of poor Sandho, the deep, muttering roar of the lions seeming to make the ground tremble and the air vibrate. If they scented my horse and drew near I was perfectly defenceless, and could do nothing to save the poor beast. So alarmed did I grow at last upon his account that I determined to risk being seen, and hurriedly began to collect scraps of dead wood, twigs, and such pieces of dry grass as were likely to burn. I did not stop to find many; but, startled by a loud barking roar that, in my nervous state, sounded very near, I knelt down and struck a match, holding it well sheltered with my hands till the splint was fully alight, and then started the grass and wood. Fortunately these were thoroughly dry and caught readily; but the quantity was very small, and the blaze a mere trifle compared with what I wished to obtain. So, as actively as I was able, I started collecting everything I could, and carefully piled it up; but with small success, for I had to depend entirely upon my hands to break off scraps, and they burned away almost as fast as I could reach the fire.

I had just thrown on as much as I could hug to my breast when I was startled by a heavy breathing; and, turning sharply, for a moment or two I was certain that one of the fierce beasts had crept up. There, only a few feet away, were a pair of glistening eyes reflecting the fitful flames, and I began to back so as to get the fire between me and my foe.

Chapter Seven
My Nocturnal Visitor

As I moved it moved too; and I dimly saw the outstretched head and body, as I supposed, of a monstrous lion about to spring, when, the fire having flashed up more brightly, I uttered a gasp of relief. It was Sandho, who had come quietly up to the fire for company and protection.

I worked the harder then, and kept on hour after hour, having to take longer and longer journeys as I exhausted the supply close at hand; and all the time I was perfectly conscious that lions were near, prowling round our little apology for a camp so as to spring upon the horse and pull him down. Every time I started for more fuel I expected to hear a roar and feel one of the savage creatures spring upon me; but the night wore on, with the fire giving a steadier glow as the time passed. I suppose the fact of my keeping up a hurried movement, making a desperate rush here and there, with the light from the fire throwing up my figure plainly, was too much for the great cats, and they feared to attack. Whatever it was, they were kept at bay; and daybreak found me thoroughly exhausted, the last growl having died out, the light showing the great soft footprints of our enemies round and round the clump of bushes, crossing and recrossing, and suggesting that there had been a party of four—an old lioness and her nearly full-grown cubs.

It was a narrow escape; and, as if only too glad to get away from so dangerous a spot, Sandho so fidgeted to start that I had hard work to secure the broken end of his rein to the ring of the bit without shortening it so much that I could not hold it in my hand.

I took a good look round, however, before starting, and it was well I did so, for, clearly seen now in the level sunbeams away to the north, there was a party of horsemen riding in my direction, and discovery seemed certain, even if I had not already been seen.

My first idea was to spring into the saddle and gallop off; but I was in no condition for springing into my saddle. Crippled as I was, it meant a slow and painful climb, and then in all probability the utmost I could do would be to walk my horse slowly away.

To mount, lie down, and urge the horse round to the back of the clump of bushes which had formed my shelter during the past night, and then cautiously strike off straight away towards the mountains at a walk, doing my best to keep the shelter of scrub between me and the enemy, seemed the wiser plan, and this I put into execution.

I had several things in my favour by doing this: the distance between me and the horsemen was great; and I felt certain that, if it were a portion of the captain's troop, they had no glass of any kind. If they caught sight of me in making my retreat, they would only fancy they saw the figure of some peculiar, humpbacked-looking animal; and on making for the mountains my position upon Sandho's back would never lead them to suppose it was a horse bearing a rider. This supposition, too, would be helped by the fact that there were still little herds and single wanderers, the relics of the vast hosts of antelopes of various species, from the tiny gazelle-like animals up through the clumsy hartebeeste and wildebeeste to the huge eland; and at a distance I felt it possible that myself and steed might be taken for one of these.

While thinking thus, and going through a painful struggle to get upon my horse properly, it seemed to me that the party were visibly coming nearer; but, hidden as we were by the bushes, I could see, from where I lay on my horse's back, as I turned my eyes in their direction, that so far I was not discovered. The crucial test, however, was yet to come; for, though I could keep Sandho out of sight for half a mile possibly, the land was gradually rising, and in that distance or less, I knew, we should stand out plainly in the clear air. Then, if seen, suffer what I might, I was determined to urge my horse on to his greatest speed, leaving the rest to fate.

I had no trouble with my well-trained steed, which obeyed every word or pressure; and with eyes so turned that I could keep the bush between us, I guided Sandho on till, as I had anticipated, the party of mounted men came gradually into view—first only the men, but soon after their horses. So far, they were going only at a walk, to pass the track diagonally to my course and some distance away.

As they were so visible, I felt they must soon see me, and tried hard to efface myself as much as possible, knowing that my dusky-brownish, homespun breeches, flannel shirt, and tanned high boots must assimilate well with the coat of my chestnut horse, and this cheered me a little.

Then, suddenly, I knew I was seen, for one of the men drew rein, letting the others go on a few horse-lengths before; and, as if in answer to a summons from the man behind, the rest of the party halted and sat gazing in my direction.

The next minute the man who had halted by himself now dismounted, and I saw a gleaming light glance from where he stood and then dropped down. It was too far off for me to see distinctly; but knowledge supplied what my eyes failed to grasp, and I knew the gleam was from his rifle-barrel reflecting the sun's rays, and the man's attitude that of one about to try a long shot at the uncouth animal in view beyond the thorny scrub.

There is an old-fashioned saying about people's feelings in critical moments: that their hearts stood still. Now, I don't believe for a moment that mine ceased to beat; but it certainly felt as if it did, while I lay rising and falling, yielding to Sandho's movements, and gazing straight back at the little hole which I knew must be pointed straight at me—invisible, of course; but the little puff of white smoke which suddenly jetted into the air was plain enough to my eyes, and so was the peculiar buzzing sound to my ears as the bullet passed over me like some strange bee in a violent hurry to reach its hive. Then came the sharp crack as of a sjambok wielded by a strong and well-accustomed arm.

"A miss, and no wonder!" I exclaimed; and I suppose I must have started and given Sandho a familiar pressure, or else it was the instinct of self-preservation at work in the sensible animal, for he suddenly made a bound forward so unexpectedly that I was nearly unseated; but my arms were now free, and, reaching down and getting tight hold of his leathern breastplate, I held on and let him go. The instinct of self-preservation was also strongly to the fore in me, and I lay fully expecting to hear the whizzing of half-a-dozen more bullets and the cracking of the rifles, since naturally I could see nothing then, my face lying against the horse's neck, as he bounded on at an easy gallop.

Were the enemy in pursuit?

I strained my hearing, but I could make out nothing more than the regular beat of my horse's hoofs; while, as no shots came, I felt certain they had made out my figure and were coming on in full chase.

"They'll have a long one," I thought; for, though I was in great pain, I found, to my intense delight, that I could accommodate myself to Sandho's long swinging gallop as he spurned the soft loose earth behind him, the ascent being exceedingly slight; and we were progressing in a series of antelope-like bounds.

At last, after galloping for quite ten minutes, something in front made Sandho swerve round to the left; and, before raising my head to see what it was, I turned my face sidewise so as to get a glance back at my pursuers, and could hardly believe my eyes when I saw that no Boers were there. It was not until I raised my head a little to gaze back in the other direction that

I could see them far away in the distance, evidently pursuing the course they had followed before the incidents of the halt and shot occurred.

Now I held on tightly and raised my head, endeavouring to make out why my horse had swerved. There it was plain enough: another of the stony kops which rose up to block our way had forced him to gallop along the unencumbered ground at the foot of a great line of hills, beyond which was the peak I had marked down as being in the neighbourhood of Echo Nek.

Unfortunately the land here was all strange to me, my journeys never having led me so far on this side of the mountains. Still, I felt I must be going in the direction of the Nek, and that sooner or later I should come to some valley into which I could strike off to the right, and get through and round by the peak beyond which I now certainly believed Echo Nek must be.

I made no effort to check Sandho, who was keeping on nearly level ground, but now raised myself upright in the saddle to watch for that which I had forgotten during the time I was in danger, but now that I was comparatively safe seemed to be the very first thing I should seek.

Many hours had now passed since, I had broken my fast; and at eighteen the desire for food is a tyrant against which no growing boy or young man can fight. But no. To my right were the rugged, barren hills undotted by bullock or sheep; to the left a far-spreading stretch of unfertile veldt; and though I cantered on for another full hour not a homestead came into sight.

At last, however, I saw a break in the continuous ridge of hills on my right, and eased Sandho down into his gentle amble, not willing to press him hard, for I knew that at any minute I might be obliged to urge him to his greatest speed.

In another half-hour we were bearing off to the right, for the hills had opened into a broad valley, at the head of which the great peak I had seen now rose up as if to block the way; and in spite of my hunger I felt lighter-hearted, for I was getting sure of my bearings. Yes, there beyond the shoulder of the peak was the crag just below which lay Echo Nek only a few miles away, not more than an hour's canter along the fairly even valley, and then— Oh, if Joeboy should not be there!

"He must; he is sure to be," I said half-aloud. "Even if he were not there, father would know how I should be pressed for food, and be there himself."

This was an encouraging and cheering thought; and, inspired with fresh hope, I rode on, wondering that, though the veldt looked so unpromising, some one had not taken up land, if only in the hope of finding minerals where the soil forbade the fruits of fertile earth; but no. All was barren and strange; even the granite blocks and kops were rare, and I looked still in vain for some sign of human habitation, some track of wheel or print of foot. The last I did begin to see now; but they were not the prints of ironshod hoofs, only those of antelopes, large and small, and not too frequent. Still, here was sign; and as I looked more closely I twice saw the soft round prints of the great sand-coloured cats, and my eyes began now to roam afield in the expectation of perhaps seeing those which had made the marks. No; the open valley that twenty or thirty years earlier might have been alive with game was absolutely desolate; not one of the vast herds which used to roam there, as the old Boers had often told me, was to be seen.

There was nothing whatever to break the long slopes of sand-coloured soil.

Ah! what was that on the ridge to my left, which ran down till it lost itself in the open bottom of the valley along which Sandho gently cantered? Some white-feathered and familiar birds, displaying their soft plumes, which looked ostrich-like in the distance. What could it be? I knew no bird, in spite of my wanderings, that ever looked like that. Still, a bird was a bird, and game, and the thought of game at such a time was glorious; but my spirits sank again, for I had no weapon, and then the grapes seemed to be sour.

"It isn't a bird; only a feather or two dropped by some old cock ostrich," I said aloud.

No. The feathers began to rise from the edge of the ridge, and there was a black face beneath them, then the broad breast, and finally the full figure of a stalwart Kaffir warrior, his thin arms and ankles ornamented with wool, his savage panoply of shield and assagai in his left hand, and his eyes shaded by his right hand, which cut straight across his forehead just below the fillet holding the three white ostrich feathers. He was evidently watching me.

Chapter Eight
Perils Which Grow

Upon making out what was before me, the little I had heard about the war rushed across my mind, and I saw at once that, catching the infection, at least one of the native tribes which had been disarmed, and were previously living at peace, had broken out, seizing the opportunity of their Dutch and English masters being at enmity to take one side or the other, possibly with some vague idea that they would thus regain their independence.

What this warrior might be I could not tell at a distance, for he might prove a Zulu still smarting under the defeat inflicted upon his nation by the British, or a Swazi who bitterly hated the Boers for their brutal treatment during the past.

I felt I ought to be able to tell at once by his appearance; but my knowledge was, after all, imperfect, and I certainly could not at a distance make out to what nation the man belonged.

I had not long time for consideration, as Sandho was steadily carrying me nearer; but I decided to go as close as I could without getting within range of an assagai; for it was worth some risk to get in touch with a friendly native in my emergency, since I knew he would try all he could to furnish me with food.

So I rode slowly on, straining my eyes the while to scan the various points in his slight dress, but keeping a sharp lookout right and left to make sure that his companions, if he had any, were not, after their fashion, crawling along under cover to outflank me. However, all seemed safe, for there was no cover on either side; but below the black warrior, and behind the ridge, there was ample space for a couple of hundred of his kin to be lying out of sight, ready at a signal to spring up and make a furious onslaught.

"And turn me into a sort of human pin-cushion, which they would fill with their assagais," I said half-aloud. "That wouldn't do, Sandho, old boy; so be ready to gallop off when I pull your rein."

My horse threw up his head and laid back his ears, beginning to bound off at once; but I checked him.

"Not yet, old boy; not yet. When I give the word you must make a half-turn, and we must try and circumvent them—if it is them, and not only one.—How near dare I go?" I asked myself; and I decided that forty yards would be as far as I ought to venture, being of course well on the *qui vive*.

The black—Swazi or Zulu—looked a terribly formidable enemy as he stood above me, clearly seen against the sky, and I was beginning to feel that I must not go much farther; but I was still in the dark as to what he might be, friend or enemy, when he mystified me still further by suddenly striking an attitude, standing as if suddenly turned into a bronze figure defying some one on his right. Directly after, he dashed into a kind of war-dance, advancing, retreating, throwing imaginary assagais at invisible foes, and then coming apparently to close quarters, screening his body with his long elliptic shield, and stabbing away at men standing and others falling all around.

I need hardly say I drew rein at once and sat ready to urge Sandho to his greatest speed at a moment's notice, for I felt that these evolutions might either mean defiance and a display of what he would do to me when I came within reach, or a feint to show his friendliness.

I cast the latter idea aside at once, and came to the conclusion that my warlike gentleman was on the watch for an opportunity to dash in after throwing me off my guard, and then I knew only too well what would happen—that which had befallen many an unfortunate settler in the past: a couple of small assagais darted at him like lightning, and the thrower rushing in after them with his stabbing weapon, followed by the fatal termination.

Still the grotesque dance went on, yet I felt pretty safe, for I was fully fifty yards distant, and had often proved Sandho in encounters with wild beasts; so I had no doubt of getting away in time when the savage made his rush which was certainly coming, as I saw the lithe actor was gradually working himself up to a sufficient pitch of excitement. His eyes were rolling, his powerful black limbs shone, and he darted here and there, leaping in the air to deliver some thrust with greater effect, and generally carrying on in a way that would have made me burst into a hearty fit of contemptuous laughter at the childish exhibition, evidently meant to impress me with the fellow's great bravery, had there not been, as I well knew, so terribly bloodthirsty an element beneath it all.

"There, Sandho," I said softly as I leaned forward to stroke my horse's soft arching neck, "I think we've had enough of the idiot's nonsense, and we'll go."

I was in the act of saying these words, keenly watching all round for danger, as well as beyond the bounding black in the full expectation of catching sight at any moment of the plumed heads of a party of his companions rising above the ridge, when, as if in a final effort or an attempt at a climax to the weirdly absurd performance, the black warrior proceeded to finish off with the slaying of about a dozen invisible enemies around him. Bang went his stabbing assagai against his shield, and then *stab, stab, stab,* when he turned upon his feet as if upon a pivot, darting his weapon as if he were some fierce creature armed with a terrible sting. I seemed to see in imagination an enemy go down at every thrust; a strange thrill of horror ran through me, and an awful kind of fascination held me seated there on my horse, as the black warrior stabbed away till his back was completely turned to me and he delivered a tremendous thrust, uttering a horrible yell. Then I burst out into a hysterical peal of laughter, and nearly fell out of the saddle.

Why? Because never was anything more absurd. The warrior's face was averted, and the long elliptically-shaped shield no longer covered the greater part of his person; and though I had failed in recognition before, I knew him now by the tremendously cut-down trousers he wore.

"Go on, Sandho," I said, and my horse walked gently forward, while the actor gave three or four more thrusts to kill the rest of the dozen invisible enemies, bringing himself face to face with me; and after leaping high in the air, uttering a triumphant yell, he grinned at me from ear to ear, as he breathlessly cried:

"'At's a way kill um all, Boss Val."

For it was Joeboy on the war-path, ready in his own opinion to slay all the Boers in the state.

Chapter Nine
The Friend In Need

"Why, Joeboy," I cried, wiping my eyes, "you're splendid. But where's Echo Nek?"

"Dah!" he said, pointing behind him with the dangerous-looking assagai he carried.

"Did you see me coming?"

He nodded, it being one of his habits to say as little in English as he could.

"Tell me: have you got anything to eat?" I said. "I'm starving."

He darted back to the other side of the ridge, and came back with the strap of a big canvas satchel over his shoulder, the bag-part looking bulky in the extreme.

"Um Tant Jenny," he said, frowning, as he shook the satchel, and then proceeded to scrape off with the blade of his stabbing-assagai the large ants which had scented the contents and were swarming to the attack. "Is there any water near?" I asked.

"Um," said Joeboy, pointing towards the other side of the ridge.

"Then there will be grass too," I said. "Go on, and show the way. Quick!"

The great black nodded and went off at a trot, taking me over the ridge and down a steep slope into a large gap in the side of the hill; and a quarter of an hour later we were alongside a bubbling stream, where long, rich, juicy grass grew in abundance.

Directly after Sandho was grazing contentedly; and when I had drunk from the pure fresh water, I was devouring rather than eating the magnified salt-beef sandwiches of which the satchel contained ample store, while Joeboy grinned to see the way in which one disappeared.

"Catch hold," I said, pushing a great sandwich towards my black companion; but he shook his head and shrank away.

"Tant Jenny say all young Boss Val," he said, and then he laughed and displayed a large packet carefully fastened to the inside of his shield. This packet he opened, took out a sandwich similar to mine, then squatted down and began to eat.

"Joeboy had plenty yes'day," he said, and he gave his front a circular rub as if to suggest that it was still fairly stored, after which he went on munching slowly as if to keep me company.

"Now," I said after eating a few mouthfuls, "what did my father say?"

"Big Boss say Joeboy go Echo Nek. Stop till son Val come."

"Is that all?" I said wonderingly.

"Yes; all Boss say."

As he spoke, however, Joeboy laid his sandwich upon the shield beside him, and then began to fumble behind him in the band of his cut-down trousers, out of a leopard-skin pocket attached to which he drew a packet of common leather tied up with a slip of the same.

I opened the leather packet with trembling fingers, and found a letter, which I eagerly read:

"Dear Val,—I take it for granted, my boy, that you will escape from those ruffians and be lying in wait for my message. I find, though, that Joeboy is missing, and if he does not return I shall have to come and meet you myself, and then I can tell you what to do. I will, however, write this in the hope that I can send it, as I do not want to leave your aunt and Bob, for there is much to do, burying and hiding a few valuables in case we are ever able to come back."

"Oh!" I exclaimed, and Joeboy half-sprang to his feet, but subsided as I went on:

"War has broken out, the Boers having defied the British Government. It has, of course, all been a surprise to me; but the news is coming in fast. Hodson has been here, and he tells me the English are all receiving orders to go. It is ruin to us, and after making such a home; but, God help us! we must do our best.

"Of course you cannot serve against your own countrymen, and I don't like your having anything to do with the horrible business; but if you feel that you must join in with our people and act as a volunteer against what is a cruel tyranny, I know you will act like a man.

"I can write no more, and Heaven knows when we may meet again. I shall make for Natal, of course, with as much as I can save out of the wreck—that is, as much as the enemy will let me carry off. Perhaps, though, that will be nothing; and I must be content with getting away with our lives, for I hear that the blacks are getting uneasy, as if they smelt blood; and Heaven knows what may happen if they break out, for the white man is their natural enemy in their eyes, and, friends now, they may be our foes to-morrow.

"God bless and protect you, my boy! Aunt Jenny's dear love to you, and she is going to help me to hold Bob in, for the young dog is mad to come after you.

"Your father, in the dear old home he is about to quit, perhaps for ever.

"John Moray.

"PS:—Good news, my boy. Joeboy has just come back, in full fighting fig. He will bring this, and some provision for a day or two. I feel sure you may trust him. He has been showing me what he would do to any one who tried to hurt young Boss Val. He is like a big child; but he is true as steel. Good-bye.

"Heaven be with you, my boy!"

That last line was in Aunt Jenny's handwriting, and there were big blotches on the paper where the ink had run, and over them came a few lines in Bob's clumsy hand:

"Val, old chap, the dad says I'm not to come along with Joeboy to join. I told him it was a shame, for I felt in a passion, and he knocked me down.

"That's only my larks. He did knock me down, but not with his fist or the handle of a— I don't know how you spell it; but I mean chambock. He knocked me over with what he said. He told me it was my duty to stop and help him and auntie. He might want me to fight for him and her. If he does, I'll shove in two cartridges—I mean only one bullet; and I don't care if the old rifle kicks till she breaks my collar-bone. I mean to let the Boers have it for coming and upsetting us. I never knew how nice dear old home was before. Old—"

That was the bottom of the paper; but upon turning it over, there at the very top on the other side, and in the left-hand corner above the word "Val," where my father had begun, was the word "Beasts," which I had passed over unnoticed as being part of some memorandum on the paper when my father took it up hurriedly to write.

I always was a weak, emotional sort of fellow—perhaps it was due to the climate, and my having had the fever when we first came there—and the writing looked very dim and blurry before my eyes; and yet I felt inclined to laugh over what Bob had scribbled. I did laugh when my eyes grew clear again, for Bob had, apparently at the last, taken up the pen to write along the edge of the paper, and so badly that it was hard to read:

"I say, Joeboy looks fizzing. He's been oiling himself over to make him go easy, and sharpening his saygays with the scythe-rubber."

"And so there's to be no more home," I said softly as I carefully folded up the paper and placed it in my breast. Then somehow the terrible feeling of hunger died out, and I only drank some more water.

"Boss Val eat lot," said Joeboy, his voice making me start.

"No more, now, Joeboy," I said. "I'll wait a bit."

"Wait a bit," he said, nodding his head, and then carefully replacing what I had left in the satchel.

"Fasten that to the back of my saddle," I said.

"Um! Joeboy carry."

"No, no," I replied. "We must part now, Joeboy. I can't go back home, nor stay here."

Joeboy shook his head.

"No stop," he said. "All bad."

"You don't understand," I said.

"Um!" he said, nodding. "Joeboy know. Boss Val fight Boers."

"Perhaps; but you must go back and help my father if he has to leave the farm."

There was another shake of the head and a frown; then a silence, during which the great black seemed to be thinking out what he was to say in English to make his meaning clear. At last it came as he sat there with his shield on one side, his assagais on the other; and, to my surprise, he took up the big stabbing weapon and one of the light throwing-shafts before touching me on the chest with a finger.

"Boss John big boss," he said solemnly. "Boss Val little boss;" and he held up the two spears to illustrate his words. "Big boss say, 'Go 'long my boy.' Little boss say, 'Go 'long my dad.' Joeboy say, 'Don't car'; shan't go. Got to go 'long Boss Val.'"

"My father told you this?"

"Um!" said the great fellow; "dat's all right."

"But you would be so much use to my father, Joe, to manage the bullocks in the wagon."

"No," he said. "No bullock. Boer boy take 'em all away. Boss John no got nothing soon."

"You are sure my father said you were to go with me, Joeboy?" I said after a few minutes' pause.

"Um," he said, nodding his head fiercely. "Say, 'Take care my boy, Joeboy.' Joeboy take care Boss Val."

He caught up his shield and sprang to his feet, with the assagais trembling in his big hand, looking as if he could be a terrible adversary in a close conflict, though helpless against modern weapons of war.

This thought made me think of myself and my own position.

"Very well, Joeboy. I say you shall come with me."

He nodded.

"But you'll have to lend me one of your assagais till I can get a rifle."

"Boss Val got rifle gun," he said sharply.

"Where? No; I have only my knife."

Joeboy laughed, and ran to the side of the rift, where he began to scratch in the sand, and a few inches down laid bare the muzzle of my rifle, gave it a tug, and it came out with the well-filled bandolier attached.

I caught at it with a cry of eager joy, and began to carefully dust away every particle of sand that clung to it before slipping on the belt, forgetting the aching pains in my wrists and left leg, as something like a glow of confidence ran through me. Then came back the thought of home, with its smiling fields, orchard, and garden around the house we had raised upon the land won from the wilderness; and the thought that I was to be exiled from it all in consequence of this war; and the injustice of the Boers raised a spirit of anger against them which helped me to pull myself together and frowningly resolve to prove myself a man.

"Action, action," I muttered. "I should have liked to go back and see them all again; but I must begin at once, before I am taken. What would they do with me?" I said aloud; and a glance at Joeboy's face showed me that, awkward though he was at speaking, he comprehended every word I had said.

"Big Boss Boer," he said, nodding, "say Boss Val come fight. No Boss Val fight? *Whish, whish, whish, crack, cruck!*"

He went through the movement of one wielding a bullock-lash, and imitated the sound it made through the air and the loud cracking when it struck home upon quivering flesh. Then he went on, "Boss Val no fight now! *Bang, bang!*"

"Flog me the first time I refuse, Joeboy, and shoot me the next time."

"Um."

"Well, then, we will not give them the chance."

Joeboy shook his head violently.

"What Joeboy do now, Boss?"

"Rub my wrists, Joeboy," I said, stripping up my sleeves and showing him their bruised state and my swollen arms.

He understood why they were so, and took first one and then the other in his big soft grey palms, to mould and knead and rub them with untiring patience for long enough, the effect being pleasurable in the extreme.

But I checked him when he was in the midst of it, and pointed to my leg.

"Boer tie up leg?" he said wonderingly.

I explained what was wrong, and he knelt before me, carefully removing my laced-up boot, and giving me sickening pain as he drew off my coarse home-knitted stocking, to lay bare the wrenched and swollen foot and ankle.

"Um!" he said. "Boss Val come to water."

He lifted me to the edge of the stream as easily as if I had been a child, and when I sat down, carefully bathed the joint for fully half-an-hour, dried it by pouring sand over it again and again, and then as tenderly as a woman replaced stocking and boot, which latter he laced very loosely.

"Boss Val go one leg when off Sandho."

"Yes, Joeboy," I said; "but it will soon get better."

"Um!" he said, and he looked at me inquiringly, as if for orders.

"Now we must be off, Joeboy, before the Boers hunt me out."

"Um!" he said, in token of assent; and upon my calling Sandho to my side Joeboy helped me to mount, securing the satchel to my saddle in obedience to my orders; and, making for Echo Nek, we went steadily on, my intention being to get through the pass and some distance on the other side towards the Natal border before dark.

"We shall know the road better there, Joeboy," I said after we had been walking some time; "it all seems strange to me here."

"Joeboy know," he said.

"What! the way about here?" I said, in surprise. "When did you come?"

"Long while," he replied. "Lost bullock. Come here."

"Oh!"—then I remembered. "Of course. You were gone a fortnight."

"Um!" said Joeboy.

"And my father thought you had run away, and that we should never see you again."

"How Joeboy run away? Bullock no run. Run other way."

"Yes," I said, laughing; "they are always ready to go in the wrong direction. Do you know"—I was going to say something about the rising of one of the rivers up in the mountains somewhere near, but I stopped short, for my companion suddenly darted to Sandho's head and pressed him sidewise towards a pile of rocks which offered plenty of shelter from anything in front.

"What is it, Joeboy?" I said. "A good shot at something?"

For answer he pointed upward at the rocks beside the pass which went by the name of Echo Nek—the place which we had nearly reached, this great gap in the mountains being the only spot for many miles on either side where a horse could cross. As to wagons, a far greater détour was necessary to find a road.

I looked in the direction he pointed out, but for some moments I could see nothing. Then a faint gleam from something moving gave me warning of what had taken place, and directly after I caught sight of the bearer of the rifle from whose barrel the sunlight had flashed.

Chapter Ten
Running the Gauntlet

Under other circumstances I should have leaped down from my horse and crouched; but my leg had grown still and cold, so I sat perfectly motionless, trying to make out some plan of action I might follow out. To my dismay, the Boers had been quicker than I had given them credit for, and had, so to speak, shut the principal gate in the huge wall which in that particular part closed in their country from Natal. The man I had seen was doubtless one of their outposts, and for aught I knew to the contrary the pass might be held by hundreds of the sturdy burghers, every man a born rifleman. To go back by the way I came meant running into the arms of those who were scouring the country to retake me, while to make a détour and get round to the other side of the opening meant getting farther into the Boer country, the more populous part, where their troops would for certain now be on the move.

It seemed there was no going backward; and upon turning to look at Joeboy he showed he was of the same opinion. "No go back," he said; "all Boer. Wait till sun gone."

"And try to steal through the pass then," I said eagerly, "in the dark?"

"Um!" he said. "All dark. No see Boss Val; no see horse."

"But they'll hear his hoofs. There are sure to be plenty of sentries."

"Um, plenty much Boer. Go soft, soft. Then Sandho gallop."

"And what about you?" I said, as I grasped that he meant we were to steal along softly in the darkness till we were heard, and then that I was to gallop. "What about you?"

"Joeboy hold stirrup and run," he said, with a laugh. "Boer better get out o' way."

This seemed to be our only road out of the difficulty, and I carefully dismounted, Joeboy leading the horse farther in amongst what was now becoming a chaotic wilderness of stones; and here, pretty well hidden, but quite open to discovery by a wandering party of Boers at any time, we sat down to wait, listening to the steady *crop, crop,* as Sandho calmly set to work to improve the occasion on grass.

As far as I could make out, the sentry we had seen was about a fifth of a mile distant; but in all probability there were others perched up on the lookout in various points of vantage high on either side of the pass; while those below, I felt sure now, would be in strong force, fulfilling the double duty of preventing English settlers from passing out of the country save as the Boers pleased, and defending the place.

"All Boer," he said, pointing in various directions. "Can't go. Wait."

"Yes," I said; "we must wait till it is dark."

"Boss Val wait. Sandho eat and rest," he said. "Boss lie down."

"No," I replied. "I must sit here and watch. You lie down now."

"Boss Val lie down," said the black, shaking his head. "Boer see um."

"Well, they'll see you," I said.

"Um!" he replied, with a nod. "Only black man. See Boss Val; come and catch um."

It was my turn to nod now, for his meaning was plain. If the Boers saw me, my chances of escape were gone; while if by ill-luck they caught night of him, the probability was that they would not trouble themselves about a solitary Kaffir.

"You are right, Joeboy," I said. "I'll keep hidden till it grows dark."

"Um!" he said softly; "get dark. Then not see Boss Val. Joeboy go and look how many."

I was about to oppose this part of his plan, but upon second thoughts I did not, but selected a better spot for my hiding-place by creeping among the stones towards where Sandho was grazing, so as to keep him well under my observation for fear he should stray too far, and not be within reach should danger arise. There he was, in a snug nook where the grass grew thickly consequent upon there being suggestions of a trickling spring. The spot was well surrounded, too, by stones, which on three sides fenced him in, and between two of these, and with a larger one to form a support for my back, I settled myself as comfortably as I could, for my leg was still very painful and my arms ached terribly. In fact, I was so weary now the time for action was over that I was quite content to subside, and sit leaning back watching the black while he crawled on hands and knees to Sandho, who suddenly raised his head with a start at Joeboy's approach; but on seeing who it was, he uttered a low whinnying sound and went on cropping the grass once more, paying no further heed to the black, who proceeded to hobble, his two fore-legs to keep him from going too far, and then returned to me.

"No go away now," whispered Joeboy.

"It wasn't necessary," I said. "I shall watch him."

"Um!" said the black, and then he pointed in the way he intended to go, laid the shield and two throwing-assagais by me, and then went rapidly off on all-fours, trotting like a huge black dog.

I watched till he disappeared among the stones between me and the sentry, and twice I caught sight of him again, or rather, I should say, of his back; but only for a moment or two, and then he was gone, while I let my eyes rest again upon the spot where I had last seen the sentry. Then I watched my horse, and afterwards began to take more note of my surroundings.

It did not take long. There were blocks of stone everywhere in the wildest confusion, and among them here and there great straggling patches of unwholesome-looking, fleshily-lobed prickly-pears with their horrible thorns. Now and then, too, were miserable, dried-up karroo-bushes, starved among the great blocks above the rich green hollow where Sandho grazed. Everywhere else was parched loose red sand, and beyond rose up the sterile mountains on either side of the pass.

Joeboy knew me better than I knew myself when he hobbled the horse, for as I sat there watching and thinking how solitary it all was, wondering how they were getting on at home, and whether the Boers were really in force by the pass, a pleasant feeling of restfulness came over me, and the mountains in the distance seemed to grow hazy and of a delicious blue; the coarse bushes did not look so dry, nor the sickly prickly-pears so unwholesome and like flat oval cakes of horribly unwholesome human flesh joined together at their edges; while the little patch of pasture where Sandho was feeding appeared to be of an indescribably beautiful tinge of green.

"I wonder how long Joeboy will be," I remember thinking, as I drew my injured ankle across my right knee and began to rub it softly. "He ought to come back soon."

Then I ceased chafing the ankle, for it was very tender, and I wondered how long it would take to get well again, so that I could leap from stone to stone as sure-footed as ever.

It was a relief to leave it alone, and I let it glide back till it was outstretched upon the sand beyond the stones, where it lay resting, and the pain began to die out. It was restful, too, for my arms; for as soon as I began to put any strain upon the muscles a peculiar gnawing sensation was set up, which was complete torture till I let them lie inert.

"The brutes!" I muttered; "they must be half-savages still to treat one like this; but it was all that wretched renegade's work. I wonder whether I shall ever meet him again. I believe he's a miserable coward. I'll soon see if I do. Oh, if I can only get amongst our people, and join them!"

These thoughts made me feel hot, and I lay back picturing all that had taken place at our farm; but as the pain in my limbs died down, so did my rage against the Irish captain, and I began looking round again, thinking how beautiful the desert place looked, and what effects were produced among the mountains by the changes in the atmosphere. Then I fell to watching Sandho, and then the soft effects grew hazy, and—then hazier— and very dark, but not so dark but that I could see Joeboy's big face as he leaned over me and said softly, "Boss Val been asleep?"

"No," I said sharply.

"Um!" whispered Joeboy, laying his hand across my mouth. "Boer jus' there. Lots. Plenty horses."

"Why, it's night," I said in a whisper as I looked round in wonder.

"Um!"

"Where's Sandho?"

Joeboy nodded his head; and, looking in the direction indicated, I could just see the shadowy form of my grazing horse, not above eight or ten feet away.

"Have I been asleep all this time?" I said, with a strange feeling of shame troubling me.

"Um! Plenty sleep," replied Joeboy. "Now ready? Come 'long."

"Yes, I'm ready," I said eagerly; "but tell me, have you been up towards the pass?"

"Um!" he said. "Plenty Boer. All dark."

"Do you think we can get through?"

"Um. Mustn't talk."

He led Sandho forward, and went down on one knee to unfasten the strap with which the horse was hobbled; then he offered me a leg up, and so enabled me to spring into the saddle without much difficulty. The next minute he was leading the horse in and out among the rocks, Sandho's hoofs striking a stone with a sharp click; after which he checked the active little animal, and we stood together listening. But all was still, and the night looked as if a black cloud had been drawn across the sky.

"Nobody can possibly see us," I said half-aloud; "and if they do they'll think it some of their own people."

"Um!" said Joeboy, and as he said it I knew I was wrong, for I recalled what I had read, that in time of war sentries challenge, and, failing to receive the password of the night, fire at once. It was a startling thought; but we went on all the same, I for my part feeling I must trust to my good-luck.

As we got farther in towards the mountains the obscurity increased and the air grew cooler. I now began to feel how impossible it would have been for me to have come alone and found my way in the darkness, for in a few minutes I was quite helpless; but Joeboy seemed in nowise confused, and did not hesitate once. It was as much as I could do to make out his black head and shoulders, and only at times found that the nodding ostrich-plumes were bobbing about just in front of me, as their wearer walked steadily on, holding my horse's head. So we went on for nearly an hour, with Joeboy leading Sandho in and out among the great blocks of stone which strewed our way, keeping him where the sand was soft by getting well in front, so that the horse's steps were pretty nearly in his own. I could make out that we were gradually rising, and that the rocks towered up to a great height left and right; but though I rode with every sense upon the strain, I could neither hear nor see sign of the enemy.

Fortunately the night was cloudy, and I knew it would be long before the waning moon rose—not, I hoped, till we had been right through the pass. In fact, as we went steadily on without interruption, I began to believe the Boer I had seen must have been one of a small outpost placed there for observation during the daylight, and that they must have retired at dusk, while I was asleep; for I thought we must now be pretty well through the highest part of the opening, and had there been any one there I must have heard a challenge.

I was just about to whisper my opinion to Joeboy when he stopped our progress and stood holding the horse's head tightly, showing me something was wrong. I raised myself in the stirrups to peer forward, but everything in front was nearly black; and though I listened, holding my breath, there was not a sound. Then suddenly a voice from somewhere above on the right front demanded in Dutch, "Who goes there?"

For answer Joeboy stepped on at once, and for the first time Sandho kicked against a stone, one of his shoes not only giving out a sharp *clink*, but striking a spark of fire.

It was as if that spark of fire struck by iron off stone had ignited the powder in the pan of an old-fashioned gun; for from close at hand there was a flash, the heavy report, and then a rolling volley of echoes. I felt Sandho bound beneath me; but the next moment he was walking steadily along, following the hand holding his bit, and he paid no more heed when directly after another shot was fired on ahead, another behind, and again another and another, raising what seemed to be a continuous roar of echoes right, left, and in front, to go rolling among the mountains.

The hot blood flew to my face, and a thrill of excitement ran through me as I involuntarily cocked the rifle I held across the saddle, sitting ready to fire at the first enemy who presented himself; in fact, I nearly drew trigger once, but my common-sense prevailed, as I felt that we could not be seen, neither could we be heard in the roar of echoes which took up and magnified the reports. Joeboy was doing exactly what was right under the circumstances—going straight on; and, unless we found a body of men confronting us and stopping our way, or an unlucky bullet struck one of us, it seemed probable that in a very short time we should have achieved our purpose.

I had often heard of Echo Nek before, and had some vague idea that if any one shouted there the tones of his voice would be reverberated from the face of the cliffs; but I had never realised the true reason as I did now.

The firing went steadily on, the Boer outpost being evidently under the impression that their action would drive back the force approaching to get into their country. This being so, the reports increased to an extent that showed plainly enough the presence of a strong body of men, who had been lying inside the valley, ready to hurry forward to the defence of the pass upon an alarm being given.

I now began to wonder how it was that we were not seen through some one of the flashes and hit by bullets sent spattering among the stones among which we wended our way; but none came near. Every now and then I heard a sharp shock against the rock, followed by a pattering downpour of fragments. Every shot struck high above our heads, and at the end of a few minutes, higher still; at which I wondered, till it suddenly occurred to me that Sandho was not climbing higher and higher up the pass, but descending.

All this time Joeboy kept steadily on, apparently as unconcerned as if he were leading the horse home from grazing peacefully away upon the veldt.

I too began to feel more at my ease, for we had gone on so far that there was a strong hope that we might be successful, unless there should prove to be another body lower down the pass. The next minute, though, I felt convinced this could not be the case, for if another body were lower down they would have been firing; or, on second thoughts, I concluded they must have fired first, since the Boers would never conclude that a body of men was leaving their territory.

The firing kept on for a few minutes longer, and then suddenly ceased; while as we proceeded, with Joeboy leading on as fast as Sandho could walk, we could hear voices behind us; men shouting and answering one another, though it was impossible to hear what was said; but it seemed as if they were asking one another what the firing was about, and whether any one had seen the attacking party. Of course this is only what I surmised; but it satisfied me at the time, and I could not help laughing at the waste of powder and lead occasioned by the harmless incident of a spark being struck from a stone by a horse's foot.

We were soon, however, satisfied about one thing: that we were not being pursued; for there was no more firing, and the voices soon died out as we went steadily on along a rough winding track pretty free from stones.

We must have been carefully making our way onward for about an hour, when suddenly we walked right into a mist, which made our progress more difficult, for the great blocks of stone seemed to loom up suddenly right in our way; and in avoiding these we somehow missed the track, good proof of which was given me by Joeboy's action; for he suddenly checked the horse, stooped down, felt about, and ended by lifting a stone as big as my head and casting it from him.

"Why did you do that, Joeboy?" I said.

"Boss wait," was the answer, and I waited, to hear the stone strike directly after, and then keep on striking, as it went on by leaps and bounds, making me shudder slightly as I grasped the fact that Joeboy had checked the horse suddenly just on the brink of some precipice, down which the stone went rolling and plunging till the sounds of its blows died away along with the echoes it raised.

Chapter Eleven
Out of the Frying-Pan

"What a narrow escape, Joeboy!" I whispered.

"Um!" he said. "No good go that way. Sandho break knees."

"Break his knees?" I said. "Yes, I should think he would! Can you find the way back to the track?"

"Um! No. All thick; all dark. Come back little way. Sit down and wait."

It was good counsel, and I sat fast—rather nervously, though—while Joeboy backed the horse. And I had cause for my nervous sensation. In fact, what followed proved that, in the darkness and confusion caused by our ignorance, Joeboy backed the horse along the edge of the precipice instead of right away from it; for there was a sudden slip, and one of Sandho's hind-legs went down, making the poor beast give a frantic plunge which nearly unseated me and drove Joeboy backwards. Then, as the horse leaped up again, he made three or four bounds before standing snorting and trembling; while I heard the rush and rattle of the dislodged stones as they went hurtling down into the gorge.

"Um! Mustn't try any more," said Joeboy coolly as he took hold of Sandho's bridle again, and petted and caressed the poor beast till he was calm once more.

"He'll stand now," I said, rather huskily, as I mastered a strong desire to get down. "Feel round for this edge, Joeboy, and find out which is the safe way to go."

"Um!" grunted the black; and after giving Sandho a final pat on the neck, he went down on all-fours and crawled away through the darkness so silently that at the end of a few minutes I began to feel alarmed, wondering whether he had made some terrible slip and gone over.

It was vain to argue with myself, for the shock I had received when the horse slipped had not passed away. No doubt my previous experiences had weakened me, and made me less able to fight against what was a very ordinary trouble for a mountain rider.

Another five minutes passed away—minutes which seemed terribly prolonged as I sat there in the darkness knowing I dared not stir, and convinced that we must be upon a projecting bracket of rock whose shape I could mentally picture, with only one narrow pathway off, and that hidden by the mist. At last I could bear it no longer, and, leaning forward to try and penetrate the darkness beyond the horse's head, I called twice:

"Joeboy! Joeboy!"

"Joeboy here, Boss," came from behind me, and I uttered a sigh of relief as the great fellow seemed to rise up close by and laid his hand upon my arm.

"Where have you been?" I said in a querulous, excited way.

"Where, Boss Val say? Go all round. Better stop till morning."

"Yes," I said, with a sigh of relief. "Let's stop till morning. Here, help me to get down."

I was obliged to ask for help, for the cold and damp air had made my injured limbs so stiff and painful that I could hardly move them, and it required a good strong effort to keep down a groan when I lowered myself on to my feet, and then gladly sat down upon the damp rock.

I had no fear about Sandho, whose rein had been passed over his head and allowed to hang down, for he had been trained to stand, and having grazed for many hours, had no temptation to stir.

Joeboy soon settled himself close to my feet, and then began our long and painful watching, hour after hour, through a night which seemed as if it would never end. I had no desire to question the black, for his action fully proved to me that our position must be perilous unless we left the horse to shift for himself, and all this was sufficient to keep off any desire for sleep; while a whisper from time to time was sufficient to satisfy myself that my companion was as wakeful as I. As the time passed on the mist seemed to thicken around us, with this peculiarity striking me: it seemed to shut us completely in, so that not a sound reached our ears, the silence being to me perfectly awful.

At last the morning was heralded by a faint puff or two of chilly air which came and went again, till at last it settled into a soft breeze, whose effects were soon apparent. All at once, as I looked up, a cloud of mist became visible, then floated away; and as if by magic the sky, of a soft dark grey, dotted with a faint star or two, came into sight.

Then day began to advance with rapid strides, and I found my notion of our being upon a bracket of rock was not too far-fetched, for we were upon a jutting-out promontory of some fifty feet across, from whose edges the rock went down in places perpendicularly, in others with a tremendously steep slope, while the way by which we came on was not above half-a-dozen yards wide.

"You were very wise, Joeboy," I said as I rose to look round. "It would have been madness to try leading Sandho off there in the fog."

"Um!" said Joe quietly; and then: "Look!"

He pointed away to our right, and, following his direction, I could here and there make out the missing path down the pass, winding along in rough zigzags till lost in the distance.

I was soon in my saddle again, and Joeboy led the horse off the perilous place where we had passed the night, and then up the pass again for a couple of hundred yards to where the track had borne off a little to the right, but where we had kept on through the mist perfectly straight, with nearly fatal results.

We looked anxiously up now as we turned off into the proper track, fully expecting to see outposts of the Boers who had fired as we crossed the head; but none were visible. So we began to descend as rapidly as we could, but only at a walk, for the track was terribly rough.

It was only very gradually that the valley began to open out, our way at times being along the stony bed of a mountain torrent; while right and left the sides of what looked like a tremendous rift in the mountain, split open in some terrific convulsion of nature, towered up.

We went along cheerily, for every yard carried us farther from risk of capture by the Boers; and once we were well clear of the pass a couple of days would, I felt sure, place us safely in the land of my countrymen with whom the Boers were at war.

"How soon shall we stop and have breakfast, Joeboy?" I said as we were passing through a perfect chaos of great stones which now hemmed us in front and back. "No fear of seeing any Boers now."

The words had hardly left my lips when Sandho stopped short, and uttered a sharp challenging neigh, which was answered from some distance in front; and directly after, as I turned my horse sharply to get under the cover of a huge block we had just passed, there came the loud clattering of hoofs and a shout, as a party of some five-and-twenty well-mounted horsemen cantered out to bar the way.

"Then they are there," I muttered as I swung Sandho round again. Joeboy laid his left hand on the saddle, and away we cantered forward to circumvent, if possible, the party in front whose horse had answered Sandho's challenge.

The men behind yelled to us to stop. We paid no heed, but, regardless of the stones, cantered on, Joeboy taking them at a stride in company with Sandho's bounds.

The next minute I was looking upon fully twenty mounted riflemen right across our path, and a glance right and left showed me that any attempt to get round them would be an act of madness, for no horse could pass.

I turned in my saddle and looked back, to find that the party there were closing in upon us; and for a moment I felt ready to turn Sandho and go at them at full gallop, so as to try and cut my way through. I saw, however, this would be a greater risk than going in the other direction.

"It's of no use, Joeboy," I said hoarsely; "we're trapped."

"Boss Val going to fight?" he said inquiringly, and as he asked his question he fitted his long, elliptical shield well upon his left arm and arranged his assagais handy for throwing.

"Two against all those, Joeboy? No; it would be folly."

There was no time for more words, for the party which had remained in hiding till we had passed were closing in fast; and then a couple of young men suddenly darted out from those in front, set spurs to their horses, and seemed to race at us, leaping the stones in their way steeplechase fashion.

In almost less time than I take to describe it, one of them, a good-looking, frank young fellow in an officer's uniform, rose in his stirrups and made a snatch at my arm; but, in answer to a touch of the heel, Sandho leaped forward, and my would-be captor passed me, riding on several horse-lengths before he could turn and come at me again; while, by a quick leap aside, Joeboy avoided the man who came at him, and stood with his back to a great stone, with his assagai raised to strike.

"Surrender, you Dutch scoundrel!" roared my antagonist, drawing his sword, "or I'll cut you down."

"Dutch scoundrel yourself, you ugly idiot of a Boer!" I cried as angrily, and I brought my rifle to bear upon him, holding it like a pistol.

"Here, don't shoot," cried my adversary. "You don't talk like a Boer."

"Why should I?" said I. "But you're not a Dutchman—are you?"

"Hardly," he said, with a laugh.

"What are you, then?"

"Making a mistake, it seems," he replied.

"But your people are Boers?"

"They're going to beat them," he replied, "as soon as they get a chance. Have you seen them up the Nek yonder?"

"Yes; I was running away from them. They were shooting at us last night."

"Hi; Robsy! Steady there!" roared my new acquaintance. "Steady, I say! Friends.—You, Black Jack, put down that spear, or it'll be the worse for you.—It's all right, sir," he continued as a grey-haired, military-looking man now rode up, followed by half-a-dozen more. "This is an Englishman running away from the Boers."

"Then he's not an Englishman," said the officer sharply. "Here, arrest this man.—Now then, give an account of yourself, for you look confoundedly like a spy. Here, some one, cut that black fellow down if he resists."

"Be quiet, Joeboy," I cried; "these are friends."

Joeboy dropped into a peaceable attitude and stood scowling at the horsemen who surrounded us.

"Now, sir," said the officer, "why don't you speak?"

"Because you called me a spy," I said.

"Well, that seems to be what you are, you young scoundrel. How many of your friends are there up yonder?"

"I don't know," I said.

"Say 'sir' when you speak to a gentleman," cried the officer angrily, "and no nonsense. Speak out—the truth if you don't want to be shot."

"Of course I don't want to be shot," I said scornfully; "and I'm not in the habit of telling lies."

"How many Boers are there, then, up in the pass?"

"I don't know," I said. "We crept by them in the dark."

"Why? To come and see what forces we had here?"

"No," I said.

"Then why did you come?"

"To get away from the Boers."

"Why did you want to get away from them?" cried the officer, gazing at me searchingly.

I was so hot and indignant that I would not speak for some little time.

"I thought so. Making up a good story—eh? You've caught the first spy, Lieutenant."

"No, sir, I think not," said the young officer.

"I think you have.—Now, sir," he continued, "if you wish to save your skin, speak out. Why did you want to get away from the Boers?"

"Because I was commandoed," I said rather sulkily.

"Oh, then you were afraid to fight—eh?"

"No; but I was not going to fight my own countrymen."

"Oh!" said the officer, staring. "Here, tell me, how were you summoned?"

I told him, and that the party was led by an Irishman named Moriarty.

"Ah! yes, I know him. Tall, handsome, dashing young Irish cavalier—isn't he?"

"No," I said; "a middle-aged, bullying, ruffianly sort of a fellow, with a red nose," I replied.

"Humph! Then where do you come from?"

"Cameldorn Farm."

"Eh? Hullo!" cried the young man who had captured me. "I say, take off your hat."

"What for?" I asked.

"Because I want to look at you. How's that scratch you got on the arm from the lioness?"

"What do you know about the scratch?" I said, leaning forward to look the speaker full in the eyes.

"Why, only that I shot her. What's your name? Of course, Val."

"Mr Denham!" I cried in astonishment.

"That's your humble servant, sir."

"But you've got a beard now," I cried, holding out my hand. "Oh, I say, I am glad to see you!"

"The same here, Val, my lad. I say, how you've grown! Here, Colonel, it's all right. I'll answer for this fellow. Why, Val, you were commandoed, and cutting away?"

"Yes," I cried excitedly. "Here, Joeboy, this is Boss Denham."

"Um!" ejaculated the black, showing his teeth.

"I was running away from the Boers so as not to serve, Mr Denham," I said eagerly, for I wanted to wipe off the slurs of coward and spy.

"Well, quite right, my lad," said the Lieutenant. "But what were you going to do?"

"Get into Natal, sir, and join the Light Horse."

"Well done!" laughed the Colonel, clapping me on the back; "then you've regularly fallen upon your legs, my lad. That your horse?"

"Yes, sir."

"Good," he cried, looking me over, "and you ride him well. We're the Light Horse. I'm the Colonel, at your service, and I accept you at once as a recruit."

"You can go through the swearing-in business some other time, Val," said the Lieutenant. "Now then, are the Boers in force and coming down the pass?"

I told him all I knew, and the Colonel laughed.

"You've seen a sentry and heard a few shots fired, my lad," he said. "Why, you're not worth calling a spy."

"Am I one of the Light Horse now, sir?" I said eagerly.

"Certainly."

"Then send me back up to the Nek, and I'll try and prove myself a better one."

"I'll send you up, sir," said the Colonel stiffly, "with a vidette, to feel for the enemy and try to draw him out; but we don't call members of the Light Horse spies. If you go on such an adventure it will be a reconnaissance."

I felt humbled, and was silent.

"This is an old friend of yours, then, Denham?" continued the Colonel.

"Oh yes," replied the Lieutenant. "His father, Mr Moray, was a most kindly host to me during a long shooting expedition, and I am very glad to have his son with us. I hope, sir, you will place him in the same troop as I am."

"Certainly," said the Colonel, who then turned to me in a frank, bluff way, and held out his hand.

"Glad to have you with us, Mr Moray," he said; "and I beg your pardon for being so rough with you. Your appearance was a bit suspicious, though. But what about this black fellow?"

"He is my servant, sir," I replied.

"Humph! But we can't allow privates in this corps to bring their servants. It is not a picnic nor a shooting expedition."

Some one who heard these words cried "Oh!" loudly.

"I beg your pardon, gentlemen," said the Colonel, smiling; "it is. I should have said this is not a hunting expedition. We all have to rough it."

"I beg pardon, Colonel," said Lieutenant Denham, giving me a quick look. "Private Moray meant to say the black had been the servant at his home. I had forgotten the man. I remember him now. He was a good hunter and manager of the bullock-wagon we took up the country."

"Yes, sir," I said eagerly; "and most useful in all ways."

"Be able to forage a little for game—eh—if we run short of food?"

"Oh, yes, sir!" I cried.

"That will do, then; let him stay with us."

Joeboy was straining his ears to catch every word, and I saw his face light up as he caught my eye, and he gave his assagai a flourish.

"Yes," said the Colonel dryly, for he had had his eye upon the big athletic black; "but tell him that he must obey orders, and not be getting up any fighting upon his own account."

"He'll obey me, sir," I said, speaking so that Joeboy could hear; and he looked at me and nodded.

"That incident is over, then," said the Colonel sharply. "Now, Mr Denham, take a dozen men and continue the advance. We know now the meaning of last night's firing; but see what you can find out about the strength of the party holding the pass. Be careful of your party. We are good shots; but recollect they are better, and I want information, not to see you bring back half-a-dozen wounded men."

"I'll be careful, sir;" and ten minutes later, to my surprise and delight at the way in which my position had altered during the last half-hour, I was riding close behind Lieutenant Denham, while, proud of his position, Joeboy was on in front, his knowledge of the pass we had just descended being most valuable at such a time, the probabilities tending to point out that he might be able to get well up to right or left of the track and gain a pretty good idea of the strength of the Boers without drawing a shot, whereas the sight of the horsemen, we felt, would have been the signal for a shower of bullets.

Chapter Twelve
Into the Fire

"What about breakfast? Have you had any?" said Denham.

"No," I replied; "but I have some with me;" and taking out a portion of what was left over from the previous afternoon, I proceeded to make up for what was lacking, eating with the better appetite for seeing that Joeboy was busy over one of the big sandwiches provided for him by Aunt Jenny.

This done, I seemed to forget my injuries, and rode on with the little troop, watching the agile way in which Joeboy made his way forward, well in advance and showing no sign of fear.

Mounted men advancing up the rugged pass had very little chance of keeping themselves concealed. Here and there a bend in the narrow valley helped us; but there was always the knowledge that, if the enemy were in force up by the neck of the pass, they had plenty of niches among the mountains on either side to which they could climb and watch us till well within range of their rifles, when shot after shot and puff after puff of white smoke would appear, with very different effect, I felt, from those fired in the darkness of the past night's scare.

All this was very suggestive of danger; but somehow I did not feel alarmed. There was too much excitement in the business, and I was flushed with a feeling of triumph at being so soon in a position to retaliate upon the people who had used me so ill.

I rode on, then, for some distance behind my officer, as I now began to consider him, till the valley opened out, and he reined up a little to allow me to come alongside, so that he could question me about the track higher up. I told him all I could, and endeavoured to impress upon him that it would be a very bad position for his men if the Boers sighted them.

"You would find the ground so bad and encumbered with rough stones," I said, "that it would be impossible to gallop back."

"But we don't want to gallop back," he said, with a laugh. "That's all capital about the bad road, and sounds sensible as a warning; but you must not talk about galloping back. If the enemy does show we shall dismount and use our rifles, retiring slowly from cover to cover. But you'll soon know our ways in the Light Horse."

"I hope so," I said; "but of course I am no soldier yet, and very ignorant."

"Not of the use of your rifle, Val, my lad," he said. "I used to envy you."

"Oh, nonsense!" I said. "Of course I could shoot a bit. My father began to teach me very early."

"I don't believe I can shoot so well now as you did two years ago, when we went up the country. I don't know what you can do now. Why, Val, I expect you'll soon prove yourself to be a better soldier than any of us, for our drill is precious rough; but we are improving every day."

"You have been farther up than this?" I said, to change the conversation, which was making me, a lad accustomed only to our solitary farm-life, feel awkward and uncomfortable, with a suspicion that my companion was bantering me.

"No," he replied; "only about a hundred yards farther than where we met this morning."

"Then you'll find the riding worse than you expect."

"Well, it will be practice," he said. "But I say, how that nigger of yours scuffles along! He's leaving us quite behind."

"He is sure-footed and accustomed to the rocks," I said as I watched Joeboy, who was getting higher and higher up the precipice to our left, as well as higher up the pass. "He wants to get up to where he can look over the Boers' position."

"He had better mind," said Denham. "You ought to have taken away those bits of vanity before he went into action."

"What bits of vanity?" I said.

"Those white ostrich-feathers. They make him stand out so clear to a shooter. Ah! he's down."

Just then Joeboy was seen to drop forward right out of sight.

"No," I said; "that was one of his jumps;" and I spoke confidently, for I had often seen him make goat-like leaps when we had been out shooting among the hills.

"You're wrong," said my companion confidently. "Poor fellow! let's get level with the place where he tumbled. I'm sure that was a fall."

"Wait a few minutes," I said, "and you'll see him perhaps a hundred yards farther on."

I proved to be quite right, for we soon saw Joeboy climbing steadily on just as I had said, and he kept on getting higher and higher till we were up to the spot where I had passed so unpleasant a night.

"My word, you did have a bad time of it! Why, if you had gone over there it would have killed this beautiful little horse of yours."

"Then I shouldn't have found the Light Horse," I said quietly; but I couldn't help feeling a bit of a shiver as I gazed at the depth below where we had stopped.

After that, as we rode on, keeping a good lookout, I began to ask a few questions about the war which had so suddenly broken out and come like a surprise upon us at our quiet and retired home.

"Oh," said my companion, "it is only what many people expected. The Boers have never been satisfied about being under England. Plenty of them are sensible enough, and think that the proper thing to do is to attend to their farms and grazing cattle; but there are a set of discontented idiots among them who have stirred them up with a lot of political matter, telling them they are slaves of England's tyrannical rule, and that it is time to strike for their freedom, till they have believed that they are ill-treated. So now they have risen, and say that they are going to drive all the Rooineks, as they call us English, into the sea, quite forgetting that if we had not helped them the savage tribes around them would have overrun their country and turned them out."

"Will they drive us into the sea?" I asked.

"What do you think?" said Denham, with a laugh. "Do you think we are the sort of people to let a party of rough farmers turn us out of Natal, just because they have been stirred up to fight by a gang of political adventurers? Is your father going to give up his farm that he has spent years of his life in making out of the wilderness?"

"What?" I cried angrily. "No! I should think not."

"Well, that's bringing it home to you, my lad. I said your father's farm. His is only one instance."

"It isn't as if we wanted to turn the Boers out," I said.

"Of course not. All we want is for them to behave like peaceable neighbours, and obey the laws. They want what they call freedom, which is as good as saying that English laws make people slaves. We don't feel much like slaves—do we?"

"Is that the reason they are at war with us?"

"Something of that kind," said the Lieutenant, "as far as I understand it. All politics, and they are the most quarrelsome things in the world. People are always fighting about them somewhere."

"But—" I began.

"Oh, don't ask me," said my companion; "that's as much as I understand about it. All I say is that it's a great pity people should be shooting at one another over what ought to be settled by a bit of talk. But, I say, look out. What does that mean? Halt!"

The men drew rein on the instant, as I looked forward, expecting to see a puff of white smoke ahead, for Joeboy suddenly dropped down behind a block of stone high up in front, and from there began to make signals, just as if he were out in rough ground with me on the veldt and had sighted game.

"He has seen the Boers," I said excitedly. "Look! He says there are hundreds of them."

"No, he doesn't," said my companion gruffly; "he's only flourishing his arms about like a windmill gone mad."

"But that's his way of signalling a big herd of game," I said, "and—"

Before I could say more, *puff, puff, puff* arose the tiny white clouds of smoke, followed by the cracking of the rifles, taken up by the echoes till there was a continuous roar; while *phit, phit, phit*, bullets began to drop about us, striking the stones, and others passed overhead with an angry buzz like so many big flies.

"Retire!" shouted my companion. "It's of no use to waste ammunition. They're in strong force up yonder.—Here, you, Moray, what are you about?"

"Nothing," I said sternly; "only looking for my man."

"But didn't you hear my order?" shouted Denham; and before I could do anything to prevent him he caught Sandho's rein and put spurs to his horse.

"Don't do that," I cried angrily. "I can't go and leave my poor fellow in the lurch. I'm afraid he's hit."

"I can't stop here and have my little troop shot down on account of your black."

"But—"

"Come on, sir!" shouted Denham; "obey orders. Here, you're a pretty rough sort of a pup for me to lick into shape," he added, in a friendly way, as he trotted back amongst the stones. "Recollect you're a soldier now, without any will of your own. You hand everything over to your officer, and obey him, whether it's to ride forward into the enemy's fire or to retire."

"But it's horrible to leave that poor fellow to his fate," I said.

"More horrible to lose the lives of the party of men entrusted to me. Look here, my lad; it's an officer's duty never to throw away a man. If he is obliged to spend a few to carry some point, that's war and necessary; but to dash them bull-headed against double odds to gain nothing is folly."

"But I can't go on. Let me stay back and try and help him," I said passionately.

"Certainly not. Be sensible. Look here: you don't know that he's hit."

"But he dropped from behind that stone."

"Yes; but that may be his dodge. Perhaps he's gliding back under cover from stone to stone."

"Perhaps," I said bitterly. "Look here: if this is your way of going to work I've had enough of soldiering."

I rode on unwillingly, expecting to hear a furious tirade from my companion, who still held my rein; but he was silent for a few minutes, while the bullets kept on spattering and whizzing about us without hitting any one.

"So you're tired of soldiering—are you?" said Denham at last.

"Yes," I said hotly. "I never felt such a coward before."

"Rubbish! Look here: you want me to expose my little detachment to the fire of that strongly-posted crowd of Boers, and get half of them shot down, so as to try and pick up your servant."

"No, I don't," I replied sharply. "There's plenty of cover here. I should have got the men behind some of these blocks of stone and returned the fire, so as to keep the enemy in check while I sent two men dismounted to try and bring my man—our guide—in, alive or dead."

"Humph!" said my companion shortly. "Why, I begin to think you are a better soldier than I am;" and, to my intense surprise, he halted the party behind a huge block which divided our way, dismounted half, and sent them out right and loft to seek cover from whence they could reply to the enemy's fire. Then he turned to me.

"You must hold two horses," he said. "I'll send two fellows to steal up the gap from stone to stone to try and pick up your man."

"No, no," I said excitedly. "I'll go alone."

"Suppose you find him wounded, or—"

"Dead?" I said, finishing his sentence.

"Yes: you couldn't carry him in."

"No," I said, with a sigh. "I'm lame still from the injury to my foot. It hurts me so badly at times that I can hardly ride."

"Hurrah!" came from the right, and the cheer was taken up from the left, while *crack, crack, crack,* rifles were being brought well into play.

"What does that mean?" said Denham. "Have they brought down one of the Dutchmen?"

He pressed his horse's sides and rode out from behind the great stone, while I followed him, to learn directly what was the meaning of the cheering. It was plain enough, for there, about five hundred yards up the narrow pass, was Joeboy coming after us at a quick run, dodging round the great stones, and pretty well contriving to keep them between him and the enemy, whose rifles kept on spitting bullets fiercely after him.

It was as Denham had suggested. Joeboy had leaped down from behind the stone as soon as he had drawn the enemy's fire, then started to follow us, running the gauntlet of their bullets, and reaching us in a very short time, flushed, triumphant, and very little out of breath.

"Well," cried Denham, "see the Boers?"

"Um!" replied Joeboy.

"Were there a great many of them?" I said eagerly, as I sat hoping the poor fellow did not give me the credit of forsaking him in a cowardly way.

For answer he held up both hands with fingers and thumbs outspread; dropped them, and raised them once more; and would have kept on for long enough if I had not checked him.

"You see," I said to Denham, "they are in great force up there."

"Yes, and no wonder," was the reply, "for it's a very strong position. Now then, all here, and forward once more."

The men ran back into the rallying-place as quickly as so many rabbits, mounted, and once more we were in full retreat, with Joeboy trotting beside my horse holding on to the stirrup-iron, while Denham kept coming to me, to talk.

"Just to give you a few lessons in the art of war," he said, with his eyes twinkling and a laugh beginning to show at their corners. "There, you see we have done exactly what the Colonel wanted us to do: made a regular reconnaissance and drawn the enemy's fire, proving that he is holding the pass. What the old man will do now remains to be seen. He won't go up here with us to try and dislodge them, but will try, I expect, to lure them down into the open somewhere, so as to give us a chance at them."

"They'll be too cunning," I said. "They fight only from behind stones, and in holes."

"Yes, they're cunning enough," said Denham; "but, like all over-clever people, they make mistakes, or find others quite as cunning. Look here: you'll have to propose some dodge to the Colonel to coax them out to give us a chance."

"I propose a plan to the Colonel?"

"Yes. Why not?" said Denham, laughing. "You've begun your soldiering by teaching me, and— Oh!"

He uttered a sharp cry, and clapped his right hand round to his back.

"What is it?" I said excitedly. "Not hit?"

"Yes, I've got it," he muttered. "Just look. It hurts horribly. I say, though, that's a good sign—eh?"

The men halted involuntarily behind the stones, and Denham bravely kept his seat till all were under cover, when, refusing to dismount, he slipped off his bandolier and began to unbutton his tunic.

"You had better let us help you down," I suggested.

"No; I don't feel bad enough," he said through his teeth, speaking viciously as if in great pain. "I don't think I'm much hurt. See any blood?"

"No," I replied as he threw off his tunic and laid it across his horse's neck. "Here, look. That's it. All! there it lies." For I had made a snatch at a long-shaped bullet, missed it twice, and then sat pointing out where it had fallen. Joeboy snatched it up and handed it to me.

"Humph!" said Denham; "then it hasn't gone through me, or it would have fallen from my back."

"Instead of your chest," I said. "It must have been partly spent with the long distance it travelled."

"I wish it had been quite spent," said Denham through his teeth, "Oh, what a fuss I'm making about such a trifle! Nothing worse than having a stone thrown at one."

"It's gone right through the back of your jacket," said one of the men. "Look, there's quite a big hole."

"It has not broken the skin," I said, examining his back.

"No, of course not. Here, give me that jacket again, you. Let's get it on. This is all waste of time."

He winced a good deal and looked very white; but he bravely mastered his feeling of faintness, and struggled once more into his tunic, suffering greatly, as I could see by the pallor breaking through his sun-browned skin.

"Stings a bit," he said to me as he fastened the buttons; "but it might have been worse—eh, Val? I always was a thick-skinned fellow, and it turns out lucky now. How far is the nearest skirmisher?"

"A good thousand yards, I should say," I replied.

"Good, and no mistake, for the distance has saved me, Val, my lad. But what's that: over half a mile—eh? Not bad shooting, and shows they must have good rifles, bless 'em! Now then, hand me that cartridge-belt, and I should be glad if you'd pass it over my head, for I'm not very ready to move."

"You will have to let the doctor see the place," I said as I extended the bandolier so as to pass it over his head.

"Doctor? Faugh! What do I want with a doctor for this? I'm going to keep quiet, my lad, or the doctor and the Colonel between them will be wanting to invalid me."

"Oh!" I exclaimed sharply.

"Hullo!" he cried. "Don't say you've got it too, lad!"

"No, no. Look here," I said, and I held out the cartridge-belt to show where a case was flattened—the brass exterior and the bullet within—while the spring-like holder was broken, and the leather beneath sprayed with lead.

"What's the matter?" said Denham, looking round, and wincing with pain as he changed his position.

"It was no spent bullet that struck you," I said, dragging out the damaged cartridge. "You have the bullet in its brass case to thank for saving your life. Look how they're flattened."

He took the bolt in his fingers, and then held them out, examining all carefully without a word.

"Humph!" he ejaculated at last. "That was a narrow escape. I think I shall save that flattened bullet. Not the sort of thing a man would choose for a back-plate, but it did its work. Yes, I must save that flattened bit and the bullet the Boer shot. They'll be worth taking out of a drawer some day to show people, if we got safe through the war. There, I'm all right now. Attention! March!"

The firing had ceased as he gave the orders, the first word in a sharp military way, the second with a catching gasp, and he fell over sidewise. Fortunately I was close upon his left and caught him in my arms, which were none too strong or ready for such a task; but I managed to hold him tightly clasped round the chest as his horse moved off and his legs sank to the ground. A couple of the men drew rein and dismounted directly to come to my help, they taking him from my arms to lay him upon the stony ground.

"Fainted," I said, dismounting painfully. "Who has a water-bottle?"

One was produced directly, and I was busily bathing the poor fellow's face and trying to trickle a little water between his lips, when we became painfully aware of the fact that we had moved out from cover, for *spat, spat, spat*, three bullets struck stones near us, making it evident that we were well in view, and that the Boers were making targets of the different members of the group. This was remedied directly; but in spite of the shaking he received in being moved to the rear of the biggest stone, Denham did not open his eyes, but lay there perfectly insensible; while, to add to our difficulties, one of our men, who had retaken their places in cover, to be ready to reply to the fire if a favourable opportunity presented itself, announced that the enemy was steadily advancing down the pass, and evidently with the intention of clearing it of the party of cavalry which had entered between its barren walls.

Chapter Thirteen
Realities of War

I glanced round at the little group of men, every face wearing the same serious aspect; then I lowered my eyes to continue my task of trying to restore Denham to his senses, while the moments glided by, and many shots were fired at our position; yet there was no change in the officer's condition.

"He isn't dead—is he?" said one of the troopers. "Dead? No!" I cried angrily; but even as I spoke a chill of horror ran through me, for the utterly inanimate state of my new friend suggested that the shock of the blow might have been fatal.

"But he doesn't seem to have a spark of life in him, poor chap!"

"He'll recover soon," I said as firmly as I could, and determined to put the best face upon the matter.

"But we can't wait for 'soon,'" cried another man impatiently. "In less than a quarter of an hour the Doppers will be down upon us, and then it's either a bullet apiece or prisoners."

"We must carry him down to where the Colonel is with the rest of the troopers," I said. "No, no. Set him on a horse."

"He can't possibly sit a horse," I said firmly; "and if you put him on one it will take two men to keep him in his place."

"We can't spare them," cried the first man who had spoken. "We want all our rifles to be speaking as we retire."

Just then a thought struck me.

"He must be carried," I said.

"It can't be done, sir," was the reply. "The men can't be spared. One of us must have him in front of the saddle as we retreat."

"No, no," I said. "Here, wait a minute.—Joeboy!" I shouted, and, shield and assagai in hand, the black dashed to my side as if to defend me from some attack.

"Can you carry this officer on your back down the valley, Joeboy?" I said.

"Um!" was the prompt reply. "You take my spears."

"Yes. Hang them to my saddle," I said. "Quick!"

The next minute I helped to raise the insensible man carefully on to the black's broad back as he bent down on one knee, Denham's arms being placed round Joeboy's neck; and then, at his request, the wrists were bound together with a sash.

"Now," I said, "can you do it?"

"Um!" was the reply; and, without a word being uttered by way of order, the man rose softly to his feet and set off at a slow, steady walk down towards the little force of mounted rifles waiting, a couple of miles or so away, to receive our news.

No sooner were we well out of the cover which had sheltered us than the firing increased, showing that our movements were under observation; but the pattering shots, which seemed to strike every spot save where we moved at a pace regulated by Joeboy's steady walk, had no effect upon the discipline of the little party. The sergeant, a middle-aged man, like a Cornish farmer, now took the command. He ordered half the party to follow close after their wounded officer, and halted the second half, who stood dismounted and covered by their horses, to reply to the enemy's fire.

Instead of checking the shots, our reply seemed only to increase them; but we had the satisfaction of knowing that the fire was concentrated upon us, and that Lieutenant Denham and his bearer were running no risk of being brought down. This was kept up for fully ten minutes, during which our friends had got some distance. Then the order was given to mount; and, giving our horses their heads, we went in single file clattering along the stone-strewn and often slippery track, followed by a scattered shower of bullets, horribly badly aimed, for we had taken our enemies by surprise.

We could not go very fast; but the pace was fast enough to overtake our companions soon, who formed up under the best cover they could find, leaving us room to pass and ride on to where Joeboy trudged manfully on, and then draw rein and walk our horses, listening to the pattering of the Doppers' bullets and the steady and regular reply of our men.

"Has he moved or spoken, Joeboy?" I said anxiously as I rode alongside.

"Um!" replied Joeboy.

"'Fraid he gone dead, Boss Val."

"No, no!" I said, laying my hand against Denham's neck. "I believe he is only stunned. Are you getting tired?"

"Um!" growled the great black. It seemed wonderful what expression he could put into that one ejaculation, which sounded now as if he were saying, "Tired? No: I could go on like this till dark."

I said no more, but fell back into my place, where I found the next man eager enough to talk.

"They brag about the Boers' shooting; but I don't think much of it, nor of ours neither, if you come to that. I don't wish any harm to them who made all this trouble; but I should like for our boys to bring down a man at every shot. It would bring some of the rest to their senses. I say, you don't think young Mr Denham's going home, do you?"

"No," I said sharply. "I think he only wants getting on to a bed, to lie till the shock of his hurt has passed away."

"Yes, that's it," said the trooper; "bed's a grand thing for nearly everything. I never knew how grand it was till I came on this business and had to sleep out here on the stones. You haven't begun to find out what it is to be away from your bed at times."

"I've slept out on the veldt or up in a kopje scores of times," I replied, "and have grown used to it."

"Oh!" said my companion, glancing at me to see if I was telling the truth. Then, apparently satisfied, he continued: "I wish those who made this war had to do all the fighting. I'm sick of it."

"Already?" I said.

"Yes; I was sick of it before we began to hit out. What's the sense of it? Here am I, five-and-twenty, hale, hearty, and strong, trying to get shot. But of course one had to come. I mean to make some of them pay for it, though."

"But you volunteered."

"Of course. I say, though, I don't wonder at you making a run for it. Nice game to have to fight on the enemy's side! I should like that—oh yes, very much indeed! My rifle would have gone off by accident sometimes and hit the wrong man. I say, though, oughtn't the Colonel to hear all this firing, and come up to help us?"

"That's what I've been thinking," I replied. "I should be very glad if we saw him on ahead. But we must have a couple of miles to go yet to join them—mustn't we?"

"Yes, quite that; but, my word!" cried my companion, "they're going it now. They're firing shots enough to bring down every one of our rearguard."

"Yes; and it will be our turn again directly, when they trot on."

"They ought to be here by now," continued my new comrade. "I don't believe they'll come."

"Why?" I said anxiously.

"They'll all be shot down."

"Nonsense," I said. "Listen; those are their rifles replying."

"I suppose so," was the reply, given thoughtfully. "But what a strange echo the hills give back here!"

"Yes," I said. "That's why it's called Echo Nek."

"I suppose so; but—but— Here, I say, those are not echoes we can hear now."

"Nonsense! What can they be, then?"

"Some one else firing. Can't you hear? It sounds from right in front."

"Well, that's how echoes do sound. The reports come down the pass and strike against the face of the rocks, and are reflected off."

"That's all very nicely put, comrade," said the young man, "and I dare say it's scientific and 'all according to Cocker,' as my father used to say; but you're not going to make me believe those are echoes we can hear right in front. Now, you listen."

I did as he suggested, and the rattling of the Boers' rifles came plainly enough, their many reverberations, as the reports seemed to strike from side to side, almost drowning the feeble replies of our own men. Then, after a perceptible pause, fresh reports were heard, and certainly these seemed to come from some distance away in front.

"There!" cried my companion triumphantly. "What do you say to that?"

"That the shots echo again from some high hills in front."

"Boss Val," cried Joeboy just then, and I touched Sandho with my heels, making him spring on to where the big black was straining his neck to look back, but trudging steadily on all the while.

"What is it, Joeboy?" I said anxiously. "Has he moved or spoken?"

"Um! Not said a word; but some one shooting over-over."

He nodded his head in the direction we were going, and now I grasped the fact that I had before doubted—namely, that firing was going on in our front.

I drew the sergeant's attention to it directly, and he nodded.

"That settles it at once," he said. "Here have I been telling myself it was all my fancy; but now you hear it I feel it must be fact."

"I hear it; so does my man, and the trooper who rides next to me."

"Yes; and we can all hear it now," said the Sergeant. "Well, it's plain enough. We're in a tight place, my lad, for there's only one answer to it, and it explains why the Colonel hasn't sent us some support, for he must have heard the firing."

"What do you make of it, then?"

"That the Doppers are better soldiers than we give them credit for being, and they've got round to the Colonel's rear somehow, and shut him in this giant hogs'-trough of a valley."

"Think so?" I said anxiously, as I thought of the Lieutenant.

"I'm sure of it. Now then; that's not our business. Halt! Right about! Take position behind those stones. Dismount and cover the retreat. Here they come."

The clatter of the horses of the other party came plainly to our ears as we took our places ready to reply to the Boers' fire. I had intended to have another look at the wounded man before this took place, and was therefore much disappointed; but there was no help for it, and I stood with Sandho fairly well sheltered behind a stone five feet high, upon which my rifle rested. Then the party we were to relieve cantered by, with two men wounded and supported on their horses; and as I watched the puffs of smoke and listened to the bullets spattering and splaying the rocks, with the buzz of the high shots now sounding so familiar, I wondered at being able to take it all so coolly.

"I suppose it's because I'm beginning to get used to it," I thought. Then I began to speculate as to what would happen now if the sergeant was right, and we were to be attacked front and rear; and what it would feel like if I were hit, as seemed very likely now that the enemy were getting so near. But I glanced right and left at my companions, just in time, to see the Sergeant start back, to stand shaking his right hand vigorously, and directly after I saw the blood beginning to drip from his finger-ends.

"Much hurt?" I asked, hurrying to his side, dragging out my handkerchief the while.

"No!" he roared; "only a scratch. Back to your place, sir! Who told you to leave? Here; stop! As you are here you may as well tie that rag round it."

He said these last words more gently, and smiled as I rapidly bound up his injury as well as I could.

Charge! A Story Of Briton And Boer | 83

"Thank ye, my lad," he said. "I must preserve discipline, and we're getting pressed. Taken off a bit of the middle finger—hasn't it?"

"Half of it, I'm afraid," I said.

"What have you got to be afraid of? Might have been worse. Suppose it had been the first finger; then I shouldn't have been able to draw trigger—eh? That'll do—won't it? I'm in a hurry."

"I haven't stopped the bleeding," I replied.

"Never mind. Mother Nature will soon do that. Now then, back you go. Show them how you young farmers can shoot."

I was on my way back to my place when the clattering of hoofs made me turn my head, and I saw a man in the Light Horse uniform come galloping up, utterly regardless of the danger he ran from obstructing stones.

"Back!" he shouted. "Retire on the main body as fast as you can go. Colonel's orders."

We were in full retreat at once, after emptying our rifles upon the steadily advancing enemy, who came on, running from stone to stone, cleverly taking advantage of every bit of cover. We soon came in sight of the men we had relieved, who were hurrying to the rear as fast as they could get their wounded men along; while, to my great satisfaction, there was Joeboy striding along at a tremendous rate: it was a walk, but such a walk as would have compelled me to trot to keep up with him. He could not have kept it up much longer, I could see, for the perspiration was streaming down his face and neck, and he was breathing hard; but at the end of another quarter of a mile, as the firing in front grew louder and louder, I saw about a couple of dozen of the troopers coming to our help, four of whom dismounted, giving up their horses to comrades, and quickly spreading a blanket upon the ground.

It struck me at once that Joeboy would refuse to give up his load; but I got up to him just in time, and at a word from me the young officer, still perfectly insensible, was lifted from the big black's shoulders, laid upon the blanket, and then the four men took the corners in a good grip and trotted off at the double. Joeboy, grinning with satisfaction, now took hold of my saddle-bow and ran by my side till we reached the strong position in a great notch in one side of the valley, where the Colonel was defending himself against a large body of the enemy coming on from the plains below.

It was a capitally chosen spot, as I soon saw, for there was a smooth open part in front of the notch, which backed right into the side; and the stones across the path, front and rear, formed capital breastworks for the dismounted men who lined them, all the horses having been turned into the gap in the huge wall, where they were quite out of the line of fire.

"Splendid!" said the Sergeant to me, as we waited to take our turn at the defence.

"But we shall be attacked on both sides," I said. "Oughtn't we to get in there with the horses?"

"No, you recruit, you," said the Sergeant. "We shall be between two fires; but don't you see how the enemy will be crippled? Every shot that goes over us, whether it's upward or downward, goes among the Doppies. They're firing at us, but at their own friends as well."

"Of course," I replied. "I did not see that."

"I didn't at first," he said; "but our Colonel's got his head screwed on the right way, and the position is famous. Well, why don't you say 'Hurrah!' or 'Bravo!' or something of the sort?"

"Because I don't feel satisfied," I said.

"You young fellows never are," said the Sergeant. "What's the matter with you now?"

"We can hold out, of course," I said, "as long as our ammunition lasts; but what about afterwards?"

"Bother afterwards!" he said sharply; "a hundred things may happen before it comes to afterwards."

"Then, if they determine to hold on, they can force us to surrender."

"Never," said the Sergeant; "so no more croaking."

"But what about provisions?"

"Every man has his rations in a satchel."

"But water?"

"Every man has his bottle well filled, my lad."

"But when the water-bottles are empty and the food is done? What about feeding the horses? What about watering them?"

"Yah!" growled the Sergeant savagely. "Call yourself a volunteer? What do you mean by coming here prophesying all sorts of evil? Do you want to starve the horses and see 'em die of thirst? Here, I say, my lad," he whispered, "don't let any of the boys hear that. You've hit the weak point of the defence a regular staggerer. You're quite right; but we must hold on, and perhaps after a good peppering they'll draw off. If they don't, it means forming up and making a dash, and that's what the Colonel won't do if he can help it, on account of the loss."

I had no more time for talking, for directly after I was ordered to take my place behind one of the stones to make the best use I could of my rifle in keeping back the enemy, who were now descending the pass in great numbers, while the firing from the rear was so furious that it was plain enough that the ascending force was stronger than the one with which they were trying to join hands.

Chapter Fourteen
How I Used My Cartridges

It was a strange experience for one who had come fresh from a home life; and in the intervals of tiring I could not help wondering whether it was not all a dream. The reality, however, forced itself on me too strongly as the light went on, the spaces about the stones being literally littered with battered bullets which had assumed all kinds of strange shapes after coming in contact with the stones—flat, mushroom-shaped, twisted, the conical points struck off diagonally, and the like; but we were so sheltered that if the Boers fired low we were unhurt, and if they fired high their shots went over among comrades. Signals were now made from above and below, with the result that the attacking party coming down the pass divided, to line the sides of the place as far as they could, so that their shots crossed our defences, and the attacking party from below followed their old tactics; thus our defences were swept by a cross-fire, and fewer Boers fell by the bullets of their friends. But these movements on the part of the Boers had brought them better within range of our pieces, for they were more exposed upon climbing up the slopes; and I had plain evidence of the loss they sustained.

At last night began to fall, and the firing of the attacking force, dropped off. It was plain that the Boers were retiring, possibly disheartened by their heavy losses. Then, soon after dark, lights began to appear, just out of range, both up and down the pass; but it was probable that the fight would be resumed as soon as it was daylight again.

Two-thirds of the men were now set at liberty to take what rest and refreshment they could, the remaining third being upon sentry-duty, ready to give the alarm should a night attack be attempted; but of this there was little probability.

Taking advantage of not being on sentry-duty, I made my way to the niche in the mountain-side which had been taken for hospital purposes, and here found Denham rolled up in a horseman's cloak and sleeping peacefully. I felt his forehead gently, and then his wrists and hands, to find all cool and comfortable; but I knew I must not wake him. Just then a figure close by stirred, and I started, for a voice said, "He's asleep."

"Yes, I know," I replied; "but has he been awake?"

"Yes; an hour ago."

"How did he seem?" I asked.

"Said it hurt him a deal, just as if his ribs were broken. Ah! he doesn't know what pain is."

"Do you?" I said.

"Rather!" said the man. "One of their bullets went right through my thigh just about six inches below my hip. That is pain. It's just as if a red-hot iron was being pushed through."

"Can I get anything for you?" I said.

"No," was the gruff reply; "unless you can get me a heap of patience to bear all this pain."

I tried to say a few comforting words to him, but they only seemed to irritate.

"Don't," he said peevishly. "I know you want to be kind, my lad; but I'm not myself now, and it only makes me feel mad. There, thank ye for it all; but please go before I say something ungrateful."

I crept away and tried to find the doctor who was with the corps; but he was busy with his wounded men, of whom he had about twenty. Giving up the satisfaction of getting his report about the young Lieutenant, I went to where Sandho was picketed with the rest, and stood by his head for about half-an-hour, petting and caressing him, before going back towards the rough breastwork—partly natural, partly artificial—which served as a shelter from the bullets.

I soon came upon one of the sentries, who challenged me; but he made room for me beside him after a few words had passed.

"Oh yes," he said, "you can stay here if you like; but why don't you go and lie down till you have to relieve guard?"

"Because I feel too excited to sleep," I replied.

"Humph! Yes, it has been warm work," said the sentry; "but I suppose we shall get used to it. I'm excited; but I feel as if I'd give anything to lie down for an hour."

"Well, lie down," I said. "I'll keep watch for you."

"You will?" he said joyfully. "No, no; I'm not going to break down like that. Don't say any more about it. It's like tempting a man. Here, I say," he whispered eagerly, "how quiet they are! You don't think they're going to make a night attack—do you?"

"No," I said; "it's not likely. What good could they do when they couldn't see to shoot?"

"None, of course. It's not as if they were soldiers with bayonets. The only thing they could do would be to stampede the horses."

"What!" I whispered excitedly. "Oh, I say, don't talk like that."

"Only a bit of an idea that came into my head. Don't see anything—do you?"

"Nothing," I replied. "It's dark; but there's a curious transparent look about the night, and I think we should see any one directly if he were advancing."

"How? I don't see that's at all likely."

"If any one passed along it would be like a shadow crossing the grey stones. They look quite grey in the starlight."

"Well, yes, they do," he said; "and—I say, what's that?"

He pointed towards the Boers' camp-fires, and, startled by his tone, I looked eagerly in the direction pointed out; but there were the piles of grey stones looking dull and shadowy, but no sign to me of anything else.

"Fancy," I said.

"No. Just as you spoke I saw something dark go across one of the stones. Shall I fire?"

"Certainly not. It would be alarming every one for nothing. We talked about seeing things pass the grey stones, and that made you think you saw some one."

"Perhaps so," he said thoughtfully. "Anyhow, there's nothing here now. I say, that seems to have woke me up."

"It would," I said; and then I crouched a little lower, shading my eyes from the starlight and keenly sweeping the chaotic wilderness of rocks again and again, but seeing nothing.

I heard, though, the steps of the sentry away to my left, and soon after a faint cough to my right sounded quite loudly.

"It wouldn't have done for you to have gone to sleep with me taking your place, for I suppose some officer will be visiting the posts before very long, and then you'd have been found out if I hadn't woke you in time."

I said this in a low tone not much above a whisper, in case any one was going the rounds; but he did not take any notice.

"It wouldn't have done, you know," I said.

There was a low, heavy sighing breath, which made me start in wonder, and then turn towards my companion, to find that his rifle was resting against the stone, and that he had sunk sidewise against another and was fast asleep.

"Completely fagged out," I said to myself, with a feeling of pity for him. "He did fight bravely against it; but the drowsiness was too much for him."

One moment I felt ready to take hold of his arm and shake him, but I did not. I was there with his rifle ready to my hand, and if I kept his watch, perhaps only for a few minutes, he would wake up again, refreshed and better able to keep it till he was relieved.

"It often is so," I said to myself. "One drops asleep after dinner, and then wakes up ready to go for any length of time. It's being a good comrade to the poor fellow," I thought; and, picking up his rifle, I took over his duty just as if it were my own, keeping my eyes wandering over the dark grey stones in front, and sweeping the whole space. Then my breath suddenly felt as if checked in my surprise, for about thirty yards away, as near as I could guess, there was a dark shadow passing one of the great blocks.

"Fancy," I said to myself as soon as I could recover from my surprise; and, treating myself as I had treated my fellow-trooper, I mentally declared I had thought about it till I seemed to see it.

"It's all imagination," I said again; and then I lowered the rifle I held, a thrill running through me as I distinctly saw the dark shadow again, but nearer than before. This time I was certain it was not imagination. A figure—enemy or no—was cautiously stealing towards our lines! My first impulse was to fire at the figure and give the alarm; but on second thoughts I hesitated to go to such an extreme. Fixing my eyes upon the dark, shadowy form, I cocked my rifle, and called hoarsely upon whoever it was to stop.

"Ah! No shoot, no shoot," cried a familiar voice.

"Joeboy!" I exclaimed.

"Um!" was the reply; and, to my astonishment, the black came hurrying towards me, bending under a load which stuck out curiously from his sides and back.

"Why, what have you been doing out there?"

"Been get all these," he said as he forced his way between a couple of stones, which caught his bulky load and checked him for a few moments.

"You idiot!" I said in a low tone, for I was afraid now that I had alarmed the sentries on either side; but though Joeboy's load on one side bumped against my companion sentry, he was so utterly wearied out that he did not stir.

"Um? Idiot?" said Joeboy. "Boss Val going to be hungry. Joeboy hungry. Been to get all these."

"What are they—forage-bags?"

"Um!" he said.

"But where did you get them—whose are they?"

"Doppies'. All in a heap. Brought them all along."

A little further questioning made it all clear—that under cover of the darkness the plucky fellow had crept up the valley, taking advantage of the shelter afforded by the stones, passed the lines of the Boers, and hunted about till he came upon something worth having in the shape of a pile of canvas forage-bags containing the men's provender, which they had left together and in charge of a sentinel, so as to be unencumbered in their attack upon us.

"But what about the sentry?" I said suspiciously.

"Um? Fast asleep," said Joeboy.

"What! all the time you were loading yourself with these bags?"

"Um!"

"You did not send him to sleep, did you?" I said suspiciously.

"Um? Killum?"

"Yes."

"No," said Joeboy coolly. "Didn't wake up. Lot more couldn't carry. Plenty to eat now."

"Then you actually went foraging up there, and got back safely with this load?"

"Um!" said Joeboy. "Boss Val must have plenty to eat. Doppies nearly caught um."

"So I should expect," I said. "But you nearly got shot, stealing up to the lines like this."

He laughed softly.

"Boss Val wouldn't shoot Joeboy. Doppies nearly ketch him. Big lot coming down now."

"What!" I said excitedly. "Some of them coming down?"

"Um! Big lot coming down to fight."

I began to grasp now that after all there was some night expedition on the way, and that the pile of haversacks Joeboy had found had been deposited there to leave the men free and unfettered.

"Look here," I said sharply; "are you sure that the Doppies are coming down?"

"Um! Great big lot."

"Here, you," I whispered, "wake up!" and I shook and shook the sentry roughly, making him spring up and make a snatch at his rifle.

"Thank ye," he said. "I say, I was nearly dropping off to sleep."

"Very," I said dryly; "but keep awake now. My man here has just brought in news that the enemy are coming on down the pass."

"What—for a night-attack?"

"Yes."

"The beasts!" he cried, and he raised his rifle to fire and give the alarm.

"No, no," I said; "don't fire unless you see them. I'll go and give the alarm. Stand fast till reinforcements come.—Here, Joeboy, bring your load into camp."

I led the way straight to the Colonel, being challenged twice before I reached the side where he, in company with his officers, lay sleeping in their horsemen's heavy cloaks.

All sprang up at once, and each started to rouse his following, with the result that in a few minutes the whole force was under arms and divided in two bodies to join the line of sentries who paced up and down the pass.

It was only now I became aware of the Colonel's plan of strategy, which was to defend the position as long as seemed wise, and then for each line to fold back, making the pivot of the movements the ends of the lines by the niche in the hillside where the horses were sheltered. Then, on the performance of this evolution, there would be a double line facing outward for the defence of the horses, in a position enormously strong from the impossibility of there being any attack from flanks or rear.

So far we had no news of any attack threatening from the Boers who held the lower part of the pass; but scouts had been sent out in that direction to get in touch with the enemy, and their return was anxiously awaited where the men were in position; but the minutes glided by in the midst of a profound silence, and I began to feel a doubt about the correctness of Joeboy's announcement.

I was in the centre of the line which would receive the shock of the descending Boers, and Joeboy had stationed himself behind me as soon as he had bestowed his plunder in safety; and at last, as there was no sound to indicate that the enemy was on the move, I began to grow terribly impatient, feeling as I did that before long the Colonel and his officers would be reproaching me for giving a false alarm.

"Are you quite sure, Joeboy?" I whispered, turning to him where he squatted with assagai in hand and his shield spread across his knees.

"Um?" he whispered. "Yes, quite sure. Come soon."

They did not come soon, and I grew more and more excited and angry; but I refrained from questioning the black any more, feeling as I did the uselessness of that course, and being unwilling to bring down upon myself the reproof of the officers for talking at a time when the order had been passed for strict silence, so that the Boers might meet with a complete surprise.

It seemed to me that an hour had passed, during which I stood behind the natural breastwork of a stone upon which my rifle rested, gazing straight away up the pass, and straining my sense of hearing to catch something to suggest that the enemy was in motion; but there was not a sound in the grim and desolate gap between the hills, and my beating heart sank lower and lower as I glanced back at Joeboy, who reached towards me.

"Doppy long time," he said, hardly above his breath.

"They won't come," I whispered back angrily. "You fancied it all."

"Um?"

"You fancied it all. They would not come on in the night."

"Boss Val wait a bit. Come soon."

"Ugh!" I ejaculated; and a voice somewhere near whispered, "Silence in the ranks!" The command was needed, for a low murmur was beginning to make itself heard.

All was still again directly after, and the time glided slowly on again, till that which I expected came suddenly; for I heard the trampling of feet behind me in the darkness, and a voice whispered, "Where's that new recruit Moray?"

"I am here, sir," I said.

"Quick! the Colonel wants you."

I left my post, and another man stepped into my place, while I followed the sergeant who had summoned me.

"I say, young fellow," he said, "you're in for a bullying. The Colonel's horribly wild about your false alarm. Are you sure the Doppies were coming on?"

I told him what I had learned, and that I had felt obliged to report it.

"Humph! Yes, of course; but it's a great pity, when the men wanted rest."

The next minute I was facing the Colonel in the middle of the pass, where he stood with a group of the officers, about half-way between the two lines of men facing up and down, but lying so close that they were only visible here and there.

"Oh, here you are, young fellow!" were the words that saluted me, spoken in a low, angry whisper. "Now then, where are these two attacking parties of Boers?"

"I only reported that one was coming, sir—one descending the pass."

"Very well; you shall have credit for only one, then. Well, where is it?"

"I can't say, sir," I replied. "I was warned of it by my native servant."

"Then just go back and flog your native servant till you have given him a lesson against spreading false alarms to rob tired men of their rest. It is perfectly abominable—just when we want all our strength for the work in hand for us to-morrow."

"I'm very sorry, sir," I said.

"Sorry? What must I be, then? I can't fight unless I have plenty to eat and as much sleep as I can get. There, get back to your post. I wish to goodness you had stopped at home or joined the Boers, or done something else with yourself, instead of coming and giving this confounded false alarm. Be off.—Here, call in the men again, and— Yes, what now?"

"Enemy coming up the pass in great strength, sir," said one of the scouts, who had come breathlessly back.

"What!" said the Colonel in a hurried whisper. "Could you make them out?"

"Yes, sir; two or three hundred, I should say."

"You got near enough to see?"

"I couldn't see much, sir; but I could hear. They seemed to spread right across from the side I was on."

"Here, you, Moray," said the Colonel, turning to me, for at this announcement I had stood fast. "Get back to your post; and I beg your pardon.—Yes; who are you?"—for another scout came in to endorse the words of the first. He had scouted down the other side of the widening pass, and according to his report the enemy could not be a quarter of a mile away.

"Thank goodness!" said the Colonel fervently. "Mr Moray, I spoke in haste and disappointment. Now then, gentlemen, perfect silence, please. I believe we shall hear some signal from below, and that is what the party above are waiting for. Then they will attack simultaneously, to give us a surprise, and we're going to surprise them. Every one to his post, please; and then, at their first rush, let it be volleys and slow falling back, so as to keep them from breaking our too open formation."

The next minute every man was in his place, and the pass so dark and still that it was impossible to believe that a terrible conflict was so close at hand. As I stood waiting and listening for the enemy's order to attack, I could feel my heart go throb, throb, throb, throb, so hard that I seemed to be hearing it at the same time making a dull echo in my brain.

Still there was no sign; and at last I began to go over my brief interview with the Colonel, and to wonder whether he would turn now upon the two scouts and charge them with having deceived themselves, for according to their report the enemy ought to have been upon us long before. I had got to this point when all at once I felt an arm upon my shoulder, and could just make out at the side and front of my face a big hand pointing forward towards the stones a hundred feet away.

"Um!" whispered Joeboy, with his lips close to my ear. "See um now. Big lots."

"I can see nothing," I whispered.

"Joeboy can. Lie down ready. Boss Val going to shoot?"

"When I get the order," I said softly, and my heart beat more heavily than ever, for I felt now that the black must be right. I had had for years past proofs of the wonderful power of his sight, and had not a doubt that, though they were invisible to me, a large body of the enemy were clustering among the stones ready for the assault upon our position.

Then I heard from somewhere below a faint, rushing, whistling sound, as of a firework, followed by a crack, and the white stars of a rocket lit up the sides of the pass and made the stones in front visible in a soft glare. The next instant from front and rear, almost simultaneously, there were flashes and a scattered roar, while the sides of the pass took up the reports, forming a deafening roll of thunder running down towards the plain.

Before this was half-over there was the rush of men before us, the stones and the spaces between seeming to be alive with running and leaping Boers, shouting and cheering like mad as they came on, their purpose being to scare us and frighten the horses into a stampede, which, if it had followed, must have been equally fatal to their comrades attacking from the rear as it would have been to us; but, instead of the enemy being gratified by hearing the clattering of hundreds of hoofs, they were received by a series of sharp volleys proceeding from our two lines of men. These were so inadequately returned that the officers in the rear ran to and fro bidding us stand firm and keep up the fire, no attempt being made to fall back towards the gap where the horses were tethered.

Those were tremendously exciting minutes, and in the confusion, the crack of the rifles, and the reverberations, I hardly know what I did, except that I kept on firing without taking aim, for the simple reason that there was nothing visible in the smoke and darkness unless one had tried to aim at a spot from whence flashes came; and as the men attacking us were constantly on the move, that would have been useless.

I found afterwards, on talking to the men above me, that they had behaved in precisely the same way as I did—they kept on firing; while all were in constant expectation of having to club their rifles to beat back the enemy should they come on with a rush.

However, we never came to close quarters that night; for, failing in sweeping our men back in the first surprise, the enemy drew off a short distance till all were well under cover, and then kept up their fire, each party of the enemy seeming utterly regardless of the risk to their own comrades beyond us.

In the midst of the roar and reverberation I was startled by a hand laid upon my shoulder, and, turning sharply, I found the sergeant by my side.

"Fall back," he said; and as I obeyed I thrust my hand to my cartridge-belt so as to reload, when, to my utter astonishment, I found it was two-thirds empty. This was soon remedied; for, as we—that is to say, about half the defenders of the upper side of our stronghold—stood fast, non-commissioned officers came running along and thrust packets of cartridges into our hands.

It was, as I have said, very dark; but I could just manage to see beneath the canopy of smoke which rose slowly that half the lower line of defenders had fallen back. Directly after, we were all hurried to the front of the great niche and ordered to man the rocks there in front of the horses.

While settling ourselves in every advantageous position we could find, the firing went on as briskly as ever, the Boers blazing away at our two lines of men, who replied as fast as they could load; and, as far as I could tell by the sound, the fusillade did not slacken.

Then I began to understand what was about to happen, and could not help laughing to myself when I saw the part of our line we had left firing suddenly come hurrying in, to pass through an opening in our ranks; and no sooner were they safe than the lower line fell back and came running into the shelter, to join up with the others.

As soon as these detachments were out of the way we had orders to fire four cartridges each, half of us firing as well up the pass as possible, the other half to fire as far downwards as they could. After these four rounds each we were to cease firing: this was, of course, to prevent the Boers from noticing that our fire had slackened and then ceased; and it answered exactly as the Colonel had intended, for the bull-headed and obstinate enemy went on for the next half-hour firing away at the stones where we had been, each side believing that a portion of the reports and echoes were caused by our firing, and all the time our men stood laughing and enjoying the blunder, and pretty sure that the enemy must be bringing down some of their own comrades. Whether the enemy found this out at last, or were dissatisfied at not being able to silence our fire, I don't know; but suddenly there was another train of sparks rushing up through the smoke, and the bursting of a rocket far on high, sending down a dingy bluish light through the overhanging cloud. Then the firing stopped as if by magic.

Instantly every man was on the *qui vive*, the front of the niche bristling with rifles ready to deliver volley after volley as soon as the rush we all expected began; but we waited in vain. When skirmishers were sent out to feel their way cautiously in the darkness, through which the smoke was slowly rising, we still waited and listened, expecting to hear them fired upon; but again we waited in vain. Both parties of the enemy had retired for the night; and, as soon as the Colonel was satisfied of this, the necessary advance-posts were sent out and stationed, and the men then ordered to lie down on their arms and get what sleep they could.

Chapter Fifteen
The Sergeant's Wound

There were the hard stones for our couches, and the air up in the pass was sharp and cold; but we were all pretty close together, and in five minutes it did not seem as if any one was awake, though doubtless the few poor fellows who had been wounded—I may say wonderfully few considering what we had gone through—did not get much sleep. I was one of those who did lie awake for a time, gazing up at the clear, bright stars which began to peer down through the clearing-off smoke, but only for a few minutes; then a calm, restful feeling began to steal over me, and I was sleeping as sound as if on one of the feather-beds at the farm, where in course of years they had grown plentiful and big.

We were not, however, to pass the night in peace; for directly after, as it seemed to me, I started up in the darkness, roused by firing. Then the trumpet-call rang out, and we were all up ready for the rush that was in progress; while I was startled and confused, and unable to understand why the now mounted Boers should be guilty of such an insane action as to attack us there, nestling among the stones. We were all ready, but no orders came to fire, and all crouched or stood with finger on trigger, gradually grasping what it all meant, and listening to the trampling of hoofs going steadily on, till at last the Colonel's familiar voice was heard from close to where I stood.

"Hold your fire, my lads. We should be doing no good by bringing a few down. Let them join their friends. They've come to the conclusion that this is too hard a nut to crack."

This is what happened: the enemy's lower party had waited till nearly daylight, and then approached quietly till their coming had been noticed by our outpost sentries, who fired to give the alarm, when they made a sudden dash to get up the pass to join the detachment of Boers above. This they were allowed to do unmolested, the Colonel saying that nothing was to be gained by stopping them, and that an advance up the pass was work for infantry, not for a mounted force.

Daylight came soon afterwards, I suppose; but I did not watch for the dawn, for, as soon as the last of the horsemen had passed and the word was given, I sank down again and slept as a tired lad can sleep. Again, as it seemed, only a few minutes expired before the trumpet once more rang out, and I had to shake myself together, when the first face that looked into mine was that of Joeboy, who was standing close by me with a heap of haversacks at his feet, and grinning at me with a good-humoured smile. I didn't smile, for I felt stiff and full of aches and pains; but before long fires were burning and water getting hot. I had a good shower-bath, too, in a gurgling spring of water which came down a rift by the gap in the pass. Then sweet hot coffee and slices of bread and cold ham out of one of the haversacks Joeboy had foraged for seemed to quite alter the face of nature. Perhaps it was that the sun came out warm and bright, and that the blue sky was beautiful; but I gave the bread, ham, and coffee the credit of it all. Ah! what a breakfast that was! It seemed to me the most delicious I had ever eaten; but before it was begun I had been to see Denham, who was sitting up with his chest tightly bandaged. He was ready to hold out a hand as soon as he saw me.

"Hullo, Moray!" he cried, "how are you this morning?"

"It's how are you?" I replied.

"Oh, I'm all right. A bit stiff, and I've got a bruise in the back, the doctor says, like; the top of a silk hat."

"You haven't seen it?" I said.

"Have I got a neck like an ostrich or a giraffe? No, of course I haven't."

"But is anything broken?" I asked anxiously.

"No, not even cracked. The pot's quite sound, so the doctor hasn't put in a single rivet."

"I am glad," I said heartily.

"That's right—thank you," said the poor fellow, smiling pleasantly, and he kept his eyes fixed upon me for some moments. Then in a light bantering way he went on, "Doctor said the well-worn old thing."

"What was that?" I asked.

"Oh, that if it hadn't been for that bullet and brass cartridge-case, backed up by the thick leather belt, that Boer's bullet would have bored— now, now, you were going to laugh," he cried.

"That I wasn't," I said wonderingly. "What is there to laugh at?"

"Oh, you thought I was making a pun: bored a hole right through me."

"Rubbish!" I said. "Just as if I should have thought so lightly about so terribly dangerous an injury."

"Good boy!" he cried merrily. "I like that. I see you've been very nicely brought up. That must be due to your aunt—aunt—aunt— What's her name?"

"Never mind," I said shortly; "but if you can laugh and joke like that there's no need for me to feel anxious about your hurt."

"Not a bit, Solomon," he cried merrily. "There you go again, trying to make puns—solemn un—eh? I say, though, you do look solemn this morning, Val. I know: want your breakfast—eh!"

"Had it," I said, smiling now.

"I do, my young recruit. I'm longing for a cup of hot coffee or tea. But I say, Val, my lad," he continued, seriously now, "I haven't felt in a very laughing humour while I lay awake part of the night."

"I suppose not," I said earnestly. "It must have been very terrible to lie here listening to the fighting—wounded, too—and not able to join in."

"Well, yes, that was pretty bail; but I didn't worry about that. I knew the Colonel would manage all right. I was worried."

"What worried you?" I said—"the pain?"

"Oh no; I grinned and bore that. Here, come closer; I don't want that chap to hear."

"What is it?" I said, closing up.

"It was that business yesterday, when I was hit."

"Oh, I wouldn't think about it," I said.

"Can't help it. I did try precious hard to carry it off before I quite broke down."

"You bore it all like a hero," I said.

"No, I didn't, lad. I bore it like a big boarding-school girl. Oh! it was pitiful. Fainted dead away."

"No wonder," I replied, smiling. "You're not made of cast-iron."

"Here, I say, you fellow," he cried; "just you keep your position. None of your insolence, please. Recollect that you're only a raw recruit, and I'm your officer."

"Certainly," I said, smiling. "I thought we were both volunteers."

"So we are, old fellow, off duty; but it must be officer and private on duty. I say, tell me, though, about the boys and the Sergeant. Did they sneer?"

"Sneer?" I cried indignantly. "You're insulting the brave fellows. They carried you down splendidly, and I believe there wasn't a man here who wouldn't have died for you."

"But—but," he said huskily, "they must have thought me very weak and girlish."

"I must have thought so too—eh?"

"Of course," he said, in a peculiar way.

"Then, of course, I didn't," I cried warmly; "I thought you the bravest, pluckiest fellow I had ever seen."

"Lay it on thick, old fellow," he said huskily; "butter away. Can't you think of something a little stronger than plucky and brave—and—don't take any notice of me, Val, old lad. I'm a bit weak this morning."

"Of course you are," I said sharply, and dashed off at once into a fresh subject. "I say, I must go and hunt out the Sergeant. That was a nasty wound he got after you were hit."

My words had the right effect.

"The Sergeant?" he cried. "Oh, poor old chap! we can't spare him. Was he hurt badly?"

"Oh no, he laughed it off, just as you did your injury; but I am afraid he has lost one finger."

"Ah, my young hero!" cried a cheery voice, and I started round and saluted, for it was the Colonel. "How's the wound—eh?"

"Oh, it isn't a wound, sir," said Denham rather impatiently. "Only a bad bruise."

"Very nearly something worse.—Morning, my lad:" this to me, and I felt the colour flush up into my cheeks. "You behaved uncommonly well last night, and we're all very much indebted to you. Pretty good, this, for a recruit. I heartily wish you had been with us two or three months, and you should certainly have had your first stripes."

I mumbled out something about doing my best.

"You did," said the Colonel. "I'm sorry I spoke so hastily to you in my error. I didn't know you two were friends."

"We are, sir," said Denham warmly.

"Oh, of course; I remember. You shot together some time ago."

"Yes, sir," said Denham, "and I had a grand time with Val Moray, here—big game shooting."

"Not such big game shooting as you are going to have here," said the Colonel. "I'm glad to see you so much better, Denham. Be careful, and mind what the doctor says to you."

He hurried away, and as soon as he had passed out of sight the Sergeant, with his arm in a sling, came up from where he had been waiting to ask how his young officer fared, giving me a friendly nod at the same time.

"Oh, there's nothing the matter with me, Briggs," said Denham. "I shall be all right now. Thank you heartily, though, for what you did for me."

"Did for you, sir?" said the Sergeant gruffly. "I did nothing, only just in the way of duty."

"Oh, that was it—was it?" said Denham. "Then you did it uncommonly well—didn't he, Moray?"

"Splendidly," I said, with a fair display of enthusiasm.

"Look here, you, sir," said the Sergeant very gruffly as he turned upon me; "young recruits to the corps have got all their work cut out to learn their duty, without criticising their superior officers. So just you hold your tongue."

"That's a snub, Moray," said Denham; "but never mind.—Look here, Sergeant, how's your wound?"

"Wound, sir?" he replied. "I haven't got any wound."

"Then why is your arm in a sling?"

"Oh, that, sir? That's a bit of the doctor's nonsense. He said I was to keep it on, so I suppose I must. But it isn't a wound."

"What is it, then?" said Denham sharply.

"Bullet cut my finger; that's all."

"Did it cut it much?" asked Denham.

"Took a little bit off, and I went to the doctor for a piece o' sticking-plaster, and he as good as called me a fool."

"What did you say, then, to make him?"

"I said nothing, sir, only that I wanted the plaster."

"Did he give you some?"

"No, sir; but I suppose he wanted to try his new bag o' tools, and got hold of me. 'Hold still,' he says, 'or I shall give you chloroform.' 'Can't you make it a drop o' whisky, sir?' I says. 'Yes, if you behave yourself,' he says. 'Look here, I can't plaster up a place like this. Your finger's in rags, and the bone's in splinters.' 'Oh, it'll soon grow together, sir,' I says. 'Nothing of the kind, sir,' he says; 'it'll go bad if I don't make a clean job of it. Now then, shut your eyes, and sit still in that chair. I won't hurt you much.'"

"Did he?" said Denham.

"Pretty tidy, sir; just about as much as he could. He takes out a tool or two, and before I knew where I was he'd made a clean cut or two and taken off some more of my finger, right down to the middle joint. 'There,' he says, as soon as he'd put some cotton-wool soaked with nasty stuff on the place, after sewing and plastering it up—'there, that'll heal up quickly and well now!'"

"Of course," said Denham. "Made a clean job of it."

"Clean job, sir?" said the Sergeant. "Well, yes, he did it clean enough, and so was the lint and stuff; but it's made my finger so ugly. It looks horrid. I say, sir, do you think the finger'll grow again?"

"No, Briggs, I don't; so you must make the best of it."

"But crabs' and lobsters' claws grow again, sir; for I've seen 'em do it at home, down in Cornwall."

"Yes; but we're not crabs and lobsters, Sergeant. There, never mind about such a bit of a wound as that."

"I don't, sir—not me; but it do look ugly, and feels as awkward as if I'd lost an arm. There, I must be off, sir. I've got to see to our poor fellows who are to go off in a wagon back to the town."

"How many were hurt?" said Denham eagerly.

"Five; and pretty badly, too."

"Any one—" Then Denham stopped short.

"No, sir, not one, thank goodness; but those lads won't be on horseback again these two months to come. Doctor wanted me to go with the wagon, but I soon let him know that wouldn't do."

"Poor fellows!" said Denham as soon as the Sergeant had gone. "That's the horrible part of it, getting wounded and being sent back to hospital. It's what I dread."

"You won't attempt to mount to-day?" I said. "You'd better follow in one of the wagons."

"Think so?" he said quietly. "Well, we shall see."

I did see in the course of that morning. For, when the order was given to march, and the column wound down in and out among the stones of the pass, Denham was riding with the troop, looking rather white, and no doubt suffering a good deal; but he would not show it, and we rode away. For a despatch had been brought to the Colonel from the General in command of the forces, ordering the Light Horse to join him on the veldt a dozen miles away as soon as the British regiment of foot reached the mouth of the pass; and, as I afterwards learned, the Colonel's orders were to keep away from the kopjes and mountainous passes, where the Boers had only to lie up and pick off all who approached, and wait for opportunities to attack them in the open.

It was Denham who told me, and also what the Colonel said, his words being, "Then we shall do nothing, for the Doppies will take good care not to give us a chance to cut them up in the plains."

As we rode down the pass we could see some of the enemy's sentries high up among the mountainous parts; but we were not to attack them there; and, with a good deal of growling amongst the men, we kept on. Then every one seemed to cheer up when, a couple of hours later, we came in sight of a long line of infantry steadily advancing, and the rocks rang soon afterwards with the men's cheers as they drew up to let us pass.

"No fear of the Boers getting past them," said Denham to me. "I shouldn't wonder if their orders are to mount the pass, go over the Nek, and hold it. Maybe we shall meet them again after we've made a circuit and got round the mountains and on to the plain."

Chapter Sixteen
On the March

Our next week or two seemed to be passed in doing nothing but riding from place to place for the purpose of cutting off parties of Boers. Information was sent to the Colonel, generally from headquarters; but, whether because we were too long in coming, or because the Boers were too slippery, we always found they had not stopped to be cut off, but were gone. There was no doubt they had been at the places we reached, generally some farm, where the old occupier and his people received us in surly silence, and invariably declared there was nothing left to eat, for the Boers had stripped the place. This sullen reception was not because we were going to plunder them, for the orders were that everything requisitioned was to be paid for; it was solely from a feeling of pitiful racial hatred.

We reached a big and prosperous-looking farm one afternoon after a long hot ride, and I had been chatting with Denham more than once, and remarking how rapidly he had recovered from his injury, which he attributed to the healthy open-air life, and had also spoken with the sergeant, whose injury troubled him very little; while of our men, thirty who had received slight injuries had refused to go into hospital, and were now ready to laugh at any allusion to wounds.

We had reached, as I said, a big and prosperous-looking farm on the open veldt, hot, fagged, hungry, and thirsty; and the first thing we saw was the disorder left after the encamping of a large body of men. There were the traces of the fire they had made, the trampling and litter left by horses, and the marks where wagon after wagon had been placed to form a laager; while in front of the long, low house a big, old, grey-bearded Boer stood smoking, with his hands in his pockets.

One of the officers rode forward to tell him that we were going to camp there for the night, and that he must supply sheep, poultry, grain for the horses, and fuel for the corps, at the regular market-prices, for which an order for payment would be given to him.

The officer was received with a furious burst of abuse in Dutch. There was nothing left on the farm. The Boers had been there and cleared the place; and if we wanted provisions of any kind we must ride on, for we should get nothing there.

The officer was getting used to this kind of reception, and he rode back at once to the Colonel, who nodded and gave an order, riding forward with the other officers to take possession of one of the rooms. In an instant the men began to spread about and search, and the farmer dashed down his pipe in a fury, to come running towards the officers, raging and swearing in Dutch as to what he would do; while, as soon as he saw half-a-dozen men approach the corrugated-iron poultry-house and proceed to wrench off the padlock, the old man rushed back into his house, and returned followed by his fat wife and two daughters, all well armed in some fashion or another, the farmer himself bearing a long rifle and thrusting his head and arm through a cartridge-belt. There seemed no doubt about his meaning mischief, but before he could thrust a cartridge into his piece it was wrested from his hands by one of the troopers; and others coming to the trooper's aid, the fierce old fellow was bundled back into his house, his people following, and a sentry placed at the door.

Rude and cruel? Well, perhaps so; but we were in an enemy's country—the country of a people who had forced a war upon us—and the Colonel had a couple of hundred people waiting to be fed. So we were fed amply, for the farm was amply stocked; and the order the officer left in the old Boer's hands in return for his curses was ample to recompense him for what had been forcibly taken.

Denham and I slept pretty close to one another in one of the barns that night, revelling in the thick covering of mealie-leaves which formed our bed. Sweet, fresh, and dry, it seemed glorious; but I did not sleep soundly all the time for thinking of what might happen to us during the darkness. Once it was whether the farmer would send on messengers to bring back the Boer party who had preceded us, and give us an unpleasant surprise. Another time, as I lay on my back peering up at the openings in the corrugated-iron roof through which the stars glinted down, I found myself thinking of how horrible it would be if an enemy's hand thrust in a lighted brand; and in imagination I dwelt upon the way the dry Indian-corn leaves would burst into a roaring furnace of fire, in which some of us must perish before we could fight our way out. It was not a pleasant series of thoughts to trouble one in the dead of the night, and just then I heard a sigh.

"Awake, Denham?" I whispered.

"Yes—horribly," he replied. "I say, smell that?"

"What?" I replied, feeling startled.

"Some idiot's lit his pipe, and we shall all be burned in our—beds, I was going to say: I mean in this mealie straw."

"I can't smell it," I said.

"What! Haven't you got any nose?"

"Yes: I smell it now," I said; "but it's some one outside—one of the sentries, I think."

"Don't feel sure—do you?"

"Yes, I do now. Strict orders were given that no one was to smoke in the barns."

"Did you hear the order given?"

"Yes; and Sergeant Briggs muttered about it, and said it would serve the old Boer right if his hams were burned down."

"So it would," said my companion; "but I don't want us to be burned in them. Oh dear!"

"What's the matter?" I said.

"I wish this old war was over, and the same wish comes every night when I can't sleep; but in the daytime I feel as different as can be, and begin desiring that we could overtake the Boers and all who caused the trouble, and give them such a thrashing as should make them sue for peace. I say—"

"Yes," I replied.

"That's all. Good-night. I can't smell the smoking now."

Neither could I.

Chapter Seventeen
We Make a Discovery

"Oh, I don't like it; I don't like it," cried Denham to me, as he rode up to my side while we were cantering over the veldt one day. "We always seem to be running away."

"Manoeuvring," I said, with a laugh.

"Oh, hang so much manoeuvring!" he muttered. "The Boers set it all down to cowardice, and hold us in contempt."

"It doesn't matter what they think," I said, as we rode on over the splendid open highland, with the brisk bracing air whistling past our ears, and our horses seeming thoroughly to enjoy the run; "we've shown the enemy time after time that we are not cowards."

"But we're running away again; we're running away again."

"Nonsense," I said; "we're altering our position. I declare I'm getting to be a better soldier than you are. Would it be right to stand fast here and let the Boers surround us and lie snugly behind the rocks to take careful aim and shoot us all down, horse and man?"

"Oh, I suppose not," groaned my companion; "but I hate—I loathe—running away from these bullet-headed double-Dutchmen. They think it so cowardly."

"Let them, in their ignorance," I said. "It seems to me far more cowardly to hide one's self behind a stone and bring down with a rifle a man who can't reach them."

"Perhaps so. But where are we making for?"

"That clump of rocks right out yonder, that looks like a town."

"But they're making for that too," said Denham, shading his eyes by pulling down the rim of his soft felt hat.

"Yes," I said; "and there's another body behind us, and one on each flank. We're surrounded."

"Then why doesn't the Colonel call a halt and let us stand shoulder to shoulder and fight it out with the ring?"

"Because he wants to save all our lives, I suppose."

"'He who fights and runs away will live to fight another day,'" said Denham, with a bitter sneer. "Oh, I'm sick of it. Look here; those brutes of Boers will reach that great kopje first, drop amongst the stones, and shoot us all down just when we get there with our horses pumped out."

"Yes," I said, "if you keep on talking instead of nursing your horse."

"Are you aware that I am your officer?" he cried angrily.

"Quite," I replied; "but I was talking to my friend."

"Friend be hanged!" he snapped out. "Keep your place."

"I am keeping my place," I said—"knee to knee with you; and our horses are going as if they were harnessed together. I say, what a race!"

"Yes, it's splendid," said Denham excitedly. "Oh, how I wish the brutes would stand fast and let us charge right into them—through them—cut them to pieces, or ride them down! I feel strung up for anything now."

I nodded at him, and panted out something about his knowing that the enemy would not stand for a charge.

It was exciting. By accident, of course, in following out certain instructions from the General in command, to take a certain course and cut off a commando of the Boers, we had somehow managed to get into an awkward position, no less than four strong bodies of the enemy hemming us in.

There was nothing for our commander to do but make for the nearest shelter, and this presented itself in the distance in the shape of what looked like one of the regular piles of granite rocks, which, if we reached it first, we could hold against the enemy, however greatly they outnumbered us; though even then it seemed plain enough that they were far more than ten to one.

"Shall we do it?" said Denham as we rode on, having increased our pace to a gallop.

"Yes," I said; "I don't think there's a doubt of it now. We're on better ground, and they're getting among rocks."

"The flanks are closing in fast," said Denham.

"Yes; but we shall be out of the jaws of the trap before it closes," I said, "and we're leaving the last lot behind fast."

"Oh," said Denham between his teeth, "if we can only get time to hurry the horses into shelter and give the enemy one good volley before they sneak off!"

"Well, it looks as if we shall. But look! look!" I said excitedly; "that's not a kopje."

"What is it, then?"

"A town, with a fort and walls. We're riding into a solid trap, I'm afraid."

"Nonsense; there's no town out here."

"But look for yourself," I said excitedly. "It's a fort, and occupied. I can see men on the walls."

"Impossible. There's no fort or town anywhere out here."

"I tell you I can see plainly," I said stubbornly, for I had in those days capital eyes, well trained by hunting expeditions to seeing great distances.

"I tell you you can't," cried Denham.

"I can, and that's what the Boers are doing. They're driving us into a trap, and that troop that has been racing us is fighting to get here first so as to cut us off when we find out our mistake and try to get away."

"I say, are you talking foolishness or common-sense?" said Denham.

"Common-sense," I replied; "the sort that nobody likes to believe."

"If you are we're galloping into a horrible mess; the Colonel ought to be told. Yes, I'm beginning to think you're right. Ah! I can see the people there. They're manning that tower in the middle; I can just make them out. Val, lad, your horse is faster than mine. You must try and drop out, or spin forward, or do something to get to the Colonel's side and tell him what you can see."

I made no reply, but rode on stride for stride with my companion; but I kept my eyes fixed upon the strange-looking rocks and edifices in front, and made no effort to change my position.

"Did you hear what I said?" cried Denham.

"Yes, I heard," I replied. "But how is it to be done?"

"Don't ask me how it's to be done," he said angrily; "do it."

"There's no need," I said; "the enemy is scuttling off as fast as he can go."

"Retreating?"

"Seems like it. Why, Denham, can't you see?"

"See? No! What? Speak out, before it's too late."

"Look again," I said, laughing. "It's a troop of baboons."

"What!" cried Denham. "Well, of all the absurd things! So it is."

There was no doubt about the matter, and five minutes' gallop brought us close up to where a mob of two or three hundred of the fierce and hardy half-doglike creatures were racing about over the rocks, after leaving the walls and battlements of the great buildings in front of us, and leaping higher and higher amongst the rocks of the great clump which stood like an island in the midst of a dried-up sea.

There was no time for natural-history studies of the ape. The squadron of Boers we had been racing to get first to the ruins—as we now saw them to be—were only far enough off to afford us time to pull up, spring from our horses at the foot of a huge wall, and, from our steady position, give the advancing enemy a volley with such good effect that over a dozen saddles were emptied, and the whole body wheeled round and dashed off to join the rest of the advancing force.

This gave us a few minutes' respite, during which the horses were rapidly led into shelter by half our party, who found a way through the great wall; while the other half rapidly manned wall, rock, and tower, ready to receive the enemy with a steady fire, which they were not likely to stand, for in every direction now the veldt stretched away, bare of such cover as our enemies loved to use.

It was close work, and the Boers swept round right and left to attack us in the rear. Our men were, however, too quick for them; and, climbing higher, knots of them reached the highest portions of the rocks beyond the ruins, and opened fire upon the enemy, so that in a short time our assailants drew back to a distance, but kept their formation of four parties. As soon as they were beyond range, we could see three men from each of three bodies gallop off to join the fourth, evidently to hold a council of war concerning their next movements. This afforded us time to make something of an examination of the stronghold so opportunely offered as a refuge, and gave the Colonel an opportunity for taking the best advantage of our position.

The ruined buildings had undoubtedly been constructed for purposes of defence; and, to every one's intense delight, on passing through an opening in what proved to be a solid cyclopean wall, strengthened with tower-like edifices, there was a wide courtyard-like enclosure, quite beyond the reach of bullets, into which our horses were led, the walls themselves being of ample width to be manned, and with sufficient shelter from which our marksmen could command the whole kopje; and on these walls about fifty of our men were stationed.

"We're safe enough here from any attack they can make," said the Colonel. "What we have to fear is the want of water and provisions if they try to invest us."

Which they would not do, was the opinion of all who heard his words. We had our haversacks pretty well lined, and each man had, of course, his water-bottle; but the possibility of being held up for over twenty-four hours was enough to make the Colonel give orders for an examination of the ruins and the rocks of the kopje around, to see if water could be found.

To Denham was given the task of making the search, and he nodded to me to accompany him, and afterwards called to Sergeant Briggs, who eagerly came to our side.

"We're to go upon a foraging expedition, Briggs," said Denham, "in case we want food and water."

"Well, it won't take much looking to prove that there isn't a mouthful of food to be got here, sir," said the Sergeant, "unless we take to shooting some of those pretty creatures hiding amongst the stones. They're as big as sheep, but I should want to be more'n usually hungry before I had a leg or a wing."

"Ugh!" shuddered Denham. "I'd sooner eat hyena."

"Well, no, sir; I won't go as far as that," said the Sergeant.

"As to water," said Denham; "this has been a city at some time, so there must have been wells somewhere, for no river has ever been hereabout in the plain."

"Wells or tanks, no doubt, sir, if we can find them," said the Sergeant; "but I expect we shall find they have been filled up or covered by the stones that have crumbled down from these towers and walls."

"What a place to build a city in, out in the middle of this wide veldt!" I remarked.

"It's more a fort or castle than the ruins of a city," said Denham. "It's a puzzle, and it must be very, very old; but I say bless the people who built the place, for it's a regular haven of refuge for us. Why, we could hold these old walls against the whole Boer army."

"Two of 'em, sir, if we'd got anything to eat."

"And drink," I added.

"Yes," said Denham. "That's the weak point; but there must be a big well somewhere, and we've got to find it."

"I believe the horses would find it, sir, if we led one about—a thirsty one. They're good ones to smell out water when they want it."

"Well, we'll try one if we can't find it without," said Denham. "Come on."

We "came on," searching about in the inside of the place, while the outer works and the rocks were held by our troops; and after carefully examining the enclosure where the horses stood looking rather disconsolate, as they snuffed at the chaotic heaps of broken and crumbling stones, we passed through what must have been a gateway built for defence. The sides of this gateway were wonderfully sharp and square, and the peculiarity of the opening was, that it opened at once upon a huge blank wall not above six feet away, completely screening the entrance to the great court, and going off to right and left. So that, instead of going straight on to explore the exterior of the court, we had the choice of proceeding along one of two narrow passages open to the sky, but winding away just as if the court had originally been built with two walls for an enemy to batter down before they could reach the centre.

No enemy had battered down these walls, not even the outer one. Time had been at work on the upper part some thirty or forty feet above our heads, where many stones had been loosened and others had fallen; but the greater part of the walls stood just as they had been built by the workmen when the world was much younger, possibly two or three thousand years ago. Had time permitted, I for one should have liked to wander about and climb here and there, and try to build up in imagination a theory as to what race or age the old builders of the place belonged.

"It's a puzzle," said Denham, in answer to a remark of mine; "but they were not of the same race or kind of people as the tribes of niggers who have lived here since, and who have never built anything better than a kraal. But look here, Val; we mustn't stop mooning over old history; we've got to find water for the horses, and there must be some about, for people couldn't have lived here without."

I roused myself at once to my task, and we struck off to the left, walking and climbing over blocks of stone which had dropped in from the outer wall and encumbered the narrow passage, every now and then being saluted by one of the men, who, rifle in hand, was perched on high, watching the Boers, and ready, as Denham put it, to administer a blue pill to any one impudent enough to come too close.

After getting along for about a hundred feet we came to a big opening on our right—a wide gap where the huge stone wall had been broken down by man or through some convulsion of nature, and now forming a rugged slope full of steps, by which our men had mounted on either side of the opening to the top, where, as stated, they had ample space for moving and shelter from the enemy's bullets.

"What are you looking for?" said one of the troopers from the top. "There's no one here."

"Water," said the Sergeant gruffly.

"Then you'll have to wait till it rains," said the sentry.

"Humph! we shall see about that," said Denham in a low tone, intended for my ears only; and we climbed on over a heap of débris, at the top of which we had a good view outward to where one of the Boer parties had dismounted and were resting their horses before retiring or making another attack.

Upon descending the farther side of the heap of broken stones, there was a continuation of the open passage, always about six feet wide, but winding probably in following the course of the rock upon which the place was built, so that we could not at any time look far along the passage.

"This doesn't seem like the way to find water," said Denham.

"One never knows," I said. "Let's see where the passage leads to."

"Of course; but it seems waste of time. The old city, or temple, or whatever it was, must have been built with two walls for security, and I dare say once upon a time it was covered in so as to form a broad rampart."

"Right!" I said eagerly, and pointed forward. For we had just come in sight, at a bend, of a spot where great stones were laid across from wall to wall; and on passing under them we found our way encumbered beyond by numbers of similar blocks, some of which seemed to have crumbled away in the middle till they broke in two and then dropped.

"Oh yes," said Denham, in reply to a remark, "it's very interesting, of course, but we're not ruin-grubbers. I dare say the place was built in the year 1; and the knowing old codgers who understand these things would tell us that the people who built the place had dolly something, or square heads; but we want to find out which was the market-place where they kept the town-pump."

"And as the pump is most probably worn out," I said laughingly, "we'll be content with the well."

"Oh, if we find the well the pump-handle's sure to be at the bottom, and— Hullo! what have we got here?"

I shared my companion's wonder, for upon rounding a curve of the passage we came upon an opening in the great stones of the inner wall—an opening that was wonderfully perfect, being covered in by the cross-stones, which were in place over the passage where the doorway showed.

"Dark," I said as I passed in. "No; only just here. There's another wall, and quite a narrow passage not above three feet wide, and then it's light again."

"Let's look," said Denham. "Stop a minute, though. Don't go in, or you may drop down some hole. Here, I'll strike a light."

The next minute a little match was lighting up the narrow place, with the wall close in front and then a passage going off to the right.

"Why, it's like Hampton Court Maze done in stone," said Denham. "But there, what did I say? Look at that hole."

He pitched the remains of the burning match to the right, and it dropped down out of sight, lighting up the narrow way and then going out.

"That's the well, I believe," I said.

"Let well alone," replied Denham. "We don't want to tumble down there.—I say, Briggs, pick up that bit of stone, and reach in and pitch it down."

The sergeant rested his rifle against the wall, picked up a block of stone, and reaching in, threw it to his left so accurately, by good chance, that it must have dropped right in the middle of the opening and gone down clear for some distance before it struck against stone, and then rebounded and struck again, rumbling and rolling down for some distance before it stopped.

"Cheerful sort of place to have gone down," said Denham. "Tell you what; that's the way down to the wine-cellars. The old races were rare people for cultivating the grape and making wine."

"I believe it's the way down to the vaults where they buried their dead," I said.

"Ugh! Horrid," cried my companion. "Here, let's light another match."

He struck one, held it low, and stepped in and then to his right, and stood at the very edge of a hole in the rough floor of crumbled stone. Then, to my horror, the light flashed in the air as if it was being passed through it rapidly.

Then Denham spoke.

"It's all right," he said. "You can step across. It's only about three feet over. Wait till I've lit another match. Yes," he said as the light flashed up, "it's just as wide as it is across. I believe that originally the place was quite dark, and this hole was a pitfall for the enemies who attacked. There, come on."

It was easy enough to spring over, and the next minute Briggs followed, and we continued our way down a narrow passage whose roof was open to the sky at the end of a couple of dozen yards, so that there was no risk of our stumbling upon a pitfall; and, after passing along this passage for a time in a curve, we came upon what seemed to be its termination in a doorway, still pretty square, but whose top was so low that we had to stoop to enter a kind of building or room of a peculiar shape, wider at one end than at the other, in which there was a rough erection; while at one corner, some ten yards away, there was another doorway leading, probably, to another passage.

"Why, it must be a temple," I said, "and that built-up place was the altar."

"Does look like it," said Denham thoughtfully.

"You gentlemen know best, I dessay," said the Sergeant; "but it strikes me that this here was a palace, and the bit we're in was kitchen."

"Nonsense," said Denham. "It was a temple, and that was the altar."

"Wouldn't want a chimbley to a temple, would they, sir?"

"Chimney?" I said. "Where?"

"Yonder, sir. Goes back a bit, and then turns up. You can see the light shining down."

"Yes," I said, as we stepped close up to the supposed altar; "that must have been a chimney."

"That's right enough," said Denham sharply. "Burnt sacrifices, of course. This place was covered in once, and that chimney was to carry off the smoke. But there, let's get on. We're not finding water. Is it dark through this doorway?"

Inspection proved that it was rather dark; but the absence of stones in the roof enabled us to see our way without a match. At the end of ten feet of narrow passage, whose floor was very much scored and broken up, there was a square opening similar to that which we had passed before entering the so-called temple.

"I shouldn't be surprised if that hole communicates with the first," I said.

"Pretty well sure to," said Denham. "Here, sergeant, fetch one of those square bits of stone that lay by the other."

Briggs stepped back, and returned with a curious-looking and roughly squared piece of stone, handing it to Denham for throwing down; but as he took it I checked him.

"Don't throw that," I said; "it has been chiselled out, and is curious. It may show who the people were that did all this."

"Humph! Maybe," said Denham. "Take it back, Sergeant, and bring us another."

Briggs went back and fetched another block.

"This here's the same, sir," he said, "and cut out deeper, as if to fit on something."

"Yes, that's more perfect," I said. "Throw the first one down."

"Seems a pity," said Denham, looking first at one block and then the other. "They are curious; why, they look as if some one had tried to chisel out a hand-barrow on a flat piece of stone."

"Yes, sir," said Briggs gruffly, "or one o' them skates' eggs we used to find on the seashore at home in Mount's Bay."

"Look here," I said, kicking at the flooring and loosening a shaley piece of stone about as big as my hand; "I'll throw this down."

I pitched the piece into the darkness below, and we listened for it to strike, but listened in vain for a few seconds, and then:

Plosh!

"Water!" I cried. "Why, we've found the well."

"Hurrah!" cried Denham; "well done us!" and he stepped back to where I had kicked out the piece of broken stone, and was about to throw another piece down, when, as the light from above fell upon it, I snatched it from his hand.

"Don't do that," he cried angrily. "I want to judge how deep the place is."

"Don't throw that," I said huskily.

"Why not?"

"It isn't a well."

"What is it, then?"

"Look at this piece of stone," I said, and I held the under part upward so that the light fell upon two or three scale-like grains and a few fine yellowish-green threads which ran through it. "It's an ancient mine, and this is gold."

"Right!" cried Denham excitedly. "Then that old place back there with the chimney is the old smelting-furnace."

"Right you are, gentlemen," cried Briggs, slapping his thigh; "and I know what those two hand-barrow stones are. I've seen one like 'em before."

"What?" I said eagerly.

"Moulds, sir, as the old people used to pour the melted stuff in. They used to do it near my old home in Cornwall, only the metal there was tin."

Chapter Eighteen
The Old Folks Work

"Then this isn't a well, after all," said Denham, who seemed struck with wonderment.

"No," I said excitedly, as all kinds of Aladdin-like ideas connected with wealth began to run through my mind; "but there's water in it, and it will serve us as a well."

"Yes, of course," cried Denham. "I say, you two have made a discovery." Then he lit a match, got it well in a blaze, and let it drop down the square shaft, when it kept burning till, at about a hundred feet below us, it went out with a faint hiss, which told that it had reached the water.

"It'll do for a well, sir," said Briggs; "and I wouldn't mind getting down it at the end of a rope. I've done it before now, when a well's been rather doubtful, and we've had to burn flares down it to start the foul air. That hole's as clear as can be."

"How do you know?" said Denham.

"By the way that match burned till it reached the water, sir. If the air down there had been foul it would have been put out before it reached the surface."

"But there will be no need for you to go down, sergeant," I said. "We can reach the water with a few tether ropes."

"To get the water—yes, my lad," said the sergeant, with a queer screwing up of his face; "but I was thinking about the gold."

"Oh, we've no time to think of gold," said Denham shortly. "But I say, Val, isn't this all a mistake? Who could have built such a place and worked for gold—making a mine like this?"

"I don't know," I said, "unless it was the ancient traders who used to go to Cornwall in their ships to get tin."

"What! the Phoenicians?" said Denham.

"Yes," I said. "They were big builders too. They built Tyre and Sidon."

"Val," cried my companion, slapping me on the shoulder, "you've hit it right on the head. They were the builders. We know they went to Scilly and Cornwall for tin. They must have come here for gold."

"Oh no," I said. "They could sail from Tyre and Sidon, keeping within sight of land all the way along the Mediterranean, through the Straits of Gibraltar, and then up the coasts of Spain and France, and across to our country; but they couldn't sail here."

"Well, not all the way; but I can recollect enough of the map to know that they'd most likely have ships at the top of the Red Sea, and could coast down from there till they got somewhere about Delagoa Bay or Durban, and gradually travel across country till they got here."

"Rather a long walk," I said.

"Long walk? Of course; but it was done by the people in the course of hundreds of years perhaps—settlers who came into the country after its products. There, I believe it, and we must have made a find. Here, come back and let's have a look at the old furnace and chimney."

We went back, and were soon satisfied that we had the right idea. On further examination we found that some of the stones were calcined, and at a touch crumbled into exceedingly fine dust; while one corner at the back—below the chimney opening, where it was a good deal broken—showed signs of intense heat, the face of one angle being completely glazed, the stone being melted into a kind of slag like volcanic glass.

"Oh, there's not a bit of doubt about it," cried Denham. "What do you say, Sergeant?"

"Not a bit o' doubt about it, sir. I've seen smelting-furnaces enough our way for copper and tin, and this might have been one of such places, made by old-fashioned folks who didn't know so much as we know now. It's an old smelting-shop for certain; but I don't see as we've anything to shout about."

"What!" cried Denham; "when we've made a discovery like this? Are you mad?"

"Not as I knows on, sir. It's only like coming to a corner of the beach at home and finding a heap of oyster-shells."

"What do you mean?" said Denham angrily.

"Why, sir, it only shows as there was oysters there once, and that somebody came and dredged them, opened 'em, and ate 'em, and left the shells behind. Here's the shell, plain enough; but the old Tyre and Sidems, as you call 'em, took away all the gold, sure enough. Trust 'em!"

"What!" cried Denham, laughing. "Is it likely? Here's a gold-mine, sure enough; but if there's one here, don't you think there must be plenty more places in this country where people could dig down and get gold?"

"May be, sir," said Briggs, scratching his ear.

"Is there only one tin-mine in Cornwall, Sergeant?" I said.

"Only one tin-mine in Cornwall!" cried Briggs in disgust. "Whatcher talking about? Why, the country's full of 'em. You find tin wherever you like to cut down to one kind o' rock as is what they call quartz, and where there's tin in it there's a lot o' red powder as well; and when you break a bit there's the tin, all in pretty little black shiny grains. Oh, there's plenty o' tin in Cornwall, only it costs a lot to dig and blast it out o' the mine."

"So you may depend upon it there's plenty of gold here, sergeant," said Denham, taking the piece of stone I had picked up and holding it out to the sergeant. "There's a specimen of the ore, and I'll be bound to say there's tons of it to be found."

"Humph!" said the Sergeant, examining the piece of stone; "p'r'aps them bits o' threads and them scrappy bits may be gold; but if you broke that up and melted it, the gold you'd get would be such a tiny bead that it wouldn't be worth taking away."

"Perhaps not," said Denham, giving me a look; "but there'd be a good-sized bead out of a ton. The ancient miners didn't work for nothing, I'll be bound. But come along; we've found what we were looking for, and—"

He stopped short, for just then a shot was fired, which made us start on our return along the narrow passage.

"Mind the hole," I shouted to Denham, who was first.

"Jingo!" he cried, "I'd forgotten it;" and he made a bound which took him clear, proving that I had spoken just in time.

Before we were out into the wider passage open to the sky, three or four more shots rang out, followed by a volley, and then there was a cheer.

"Ahoy, there!" cried Denham, hailing the men on the top of the outer wall. "What is it—enemy come on?"

"Eh? Oh, it's you, sir," cried one of our troopers, looking down. "Yes, and no. Enemy, but not the Boers."

"What do you mean?" cried Denham sharply.

"Troop of those baboons got together and making a rush, barking like a pack of dogs, at our fellows out yonder among the rocks. They had to give 'em a few pills to scatter 'em. The savage little beasts have gone off now."

"I thought we were going to be out of a fight," said Denham to me as we quickly retraced our steps, to make our way to the Colonel, whom we found at last in the court amongst the horses, talking anxiously to a knot of officers.

"Oh, there you are, Mr Denham," said the Colonel as we went up. "I was beginning to think you'd come to grief. I could have searched the place half-a-dozen times over by now. You've come to say there's no water, of course?"

"No, sir; I've found plenty."

"What!" cried the Colonel, whose whole manner changed in an instant. "You've found plenty?"

"Yes, sir."

"Splendid news, my dear boy. There, I forgive you for being long," he added good-humouredly. "The horses want a drink badly. Show the men where to lead them at once."

"My news is not so good as that, sir. It's hard to get."

"What! At the bottom of a well?"

"Of a well-like place; and I think there's an ample supply."

"See to getting ropes, Sergeant," said the Colonel, "and—we have no buckets with us?"

"No, sir; but there's a couple of those zinc-lined nose-bags in the troop."

"Capital. They'll do. Take what men you want, and set to work drawing water at once. You must try and clear out some hollow among the stones near the mouth of the well, so that the horses can be led to drink as fast as the men can haul the water up."

I was in the party told off to help; and the first thing to be done was to find the nearest part of the court to the interior building where the mine-shaft was. It proved to be an easier task than we anticipated. What was better, we came upon a pile of stones in one corner, close up to the wall, which looked as if they had been heaped up there by hand for some reason or another; and they attracted me so that I drew Denham's attention to them, and told him what I thought.

"You're right," he said. "Here, half-a-dozen of you, come and help."

He was about to set the men to work to drag the stones away; but I proposed that the tethering raw-hide ropes of two of the horses should be attached to their saddles and the ends made fast to the great rough slabs of stone. This was done, and the horses set to draw, when one by one a dozen massive pieces were drawn aside, leaving a little opening, through which I dropped a stone, with the result that those who listened heard a deep-sounding *plosh!* and set up a cheer. Then other two slabs were dragged away, to lay bare a roughly squared hole six feet across, from which the water could be easily drawn up.

"That communicates with our shaft, then?" said Denham to me in a questioning tone.

"No doubt," I said. "I dare say there are tunnels running in several directions. Did you tell the Colonel about the gold?"

"Not yet," he replied. "He thinks a good deal more about the water now than he would do about gold. But, I say, do you think it will be good drinking-water?"

"Certainly," I said. "Gold isn't copper."

"Thank you," he said sarcastically. "I found that out a long time ago. I never could do anything like so much with a penny as I could with a sov.— Here, Sergeant," he cried as the first water-bag was pulled up, dripping, and with the sound of the water that fell back echoing musically with many repetitions underground, in what seemed to be a vast place. "Water good?"

"Beautiful, sir. Clear as crystal and cold as ice."

"Then I'll have a taste," said the Colonel, coming up. "Excellent!" he continued, after taking a deep draught from the portable cup he took from his pocket. "Now, what are you going to do?"

"Keep on pouring it into that hollow among the stones, sir," said Denham, pointing to a little depression. Into this one of our makeshift bags was emptied, and the impromptu trough proved quite suitable.

Then the men worked away at lowering and raising the nose-bag buckets, drawing up sufficient in a few minutes for watering half-a-dozen horses at a time.

While this was progressing the Colonel returned from where he had been inspecting the top of the wall, and rearranging the men so as to take the greatest advantage of our position, to make sure the Boers could not break in through the weakest spot—the opening where the wall had fallen.

"Ha!" he said to Denham and me, "you two deserve great credit for hunting out the old underground tank of this ancient fortress. Now, with plenty of provisions and fodder for the horses, we might hold this place for any length of time. I think the General ought to know of it, and place two or three companies of foot here. I see that good shelter might be contrived by drawing some wagon-sheets across the top of these double walls."

"Yes, sir—easily," said Denham. "As you say, there would be no horses to keep if the place were held by foot."

"Exactly," said the Colonel, who seemed much interested in the drawing of the water, and listened intently to the echoes of the splashing from the impromptu buckets. "Why, Denham, that tank seems to be of great size; quite a reservoir, and tremendously deep."

"It is, sir," said Denham dryly; "only it isn't a tank."

"What is it, then—a well?"

"No, sir: a gold-mine," said Denham in a low tone.

The Colonel looked at him sternly, and then smiled.

"Oh, I see. Metaphorical," he said. "Yes, to thirsty folk a perfect gold-mine. Liquid gold—eh?"

"You don't understand me, sir," said Denham quietly. "I was not speaking in a figurative way, but in plain, downright English. That really is part of an ancient gold-mine, in which the water has collected in course of time."

"Really? Are you sure?" said the Colonel.

"Yes, sir," replied Denham. Then in a few words he told the Colonel that we had discovered two shafts within the walls, as well as the old furnace-house and the ingot-moulds.

"You astound me," said the Colonel. "Here, come along and let me see."

He followed Denham, and I went too, as one of the discoverers. The Colonel examined everything with the utmost interest.

"Not a doubt about it," he said at last. "You two lads have made a most curious discovery. It may be valuable or worthless; but here it is. I think that, besides being a splendidly strong place for a base, it is otherwise worth holding."

"You feel sure it is an old gold-mine, then, sir?"

"Undoubtedly, and it must have been of great value. This explains why it was made a favourite station by the ancient settlers who discovered the riches on the spot. I've heard rumours of old workings about here in the veldt; but I never thought much about them, or that they were of any consequence. I shall begin to think now that we must fight harder than ever to hold this part of the country. Which of you two made the discovery?"

"Both of us," said Denham. "No; Moray first stumbled upon the hole there."

"We were together," I said quietly; "and Sergeant Briggs helped."

"I didn't see much of his help," said Denham dryly. "We pushed, and he did the grunting."

"You shall have the credit of the discovery, never fear," said the Colonel, "and your share of the profit, if there is any; but we have something else to think about now. Come up here; I want to see how our enemies are going on."

He led the way back to the walls, and we followed him to the highest part of our fortress. The strength of the place seemed to explain a great deal, suggesting, as it did, that the builders must have had good reasons for the tremendous labour expended in making the place the stronghold it must have been.

"Ah," said the Colonel, shading his eyes and gazing over the walls at the rocky part of the kopje, "I don't want to be unmerciful; but I'm afraid we must clear the rocks of the enemy."

"The apes?" said Denham.

"Yes; the vicious little brutes have bitten two of the men; but they had to pay for it, for three were killed and I don't know how many wounded before the pack was driven off. You should both be well on the lookout when wandering about, and ready to use your revolvers, for the apes have steel-trap jaws, and muscles nearly as strong. It is astounding the strength there is in an ape."

"But if you come to the question of strength, sir," said Denham, "it seems to me that everything in nature is stronger than a man. Look at insects."

"No, thank you, Mr Denham," said the Colonel sarcastically. "I have something else to look at, and no time to listen to your lesson on natural history. Some evening, perhaps, when there is no danger, and I am sipping my coffee over a quiet pipe, I shall be happy to listen to you."

"Thank you, sir," said Denham.

"Is that meant to be sarcastic, my dear boy?" said the Colonel, laughing.

"Oh no, sir," said Denham in an ill-used tone.

"I say 'Oh yes.' But I didn't mean to snub one of my smartest officers.— Well, Moray, this is another reason for giving you your stripes. Work away, my lad, and master all your drill. I would promote you directly; but it would seem too much like favouritism in the eyes of your seniors. You may rest assured that I am not forgetting you."

"I am quite satisfied, sir," I said warmly. "Every one treats me more as a friend than as the latest recruit."

"I'm glad of it, and that Mr Denham here seems to look upon you as a companion—a brother-in-arms, I ought to say."

"Yet I've a lot of trouble with him, sir," said Denham mockingly. "He's a very impudent young brother-in-arms sometimes."

The Colonel made no reply, but took his field-glass from its case, and sat down on the highest point of the old fortress, while he proceeded carefully to examine the country round, dropping a word or two about his observations from time to time.

"The Boers seem as if they mean to stop," he said softly, and there was a pause as he swept the horizon with his glass. "A good twelve hundred men if there's one," then came, and he had another good long look. "Let it stand at twelve hundred," he muttered; "but I believe there are more." There was another pause. "Take some grass to keep all those horses," he muttered—"that is, if they stay." Another pause. "Be next door to madness to try to cut our way through them."

"Yes, sir," said Denham.

"I beg your pardon, Mr Denham," said the Colonel, lowering his glass to look at my companion.

"Beg pardon, sir; I thought you spoke," replied Denham, and he cocked his eye comically at me as the Colonel renewed his observations.

"They evidently mean to stay; and if we made a rush for it, every man would be down upon his chest delivering such a deadly fire as I dare not expose my poor, fellows to."

"No, sir," said Denham to me silently—that is to say, he made a round "O" with his mouth, and then shaped the word "sir" as one would in trying to speak to a deaf and dumb person.

"They'd empty half our saddles, and kill no end of horses," continued the Colonel, as he kept on sweeping the plain with his glass.

There was a long pause now; and then, still speaking in the same low, distinct voice, and without doubt under the impression that he was only expressing his thoughts in silence: "That's it," he said at last, as if he had quite come to a decision as to the course he must pursue. "In the dark. A quiet walk till we are discovered by their outposts, and then gallop and get through them. Say to-morrow night, when the horses are well rested."

Another pause, during which Denham shook his head violently. Then: "No. The poor horses would be hungry. It will have to be to-night. Let me see; there is no moon. Yes, it must be to-night."

Click! went the field-glass as it was closed, and at the same moment the Colonel turned, to see Denham nodding his head violently at me in acquiescence with our chief's remarks, but in profound ignorance, till he saw my eyes, of the fact that the Colonel was watching him curiously; then he met the Colonel's glance, and blushed like a girl.

"Don't do that, Mr Denham. You'll injure your spine."

"Oh!" went Denham's mouth, and he stamped his foot, as the Colonel walked away—both movements, of course, in silence.

"There," said the Colonel loudly, as if for us both to hear; "I don't think I need try to see any more. Ha!" he ejaculated as, with a sharp movement, he began to open and focus his glass again, and looking towards the west for some time. "Worse and worse. They mean to have us. I suppose they look upon us as a danger that must be crushed out once and for all."

"If they could do it, sir," said Denham.

"They evidently mean to try, Denham," replied the Colonel, with a sigh. "Some of us will have to bite the dust before this business is over. There's a fresh commando of quite five hundred men coming up yonder under the sun, and before dark we shall be regularly ringed round."

"Well, let them come, sir," said Denham bitterly; "they can't all hit at us at once. What you said was right."

"What I said was right?" replied the Colonel, staring. "Why, what did I say?"

"Something about advancing to-night in the darkness; and then, as soon as we were discovered by the outposts, making a gallop for it."

"Did I say that?"

"Yes, sir."

"Not a bad plan either," said the Colonel, his face wrinkling up.

"No, sir; just the exciting rush I love."

"Humph!" said the Colonel. "Well, gentlemen, we may as well go down."

"'Well, gentlemen,'" whispered Denham to me, with a laugh, as soon as he had the opportunity. "I say, recruit—private—whatever you call yourself—why don't you blush?"

No more was said then, as orders were given for every man to make a good meal from his haversack; and as soon as the order was passed along, the men looked at one another and began to whisper.

"We're not going to stop here for to-night," said one. "I had picked out my corner for a good snooze."

"The Colonel was afraid the ruin would be too draughty for us, and didn't wish to see his boys getting up in the morning with stiff necks," said another; and plenty of laughing and banter went on amongst the men, who in all probability would be engaged in a deadly struggle before many hours had passed.

I thought of this for a time, and I ate my bread and cold salt pork slowly and without appetite, for the thoughts of the pleasant old farm came back; and I began to wonder how father and Bob were, and what Aunt Jenny would be thinking about. Then, between the mouthfuls, a vision of Joeboy's black face and grinning white teeth seemed to rise up; and I fell to thinking how disappointed he would be when he returned from the foraging expedition to find that the corps had been suddenly called out.

"Poor old Joeboy!" I thought to myself; "it's a pity father didn't keep him at home. It would be horrible if he were to be shot by the Boers." But I was eating again heartily soon, the conversation of the men taking up my attention, for they were discussing what was to be done that evening.

"It's only a reconnaissance," said one. "We're going to give the Doppies a stir-up to show them we're 'all alive, oh!'"

"Nonsense," said another. "We shan't do anything; the Colonel don't care about working in the dark."

"That's right," said another voice. "It would be absurd to move from such a strong place as this. Why, we could laugh at twice as many as they could bring against us."

"Don't you talk nonsense, my lads," said a familiar voice which made me turn my head sharply.

"Who's talking nonsense, Sergeant?" said one of the troopers.

"The man who spoke," was the reply. "What's the good of a strong place like this to us if we've got no provisions for selves and horses?"

"The horses might be driven out to graze under the fire of our rifles."

"How long would the scanty grass round here last? No: the chief's right enough, and as soon as it's dark the orders will come, 'Boot and saddle.' We've got to cut our way through that mob of Dutchmen to-night."

"Oh, very well," said one of the men who had not yet spoken; "this is rather a dreary sort of place, so by all means let us cut."

The men grew very quiet afterwards as the twilight began to fall, and I noticed that most of them, after finishing their meal and getting a draught of water freshly drawn up out of the old mine, walked up to their horses and began to make much of them, patting and smoothing, and then examining girths, bridles, and every buckle and strap.

The night was coming on fast now, and the Boers began to mingle with the haze in the distance. We saw they had filled up all the gaps between their lines, opening out till they formed a complete hedge of dismounted horsemen around our stronghold; and they looked a very formidable body of men.

"Yes," said Denham, who had drifted to my side again, according to what had now become a custom of his—for I could not go to him—"we're regularly ringed round, Val."

"Yes, they're very strong," I said.

"No, they're not, lad, for a ring's very weak, and bends or breaks if it's pushed from the inside; but if pushed from the outside it takes a deal to break it. We'll both bend and break it to-night."

We sat talking for a bit, and watched the Boers till they were quite invisible. Then we could do nothing but wait for orders, no one believing that any attack would be made by our mounted enemy. However, about an hour after it was quite dark an alarm was suddenly given; but every man was on the alert, and the entrances to our fort were doubly strengthened. For there was the sound of shouts and horses thundering over the plain towards the fort; and at last the order was given to fire, a sharp fusillade ringing out in the horsemen's direction. It had its effect, for the enemy turned and galloped away, the sounds of their retreat rapidly dying out; and all seemed quiet till one of the defenders of the gap in the wall challenged, with the customary "Halt! or I fire!"

"Um!" cried a familiar voice. "Don't shoot. On'y Joeboy. Want Boss Val."

Chapter Nineteen
Bathing in Hot Water

"Why, Joeboy," I cried excitedly, "how in the world did you manage to get here?"

"Um! Walk very fas'. Then crawly till Doppies hear and shoot. Then run very, very fas'. Water: Joeboy thirsty."

The faithful fellow had followed the troop as soon as he returned from his mission; and as he afterwards told me, with a broad smile upon his face, he tracked us by following the Boers.

"Joeboy know they try to ketch sojers," he said. Soon after this, the Boers having withdrawn to their former position, as was carefully tested by the scouts sent out, the Colonel and the officers held a little council of war, at which Denham was present. And then the Colonel announced his plans to this effect: He had made up his mind it was impossible to hold the ruined fortress without provisions, though he would have much liked to keep it as a base from which to make a series of attacks upon the enemy. It was perhaps possible to get help; butt this was doubtful, for the General's hands were very full. Then, by sending out several messengers with a despatch, one of them would be sure to reach headquarters; but, even if he did, the reply would probably be to the effect that it would be madness to despatch a detachment of infantry right out into the veldt at a time when the force at disposal was so very small. So the Light Horse must make a dash to extricate themselves from their awkward position. These, Denham said, were the details of the Colonel's plan.

"'That's how matters stand,' said the Colonel in conclusion, 'and I propose starting about two hours before daylight, going due east in column, and as quietly as possible, till we come in touch with their outposts, and then charge and cut our way through them before they have recovered from their surprise. Now,' he said, 'I am open to consider any better suggestion if either of the senior officers can propose one.'"

"Did any one make a suggestion?" I asked.

"Of course not. Every one thought the plan splendid," replied Denham.

"Then we're going to try it?" I said.

"We're going to do it," cried my companion warmly; "but I don't like giving up a rich gold-mine like this now we've found it."

"No," I said thoughtfully; "and, besides the gold, it is such a grand archaeological discovery."

"Well, yes, I suppose it is," replied Denham; "but I was thinking of the gold. I say, though, you'll have to sit fast, squire—regularly grow to your saddle."

"Of course; but I'm afraid we shall leave a lot of our poor fellows behind."

"Not we," cried Denham warmly. "Our fellows can ride, and there'll be no firing. The Doppies won't try to shoot for fear of hitting their own men, as it will be too dark for them to aim for us. Besides, we may steal through without being discovered."

"Not likely," I said. "They'll be too cunning. Depend upon it, they'll have vedettes out all along the line."

"Then the vedettes had better look out, for those we meet when we charge through in column will be in a very awkward position."

"Yes, very," I said thoughtfully.

"The Colonel then said all those not on duty were to lie down and sleep till they were roused up half-an-hour before the start."

"Oh yes," I said bitterly; "we shall all feel quite ready for and enjoy a good sleep with a ride like this in prospect."

"Well, why not? I know I shall sleep," said Denham. "So will you. So here goes."

As he spoke I noticed that the men were lying down in the soft sandy patches among the stones; and, after seeing to my horse—just as a matter of course, though there was no need, for Joeboy had gone to his side—I returned to where I had left Denham, and found him wrapped in his cloak, fast asleep, and announcing the fact gently to all around in what sounded like an attempt to purr.

"I may as well lie down," I thought, after seating myself on a block of stone, and gazing round at the high walls which encompassed us, and at the bright stars overhead looking down peacefully upon our camp, as if there were no such thing as war in the world. Then I began thinking about home again, and wondered what they were all doing there, and whether the Boers had interfered with my father because he was an Englishman. This brought up the thought that if the war went against the Boers they might go so far as to commandeer both my father and Bob. The thought was horrible.

"It doesn't matter so much about me," I meditated; "but for them to be dragged off, perhaps to fight against us—oh! it would be terrible."

There had until now been a sad feeling of restfulness about my position; but as I drew a mental picture of two forces drawn up against each other, with my father and brother forced to fight on one side, and myself a volunteer on the other, the rock upon which I was seated began to feel horribly hard, and I changed my position, to lie down on the soft sand at my feet.

Well, I had been very hard at work all day; and Nature intended the lying-down position to be accompanied by sleep. In less than a minute, I suppose—in spite of home troubles, risks in the future, and, above all, that one so very close at hand—my eyes closed for what seemed to be about a moment. Then some one was shaking my shoulder, and the some one's voice announced that it was Sergeant Briggs going round to all the men of his troop.

"Come, rouse up, my lad! rouse up!" he whispered. "We're off in less than half-an-hour."

I sprang to my feet, just as Denham came up. "Oh, there you are," he said drowsily. "I was just coming to wake you. I say, get right up beside me. We may as well go through it close together, and give one another a help—if we can."

That was a weird and strange business, moving about in the darkness, with the horses snorting and sighing as the saddle-girths were tightened, and bits and curbs adjusted for a ride where everything depended upon horse and man being well in accord; but the preparations did not take long, and we were soon all standing in our places, bridle upon arm, and in as regular order as the roughness of the stone-littered court would allow.

I now learned that the men posted upon the walls had been withdrawn, and that every one was in his place, waiting for the command to start upon a ride at the end of which many would not answer to their names.

Then, from out of the darkness, the Colonel's voice rose low and clear, giving the order "March!" and in single file the men moved off, leading their horses towards the openings, through which they passed; then they bore off to their right to take up position in line till all were out, our troop being last. Next came the order, softly given to the first troop, to mount; and the same order was quietly passed along from troop to troop till it reached us, and we sprang into our saddles almost without a sound.

"First come first served," said Denham to me in a whisper. "I should have liked to be in front so as to do some of the scouting and feeling for the enemy, besides having first go at them before they grew thick. I say, Val, we must mind that we don't get cut off and taken prisoners."

"Ugh! Yes," I said, with a shiver. "I say, isn't it rather chilly?"

"Be warm enough presently," said Denham bitterly. "Bah! This is too bad. I did want to be first in the column."

"Form fours—left!" came from the front.

I felt electrified as, quite accustomed to the command, the horses swung round to the left.

Then came the word "March!" and our column moved off, with Denham whispering to me.

"Talk about luck," he said. "Why, we're going round the other way, and we are to open the ball after all."

For so it was. We had made up our minds that we were to be last, but the Colonel's determination was to bear round to the left instead of the right; and in consequence of the movement the rear troop led. We rode on at a walk till we had passed round by the rocks which harboured the baboons, and then on till we were nearly opposite the opening by which we had entered the old stronghold.

Then the order came, "Right!" and we struck off straight away for the Boer force opposite, an advance-guard and supports being sent out far ahead; while the silence of the night was only broken by the softly-muffled tread of the horses, and once in a way by an impatient snort.

"That's the danger," said Denham to me softly. "Just at the nick of time our nags 'll be telling the Doppies we're coming."

"Perhaps not," I replied. "Where they are they have horses about them in all directions; and if they heard a snort, why shouldn't they think it was from one of their own ponies?"

"I hope they will," said Denham impatiently. "But, I say, the chief isn't going to keep us at this snail's-pace—is he? I want to gallop, and get it done.—Hullo! old Dark Night; I didn't know you were there."

This was to Joeboy, who was walking with one hand on the cantle of my saddle.

"Um!" said Joeboy; "come along take care of Boss Val."

"Good boy!" said Denham banteringly. "Take care of me too."

"Um! Yes! Take care too," replied the black; and just then an idea struck me, and I hastened to communicate it to my companion at once.

"Why, Denham," I said, "we ought to send Joeboy right on in front, away in advance of the guard. He wouldn't be noticed in the dark, and would be able to get close to the outposts and let us know when it is time to charge."

"Silence in the ranks there!" said a stern voice. "Not a word there! Who's here?"

"Denham, sir," replied my companion.

"Then you had better go to the rear. I want trustworthy officers in front during this emergency."

"Yes, sir," said Denham bitterly; and he was in the act of falling out from his place when, feeling unable to contain myself, I broke out:

"I beg pardon, sir; it was my fault. I spoke to propose—"

"To propose what?—Silence!"

I was mutinous in my excitement, for I continued:

"To send on this black we have with us right in front. He could get close up to the outposts without being seen."

I expected a severe rebuke before I had finished; but, to my surprise, the Colonel—for it was he who had ridden up to the front—heard me to the end.

"A black?" he said. "Is he to be trusted?"

"I'll answer for him, sir," I said eagerly.

"Here, Mr Denham," said the Colonel, "stay in your place. Yes—send the black scout on at once to creep forward far in advance of the column, and tell him to come back and give us full warning of how near we are to the enemy."

The Colonel drew rein as soon as he had spoken, and we passed on, while as soon as we were getting out of hearing Denham gripped my arm.

"You brick!" he whispered. "Now then, send on your Joeboy.—Do you understand what for?" he now asked the black.

"Um!" replied Joeboy. "Find the Doppies, and come back."

"That's right," said Denham eagerly. "Creep up as close as you can, and then come and warn us. Oh, what a blessing to have a black skin, and no clothes to hide it!"

"Joeboy go now?"

"Yes. Off," whispered Denham, and the black uttered a peculiar click with his tongue, leaped out sidewise, and then bounded forward without a sound. One moment we saw his black figure dimly; the next he seemed to have melted away or been absorbed into the blackness right ahead, and for some time we were following the track of what had been like a shadow.

I listened as our horses tramped quietly on through what was, now that the kopje had been left behind, like a sandy desert, whose soft surface completely muffled the hoofs. Once in a while there was a faint rustling as the horses brushed through a patch of thick bush or the yellow-flowered thorn; but not a stone was kicked away or sent forth a sharp metallic sound. So quiet was it that Denham turned to me and whispered:

"Who'd ever think there were four hundred of our fellows on the march behind us?"

"And somewhere about twelve or fifteen hundred of the enemy in a circle round about."

"Yes; but they're standing still," he said. "Think your Joeboy will make them out?"

"I'm sure of it," I said.

"That's right. Then in a few minutes we shall be at them with a rush. I don't like this fighting in the dark."

"It will be a shout, a rush, and we shall cut our way right through," I said.

"Perhaps; but don't you cut, young fellow. If you come at any one there in front, you give point; don't waste time in cutting. I say, Val; if I don't get through, and you can get to where I'm found—"

"What are you talking about?" I whispered sharply.

"About my will," he said quietly. "I leave you my watch and my sword."

"And I'll leave you my rifle and Sandho. He's a splendid fellow to go."

"Stuff and nonsense!" said Denham, interrupting me. "You won't be hurt."

"That's more than you know," I said peevishly, for his words upset me; and when he went on I made no reply. Even if I had replied I should not have been able to finish my speech, for Joeboy now came up at a long loping run. He caught at Denham's bridle, checking the horse, while Sandho and the three troopers on my right stopped short, and the whole line of horsemen suddenly halted.

"What is it?" said Denham.

"Doppies all along," said Joeboy. "All this way; all that way," he continued, gesticulating.

"How far?" I whispered.

Joeboy shook his head, and seemed to feel puzzled how to answer the question. At last he raised his face and whispered, as he pointed forward:

"Far as two sojers over dah," he said, "and far again."

"Twice as far as the advance-guard," I interpreted his words to mean.

At that moment the Colonel rode up, and Denham repeated the black's words.

"That's right," he said in a low tone, with his face turned so that as many of the troop as possible should hear. "Lieutenant Denham, I shall not alter our formation. Your orders are, 'Forward' at a walk, and as silently as if the horses were grazing, till the advance-posts give the alarm. Then gallop straight away. Not a shot to be fired. Forward!"

There was a low murmur as of many drawing a deep, long breath. Then the column was in motion, and I felt a thrill of excitement running through me like a wave, while unconsciously I nipped Sandho's sides so that he began to amble. This brought back the knowledge that I must be cool, so I gently checked the brave little horse, and softly patted his arching neck, when he promptly slowed to a walking pace like the others. Then I found that Joeboy had crept round to my right side, between me and the next trooper, and, assagai in hand, was holding on to my saddle with his left hand.

All was perfectly still; and though we had gone on fully a hundred yards, there was nothing to be heard or seen of the enemy in front.

Suddenly Denham leaned towards me, and gripped my shoulder for a moment before loosening his grasp and holding his right hand before me.

"Shake," he said in a low whisper.

Our hands pressed one another for a brief moment or two, and then we both sat upright, listening.

All was yet silent. Then, far away, but so loudly that the air seemed to throb, came the deep, thunderous, barking roar of a lion, followed from out of the darkness ahead by the rush and plunge of a startled horse.

"Quiet, you cowardly brute, or I'll pull your head off!" came loudly in Dutch, as a horse somewhere to our left uttered a loud, challenging neigh. This was answered directly by Denham's charger; and in an instant a horse in front followed the first horse's example.

I heard a faint rustle as every man threw his right arm over the reins to seize the hilt of his sabre, and the feeling of wild excitement began to rush through me again as I gripped my own and waited for the order to draw.

Now the darkness was cut by a bright flash of light right in front; there was the sharp crack of a rifle, and right and left *flash, crack, flash, crack,* ran along a line.

As the first report was heard Denham rose in his stirrups. "Draw swords!" he yelled; and then, "Gallop!"

There was the rasping of blades against the scabbards, three or four closely following digs into the soft sandy ground, with our horses' muscles quivering beneath us, and then we were off at full speed, tearing after the outposts, which had wheeled round and galloped back, while with our sabres at the ready we went straight ahead.

"Keep together, lads," cried Denham in a low, hoarse voice; but the order was needless, for, after the manner of their nature, our chargers hung together; and as we raced along it seemed to me that we should pass right through the enemy's lines without a check.

Vain thought! Away in front, as we galloped on, a low, deep hum seemed to be approaching; and I knew the alarm had spread, and that the Boers were rapidly preparing for us. More than that, we had convincing proof that they were prepared.

Suddenly, flashing, glittering lights, as of hundreds of fireflies playing about a hedge extending right and left as far as I could see, began to sparkle and scintillate; but only for a moment, for now came the crackling roar of irregular firing, the flashes being partially obscured. Then, in a few brief moments more, we were closing up to the long line of riflemen.

"Now for it!" cried Denham close to my loft ear, his voice sounding like a husky whisper as we raced on knee to knee, and then our horses rose, as it were, at a fire-tipped hedge to clear the smoke.

There was a crash, yells of rage and defiance, and we were through, tearing away with the roar of our long line of galloping horses close after us. There was no time to think of danger—of shots from the enemy, or being crushed down by the hoofs of the troopers tearing after us; all was one wild state of fierce excitement, which made me feel as if I must shout in triumph at the result of our successful charge.

Contrary to expectation, there was now a new sound—the buzzing hiss of bullets overhead. Then, away to my left, yet another peculiar announcement of what might happen; for, clearly above the heavy thud of horses' hoofs and the loud jingle of bits and chains, I could hear a curious *zip,*

zip, zip, zip — a sound I had learned to know perfectly well: it was the striking of the Boers' bullets upon inequalities of the ground, and their ricochetting to hit again and again, as though a demoniacal game of "Dick, duck, and drake" were being played upon the surface of the ground instead of upon the water from off the shore.

Suddenly some one tore along to the side of our column, and a voice shouted, followed by the clear notes of a trumpet.

The horses wanted no touch from rein or spur. Those right and left of me bore round, and naturally mine went with them. Left incline, and we tore on still in as wild and reckless a race through the darkness as was ever ridden by a body of men.

The bullets overhead buzzed, and the ricochets sounded *zip, zip*; but, as far as we could tell, no one was hit, nor had a man gone down from the false stop of a horse.

Unexpectedly, though, I heard a cry from somewhere behind, then a heavy fall, and another, as a couple of horses went down, and caused some confusion; but to stop to help the unfortunates was impossible at such a time. It was the fortune of war, as we all knew; and we tore on, till a note from the trumpet rose from our left; then another, and the fierce gallop was changed to a trot, and evolution after evolution was executed to bring the retiring regiment into formation of troops. Soon after this was completed a fresh call brought us to a walk, and directly after to a halt to breathe the panting horses.

"Dismount, my lads," cried the Colonel. This order was to enable the brave beasts to have the full advantage of our halt.

"Hurt?" was asked excitedly on all sides; but every answer was in the negative, and we stood there by our troopers and chargers in the darkness, listening to the wild excitement from the distance.

The firing was still going on, but in a confused, desultory way; and for the moment it seemed as if we had made good our escape, and had nothing to do but mount and ride quietly away. That was how it struck me, and I said so to Denham.

"Oh no," he said anxiously. "Didn't you see?"

"See what?" I asked.

"Why, we were riding straight on into another body of the enemy after we had cut through the first."

"No," I said. "Who could see through this darkness?"

"Well, I didn't at first; but when the Colonel dashed up with the trumpeter and turned us off to the left, I looked out for the reason, and there it was: a long line of the brutes, blazing away in our direction. You must have heard the bullets."

"Yes, I heard them," I said, "but I thought they came from behind."

"Some of them did, my lad, and I'm afraid we've left a good many poor fellows behind. But them, it can't be helped. The thing now to be settled is which way we are to go next. Listen; the officers are nearly all with the chief now, and the whole plain seems to be dotted with the enemy."

Denham had hardly done speaking when a movement a short distance from us resulted in the officers joining their troops and squadrons. Then the order to mount was passed softly from troop to troop, and we waited for the little force to be put in motion again.

"It's of no use for the chief to try the same ruse again," whispered Denham. "It was right enough as a surprise; but the enemy is on the alert now. It seems to me we are as completely surrounded as before."

"Never mind," I said, as cheerily as I could; "we shall do it yet."

"Oh yes, we shall do it yet," replied my companion; "but it must be done quietly and quickly, while it's dark. I say, though, what about your black boy? He couldn't have kept up with our mad gallop."

"Joeboy?" I said in an excited whisper. "Joeboy? I forgot all about him;" and a pang of misery shot through me.

"He was holding on by your saddle—wasn't he?"

"Yes," I said huskily; "but from the moment I drew my sword and we charged, I never thought about the poor fellow till you spoke."

"Advance at a walk!" was the next order; and as we started, the Colonel came up to where Denham and I rode at one end of the leading troop.

"Here," cried the Colonel; "where's that Matabele fellow? He may lead us out of this crowd."

"Gone, sir," said Denham quietly. "We lost him in the gallop."

"Tut, tut, tut!" muttered the Colonel; "he would have been more useful than ever now. Forward at a walk! They can't see us, nor tell us from one of their friendly troops riding about the veldt. Silence in the ranks!"

"He needn't have spoken," said Denham in a low voice, as the Colonel drew rein and let us pass. "We shall get through yet, as you say."

However, the odds seemed to be terribly against us, for whichever way we turned large bodies of the enemy were evidently in front; and after changing our direction again and again during the next two hours, the Colonel at last halted the corps.

"It's of no use," I heard him say to one of the senior officers. "We're only tiring out the horses and men. We must stand fast till daybreak, then select our route, make for it, and try what a good charge will do. We shall clear ourselves then."

Directly afterwards the order was passed for the men to dismount and refresh themselves with such water and provisions as they had, and silence once more reigned among us; for, not far off, large bodies of the mounted Boers were in motion, and twice we were passed at apparently some two hundred yards' distance, our presence not being detected.

"We ought to be able to get through," whispered Denham to me soon after the second body had gone by. "They must be thinking by this time that we have got right away. Where do you think we are facing now? North, I should say."

"East," I replied, pointing away straight in front. "That's the morning breaking."

"For the beginning of another day," said Denham softly. "Well, I shan't be unhappy when this one's work is done."

"Nor I," was my reply. "I half-wish we had stayed among the ruins."

"To be starved," said Denham bitterly. "No; this is far better. It gives us something to do."

"Yes," I replied; "and there's some more, for the Colonel's coming up."

Chapter Twenty
What People Think Brave

The Colonel was coming up, and it was quite time, for day was breaking fast, and the black darkness which had been our friend during the night was gradually dying away.

There was but one thing to be done: to select the best direction for making our dash; and, glass in hand, the Colonel stood near us, carefully scanning the country round. We who were waiting did the same, and saw the distant hills which seemed to turn the broad plain which had been the scene of our night's encounter into a vast amphitheatre. It was too dark yet to make out much of the enemy's position; but right away to our left, and not many miles distant, was the heavy-looking mass of the great kopje and the ancient buildings we had left.

For some time we sat waiting, with the grey dawn broadening, and at last I could clearly make out bodies of the mounted Boers in nearly every direction; while, as I still scanned the distance, I gradually grew less surprised that we were evidently so thoroughly hemmed in, for the plain seemed to be alive with the enemy, though the nearest party must have been about half a mile off. Still there was no movement on the part of the enemy towards us, as doubtless, in the dim morning light, our dust-coloured jackets and broad-brimmed felts caused us to be mistaken for some of their own people.

However, it was only a few minutes before a change took place. The Colonel had made up his mind, and the horses' heads were turned for the open country, where there was a gap in the hills; and away we went at a steady walk, orders being given for the corps to break up its regular military order and ride scattered in a crowd, after the fashion of our enemies. This served us for a few minutes, during which we covered a mile in the direction we were to go; but the light had grown stronger, and it became evident that a body on our right was moving slowly to cut us off. Before another minute had passed another body was advancing from the left; and, ignorant as I was of military evolutions, it was plain enough to me that, long before we reached them, the two bodies would meet and join in line to impede our advance.

I was right, though I did not feel certain; for the orders were given, "Trot!" and then "Gallop!" and away we went for the closing-up gap in front.

"We shall never do it," said Denham to me as we galloped on.

"We must," I cried, and then no more words were spoken. To a man we knew, as we went along at a steady hand-gallop, that every body of Boers within sight was aware of what was going on, and moving forward to take us in a gigantic net whose open meshes were closing in.

There was no cheer, but a savage sound as if every man had suddenly uttered the word "Ha!" in token of his satisfaction; for, as the two bodies of the enemy in front were racing over the veldt to meet and crush us as we tried to get through, our trumpeter sounded a blast which sent us along at full speed; and then another call was blown, and we swept round till, going at right angles to our former course, we were riding exactly in the opposite direction to the detachment of Boers on the right. Our object was, of course, to get round by their rear; and, being an irregular and only partially drilled body, the result of the Colonel's manoeuvre was that the enemy, in their efforts to reverse their advance, fell into confusion. Some were trying to pull up, others tried to sweep round to right or left and meet us; while, to add to their confusion and turn them into a mob of galloping horsemen, the left body charged full among their own men. The result was that we came upon the struggling rear of the enemy's right wing, scattering and riding over them; and had the country beyond been clear, we could have made our escape.

Unluckily it was the fortune, of war that, just as we had cleared the scattering mob, with every man riding for his life, there appeared in front another and stronger line, with bodies of the enemy coming in from right and left.

Our chief turned in his saddle to glance backward; but it was only to see the two bodies we had passed struggling to got into something like order, so as to pursue us. For another minute no alteration was made in our course; but the attempt was hopeless, for we should have been outnumbered twenty times over, while the enemy in front now opened fire, their bullets whizzing overhead.

The trumpet rang out, and we wheeled round as upon a pivot, our well-drilled horses never losing their formation; and away we went as soon as we were facing our loosely-formed, mob-like pursuers, straight for their centre.

The trumpet again rang out; and, sword in hand, every man sat well down in his saddle, prepared for the shock of the encounter which in another minute would have taken place.

This, however, was not the style of fighting the Boers liked; and, already upset by the collision of the two bodies resulting in a confused mob, they declined our challenge, and pulled up, tried to ride off to right and left, and again got themselves into a disorderly crowd; but as they opened out we dashed through them, tumbling over men and horses, and with, a cheer galloped to reach an open part of the plain.

It was a wild and exciting rush before we got through; and I have but little recollection of what took place beyond the fact that I struck out right and left in mêlée after mêlée, wherein blows were aimed at us with the butts and barrels of rifles, and shots fired at close quarters, but in almost every case I believe without effect. Then the call rang out, "Halt!" and, with our enemies at a distance, we formed up again, to give our panting horses breathing-time.

It was then, I remember, that Denham—who had not been missed—almost breathless, and with uncovered head, edged in to my side, and as soon as he was able to speak panted out:

"Glorious, Val! Glorious! Oh! we did let them have it; but there's nothing for it except to die game or surrender, and I'll be hanged if I'll do either, and so I tell them."

"Which way are we going now?" I said, taking off my soft hat and offering it to him, as I wiped the perspiration from my face with my hand.

"Do you want to insult a fellow?" he cried, laughing. "Who's going to wear your old hats?" Then, seriously: "No, no; keep it, old chap. Which way next? Who knows? I'm sure the Colonel doesn't. It's all chance. I don't like running; but run we must if they'll only open a hole for us."

"It's horrible," I said.

"Not a bit of it. They're getting it worse than we are."

"Yes; but look at their numbers."

"I've been looking, old fellow, and there's more than I can count. I didn't think there were so many Doppies in the country. There are too many for us to kill, and so many that they won't run away. Why, we're nowhere. Yah! Cowards! That's the Boer all over. Look at them, lying down at a distance to pick us off. I don't call that fighting. Oh, Colonel, Colonel, this won't do!"

He said the words to me, and the men within hearing laughed. There was, however, good cause for Denham's words, the bullets beginning to fall about us, aimed from different directions; and it was quite plain that, if we stood grouped together in troops, it would not be long before a perfect hail of bullets would be pattering among us, many of them going straight to their goals, and decimating our little force, or worse.

The officers needed no telling; and in a few minutes we were off again, first in one direction, then in another, our leader giving up as hopeless the idea of making straight for any particular opening in the dense ranks, but picking out the smaller parties of the enemy—that is to say, mobs not more than double our own strength; and when we could get within striking distance they were punished and scattered like chaff before the wind, in spite of the scattered volleys they sent at us before they fled.

This could not last, of course, for it was always at the cost of some of our poor fellows and of many horses, who had to be left to fall into the enemy's hands.

At last we managed to charge home right into a body of our foes at least three times our strength—numerous enough, in fact, to surround us as we fought our way through them, thus rendering us more and more helpless; but our men fought desperately, till about half of the corps forced their way through, and, making an attempt to keep well in formation, dashed on.

I was with about a dozen quite fifty yards in the rear, half-mad with pain and excitement, for one of the Boers had clubbed his rifle in the midst of the mêlée and struck at my head. I was too quick for him, wrenching myself sidewise; but the rifle glanced all down one side, giving me for the moment a terrible numbing sense of pain. Yet my head was quite clear, and I rode on, feeling a wild kind of exhilaration from the knowledge that with one quick thrust I had passed my sword through his shoulder. Now I was urging on poor bruised and frightened Sandho to keep up with the dozen or so of our men who were trying to overtake the main body. We were in no formation, only a galloping party; and, consequent upon my injury, I was last. As we tore on we passed one of the corps trying to drag himself from under his fallen horse, which was lying across his legs. I couldn't let him lie like that; so I pulled up, leaped down, and, shouting to Sandho to stand, dashed at the fallen and wounded horse's head, caught him by the bit, and dragged at him to make him rise. The poor beast made a desperate effort, and got upon three legs; but sank back again with a piteous groan, for it had stepped into some burrow and snapped its off hind-leg right in two. However, the horse's effort had saved its rider, who struggled to his feet, his face blackened with powder and bleeding, and passed his hand across his eyes. To my astonishment I saw who it was, the long drooping moustache telling me in spite of his disfigured face.

"Well done!" he said hoarsely; "but I'm hurt, and you can't help me. Mount and be off. I'm done."

I glanced behind me, and saw that the Boers were getting together again as if to come in pursuit, while a long line was coming up from the left at a steady trot, and bullets were whizzing by. It was only a momentary glance to see what our chances were; and in answer to the Colonel's words I shouted to Sandho to come round to my side.

"Poor wretch!" groaned the Colonel; "you've done your part. I can't see you suffer like this;" and, to my horror, he took out his revolver, placed it to his charger's forehead, and fired. The shot had a double effect that was nearly fatal to our chance, for at the clear-cutting report the Colonel's charger laid his head slowly down, and a quiver ran through his frame; but Sandho reared up, made a bound, and was in the act of dashing off. Almost instinctively I gave out a shrill whistle, which brought him up, and he trotted back to my side.

"Now," I cried, half-wild with excitement and the feeling of exaltation which had come over me, "mount and gallop after our men."

"What! No, boy, I can't do that," he said, smiling, as he clapped me on the shoulder. "I've played my part, and if it means exit I'll go off the stage like a man, for I suppose the brutes will shoot me for what I've done."

"Nonsense!" I cried, wildly now. "Jump on, and gallop."

"No," he said, recocking his revolver. "Mount, my lad, and ride for your life."

"I won't," I said. "You get up and go."

"What!" he shouted, with his face lowering. "Mount, sir. I order you."

"Don't be a fool," I yelled at him. "They'll be after us directly. There, some of them are firing already. Get up, or you'll lose my poor old horse."

He turned upon me in a rage, with his revolver raised.

"Bah!" he cried. Then a change came over him, and he turned to look back at the enemy. "Can you run?" he said. "I can't; my right leg's cut."

That was plain enough, for his breeches were gashed above the knee, and there was a great patch of blood spreading.

"Yes, I can run," I said stubbornly; "but I won't."

"You shall," he said, as he thrust his foot into the stirrup and swung himself up on Sandho's back. "Now then, on my right here. Catch hold of the holster-strap, and we'll escape together, or fall: the brave lad and the fool."

Chapter Twenty One
I have my Doubts

"Too late; too late," I muttered through my teeth as, sword in hand, I made a bound to keep up with Sandho, who dashed forward. It was lucky for me I did so; as it was, I nearly lost my hold. The poor beast had been sadly punished in the mêlée; and between temper and dread he was hardly controllable, and bearing hard against the curb in a wild desire to rush off. In fact, I fully expected at any moment to be shaken from my grasp, as, oddly enough, even in that time of peril, I recalled the gymnastic sport of giant strides of my schooldays, and held on; but I was certain we were now too late, and that it was only a matter of moments before we should be overtaken and cut down or taken prisoners by a strong party of the Boers who were in full pursuit.

Then my exaltation increased, and I thought that Sandho would be able to go faster if relieved of my clinging hand, and so save the Colonel; and in another instant I should have let go, when—as he told me afterwards—the Colonel seemed to divine my thoughts, and I felt his sword strike against my back as it hung loosely by the knot to his wrist, while his strong right hand was thrust under and gripped my leather cartridge-belt.

"Hold on tightly, my lad, and we'll do it somehow," he cried.

These words drove all the heroic thoughts out of my brain, and I tried to look back to see how near our pursuers were; but I could not turn my head round, but only listen to the shouts, while *crack, crack, crack* came the reports of rifles—badly aimed by the mounted men, who fired from the saddle, holding their weapons pistol-wise—the bullets from which went whizzing and buzzing past our ears.

"It's all over," I thought, and a deep sense of depression was coming on at the thought of the Colonel falling wounded and a prisoner into the Boers' hands; but the depression was only momentary, being chased away by a wild feeling of excitement as I thought I had misjudged the gallant lads of the Light Horse. For as soon as they had pulled themselves together, under command of their remaining officers, and had discovered the loss of their chief, in response to our Major's orders they drew rein and divided into two squadrons, which swung round into line, with a short distance between them, and gallantly charged down upon our pursuers.

They were none too soon. I remember feeling a strange choking sensation as, with a wild cheer, they swept round us, and, sword in hand, rode over and cut down those of the enemy who stopped to face them, the majority taking flight. Then our men came thundering back, seeming to sweep us up and carry us along with them, while the Boers in our rear and on both sides began to fire at our hurrying troopers.

I was nearly breathless, and must have dropped but for the Colonel's strong grasp; and I was curiously giddy till I heard his voice just above me give the word for the men to halt. His orders were echoed by the troop-leaders, who and the racing retreat was checked.

"Bring one of those horses here for me," shouted the Colonel; and I now noticed that just ahead were half-a-dozen of the brave beasts whose saddles had been emptied but had kept their places in retreat, charge, and retreat again.

"That's right," cried the Colonel as he released my belt, so that I stood, hardly able to keep my feet as, with swimming eyes, I saw him stagger forward and mount the fresh charger, though evidently experiencing great suffering.

"Now then, my lad—Moray—what's your name?—mount."

His words seemed to galvanise and bring me back to a knowledge of my position, while Sandho helped to rouse me by turning and coming close up.

I hardly know how I did it, but I managed to climb into the saddle, and from that moment, as we cantered away together, with the bullets whizzing after us, the terrible burning sensation of exhaustion from which I suffered began to die out, and the throbbing of my brain steadied down.

"What are we going to do now, Denham?" I said at last, as, gazing straight ahead, I leaned over a little towards the left.

"Eh? Denham?" said a voice. "I'm not—"

"Ah!" I cried excitedly; "don't, say the Lieutenant's down!"

"Well, I won't if you don't want me to," said the private at my side; "but he is, and pretty well half our poor fellows too."

I uttered a groan, and down came the horrible feeling of depression again—a feeling I now knew to mean despair.

"Can't be helped," continued my fellow-trooper. "We've fought as plucky a fight as could be; but they've been too many for us, and I suppose we shall have to surrender at last, or all be shot down. Ah! there goes another," he cried. "No; it's only one of the empty saddle-horses."

As we swept past it, I looked at the poor beast struggling to get upon its feet again; and then it was in our rear, and my companion said bitterly the one word, "Down!"

"Why, that's the old fort and the kopje yonder, a mile ahead," I said suddenly. "Are we going there?"

"Eh? Yes, I suppose so," was the reply, "if the Doppies'll let us. They're coming on again."

He was quite right, for upon glancing to my left I could see a perfect swarm of the Boers galloping as if to cut us off, while I learned from the right that they were also coming on there. Then came the news that they were advancing in force behind; and from that moment the crackling of rifle-fire ceased, and it became a hard ride for the haven of comparative safety ahead.

"They'll reach the old place just about the same time as we do," said my companion on the left, "unless something's done."

Something, however, was done, for the Colonel seemed to have recovered himself, so that he was ready for the emergency; and as we neared the place that offered safety he gave his orders, and these were cleverly carried out. Half of our flying troops drew rein and faced round, unslung the rifles from their shoulders, and proceeded to fire volley after volley with terrible effect upon the nearest of the Boers. Then this troop retired past the other one in reserve, who had halted to take their turn, and another half-dozen well-aimed volleys went hurtling through the Boer ranks with such terrible effect upon horse and man that, upon the repetition of the evolution, the pursuit was checked, and the enemy began firing in turn.

We were in rapid motion again, so their shots had no effect; and a little more firing enabled us to reach and dash round the great walls to the entrance to the old fort, where our men sprang from their horses, which filed into safety of their own accord, while their riders put in practice the Boers' tactics, seeking the shelter of fallen stones and mounting the great walls, the steady fire from the ruins soon sufficing to send our enemies cantering back.

"Water for the horses at once," cried the Colonel as he entered the court, where I was standing examining poor Sandho. "Ah, Moray!" he said as he saw me; "not hurt, I hope?"

"Only battered and bruised, sir," I said. "Nothing serious."

"Humph! I'm glad of it, boy. You did splendidly. But I'm a fool, am I?"

My words, uttered in the wild excitement of our adventure, had slipped but of my memory; and as he brought them back to my mind so suddenly, I stood staring at him as if thunder-struck.

"A nice way to address your commanding officer! Why, you insolent, mutinous young dog! you ought to be court-martialled. What do you mean!"

"Not that, sir," I said, recovering myself. "I was half-mad with pain and excitement then, and I wanted to save your life."

"Yes, I know; I know," he said, changing his manner. "I forgive you, for no one else heard; and now, thank you, my lad; thank you. If I survive to write to my poor wife and girls again, I shall tell them when they pray for me to put the name of some one else in their prayers—the some one who saved my life. Thank you, my lad, and God bless you!"

I felt astonished and at the same time overcome by his words, and in my confusion could not find words to reply, till, lowering my eyes, I found exactly what I ought to say; for they fell upon the great patch of blood-stain which had been spreading terribly upon his right leg, till his knee was suffused, and ugly marks were visible right down his brown leather boot.

In an instant my hand went up to my throat, and I loosened the silk handkerchief knotted there.

"Your wound's bleeding dreadfully, sir; let me tie it up."

"No, no; not till I've seen to the men, my lad," he replied peevishly as he turned away, only, however, to turn back.

"Yes," he said, with a smile; "thanks, lad. First aid, and—here! Water, some one. Ugh! I feel sick as a dog."

I caught hold of him and saved him from falling by lowering him down upon a stone, just as there was the soft *pad, pad* of naked feet behind me, and a familiar voice said:

"Water, Boss. Here water, sah!"

"Joeboy!" I whispered as I turned and caught a waterbottle from an extended black hand. "You here!"

"Um? Yes, Boss Val. Couldn't run no more, and come away back."

I handed the water to the Colonel, who drank with avidity; then I tightly bound up the cut on his leg, for he impatiently refused to have it examined by one of the officers who had hurried up; and then, as soon as I was at liberty, I turned to the black.

"Have you seen the Lieutenant, Joeboy?" I said excitedly.

"Um? Boss Denham!" he replied. "No; all a rush and gallop. Lost Boss Denham. Lost Boss Val. Lost ebberybody. Joeboy said, 'All come back to water. Boss Denham come soon.'"

"I pray to Heaven he may!" I said sadly; but I had my doubts.

Chapter Twenty Two
Making the Best of it

That was a terrible night which followed. We had plenty of water; but our scraps of food were sadly inadequate for the wants of the men, who, many of them wounded, were sick and despondent, and dropped down here and there to fall asleep as soon as their injuries were roughly dressed. Meanwhile the walls were as strongly manned as could be contrived under the circumstances; and the weary horses were now watered and given the last handful of grain in the bags, after which they stood snuffing about among the stones, every now and then uttering an impatient neigh—Sandho as bad as any of them, though he had fared better, for I had given him half my biscuits and a piece of bread-cake.

By nightfall the entrance had been strongly fortified with a massive wall of stones, a narrow side-opening being left, large enough to admit any straggler who might manage to reach our camp; and then all but the sentries, after a last look at the Boers' fires in the distance, lay down anywhere to sleep; but pain and weariness kept me as wakeful as a group of officers, among whose voices I was glad to hear that of Sergeant Briggs, who spoke the most cheerily of them all.

"If you'll not mind, gentlemen," he said, "I should like to say that our position isn't so bad as you think."

"Why, it couldn't be worse," said the Major.

"Begging your pardon, sir, yes," said Sergeant Briggs. "We've plenty of water, and our marksmen can keep the Boers at a distance as long as you like. They won't face our rifles."

"But the horses, man!"

"They can be taken out to graze, sir, covered by our rifle-fire. There's a good patch of green out yonder."

"But we can't go and graze," said another officer.

"No, sir; but we shall be hungry enough by to-morrow night to be ready for a raid on the Boers' provision wagons. There'll be plenty, and we must cut one out, fasten a dozen reins to it, and bring it up here."

"Humph! We might try," said the Major.

"And we will," said one of our captains. "Why, we might capture some of their ammunition too," he added.

"Yes, sir. They've got pack-mules with their small-arms ammunition; and with a bit of scheming and a night surprise it might be done," said the Sergeant. "And there's another thing I had my eyes on to-day."

"What's that, Briggs?" said the Major.

"A train of bullocks, sir; and if one of you gentlemen can shoot the train with a field-glass just before sunset to-morrow night, if we're here, and give me half-a-dozen men and that black chap as come along with young Mr Moray, I shouldn't wonder if we had grilled steak for supper just by way of a change."

"Why, Sergeant," cried the Major, "if you're not our adjutant before this war's over it shan't be my fault."

"Thank ye, sir," said Briggs stolidly; "but I should like to get the beef for the boys and a load of mealies for the horses before we talk about that. And now, if you wouldn't mind, I'll have a couple of hours' sleep."

I felt for a few minutes so much brightened up that I was ready to go off too; but the thoughts of poor Denham lying out dead or wounded somewhere on the veldt kept me awake, and I was in greater pain than ever from the blow I had received. And there I lay in my misery till about midnight, when there was an alarm from the sentries of horsemen approaching, and I sprang to my feet.

Chapter Twenty Three
"Il Faut Manger"

I felt dizzy, and every movement was painful when I arose. The air was so cold that I was half-numbed; and in addition to my bruised side I ached from the tightness of my belts, and my sword-hilt and revolver seemed to have made great dents into my flesh. However, with an effort I lifted my rifle, which had been my bedfellow on the sandy earth, and hurriedly joined the others in making good the defence of the great gateway, with its newly-made protecting screen of stones.

There was no desperate encounter, however, to send the blood rushing through our veins; for, as we reached the entrance, we heard the men on duty removing stones while they carried on a desultory conversation with the new arrivals; and directly afterwards a thrill of joy ran through me, and a curious choking sensation rose in my throat, for somewhere in front where it was darkest I heard the Major say:

"That's grand news, Denham—thirty of you, and forty horses?"

Then his voice was drowned in the loud, spontaneous cheer which rose from those about me, in which at the moment I felt too weak to join.

"Here, get in, all of you," cried the Major as soon as he could make himself heard. "You're sure there is no pursuit?"

"Quite," came in Denham's familiar voice. "We have had a very long round since we wore cut off, and have not heard a soul as we came through the darkness."

"How about wounds?" said the Major.

"Pretty tidy, sir," said Denham. "The poor horses have got the worst of it. But we're all starving, and choked with thirst."

"We can manage water for you," said the Major; "but I'm afraid to say anything about food."

"Never mind," said Denham cheerfully; and then he seemed to turn away, for his voice sounded distant as he said—to the men with him, of course—"Tighten your belts another hole, lads. We'll forage for food to-morrow."

"That we will," cried the Major; and then out of the darkness came the trampling of horses' feet, followed by a few neighs, which were answered from where the horses stood together in the court. Meanwhile I tried to get to the front, but could not, and had to wait till the men began to file in after the homes; but at last I heard Denham's voice again.

"Not a bad wound?" he said.

"A nasty but clean cut from some Boer who had one of our swords."

"But tell me," said Denham eagerly—"young Val Moray? Did he get in safely?"

"Any one would think he was a cousin or brother," said the Major pettishly. "Yes, he managed all right, after giving up his horse to the Colonel and getting him in after he had been down."

"Val did?" cried Denham eagerly. "I am glad!"

I did not wait to hear any more, and did not try to force my way through the dense pack of our men, but worked hard to get back to the spot where I had been lying down; and upon reaching it, with the satisfactory feeling that there was to be no more fighting that night, I dropped into my old place, after shifting hilt and belt so as not to lie upon them again. Then, in spite of hunger and pain, a comfortable and exhilarating sensation stole over me, which I did not know to be the approach of sleep till I was roused by the reveille, and sprang up in a sitting posture, when the first man my eyes fell on was Denham, who was peering about among the troopers as if for something he had lost.

"Oh, there you are!" he cried as he caught sight of me; and the next minute we were standing together, hand grasping hand.

"Denham, old fellow," I said huskily, "I thought you were either a prisoner or dead."

"Not a bit of it," he replied; "but it wasn't the Boers' fault. Just look at my head."

"I was looking," I said, for a closely-folded handkerchief was tied diagonally across his forehead. "Is the cut deep?"

"Deep? No," he replied. "Deep as the beast could make it—that is, to the bone. I say, what a blessing it is to have a thick skull! My old schoolmaster used to tell me I was a blockhead, and I thought he was wrong; but he was right enough, or I shouldn't be here."

"The loss is bad enough without that," I replied.

"Horrible; but they've paid dearly for it," he said. "But I say, what about rations? We can't starve."

I told him what I had overheard during the officers' talk with the Sergeant.

"Yes," said Denham peevishly; "but that means waiting till to-morrow morning. We must make a sally and get something."

"I wish we could," I said, for now that my mind was at rest I felt ravenously hungry. "Hullo! what's going on there?"

Denham turned sharply, and, to our astonishment, Sergeant Briggs was coming from the gate leading half-a-dozen men stripped to shirt and breeches, carrying in half-quarters of some newly-killed animal.

"Why, hullo!" I cried, "what luck! They've found and been slaughtering an ox."

"Yes," said Denham dryly, "and there's more meat out yonder. We shan't starve. I'd forgotten."

"Forgotten! Forgotten what?"

"It isn't beef," he said quietly. "It's big antelope."

"What! eland?" I cried joyously.

"No; the big, solid-hoofed antelope that eats like nylghau or quagga."

"What do you mean?" I said wonderingly, as I mentally ran over all the varieties of antelope I had seen away on the veldt.

"The big sort with iron soles to their hoofs. Two poor brutes, bleeding to death, dropped about a hundred yards away as we came in last night."

"Horse!" I exclaimed. "Ugh!"

"Oh yes, it's all very well to say 'Ugh!' old proud stomach; but I feel ready to sit down to equine sirloin and enjoy it. Why shouldn't horse be as good as ox or any of the antelopes of the veldt? You wouldn't turn up your nose at any of them."

"But horse!" I said. "It seems so—so—so—"

"So what? Oh, my grandmother! There isn't a more dainty feeder than a horse. Why, he won't even drink dirty water unless he's pretty well choking with thirst. Horse? Why, I wouldn't refuse a well-cooked bit of the toughest old moke that ever dragged a cart."

"But what about fire?" I said.

"Oh, there's plenty of stuff of one kind and another to get a fire together. They break up a box to start it, and then keep it going with bones and veldt fuel. Look; they're coming in with a lot now."

"I say," I cried, as a sudden thought struck me. "Here, Sergeant!"

"What do you say?" cried Denham.

I said it to the Sergeant, proposing that he should make a roasting fire under the chimney of the old furnace; and as I spoke his face expanded into a genial smile.

"Splendid!" he said, and hurried away to shout to Joeboy; and in a very short time the smoke was rolling out of the top of the furnace chimney for probably the first time since the ancient race of miners ceased to smelt their gold-ore in the place marked on the maps of over a century ago as the Land of Ophir, but which has lain forgotten since, till our travellers rediscovered it within the last score of years.

Chapter Twenty Four
A Very Wild Scheme

"Well," said Denham some two hours later, "it isn't bad when a fellow's hungry."

"No," I agreed, speaking a little dubiously; "but it would have been much better if we had not known what we were eating." I did not hear any other opinions; for the men were ravenously hungry when the cooking was over, and we had all so many other things to think about.

It had been a very busy morning. Wounds had to be dressed, the uninjured had the task of strengthening the force upon the walls, and another party led the horses out a quarter of a mile to graze. This they were allowed to do in peace, the Boers paying no heed to the proceedings. Then the lookouts, who were furnished with the officers' glasses, gave warning that strong parties were quietly on the move about a mile away—evidently making a circuit for the purpose of disarming our suspicions—with the intention of swooping round and cutting off the grazing horses. But, as Denham said, they had not all the cunning on their side, for we had taken our precautions. A red flag was hung out, and in answer to the signal the horses were headed in for the gateway at once.

That was sufficient. The Boers, instead of riding along across our position, suddenly swooped round, and came on, five hundred strong, at full gallop, getting so near that they would have cut off some of our valuable horses had not fire been opened upon them from the walls, quite in accordance with the Boers' own tactics; our men lying down and taking deliberate aim, with the result that saddles were emptied and horses galloping riderless in all directions.

However, the party gradually came nearer, till they found that our firing grew hotter and more true; then, utterly discouraged by its deadly effect, they wheeled round again, and went off as hard as their horses could gallop.

"Let them try the same ruse again," said the Colonel, as he turned from where he had limped to watch the little action, and stood closing his glass.

"Let them come again if they like; but they had the worst of it this time. Splendidly done, my lads! Excellent!"

The Boers rode right away, then turned and rode back as if about to renew the attack; but suddenly they drew rein, and a small body came on at a canter, one of them waving a handkerchief.

"Yes," said the Colonel sternly. "Hold your fire, my lads; they want to pick up their wounded."

This was soon proved to be the case, and we looked on, thinking how much better their wounded fared than did ours.

"Yes," said Denham when I said something of the kind to him; "but I hope they are behaving decently to our poor lads, wounded and prisoners. Let's give them credit for a little humanity."

The Colonel waited till the enemy had retired with their injured men, leaving a couple of dead horses on the plain. Already I could see that the carrion-birds had caught sight of the dead, and were winging their way to an anticipated feast; but they were disappointed, for the order had been given, and the horses were being led out again to graze, while four men, with strong raw-hide plaited reins attached to their saddles, rode out quickly to play the part of butchers to the beleaguered force, and shortly after came slowly back drawing a fresh supply of meat for the garrison. Then the vultures descended to clear away everything left.

"It makes one shudder," said Denham to me as we sat perched upon a broken portion of the wall, resting after the previous day's exertion, and nursing our rifles.

"Why?" I said, though I felt that I knew what he was about to say.

"Makes one think how it would be if one lay somewhere out on the veldt, dead and forgotten after a fight."

"Bah! Don't talk about it," I cried.

"Can't help it," he replied. "It makes me want to practise my shooting upon those loathsome crows."

"Why should you?" I replied. "They are only acting according to their nature, and— Hullo! Look yonder; what's the matter with the baboons?"

Away to our left a loud chattering had begun amongst the ridges of ironstone and blocks of granite which formed the kopje. The drove, herd, flock, family, or whatever it was, of the dog-faced apes was running here and there, chattering, grimacing, and evidently in a great state of excitement. There were some five or six big fellows, evidently the leaders, and these kept on making rushes right down to the bottom of the stones, followed by others; while the females with their young, which they hugged to their sides in a curiously human way, kept back, partly in hiding, but evidently watching the males, and keeping up a chorus of chattering.

"Why, the beggars are going to attack our butchers."

"Yes; but they think better of it," I said, laughing; for the leaders of the troop turned back and began leaping up the hill again, but only to come charging down once more to the bottom of their little stony home, and stand chattering and grimacing menacingly.

"They're hungry," said Denham.

"Oh no, I don't think they'd behave as badly as we do," I replied. "I don't think they'd eat horse."

"What do they eat, then?"

"It always seemed to me when I've seen them that they ate fruit, nuts, and corn. There used to be a pack of them in a big kopje not far from our place, and they would come down and make raids upon the farm till we had to make it too hot for them with small-shot, and then they went right away."

"They don't like to see those horses dragged in," replied Denham.

"Not used to it," I said. "There, they are going back into hiding now."

The horses had now been drawn in to be treated as if they were oxen, and in a few minutes not one of the baboons was to be seen. There were two or three alarms in the course of the day, but no direct attack; and the whole of the horses had a good long graze, the vegetation after the late rains being fairly abundant in places, though for the most part the veldt in the neighbourhood of the old fortress was very dry and bare. There was abundance of water, however, for a stone tied to the end of four reins carefully joined did not suffice to plumb the well-like hole.

That evening, as Denham and I sat playing the part of voluntary sentry, my companion lent me his glass to watch the distant troops of Boers, which I did diligently. We were seated on the top of the wall, for the simple reason that both of us were terribly stiff and bruised, and consequently extremely disinclined to stir. Then I uttered a loud exclamation.

"What's the matter?" said Denham quickly.

"Take the glass," I said; "the sloping sun lights up that part clearly. There, sight it upon the line below that flat-topped hill in the distance."

"Yes," he said, taking the glass and focussing it to suit. "What of it? Boers, Boers, hundreds of Boers."

"But there's something in motion."

"Ah! Yes, I see now: one, two—why, there must be half-a-dozen ox-wagons with long teams."

"What does that mean?" I said.

"Ox-wagons."

"Yes; but what are they laden with?"

"I dunno," he said, peering through the glass.

"Corn for the horses; provisions for the Boers' camp."

"Of course! Oh dear, if we could only get one of them across here!"

"Well, could it be done?" I said.

Denham shook his head.

"It could only be done in the dark. You mean stampede the bullocks; but they'd be outspanned at night, and we could never get them inspanned and away without being beaten off.—Can't see it, Solomon the Wise."

"It does seem difficult," I assented.

"Yes; and, suppose we had got a team hitched on all right, see how they move: two miles an hour generally. But it does look tempting."

"But we might get a team of oxen away without a wagon by making a bold dash."

"Might," replied Denham; "but bullocks are miserably obstinate brutes to drive. It would mean a good supply of beef, though—wouldn't it?"

"Splendid."

"Yes; but we want meal too. I say, I dare say there's coffee and sugar in those wagons as well."

"Most likely," I said; "the Boers like eating and drinking."

"The pigs! Yes, and we're to starve. I say, couldn't we make a bold night-attack and drive them away, compelling them to leave their stores?"

"Well, after last night's experience I should say, 'No; we could not,'" I replied.

"You're quite right, Val," said Denham, with a sigh. "Hullo! here's your black Cupid come up to have a look at us."

For Joeboy, whom a good hearty meal had made very shiny and happy-looking, came climbing up to where we sat, and stood looking down at us as if waiting for orders.

"Here, Joeboy," I said; "look through this."

"Um? Yes, Boss," he said; and, from long usage when out hunting with my father or with me, he took the glass handily and sat down to scan the distant Boer line.

"Lot o' Doppie," he said in a low tone, as if talking to himself. "Lot o' horse feeding; lot o' wagon and bullock. Plenty mealie, coffee, sugar."

"Yes, Joeboy," I said; "and we want one of those wagons and teams."

"Um? Yes, Boss," he said thoughtfully, without taking his eyes from the glass. "Joeboy know how."

"You do?" said Denham quickly. "Tell us, then."

"Boss Colonel send Boss Val and hundred sojer fetch um."

"It wouldn't do, Joeboy," I said sadly. "There would be another big fight, and we should lose a lot of men and horses without getting the wagon."

"Um? Yes. Too many Doppie."

"That's right, Shiny," said Denham.

"Yes," I said; "we must wait till we see a team making for the kopje, and then the Colonel can send out a party and cut them off."

"Then the Boer General will send out a bigger party and cut us off," said Denham bitterly. "I don't want another set-to like yesterday's for a week or so. So we must take to horse and water for the present, I suppose."

"Joeboy know," said the black, with his eyes still fixed on the glass.

"You know?" I cried, staring at the black's calm, imperturbable countenance.

"Um? Yes."

"Why, what could be done?" I said, excited by the black's cool and confident way, knowing as I did from old experience how full of ingenuity the brave fellow was.

"Um?" he said thoughtfully, as he still watched the Boer lines. "No good to fight; Doppie too many."

"Yes," said Denham impatiently. "You said so before."

"Um?" said Joeboy, taking his eyes from the glass a moment or two to glance at the speaker, but turning away and raising the glass again; "Joeboy know."

"Let's have it, then," said Denham, "for hang me if I can see how it could be done."

"Big fool black fellow drive wagon," said Joeboy, still gazing through the glass, as if he could see those of whom he spoke. "'Nother big fool black fellow vorloper. Both fast sleep under wagon. Boss Val talk like Boer: double-Dutch."

"Is that right?" said Denham.

"Oh yes," I said. "I can speak like a Boer if it is necessary."

"Um? Yes," said Joeboy quietly. "Think Doppie talky, Boss Val take Joeboy and go in a dark night up to wagon. Stoop down and kick big black fool driver and big black fool vorloper. 'Get up!' he say. 'Want sleep alway? Get up, big fool! Trek!'"

"What?" I cried excitedly.

"Um? Talk like Doppie, Boss Val talk. Big fool get up an' inspan. Boss Val get up on box an' keep call driver big black fool, like Doppie. Joeboy walk 'long o' vorloper. Tell 'im Joeboy 'tick assagai in um back if he talk, and drive right 'way."

"Ha!" I said, with a heavy expiration of the breath. "But do you understand what he means?"

"Oh yes, I understand," said Denham, laughing; "but where are the Doppies going to be all the while?"

"Lying somewhere about, of course, asleep," I said excitedly; "but there would be no sentries over the wagons; and, as he says, the black foreloper and driver would be sleeping underneath."

"Oh, that's right enough," said Denham impatiently. "But the noise, the rattle of the wagon, the getting of the oxen, and all the rest of it?"

"The oxen would be all lying down with the trek-rope between them, and they'll quietly do what their black driver and foreloper wish. I think it could be done."

"My dear boy, it's madness."

"It isn't," I said angrily. "Joeboy is right, and a trick like this would perhaps succeed when force would fail. We must capture one of those wagons."

"Oh, I'd have the lot while I was about it," cried Denham, laughing.

"Be sensible," I cried pettishly. "Joeboy is right. Can't you see that it is the sheer impudence of the thing that would carry it through?"

"No, old chap," he replied; "that I can't."

"Well, I can," I said firmly. "The black driver and foreloper could be roused out of their sleep, and they take it as a matter of course that they were to drive the wagon somewhere else, and obey at once, especially if they are hurried by some one who speaks like a Boer."

"Well, I grant that's possible," said Denham; "but what about the Boer sentries and outposts? They'd stop you before you'd gone straight away for a hundred yards."

"I shouldn't go straight away," I said, "but along by the front; and if we were stopped, Joeboy could tell the outpost we were ordered to change position—to go on to the other end of the line. What would the outpost care or think about it? All he would think would be that a wagon-load of stores was being shifted, and let us pass. Then I should tell Joeboy to begin creeping out towards the east yonder, and keep on till we were out of bearing before striking away for the kopje here. Once we had got clear off we could keep steadily on all through the night, and at daybreak you would be watching for us, and send out a detachment to bring us in."

"Splendid, my boy—in theory," said Denham; "but it would not work out in practice."

"Think not?"

"A hundred to one it wouldn't," cried Denham firmly.

"Well, I think it would," I said—"and from the cool daring of the thing."

"And what about your horse? That would be enough to betray you."

"No take Sandho," said Joeboy, who had been listening attentively.

"Of course not," I said. "We should walk right across to the Boer lines, getting off as soon as it was dark."

"Why not go in disguise as a minstrel?" said Denham banteringly—"like King Alfred did when he went to see about the Danes? Have you got a harp, old chap?"

"No," I said coolly.

"Well, it doesn't matter, because I don't believe you could play it. But a banjo would be better for the Doppies, or—I have it—an accordion! Haven't one in your pocket, I suppose?"

"Why can't you be serious?" I said.

"I am, old fellow. Banjo, concertina, or accordion, either would do; and if you could sing them one or two of their popular Dutch songs it would be the very thing."

"Don't banter," I said dryly.

"Then don't you propose impossibilities. There, they are cooking supper again, so let's get down and see about a bit of—ahem! you know.

Whatever it is, we must eat. I almost wish I were a horse, though, and could go out on the veldt and browse on the herbage. Here, I say, I've got a far better Utopian scheme than yours."

"What is it?" I replied quietly, for I felt that he was going to chaff me.

"Well," he said, "it's this. You know how imitative monkeys are?"

I nodded.

"Then all we have to do is to make a ring of our men round the kopje there, and drive the baboons into the court here. From the court we could turn them into one of the passages between the walls, stop up the ends, and capture the lot."

"To eat?" I said sarcastically.

"Eat, man? No; to drill, and teach them to forage for us, just as the Malays teach the monkeys to pick coco-nuts for them."

"Drill them? Ah! there is a baboon called a 'drill.' Yes, go on," I said.

"We could send them out every night, and they'd come back laden with mealies for us; and there you are."

"Nice evening, gentlemen," said Sergeant Briggs, who had just climbed to our side. "I've been using the Major's glass. My word! they've got wagon after wagon loaded with stores across yonder. Is there any way of cutting out one or two, for we must not go on living upon horse?"

I looked hard at the speaker, and then at Denham, and the result was that we astonished the Sergeant, for both Denham and I burst out laughing, and Joeboy smiled as widely as he could.

Chapter Twenty Five
A Forlorn-Hope for Food

Sergeant Briggs stared, and looked so puzzled that we laughed the more.

"Beg pardon, gentlemen," he said, speaking as if huffed, "have I said something stoopid?"

"Tell him, Val," cried Denham; and I explained why we laughed.

"Oh, I see," he said good-humouredly. "I thought I was being laughed at. Well, I don't know, Mr Denham, sir; I don't think the idee's quite so wild as you fancy."

"Oh, it's impossible, Sergeant."

"No, sir, begging your pardon, it isn't. It's the cheek of the thing might carry it off. I like it."

"Yes; your mouth waters for the stores, Sergeant."

"Maybe, sir; but if I was you I should go straight to the Colonel and tell him."

"So as to be laughed at for a fool," said Denham. "The chief's in no laughing humour, sir," said the Sergeant stolidly. "He ought to be in hospital with that cut on the leg he got; but he won't give up, though I've seen him turn whitey-brown and come out all over the face with big drops. That means pain. No; he won't laugh."

"Then he'll growl at us, and tell us to be off for a pair of idiots."

"Well, I'll risk it," I said firmly.

"Will you? Young fellow," cried Denham, "don't you presume on my friendliness and forget that you're a private in my troop."

"It's my duty to let the Colonel know," I said warmly.

"Yes, through your superior officer. Well, look here; perhaps you're right. Let's go to him at once."

We descended after another look at the Boer lines, and found the Colonel resting against a block of granite, with his injured leg lying in a bed of sand. He listened attentively, after Denham's introduction, to all I had to say. Then he sat in perfect silence, frowning, and tugging at his long moustache. I was as uncomfortable as ever I had been, and wished I had not come; but soon a change came over me, for the Colonel spoke.

"Capital," he said sharply. "But—"

My hopes went down to zero again, but rose as he went on, taking the right line of thought: "It can only be done by sheer bravado. It is the utter recklessness of the ruse that would carry it through. Do you think, Moray, you could do this without breaking down at the supreme moment?"

"I think so, sir."

"That's good," said the Colonel; "there's a frank modesty about that 'think.' But do you dare to run the risk for the sake of your officers and brother-privates, who are in a very tight place?"

"I don't think now, sir," I said: "I dare go."

"Then you shall, Moray."

"To-night, sir?"

"No: have a night's sleep and a quiet day to-morrow to think out your plans. You will be fresher then. There, I'm in pain, and I want a few hours' rest to set me up. One minute," he added as I turned to go. "How many know about this?"

"Only Sergeant Briggs, sir, and the black, of course."

"Keep the black quiet," said the Colonel, "and tell Sergeant Briggs from me that the expedition is to be kept secret."

"Yes, sir."

"You are not to go on sentry work to-night."

I saluted, and went away with Denham, who began to growl:

"The chief's as cracked over it as you are. But, look here, Val, you must alter your plans."

"I can't," I replied. "I shall go."

"Of course you will; but you must reshape them so as to take me with you."

"That's impossible," I replied. "But would you go?"

"Would I go? Of course. I should like the fun of it. Here, you must go and tell the chief you feel as if you can't curry out the business properly unless you have my help."

I looked at him, laughing.

"I say, who's cracked now?" I said.

"Well, I believe I am—half," he replied. "I say, Val, I would like to go with you."

"What! upon such a mad expedition?" I said.

"Yes. It doesn't look so mad when you come to think a little more about it. Look here; I know. I'll go as a Dutch driver."

"You'll stop along with your troop, and I'll ask the chief to let you come to my help in the morning when we're coming along with the wagon—if—if we carry it off."

Denham was silent for a few moments before he said any more. Then, with a sigh:

"Yes, you might do that; but I should have liked to be in the thick of the business."

Many of the men went hungry to bed that night, and Denham and I lay talking for long enough before sleep came; but when it did, nothing could have been more restful and refreshing.

We rose at the "Wake up" to find that there had been no alarm in the night, and our first act was to climb to the top of the wall and use a glass, to see that the Boers wore in the same positions, and the outposts were just riding in, so that I had some insight as to the way in which the enemy guarded their front during the night.

"Here, I say, look!" cried Denham suddenly. "You ought to have gone last night."

"Why?" I asked as I took the glass; and then, "Oh!" I exclaimed in a tone of disappointment.

"Yes, you may well groan," cried my companion. "Why didn't the chief let you go?"

There was good reason. We could see plainly enough that the Boers were unloading the wagons, and the Kaffirs hard at work carrying bags which no doubt contained mealies or flour. To me the sight was maddening, for it now seemed one of the easiest things in the world for us to have captured and carried off one of the laden wagons.

"There, it's of no use to cry after spilt milk," said Denham, with a groan.

"Nor is it of any use to despair," I replied as I watched the unloading. "Perhaps they may leave one of the wagons full."

"Oh, they will, of course!" said Denham mockingly. "They'll pick out the best one, containing a nice assortment, and label it, 'Reserved for the use of the Natal Light Horse. To wait until called for by Don Quixoto Valentino Morayo and his henchman Sancho Panzo Joeboyo.' I never thought of that."

"Let's go and report what we have seen," I said bitterly; and we went and found the Colonel.

"Humph!" he said shortly; "unfortunate." That was all.

Then the day glided by, with our men always on the alert, their only work being to man the walls and keep a sharp lookout while the horses were driven out to graze; but though the Boers showed in force in different directions, they made no attack. In spite of a false alarm or two, the poor brutes managed to pick up a pretty good feed; though, considering the work they had to do, it was poor and unsustaining as compared to corn.

As for the men, they made the best of things; but several knots gathered together trying to allay the desire for different food by the agency of their pipes. However, instead of endeavouring to get accustomed to the food pretty plentifully prepared for their meals—other two horses having to be shot on account of their wounds—some of the men preferred to fast; and it was these men who discussed the probability of the Colonel making a dash again that night, to cut a way through and escape.

Sergeant Briggs favoured this idea.

"I hope the chief will make another try to-night," he said to Denham and me. "The Boers mean to starve us out; and in another day or two all the fight will be gone out of the poor lads."

However, the sun often peeps out on the cloudiest days; and towards evening, just when we were feeling most despondent, Joeboy came up to Denham and me just as we were going up to our old place of observation, glass in hand. As we mounted, it was to see the horses led in, with the guard behind them; the lines of the enemy being descried very distinctly in the horizontal rays of the low-down sun. Denham was using the glass and making comments the while.

"There's a famous great gap out yonder," he said, "just to the right of where we saw those unlucky wagons, Val. I will just go and tell some one. The enemy will not be likely to fill it up; and I believe we might go softly that way and make a dash through.—Oh, you disgusting, sybaritish, gluttonous brutes! I always did think the Boers were pigs at eating. Look at their fires all along their lines. Here are we starving, and they're doing nothing but cook and eat—eat—eat."

I took the glass and looked at the opening he had noticed, but said nothing, remembering how terrible was our experience on the previous occasion. I saw too—as enviously as my companion, but in silence—how the fires were sending up their clouds of smoke in the clear, calm air all along the line, telling of preparations for the coming meal.

"The empty wagons are gone," I said at last.

"If you say wagon again I shan't be able to contain myself," cried Denham passionately. "I don't want to kick you, Val; but I shall be obliged. Look here, if I feel as bad to-morrow evening as I do now, I'll mount and desert to the Boer ranks."

"Not you," I said.

"But I will, just for the sake of eating as much as ever I can. Then I'll desert again and join our own ranks."

"Why, Denham—" I exclaimed excitedly, and then I was silent.

"Why, Denham—" he replied.

"Wait a minute," I cried; "let me make sure."

"Sure of what?" he said, growing excited in turn on hearing the elation in my voice.

"Wagons!" I cried.

"Ah, would you?" he shouted. "Didn't I say that if you spoke of wagons again—"

"One—two—three—four—five—six!" I cried, with the glasses to my eyes. "Hurrah! There's a fresh lot coming into camp, right into that opening you saw. Be quiet and let me watch"—for Denham had given me such a slap between the shoulders that I nearly dropped the glass.

"Say it again, old man—say it again."

"There's no need," I replied. "Yes, I can make them out quite plainly— six wagons, with their long teams of oxen and black drivers and forelopers. You can see the black bodies and white cloths."

"I don't want to see them," cried Denham wildly. "I'll take your word. Six teams of oxen!—that's all beef. Six wagons!—that means bread. There, you be off and tell the Colonel you're going to start; and I'll see about the troop that's to follow and bring you in. I say, pick out a wagon of meal; not one of mealies. I don't know, though. Couldn't you bring both?"

"There's plenty of time," I said.

"Time? The Colonel ought to know by now. Here, give me that glass."

"Be quiet," I said, angry with excitement. "I want to watch and make sure where the wagons are drawn up."

Denham ceased speaking, and during the next half-hour I watched till I had seen tin; six wagons drawn up pretty close together, and their black drivers moving about attending to the oxen; now all grew faint and indistinct, then completely faded out of sight; not, however, until I had made up my mind that I could go straight away from the old fort and find the place, though there were minutes when the task in the dark seemed impossible.

Turning to Joeboy, who had twice looked through the glass, I asked:

"Do you think we could find those wagons in the dark?"

"Um? Joeboy could," he replied promptly. "Go right straight."

I breathed more freely then, and suggested to Denham that I should go and report to the Colonel what I had seen.

"Yes; at once," he said. "Come along; and I want to have command of one of the troops sent out to bring you in."

We had commenced the descent when Denham stopped me.

"Look here," he said; "I have a good thought. We ought to arrange some signal to let me know your whereabouts when you are returning with the wagon."

"I haven't got it yet," I said.

"No, but you're going to get it," he said confidently; "and I want to be able to come to you with fifty men, and to make sure of bringing you in. Now then, what will your signal be? Because, if I hear it out on the veldt we can ride straight off to you. Can you yell like a hyena?"

"No," I said promptly. "Joeboy can."

"Wouldn't do," said my companion, upon second thoughts. "Those beasts are singing all over the place sometimes, and they might lead us wrong."

"So would the cry of any animal."

"Yes," said Denham thoughtfully. "I don't know, though. Here, can you suggest something?"

"I can't do it; but Joeboy can roar like a lion splendidly."

"Wouldn't that scare and stampede the bullocks?"

"Oh no," I said; "the cry would cheat the Boers, perhaps; the bullocks would know better—wouldn't they, Joeboy?"

"Um? Big trek-ox laugh, and say 'Gammon,'" replied the black, showing his glistening teeth.

"Very well, then; when you are getting within earshot let Joeboy give three roars half-a-minute apart."

"Right," I said. — "You understand, Joeboy?"

"Um? Yes, Boss Val."

"Here, give us a specimen," said Denham. "Don't make a bully row. Just roar gently so that I shall know it again."

Joeboy dropped upon his hands and knees, placed his lips close to the surface of the wall, and a low, deep, thunderous roar seemed to make the air quiver and shudder. Directly afterwards there was an excited stamping and neighing amongst the horses.

"That'll do splendid," whispered my companion. "Three times, mind. Hark! they're talking about it all over the place. There'll be an alarm directly about a lion getting into the laager."

By the time we had reached the spot where the officers made their bare, unsheltered camp, the alarm had already died away; and, after being challenged, we had leave to advance.

The Colonel heard what we had to say in silence, and then remained for a minute or two without speaking.

"It is a very risky and daring business, Moray, my lad," he said; "but we are in a desperate strait. I did mean to make another dash for liberty to-night; but since this piece of good fortune has turned up I'll wait twenty-four hours and see what you do. If you succeed I promise you that—"

"Please don't promise me anything, sir," I said quickly. "Let me go and try my best. If I fail—"

"And the Boers take you prisoner," said the Colonel quickly, "I shall, like every one in the corps, thank you all the same for a very dashing and plucky venture. — As for you, Denham; yes, certainly. Take fifty men, and go out to meet him and bring him in. You need not, of course, start till well on towards morning; and when you are gone I shall order out nearly all the rest of the force to your support, so as to bring you all in, if you are pressed."

"Thank you, sir," I said eagerly; but Denham replied in rather a grumpy tone, for he was all on fire to begin doing something almost at once.

"Then I may start when I like, sir?"

"Certainly, my lad. Of course you will take your rifle?"

"Yes, sir."

"Take two revolvers instead of one. You may want them at a pinch; but you must depend upon scheming in this, and not on strength. By the way, there are a few biscuits in my haversack; you can take them."

"Oh no, sir—" I began; but he interrupted me.

"Take them," he said shortly, and in a way that meant a command; but I compromised the matter with my conscience by only taking half.

I now left the Colonel's quarters with Denham and Joeboy, and only waited till it was as dark as it seemed likely to be before having a few final words with my companion and Briggs, who were the only men in the secret of what was about to be undertaken. Then, filling my water-bottle and placing the biscuits in my pocket—after Denham had refused a share—I saw that my bandolier was quite full of cartridges, slung my rifle, and placed one revolver in its holster-pocket and thrust the other in my breast. We now walked towards the well-barricaded gateway, gave the word, and Joeboy and I stepped out, with Denham and Briggs; but stopped to shake hands with Denham, who held mine tightly.

"Good luck to you, Val, lad!" he said softly. "Don't take any notice of what I said before—I mean of all that cold water I poured on your scheme. It's splendid. Go in and win; and when you're half-way back, or if you're pursued, make old Joeboy fill his bellows and roar. I'll come to your help, even if there's a thousand Doppies after you."

"I know you will," I said warmly as I returned the pressure of his hand. "There, good-bye."

"Good-bye, old boy! You'll do it. Oh! I wish I were coming too."

"Good-bye, Mr Private Moray," said Briggs softly, in his deep tones. "I wish you everything in the way of luck. You'll do it, my lad, I know.—Here, Joeboy, you stick to your boss."

"Um! Me stick to Boss Val—um!—alway."

"Good-bye," I said again, trying to free my hands, for Denham and the Sergeant each held one tightly and in silence.

At last, as we stood there in the darkness, they let my fingers slip through theirs, and I stepped out into the open, following Joeboy's steps, for he at once took the lead, without making a sound.

"Ah!" I said to myself, after drawing a very long breath, "this is going to be the most exciting thing I ever did."

Chapter Twenty Six
Successful Beyond Expectation

"Boss Val come close up to Joeboy," said the black a minute or two later.

I had but to take two steps, and then I could touch the speaker, who was standing with his back towards me.

"Joeboy no turn round," he said. "Boss Val keep close. Joeboy got to keep seeing wagons, and not lose them."

"But you can't see the wagons now," I said softly.

"Um? Joeboy see um inside um head. Can't see with eyes. Too far away. But Joeboy know jus' where they are, and feel see um. Come along and no talk. Take hold, and no let go."

I grasped the long handle of Joeboy's assagai, which had touched me lightly on the side as he spoke; so there was no chance of our being separated in the dark and having to call to each other with probably Boer outposts within hearing. The plunge had been made, and now I began to see how terrible was the responsibility I had undertaken. For a few minutes after leaving our friends I began to ask myself whether Denham had not been right in calling it a mad project; but these thoughts soon passed away as I pulled myself together with the determination to do what my friends had told me: "Go in and win." There was too much to do and too much excitement now to leave room for hesitation and thoughts about risk and chances of discovery. Joeboy, too, was a splendid fellow for a companion: he went steadily on as if the whole business was some exciting game in which he played the chief part.

Fortune seemed to be favouring us so far as the weather was concerned, for a brisk wind was blowing, and the clouds overhead veiled every star; so the night was profoundly dark.

After tramping on for about ten minutes, Joeboy stopped and stood motionless; then he whispered to me to come close up, without turning his head when he spoke.

"Boss Val lissum with both ears," he said. "Tell Joeboy when he hear Doppie. Joeboy tell Boss Val too."

"Right," I said; and we went on again so silently that I did not hear my own footsteps in the sandy earth.

There was no risk of meeting with any impediment, for the veldt from the old fortress right away to the place where I had marked down the wagons was a smooth, undulating plain. What we had to dread was coming across a Boer outpost or patrol; but I had little fear of that without ample warning, for I had had frequent experience in hunting expeditions of the keenness of Joeboy's senses of sight and hearing. I was just beginning to wonder how long it would be before he gave me warning of any danger being near, when he stopped short again. I closed up so that I could lay my hands upon his shoulders. Then he whispered very softly:

"Hear Doppie soon. Boss Val go down when Joeboy kneel."

"Right," I said again, straining my eyes right and left to get sight of the Boer camp; and, though I judged that their fires would be all out, I expected to get a glimpse before long of one of their lanterns. All, however, remained dark, and the time dragged slowly in the same monotonous way, making me wish I could walk side by side with my companion, who seemed to be far more cautious in the darkness than I thought necessary.

We must have gone, as I hoped in a perfectly straight direction, for what appeared to be nearly an hour, and I was getting desperate about our slow progress, when suddenly the assagai-shaft was jigged sharply and then dragged; and for a moment I saw a faint spark of light far ahead, due to the fact that Joeboy had gone down suddenly upon hands and knees. I followed suit, and lay flat, listening, but only hearing my heart throbbing slowly and heavily. Not a sound was to be heard for fully half-a-minute; and then came the familiar click of iron against iron, caused, as I well knew, by a horse champing at his bit and moving the curb-chain. Directly after there was the dull *thud, thud* of horses' hoofs coming from our right, and I knew that mounted men were approaching us at right angles to our course, and thought we must be discovered the next minute or else trampled on by the horses.

For a moment or two my heart seemed to stand still and then to go at a gallop, for the horses came nearer and nearer; and I tried to press myself closer and closer to the sand as one horse passed within two or three yards of my feet, and another a little way in front.

I could hardly believe the men had gone by without seeing us, though I had not seen them, and still crouched down, expecting to hear the riders turn and come back. Hence it was like a surprise when I heard a faint rustling which indicated that Joeboy was getting up; and, warned by a jerk of the spear-shaft, I sprang up too.

"All ride by," said the black; and I realised now that a patrol must have passed, with the men riding two or three horse-lengths apart to keep guard against any surprise parties of our troop.

We went on again for a short distance, and then there was another stoppage; for from the front came the murmur of voices talking in a low tone, suggestive of a little outpost in front.

Joeboy made a brief halt, and then we went down on hands and knees, and crawled to the right for about fifty yards before turning again in the direction of the wagons; and this movement was kept up for quite a hundred yards; then the black rose to his foot, and our walk recommenced.

We must now, I thought, have kept on for above an hour, though I dare say it was not more than half that time; but I fully believed it was nearer three hours than two after we had left the fort when Joeboy suddenly dropped down flat; and, as I followed his example, he backed himself, walking quadrupedally on his hands and toes till he was able to subside close to where I lay on my face.

"Boss Val tired?" he whispered. "Um?"

"Not a bit," I replied. "Are we near the wagons?"

"Um? Done know," he replied. "Close by Doppie. All quiet. Fas' asleep. Lissum."

I listened, and all was very still. Now and then from a distance came a faint squeal and a stamp from some horse; but there was no talking going on, and it was hardly possible there in the darkness to conceive that probably a thousand men were lying near at hand, spread out to right and left, and ready at a call to spring up, mount, and dash across the plain.

"I can hear nothing," I replied at last, with my lips close to his ear. "Think they are gone, Joeboy?"

"Um? Gone?" he whispered back. "Gone 'sleep. Joeboy going to look for wagons."

"Stop a moment," I whispered. "Are you going to leave me here?"

"Um? Boss Val lie still and have good rest. Joeboy come back soon."

"But do you think you can find me again?" I said.

He put his lips close to my ear again and laughed softly.

"Um? Oh yes, Joeboy find um sure enough. See a lot in the dark. Boss Val lie quite still."

Before I could remonstrate against a plan which, it seemed to me, might, ruin our expedition, he had crept away; and from the direction he took I knew he had gone off to the left, going quite fast, and progressing in a style which, in old days, I had often laughingly said was like that of the crocodiles of the Limpopo. This time I did not hear him make a sound, and I could, of course, do nothing but lie still, feeling in my utter misery that all was over, and that I could only lie there till near daybreak, waiting to be found again by Joeboy, and waiting in vain. Then I would have to run the gauntlet of the outposts, and make a desperate effort to return, shamefaced and miserable, to the camp.

I tried hard to fix my attention on listening and endeavouring to make out how near I was to the Boer lines; but I could not hear a sound. Again and again I fretted at my miserable position as the time glided away and there was no sign of Joeboy.

"I should have stopped him," I reflected. "I ought not to have let him take the lead."

Just then, however, my heart seemed to give a great jump; for without a sound the black was alongside again, touching my leg, and then gliding up till his lips were level with my ear.

"Boss Val 'sleep—um?"

"Asleep!" I whispered back indignantly. "No."

"Um!" he whispered. "Joeboy been very long way. No wagon there. Now go this way."

"No, no!" I whispered back. "You must stay with me, or we must go together, Joeboy!"

There was no reply, and in alarm I stretched out my left hand to seize hold of him; but he had gone. I half-fancied I heard a faint rustle some distance off as of a great serpent gliding across in front of my head; but I dared not raise my voice to stop him. Now I realised that he must have glided away from me the moment he had uttered the words "this way;" and again I had to go through all that agony of expectation and dread. Still, I began to feel a little more confidence in Joeboy, and for the next half-hour I waited anxiously, hoping against hope, till I was in despair and half-mad.

I was just at my worst again, and picturing the looks of Denham, and his disappointment if I managed to get anywhere near where he was on the lookout for us, when I jumped violently, quite startled, for Joeboy seemed to rise out of the black earth on my light.

"Um?" he said softly. "Joeboy getting tired. Couldn't find wagon."

"Then it's all over?" I whispered, my heart sinking with despair.

"Um? Couldn't find at first," he said. "Joeboy went behind um. All out before Doppies."

"Then you did find them?" I whispered joyfully.

"Um? Yes, Joeboy find um. Went long way and then come back."

"But how did you manage to find them in the dark?"

"Um? Smell um," he said quietly. "Now, wait bit. Boss Val know what to say?"

"Oh yes, I know," I said.

"Get up," he whispered. "No Doppie here."

I was startled by his words, but I obeyed; and as soon as I was erect I felt his hands about me, feeling whether my rifle was slung across my shoulder, my bandolier in place, and my revolvers ready. Apparently satisfied, he gave a grunt, and taking my hand, he whispered again:

"No Doppie here. Over this way and that way."

I yielded to his guidance, with my heart throbbing heavily now; but the feeling of excitement returned as I began to act, and in a few minutes I found that something big and dark had loomed up in front, which I knew to be a great tilted wagon.

Joeboy bore to the left, and we walked silently on together till we had passed the rears of six of the great vehicles drawn up at a fair distance apart, but pretty regularly side by side. I now realised that, though the wagons, as seen through the glass, had appeared to be in touch with the Boer troops, they really formed a line some distance in front.

From that moment everything seemed to be like a curious waking dream, in which I was the chief actor; for, passing the last tail and going forward, I walked with Joeboy to the front, all being silent about the wagons. From beyond these came the peculiarly soft, chewing sound of working jaws; and I made out, partly by hearing and partly by the peculiar but not unpleasant odour, that there were the teams in their places, all the great oxen crouching down, from the pair on either side of the dissel-boom or pole to the foremost couple right in front, pair after pair, along the trek-tow—that is, the great rope which, for the team, serves as a continuation of the pole.

"Um?" whispered Joeboy as I stood listening to the dull cud-chewing of the resting beasts. "Now make um come out."

I hesitated for a moment or two; then I made the great effort to play my part as I felt it ought to be acted, and stood alongside the black and close up to the wagon, between the wheels. Then taking a long breath, and wondering at myself the while, I stooped down so that my voice might go well beneath; but paused as I was about to speak, for I could hear in duplicate a deep guttural snore. At that moment Joeboy pinched my arm; and, drawing a deep breath, I growled out in the best imitation I could of the Boer Dutch:

"Now then; rouse up, you lazy black beggars! Rouse up and trek!"

My heart sank as the last word passed my lips.

"Suppose they are not Kaffirs?" I thought.

There was not a sound, and Joeboy again pinched my arm.

I knew what he wanted; so, raising my voice, I said hoarsely, and in an angry tone:

"Rouse up! Trek!"

There was a loud rattling noise at the same moment, for Joeboy had reached under the wagon to strike here and there with the shaft of his assagai.

In an instant, following a dull thud or two, there came low remonstrant growls, there was a scuffle and a rush, and two big figures rose near us; one Kaffir ran towards the front box of the wagon, and the feet of the other went *pat, pat* till he stopped by the foremost pair of oxen in the team. Then the great beasts began to get upon their feet and shake themselves.

"It's all over now," I thought, as I stood appalled by the noise made by the bullocks, one of them lowing loudly; and, as if my despair was not deep enough, I found from what I could hear that I had fired a train, started a conflagration, or—to use another simile—touched one end of a row of card houses and set all in motion. The action of rousing up the blacks asleep beneath this one had communicated itself from wagon to wagon on to the end. "Open sesame!" caused the cave of the Forty Thieves to open; the magic word "Trek!" had started the wagon-drivers and forelopers; and now I expected the next thing would be a rush of Boer cavalry to surround us, unless Joeboy and I could hide.

"Yah! hor! whoo-oop! Trek!" cried Joeboy in his hoarsest voice, and he ran from me towards the foreloper, leaving me half-stunned at the turn matters had taken.

"Trek!" cried the black, who had climbed on to the box; then there was a tremendous crack of the huge whip he wielded, the oxen jerked at the trek-tow, the wheels creaked, and as I involuntarily took my rifle from where it was slung and cocked it, the huge wagon began to lumber heavily through the soft earth, and I walked by its side uninterrupted, finding that in turn first one and then another of the six wagons started and followed, till the entire row were in motion, following the lead of Joeboy with the first foreloper, the whole business growing, in the darkness, more and more like a feverish dream.

Chapter Twenty Seven
Night Work

By a sudden effort I threw off the dreamy sensation—the feeling that I was half-stunned by the pressure of the task I had undertaken, now that it had suddenly grown so much greater than I had anticipated—and I walked alongside the wagon-box, breathing hard, and planning that at the first sound of approaching enemies I would rush forward to where Joeboy was tramping beside the foreloper, assagai in hand, and make a dash with him for liberty. But the minutes glided by, as the line of wagons, all going on with the regularity of some great, elongated machine, rolled easily along over the soft earth, the rested bullocks pulling steadily under the guidance of their leaders and drivers.

In vain I listened for the furious rush of horses and the challenges and orders to stop; then, by degrees, I began to grasp the fact that, though hundreds of Boers must have heard the wagons start, not one gave heed to the crack of whip, the cries of the black drivers, or the creaking and rumbling of the wheels. The moving of wagons of stores was quite a matter of course; somebody had given orders for their position to be changed, and that was all. These sounds were nothing to the weary men, rolled up in their warm blankets, making the most of their night's rest. Doubtless it awoke many; but they only listened for a moment, and then turned over to sleep again. Oxen, their drivers, and the wagons had nothing to do with the enemy. Had there been a trumpet-call, a single shot, or a loud order, to a man they would have sprung up to rush to their horses, saddled, and been ready to attack or defend; but the shifting of some wagons during the night—what was that? Nor was the Boer force a carefully drilled cavalry brigade, with its transport-corps under the strictest discipline, every man part of a machine which only moved by order, and whose stores and supplies were under the most severe regulation and guard; it was a loose, irregular horde, whose officers had to permit the men to fight very much as they pleased, so long as they fought well and advanced and retreated at the word.

It took time to reason all this out, and to get to believe that our bold ruse was succeeding to a far greater extent than I had ever dared to hope. There it was all plainly enough—all real; the wagons were going steadily along, the first guided by Joeboy, and the rest following with their black conductors quite as a matter of course.

As far as I could make out in the darkness, we were going along parallel with the lines of the sleeping Boers. Growing more excited now, I began to wonder how soon Joeboy would turn the heads of the leading bullocks and strike out for the fortress; then my thoughts drifted into a fresh rut, and I speculated as to how long it would be before we came upon some outpost and were turned back.

Hardly had this idea crossed my mind, sinking my spirits almost to despair, when a great figure loomed up before me. Joeboy was at my side.

"Got um all, Boss Val," he said in a low tone. "Doppies come and stop us soon. Say, 'Where you go?'"

"Yes; and we shall be turned back," I replied quickly.

"Um? No. Joeboy say, 'Big boss tell us to go right away other end.' Joeboy hear and know how Doppie talk, and Joeboy say right words."

"Are you sure?" I said in Boer Dutch, to test him.

"Um? Yes. Know what to say, like Boss Val know. Always talk like Boer before Joeboy come and live with Boss Val."

"Of course," I whispered, with a feeling of relief.

"Um! Boss Val jump in wagon and say nothing. Go to sleep like. Doppie coming."

He gave me a push towards the wagon and went forward at a trot. Yielding to his influence, I climbed in at the front, past the driver, and drew the curtains before me, only leaving a slit through which I could hear what passed. I was not kept waiting long. As far as I could judge, about a dozen mounted men cantered up, and a thrill ran through me as a familiar, highly-pitched voice cried in English, with the broadest of Irish accents:

"Whisht now, me sable son of your mother! What does this mane?"

"Moriarty," I said to myself; and, with my heart beating fast, and a strange feeling of rage flushing up to my head, my right hand went to my revolver and rested upon the butt as I strained my ears to listen for every word. My thoughts, of course, flashed through my brain like lightning; but the answer to the renegade captain's words came slowly, Joeboy replying in deep guttural tones, using Boer Dutch, to say:

"I don't know what you mean, Boss?"

"Ugh! You soot-coloured, big-lipped baste!" snarled Moriarty; and then in Boer Dutch, "Where are you taking the wagons?"

"Over yonder," replied Joeboy.

"Why? Who told you?"

"Big boss officer man," replied Joeboy calmly enough. "Say want more mealies there. Make haste and be quick. Ought to have gone there last night. Wake all up and say come along."

"Oh," said Moriarty thoughtfully; and then, as I waited with my trepidation increasing, to my great surprise and relief he said a few words to those with him, which I could not catch; then aloud, in Dutch, "All right. Go on."

When he began speaking Moriarty did not stop the wagons, which had crawled on in their slow and regular ox-pace, so that I was taken nearer and nearer till I was in line with the group of horsemen, and then past them; then the voices grew more indistinct. As the last words were uttered the patrol or outpost, whichever it was, trotted off, leaving me wondering what the broad-shouldered black just before me on the wagon-box might be thinking about what had passed, and my peculiar conduct in taking refuge inside. "A shout from him, if he is suspicious, might bring them back," I mused; so, under the circumstances, I decided to keep up the appearance of having got in for the sake of a rest, and sat back upon one of the sacks.

However, I was not permitted to stay long inside, for as soon as the mounted Boers were out of hearing Joeboy came to the front of the wagon and called to me in his deep tones—speaking in Boer Dutch—to come out.

I stepped out past the driver, yawning as if tired, and leaped down, to walk on with the black.

"Hadn't you better turn the heads of the leading bullocks now towards the laager, Joeboy?" I said.

"Um? Did," he replied, "soon as Doppie captain went away. Going straight home now."

"Ah!" I ejaculated. "Capital! But we shall be stopped again and sent back."

"Um? Joeboy don't think so. Doppie over there, and Doppie over there," he said, pointing in opposite directions with his assagai.

"You think we shall not meet another party, then?"

"Um? Can't hear any," he replied.

"But about the drivers and forelopers? When they find where we're going they'll want to go back to the lines."

"Um? No," said Joeboy decidedly. "Black Kaffir chap. Not think at all. Very sleepy, Boss Val. Jus' like big bullock. You an' Joeboy tell um go along and they go along."

"But suppose they turned suspicious and said they wouldn't go with us?"

"Um?" said Joeboy, and I heard him grind his teeth. "They say that, Joeboy kill um all: 'tick assagai in back an' front. All big 'tupid fool. Ha! ha! Joeboy almost eat um." He laughed in a peculiar way that was not pleasant, and it moved me to say:

"Don't attempt to touch them if they turn against us. I'll threaten them with my pistol."

"Um? Boss Val think better shoot one? No; Boss Val mustn't make Doppie come. Joeboy say 'Trek,' and they no trek, he 'tick assagai in um back."

"No, no; there must be no bloodshed."

"Um? Blood? No; only 'tick in little way. Make um go like bullock. Make um go like what Boss Val call "tampeed.' Black Kaffir boy not say 'Won't go.' Be 'fraid o' Joeboy."

I thought it very probable, and said no more. Leaving him with the foreloper of the first wagon, I stood fast and listened intently while the whole of the six great lumbering wagons, drawn by their teams averaging four-and-twenty oxen, crept past me. The forelopers walked slouching along, shouldering a bamboo sixteen or eighteen feet long, without so much as turning their heads in my direction; and the drivers on the wagon-boxes were sitting with heads down and shoulders raised, apparently asleep and troubled about nothing. They all trusted to the front wagon for guidance, as their teams, until the oxen were tired, needed no driving whatever, but followed stolidly in the track of those in front.

So slow!—so awfully slow! when I wanted them to go in a thunderous gallop! Yet I knew this was folly. I wanted to play the hare, though I knew that in this case the tortoise would win the race; for to have hurried meant some accident, some breaking of the heavy wains: a wheel off or broken, the giving way of trek-tow or dissel-boom. There was nothing for it, I knew, but to proceed at the oxen's steady crawl, which had this advantage: the wagons made very little noise passing over the soft earth, the oxen none at all worth mention. But it was agonising, now that we had started and actually been passed on by the enemy's patrol, to keep on at that dreadful pace, which suggested that, even if we did go on without further cheek, when day broke we should still be within sight of the Boer lines and bring them out in a swarm to turn us back.

It seemed to me we must have been creeping along for an hour, though perhaps it was not half that time, when suddenly the first team of oxen was stopped, the wheels of the first wagon ceased to move, and the whole line came, in the most matter-of-fact way, to a stand. No one seemed to heed, and the oxen went on contemplatively chewing their cud.

"What is it?" I said, running up to Joeboy.

"Um! Cist!" he whispered. "Doppie coming."

I could hear nothing, and it was too dark to see, so I stood listening for quite a minute, knowing well that the black must be right, for his hearing was wonderfully acute. Then in the distance I heard the sound of trotting horses coming along at right angles towards us; and as it occurred to me that the patrol would come into contact with us about the middle of our long line, I began to wonder whether Joeboy would be able to get the better of the Boer leader again.

Nearer and nearer they came, and a snort or the lowing of a bullock would have betrayed us; but the stolid beasts went on ruminating, and, to my utter astonishment, the little mounted party rode past a couple of hundred yards behind the last wagon, as near as I can tell, and the sound of the horses' hoofs and chink of bit against ring died away.

"Ha!" I ejaculated, with a sigh.

"Um?" said Joeboy, who had come by me unheard. "Yes, all gone. Doppie big fool. No see, no hear. Joeboy hear; Joeboy see wagon and bullock long way off. Doppie got wool in um ear an' sand in um eyes."

"So have I, as compared with you, my big black friend," I thought to myself; "but I don't want you to call me or think me a big fool, so I'll hold my tongue."

"Doppie can't hear now," said Joeboy. "All agone. Not hear any more.— Go on. Trek!" he cried in his deep, guttural tones; and the bullocks dragged at the great tow-ropes, the axles groaned, and away we went again in the same old crawl hour after hour, but without further alarm, though in one prolonged agony of anxiety, during which I was always looking or listening for pursuers.

Then came another trouble: the darkness was greater than ever. It was a cloak, certainly, for our proceedings; but there was not a star visible to guide us in our course towards the old stronghold.

"Think we're going right?" I asked again and again.

"Um? Joeboy think so," he always replied. "Wait till light come. Soon know then."

Words of wisdom these, of course; but though we kept on in what we believed a straight line for our goal, the line we were taking might be right away from the camp, or we might be proceeding in a curve which would bring us within easy reach of the enemy—perhaps as near as when we started. Truly we were in the dark; and as the air grew colder towards daybreak, everything looked, if possible, blacker still.

"Morrow morning," said Joeboy, suddenly coming back to where I trudged alongside one of the wagons, whose drivers appeared to be all asleep.

I looked in the direction he indicated, and there was a faint dawn low down on the horizon.

"Then we're going wrong, Joeboy," I said; "that's the east."

"Um!" he said. "Too much that way. Going right now."

I looked back in the direction of the Boer camp, but nothing was visible there. It seemed as if the darkness lay like a cloud upon the earth; but, upon turning again to look in the way the heads of the oxen were pointed, I could see what looked like a hillock in the distance. Fixing my eyes upon it, I could gradually see it more distinctly, and in a few minutes' time made out that what had seemed like one hillock was really two—the one natural, the other artificial: in other words, the pile of ironstone and granite in one case, the built-up stronghold in the other.

"Joeboy," I said, beckoning him to one side after a furtive glance at the black foreloper, "we're a long way off, and the Boers will miss the wagons and see us soon."

"Um? Yes," he said coolly.

"Do you think that you can get the bullocks to go faster?"

"Um? No," he said. "Must go like this."

"But the Boers will come after us as soon as they see us."

"Um? Yes; but can't see us yet. When Doppie see us Boss Denham see us too, and come along o' fighting boys."

"Yes; I had half-forgotten that," I replied. Not thinking of anything more to say, I trudged on. At last, as the light grew stronger, Joeboy turned to me to say:

"Boss Val see Doppie now?"

I looked back in the direction of the enemy's lines and shaded my eyes; but nothing was discernible.

"I can't see them yet," I said.

"Um? No. Joeboy can. Can't see a wagons yet."

"They can't see the wagons?" I cried. "How do you know?"

"Come on horses after us," he said. "Gallop fast."

"Of course," I replied, and looked anxiously at our great, lumbering prizes, wishing I could do something to hurry the bullocks on; but wishing was vain, and I knew all the time it would be madness to attempt to hasten the animals' pace, and likely only to end in disaster.

The darkness, which had appeared to be low between us and the Boer lines, now began to turn of a soft grey, which minute by minute lightened more and more, and rose till it looked like a succession of horizontal streaks, beneath which lay something disconnected and strange, but which gradually took the form of a long line of horses, broken here and there by little curves which, by straining my eyes, I made out to be wagon-tilts seen through the soft pale-bluish air. Next, on turning sharply to look in the direction of our comrades, there were the old piled-up walls of our stronghold clearly marked against the sky.

"It's a long, long way yet, Joeboy," I said.

"Yes, long way," he replied.

"Can you see the Boers on the move?"

He shook his head, and then hurried to the foreloper, a heavy-looking black, who was signalling to him.

Chapter Twenty Eight
An Unexpected Obstacle

"What does he want?" I muttered to myself as I looked on curiously, for I could not hear what was said; but, to my horror, there appeared to be something like a quarrel, as the foreloper suddenly threw down the long bamboo he carried and then squatted upon the ground.

In an instant the shaft of Joeboy's assagai fell with a sounding thwack across the man's bare shoulders, making him spring to his feet and snatch a knife out from his waistcloth. My hand went to my revolver, and I ran to Joeboy's aid; but there was no need. In an instant the glistening blade of my companion's assagai was pointed at the foreloper's throat, making him recoil; and then, in response to a threatening thrust or two, the man picked up his long, thin bamboo and replaced his knife, while Joeboy, pointing fiercely to me, rated the man in his own tongue.

"What is it, Joeboy?" I asked as the man went back to the head of the bullock-team.

"Um? Say want to 'top and rest bullocks and make fire for breakfast, Boss. I say he go on till we get to laager. Say he won't, and Joeboy make um. Boss Val put little 'volver pistol away and unsling gun; pretend to shoot um."

I did as Joeboy suggested, and the man went down upon his knees and laid his forehead upon the earth. I needed no telling what to say next.

"Get up! Trek!" I shouted as fiercely as I could. The man leaped to his feet and urged the bullocks on, while the driver on the box made his great two-handed whip crack loudly in the quiet of the morning. The actions of these two being taken up by the men with the wagons behind, the bullocks for a time went on at the rate of quite another half-mile an hour extra.

"Um!" ejaculated Joeboy, with a look of satisfaction in his eyes; "rifle gun reach long way. Boss Val see boy not driving well, pretend to send bullet in um head, and make um jump along. Ha!"

Noticing that the black was using his hands like a binocular glass, and looking back, I asked anxiously, "What is it?"

"Um? See Doppie coming now?"

I looked, but could make out nothing; yet I was satisfied it was so. I now gazed eagerly in the direction of our goal, for Joeboy had first turned his eyes there.

"Can you see help coming, Joeboy?" I asked anxiously.

"Um? No," he replied.

"Then it's all over," I said in despair.

"Um? Yes, here um come."

"Ah!" I cried, remembering now the signal agreed upon. "Is it the Lieutenant—Mr Denham?"

"Joeboy can't see so far as that," replied the black. "Only see horses coming fas'. Coming to fetch wagons and plenty mealies and flour. Boys all say 'Hurrah!' and make all horses laugh."

"But do you think they will get here first?"

"Um? Yes. Doppie got longer way to come."

"Ha!" I ejaculated, with a sigh of relief.

A few minutes later the foreloper on whom so much depended—guided, no doubt, by our anxious looks in one direction—made out the coming of our friends, and I saw his eyes open widely till there was a great opal ring round the dark pupils. Looking at me despairingly, he pointed with his long bamboo in the direction of the galloping troop.

I nodded, and pointed forward. After an uneasy glance at my gun, he went on with his team in the direction we wished.

"Black boy run away fas'," said Joeboy, suddenly laughing merrily, "but 'fraid lead bullet run fasser."

"I suppose so," I said slowly as I turned to look back. The light being now much increased, I readily detected a strong troop of the Boers in motion, and doubtless coming in our direction. I drew my breath hard as I looked at the long lines of slowly plodding oxen and then in the direction of our rescuers, who must have seen we were pursued, for they were galloping. Then, to my horror, Joeboy turned to me and nodded, after gazing back.

"Um?" he said in a long, slow, murmuring way, "'nother lot o' Doppie coming. Big lot."

I darted a look at our comrades, who came sweeping along over the veldt; but they were still far distant, and we seemed to be creeping along more slowly than ever.

"Not enough; not enough," I thought; but I wasted no time in regret. There were fully fifty friends, all good horsemen and able shots, coming to our help; so I need not despair. Thinking of what would be the best tactics under the circumstances, there seemed to be two ways open to us: for the troop to fall in on either side of the last wagon, and keep up a running fight; or, if the Boer party proved too strong, the six wagons could be drawn up laager-wise and turned into a temporary fort, with the bullocks outside, our men firing, till help came, from behind an improvised shelter formed by the sacks of grain and meal.

Then I reasoned despairingly that the Boers would send forward troop after troop to recover, the wagons. "If they can," I now muttered through my teeth. For I was more hopeful now, as it soon became evident that the enemy had twice as far to come as our men had. At last, when the mental strain had become almost unbearable, Denham and his troop dashed forward, cheering madly.

"Bravo! bravo, Val!" he shouted to me, pulling his horse up so suddenly that it nearly went back on its haunches. "Here, you, Joeboy, keep the teams going. Fall in, my lads! Dismount!"

The troop sprang from their saddles, swung round their rifles, and waited. In obedience to Denham's next order I followed the last wagon, rifle in hand. Seeing the uneasy glances the drivers and forelopers directed at it from time to time, I felt convinced that if it had not been for this they would have played some trick with the bullocks, or have done something to stop the further progress of our prize-convoy, now that they fully understood what was wrong.

For me the suspense was over, though the plodding of the oxen still seemed maddening; but I had active work to do yet, with Joeboy for my aid, keeping the blacks well to their work. This we did vigorously, being called upon very soon even to threaten and command.

Just when least expected, and following upon a determined charge made by our pursuers, there was a rattling volley delivered standing by our men, who, steadying their rifles upon their horses' backs, emptied many a saddle. But the Boers came on till within about a hundred yards, when a second volley was poured into them, sending horses and men struggling to the ground. The troop now divided in two, swinging round to right and left and dashing back towards the second party, who were now well in sight.

It was at the first volley that the alarmed black drivers nearly got out of hand, while the teams began to huddle together and threatened a stampede. The black boys, however, soon saw they had more to fear from us than from the Boers; and by the time our friends had remounted and trotted up to us the wagon-train was steadied again.

"Can't you get any more speed out of them, Val?" shouted Denham.

"No," I said; "this is the best they can do with the loads. You fellows must save the prize now."

"And we will," cried Denham, waving his hat, with the result that his men cheered.

Meanwhile the detachment of the enemy we sent to the right-about in a headlong gallop had settled down to a trot to meet the reinforcements coming up; but we had also a force coming to join us; so, when the enemy had joined hands and came on again, we of the wagon-train had two troops for our protection, who, coming on at a walk behind, readily faced round, dismounted, and poured forth a withering fire, which again sent the enemy scuttling away on their shambling ponies.

So the march went on for the next hour, during which troop after troop of the Boers reinforced our pursuers, but always to find that our force had been strengthened. Then the Colonel joined us with all he could command, and a fierce little battle raged. Again the Boers were repulsed. There being no cover for their men, which is so necessary for the practice of their marksmanship to the best advantage, the clever cavalry manoeuvres of the Light Horse proved too much for them.

Unsuccessful attempts to recapture the wagons were kept up till they were drawn as close to the opening in the old fortress walls as they could be got, the enemy being kept at bay while the bullocks were driven in. Then followed troop after troop of our men, who dismounted and hurried to the top of the walls, where they covered the retirement of their comrades so effectually that the enemy were soon in full retreat, gathering up their wounded as they passed without molestation from us.

That afternoon the Boers' wagons, surmounted by a white flag, were seen coming across the plain, their attendants being engaged for a long time in the gruesome task of collecting the dead.

It must not be supposed, however, that our men had not suffered; we had a dozen slightly wounded. Inside the walls that evening there was a triumphant scene of rejoicing, in which to a man the wounded took part. The wagons had been emptied, and grain and meal stored under cover; horses and bullocks had a good feed, and one of the wagons was demolished for firewood, our whole force revelling in what they called a glorious roast of beef.

I never felt so much abashed in my life, I could not feel proud; though, of course, I had done my best. I tried to explain that it was poor old black Joeboy we had to thank for the success of the raid; but the men would not listen. If ever poor fellow was glad when the sentries had been relieved and the fires were out, so that rest and silence might succeed the wild feast, I was that person. I felt utterly exhausted, and I have only a vague recollection of lying down upon some bags of mealies, and of Denham, who was by me, saying:

"Hurrah, old fellow! The chief must make you a sergeant for this."

I don't think I made any reply, for I was nearly asleep; and that night seemed to glide away in a minute and a half.

Chapter Twenty Nine
Another Discovery

Denham and I went out early next day with a small party and an empty wagon to go over the ground between our laager and the Boer lines, following the route taken with the captured wagons, to make sure that no wounded and helpless men were left on the veldt, and to collect such rifles and ammunition as had been left.

A sharp lookout was kept against surprise; but there was no need. Denham's glass showed that the Boers, probably satisfied with their reverses of the previous day, were keeping to their lines.

We went as far as the spot where the first attack on us was made, finding only a few rifles as we went, noticing on our way sixteen dead horses—ghastly-looking objects, for near every one numerous loathsome birds rose heavily, flying to a short distance; and footprints all around in the soft earth showed that hyenas had been at the miserable banquet. The ground here and there also showed the unmistakable tracks of lions; but I am not sure they had been partakers.

"Well, I'm precious glad there's no burying of the dead, or bringing in wounded Boers as prisoners," said Denham as we rode back slowly side by side. "I don't mind the fighting when my monkey's up—it all seems a matter of course then; but the afterwards—the poor dead chaps with all the enemy gone out of them, and the suffering wounded asking you for water, and whether you think they'll die—it makes me melancholy."

"It's horrible," I said; "but it was none of our seeking."

"No; it's the Boers' own fault—the beasts! Fighting for their liberty and patriotism, they call it. They won't submit to being slaves to the Queen. Such bosh! Slaves indeed! Did you ever feel that you led the life of a slave under the reign of our jolly good Queen?"

"Pooh!" I exclaimed.

"Pooh! puff! stuff!—that's what it is, old fellow. They're about the most obstinate, stupid, ignorant brutes under the sun. They don't know when they're well off as subjects of Great Britain, so they'll have to be taught."

"Of course," I said. "But they are brave."

"Well, yes, in a way," said Denham grudgingly. "They'll fight if they're ten or a dozen to one, and can get behind stones or wagons to pot us; but they haven't got sense enough to know when they're well off, nor yet to take care of six wagon-loads of good grain and meal, and nearly a hundred and fifty oxen."

"Well, no; they were stupid there," I said.

"Stupid, Lieutenant Moray!"

"What!" I exclaimed. "Do you know what you're saying?"

"Oh yes; all right. You're not a commissioned officer yet, but you will be. Promoted for special bravery and service in the field."

"Nonsense!" I said, flushing up.

"Oh, but you will be, sure. Not that I think you deserve it. There wasn't much risk."

"Oh no," I said; "only the risk of being taken, and shot for a traitor, a thief, and a spy."

"That's only what the Doppies would call it, and they're idiots."

"If a fellow is going to be shot," I said, "it doesn't make much difference to him whether he's shot by a wise man or a fool."

"Oh, I don't know," said Denham quickly. "I'd rather be shot by a wise man than by a Boer pig. But there was no risk. You and that big nigger went in the dark, and you had luck on your side, and— Oh, I say, Val, you did it splendidly! I had a good tuck-out of mealie-porridge this morning, and three big slices of prime beef frizzled. I feel quite a new man with all that under my jacket, and ready to take two Boers single-handed."

"Yes, a good meal does make a difference," I said, smiling with pleasant recollections of my own breakfast.

"Difference! Oh, it was splendid! I felt as if I could have voted for you to be made colonel on the spot, and black Joeboy adjutant, when I caught sight of you coming with six wagons and teams instead of one. My dear boy, you've won the affection of every one in the corps, from the Colonel right down to the cooks. It's only cupboard-love, of course; but they're very fond of you now. We were going to chair you round the big court last night, but the Colonel stopped it. 'Let the poor fellow have a good rest,' he said. But we did all drink your health with three times three—in water. Here—hullo! What game do you call that?"

He pointed to where, half a mile away, a dozen of our men were riding out, closely followed by the bullocks we had captured overnight.

"Taking the teams out to graze, I suppose. The poor beasts must be well fed to keep them in condition."

"Of course. But how do we know that they won't all bolt back for the Boers' camp? They're Boer bullocks, you know. Oh! I'll never forgive the Colonel if he loses all that beef."

"The poor brutes will only make for the nearest patches of grass and bush," I said, "and their guard will take care to head them back if they seem disposed to stray."

"But is any one on the lookout with a glass on the wall?"

"Sure to be," I said.

"I'm not so sure," cried Denham impatiently. "Why, there must be going on for six hundred sirloins there, without counting other tit-bits; and if the bullocks are taken care of, each one is a sort of walking safe full of prime meat for the troops."

"There—look!" I said; "they're settling down to graze, and the guard is spreading out between them and the open veldt."

"Yes, I see," said Denham anxiously; "but I hope they'll take great care. That job ought to be ours."

But it was not, and I did not want it. I said so, too.

"That's bosh," replied Denham. "You say so because you're not hungry; but just wait till you are, and then you'll be as fidgety about the bullocks as I am."

"But you're not hungry now," I said laughingly.

"Well, no—not at present; but I shall be soon. I haven't made up the balance of two days' loss yet. Ugh! only fancy—grilled cat's-meat for a commissioned officer in Her Majesty's service! Ugh! To think that I was compelled by sheer hunger to eat horse! I'd swear off all flesh-feeding for good if it wasn't for that beef."

He burst into a hearty fit of laughing then, and we rode on, chatting about our position and the fact that the Boers seemed to consider they could not do better for their side than keep us shut up as we were till we surrendered as prisoners of war.

"That's it, evidently," said Denham. "They hate us horribly, for we'd been doing a lot of mischief amongst them before you joined, as well as ever since."

"Shall we be able to cut our way through before long?" I asked.

"I don't know, old fellow," he replied.

"We ought to," I said, "because we could be of so much use to the General's troops."

"Well, I don't know so much about that," said Denham as we neared the fortified gateway, with its curtain of empty wagons. "I'm beginning to think that we're being a great deal of help to the General here."

"How?" I asked wonderingly. "Our corps is completely useless."

"Oh no, it isn't, my little man. Look here; I'm of opinion that we're surrounded by quite a couple of thousand mounted men."

"Yes, perhaps there are," I said, "at a guess."

"Well, isn't that being of use to the British General? We're keeping these fellows fully occupied, so that they can't be harassing his flanks and rear with all this mob of sharpshooters, who know well how to use their rifles."

"I say," I cried, "what's the matter yonder?"

"Nothing! Where?"

"Look at the baboons right at the far end of the kopje. They're racing about in a wonderful state of excitement."

"Smell cooking, perhaps," said Denham. "Here, Sergeant," he continued, calling up Briggs, "take Mr Moray and a couple of men. Canter round yonder and see if you can make anything out. Scout. Perhaps the brutes can see the Boers advancing."

In another minute we were cantering round the ragged outskirts of the great pile of stones, where they came right down to the plain, among which were plenty of grassy and verdant patches, little gorges and paths up amongst the tumbled-together blocks; and as we rode along we startled apes by the dozen from where they were feeding, and sent them shrieking and chattering menacingly, as they rushed up to the higher parts.

It was away at the extreme end where the main body of the curious-looking, half-dog, half-human creatures were gathered, all in motion, and evidently much exercised by something below them on the side farthest from where we approached.

"They're playing some game, Mr Moray," said the Sergeant, speaking quite respectfully to me, and, as I thought, slightly emphasising the "Mister," which sounded strange. "Tell you what it is: one of the young ones has tumbled into a gully and broken his pretty little self."

"Give the order to unsling rifles, Sergeant," I said quietly, "and approach with caution."

"Eh? What! You don't think there's an ambuscade—do you?"

"No," I said as I watched the actions of the apes keenly; "but I do think there's a lion lying up somewhere."

"A lion!"

"Yes; one of the brutes that were feeding on the dead horses in the night. He has made for the shelter yonder, and is in hiding."

"And the monkeys have found him, and are mobbing the beggar now he's sleeping off his supper?"

"That's it, I think," I replied.

"Then let's get his skin if we can. Steady, all, and don't fire till you get a good chance."

We checked our horses so as to approach at a walk, the Sergeant sending me off a few yards to his left, and the other men opening out to the right.

I fully expected to see the baboons go scurrying off as we approached; but, on the contrary, they grew more excited as, with rifle ready and Sandho's rein upon his neck, I picked my way alongside the others in and out among the great blocks of stone at the foot of the kopje, where there was ample space for a couple of score of lions to conceal themselves. But I felt sure that as soon as we came near enough, and after sneaking cautiously along for some distance, the one we sought would suddenly break cover and bound off away across the veldt.

Wherever I came to a bare patch of the sandy earth I scanned narrowly in search of "pug," as hunting-men call the traces; but I could not make out a single footprint. There were those of the baboons by the dozen, and the hoof-tracks of horses, probably those of some of our men when they made a circuit of the rocky hillock. Every hoof-mark was made by horses going in the direction we were; but still no sign of a lion.

"Keep a sharp lookout," said the Sergeant softly; and I remember thinking his words unnecessary, seeing that every one was keenly on the alert.

"Seems to me a mare's-nest," said the Sergeant to me dryly, as he cocked his eye and pointed down at the footprints.

"No," I said; "the baboons have got something below them on the other side, or they wouldn't keep on like that. Ah! look out!"

"What can you see?" cried the Sergeant.

"Marks of blood on the ground here. The lion has caught one of the baboons, I expect, and he's devouring it over yonder under where the rest are dancing about and chattering."

"And enough to make them," said the Sergeant between his teeth. "Shoot the beggar if you can, sir."

"I'll try," I replied; and Sandho advanced cautiously, with the cover getting more dense, till, just as I was separated from the Sergeant by a few big blocks of ironstone, from out of whose chinks grew plenty of brushwood, Sandho stopped short, threw up his muzzle, and neighed.

"What is it, old fellow?" I said softly, as I debated whether I should dismount so as to make sure of my shot. "There, go on."

The horse took two steps forward, and then stopped again.

"Here's something, Sergeant," I said. "Push on round the end of that block and you'll see too."

"Lion?"

"No, no. Go on."

Sergeant Briggs pushed on, and uttered a loud ejaculation.

"One of the Boers' horses?" I said.

"One of the Boers, my lad," he cried. "Close in there."

The two men drew nearer, and the next minute we were all gazing down at where one of the enemy's wounded horses had evidently pitched forward upon its knees and thrown its wounded rider over its head to where he lay, a couple of yards in advance, with a terrible gash across his forehead, caused by falling upon a rough stone. But that was not the cause of his death, for his jacket and shirt were torn open and a rough bandage had slipped down from the upper part of his chest, where a bullet-wound showed plainly enough that his lungs must have been pierced, and that he had bled to death.

"Poor chap!" said the Sergeant softly; "he's got it. Well, he died like a brave man. Came up here, I s'pose, for shelter."

"There's another over yonder," I said excitedly, for about fifty yards away from where we were grouped, and high above us, the baboons were leaping about and chattering more than ever.

"Shouldn't wonder," said the Sergeant; "and he aren't dead. Trying to scare those ugly little beggars away."

"I'll soon see," I said; and as I urged Sandho on, the shrinking beast cautiously picked his way past the dead group, and we soon got up to a narrow rift full of bushes, the path among the rocks running right up to the highest point, towards which the baboons began to retire now, chattering away, but keeping a keen watch on our proceedings.

"Another dead horse, Sergeant," I shouted back.

"Never mind the horse," cried Briggs. "Be ready, and shoot the wounded man down at sight if he doesn't throw up his hands. 'Ware treachery."

I pressed on into the gully, at whose entrance the second dead horse lay, and the next minute, as Sandho forced the bushes apart with his breast, I saw marks of blood on a stone just beneath where the apes had been chattering in their excitement; and then I drew rein and felt completely paralysed, for a faint voice, whose tones were unmistakable, cried:

"Help! Wather, for the love of Heaven!"

Chapter Thirty
Briggs's Irish Lion

"Why, it's an Irish lion!" cried the Sergeant, who was now close behind me.

I was too much surprised to say anything then; but I felt afterwards that I might have said, "Irish jackal! The Irish lions are quite different." But somehow the sight of the badly-wounded man disarmed me, and I dismounted to part the bushes and kneel down beside where my enemy lay back with his legs beneath the neck and shoulders of his dead horse, blood-smeared and ghastly, as he gazed wildly in my face.

"Wather!" he said pitifully. "I am a dead man."

"Are you, now, Pat?" cried the Sergeant, in mocking imitation of the poor wretch's accent and high-pitched intonation.

"Don't be a brute, Sergeant," I said angrily as I opened my water-bottle and held it to the man's lips. "Can't you see he's badly hurt?"

"Serve him right," growled the Sergeant angrily. "What business has he fighting against the soldiers of the Queen? Ugh! he don't deserve help; he ought to be stood up and shot for a traitor."

"Be quiet!" I said angrily as I held the bottle, and the wounded man gulped down the cool water with terrible avidity.

"All!" he moaned, "it putts life into me. Pull this baste of a horse aff me. I've got a bullet through my showlther, and I'm nearly crushed to death and devoured by those imp-like divils o' monkeys."

"Here, you two," cried the Sergeant surlily, "uncoil your reins, and make them fast round this dead horse's neck."

Our two followers quickly executed the order, and then, the other ends of the plaited raw-hide ropes being secured to rings in their saddles, they urged on their horses, which made a plunge or two and dragged their dead fellow enough on one side for the Sergeant, with my help, to lift the poor rider clear.

"The blessing of all the saints be upon you both!" he moaned. "There's some lint in my pouch; just put a bit of a bandage about my showlther. I'm Captain Moriarty, an officer and a gintleman, who yields as a prisoner, and I want to be carried to yer commanding officer."

He spoke very feebly at first; but the water and the relief from the pressure of the horse revived him, and he began to breathe more freely, his eyes searching my face in a puzzled way as if he thought he had seen me before.

I took no heed, but did as he suggested; and, finding the lint and a bandage, roughly bound up the wound, which had long ceased bleeding.

"Can ye fale the bullet in the wound, me young inimy?" he said, with a sigh.

"No," I replied, looking him full in the eyes. "Our doctor will see to that."

"Then ye've got a docthor with ye?" he said, pretty strongly now.

"Of course we have," growled the Sergeant, whose countenance seemed to me then to bear a remarkable resemblance to that of a mastiff dog who was angry because his master spoke civilly to a stranger he wanted to hunt off the premises. "Do you take us for savages?"

"Silence, sor!" cried our prisoner, "or I'll report ye to yer officer."

"Silence yourself!" cried the Sergeant. "What do you want with a doctor, you Irish renegado turncoat? You said you were a dead man."

"Whisht! I'm a prisoner; but I'm an officer and a gintleman.—Here, boy, ordher your min to carry me out of this."

"My men!" I said, laughing. "I'm only a private, and this is my sergeant."

"Thin ye ought to change places, me boy.—Give orders to your min to carry me out of this, Serjint."

"I'm about ready to tell the lads to put an end to a traitor to his country."

"Tchah! Ye daren't do annything o' the kind, Serjint, for it would be murther. This is my counthry, and I'm a prisoner of war."

"Let him be, Sergeant, and we'll get him into the camp.—Can you sit on a horse, sir?" I said.

"Sure, how do I know, boy, till I thry? I've been lying under that dead baste till I don't seem to have any legs at all, at all. Ye must lift me on."

"Officer and a gentleman!" said the Sergeant scornfully. "I never heard an Irish gentleman with a brogue like that. I believe you're one of the rowdy sort that call themselves patriots."

"Sure, and I am," cried our prisoner. "But here, I don't want any wurruds with the like o' ye.—Help me up gently, boy, and let me see if I can't shtand."

"Take hold of him on the other side," I said to the Sergeant, and he frowningly helped, so that we got our prisoner upon his feet.

"Ah!" he said, with a groan. "I think I can manage it if ye lift me on a horse."

Sandho was led up, and with a good deal of difficulty and a repetition of groans and allusions to the state of his lower members, the Captain was hoisted into the saddle, and after another draught of water he declared that he could "howld" out till we got him to the "docthor."

"He doesn't look as if he could try to make a bolt of it," growled the Sergeant; "but you'd better throw the reins over your horse's head and lead him.—And look here, Mr Officer and Gentleman, I'm very good with the revolver, so don't try to spur off."

Our prisoner waved his hand contemptuously and turned to me.

"Sure, me wound and me fall put it all out of me head; but I had a man with me when I was hit, and we were cut off in the fight."

"Yes," I said; "the poor fellow lies close here—dead."

"Thin lade the horse round another way, boy. I don't want to look at the poor lad. Ah! I don't fale so faint now. To think of me bad luck, though. Shot down like this, and not in battle, but hunting a gang of wagon-thieves."

"Ha, ha, ha! ha, ha, ha!" roared the Sergeant, slapping his thigh again and again as he laughed. "Come, I like that, Mr Moray.—Here, Mr Captain, let me introduce you to the gentleman who so cleverly carried off your stores last night."

I was scarlet with indignation at being called a cattle-thief, and turned angrily away.

"What!" said the prisoner; "him? Did—did he—did—But Moray—Moray? Sure, I thought I knew his face again. Here, I arrest ye as a thraitor and a deserter from the commando, boy;" and his hand went to the holster to draw his revolver, which had not been interfered with.

"Drop that!" roared the Sergeant roughly, and he dragged the prisoner's hand from the holster, wrenching the revolver from his grasp, and nearly making him lose his balance and fall out of the saddle. "I've heard all about it. So you're the Irish scoundrel who summoned that poor lad, and when he refused to turn traitor and fight against his own country, you had his hands lashed behind his back and treated him like a dog. Why, you miserable renegado! if you weren't a wounded man I'd serve you the same. An officer and a gentleman! Why, you're a disgrace to your brave countrymen."

"Whisht! whisht!" cried our prisoner contemptuously.

"Whisht! whisht! I'd like to whisht you with a Boer's sjambok," cried the Sergeant. "Here he finds you wounded and where you'd have lain and died, and the carrion-birds would have come to the carrion; and when the brave lad's helped you, given you water, bound up your wound, and put you on his own beast, like that man did in Scripture, you turn round in the nastiness of your nature and try to sting him. Bah! I'd be ashamed of myself. You're not Irish. I don't even call you a man."

The Sergeant's flow of indignation sounded much poorer at the end than at the beginning; and, his words failing now, I had a chance to get in a few.

"That's enough, Sergeant," I said. "You forget he's a wounded man and a prisoner."

"Not half enough, Mr Moray," cried the Sergeant. "I'm not one of your sort, full of fine feelings; only a plain, straightforward soldier."

"And a brave man," I said, "who cannot trample on a fallen enemy."

Sergeant Briggs gave his slouch felt hat a thrust on one side, while he angrily tore at his grizzled shock of closely-cut hair: it was too fierce to be called a scratch.

"All right," he said—"all right; but the sight of him trying to get out a pistol to hold at the head of him as—as—"

"Be quiet, Sergeant," I said, smiling in spite of myself. "Look: the poor fellow's turning faint. Let's get him to the camp. Ride alongside him and hold him up or he'll fall."

"If I do may I—"

"Sergeant!" I shouted.

"Oh, all right, all right. I— But here, I'm not going to let you begin to domineer over your officer."

"Sergeant," I said gently, and without a word he pressed his horse close alongside the prisoner, thrust a strong arm beneath him, and we went out into the open, passing, after all, the prisoner's Boer companion, whose fighting was for ever at an end; and at last we reached the entrance to the old fort, with our wounded prisoner nearly insensible. After the horses had been led in, the prisoner had to be lifted down and placed in the temporary hospital made in a sheltered portion of the passage. Here the surgeon saw him at once, and extracted a rifle-bullet, which had nearly passed through the shoulder.

The Colonel was soon made acquainted with all that had passed, the Sergeant being his informant, and men were sent out to give a soldier's funeral to the dead Boer, who, with the Captain, must have dashed out in one of our skirmishes, after being wounded, and tried to escape by going right round the kopje, but had fallen by the way.

"Here, Moray," said the Colonel to me the next time he passed, "you've been heaping coals of fire upon your enemy's head, I hear?"

"Oh, I don't know, sir," I said uneasily.

"I've heard all about it, my lad; and a nice sort of a prisoner you've brought me in. If he had been a Boer I'd have put him on one of the captured horses and sent him to his laager, but I feel as if I must keep this fellow. There, we shall see."

"A brute!" said Denham that same night. "He's actually had the impudence to send a message to the Colonel complaining of his quarters and saying that he claims to be treated as an officer and a gentleman."

"Pooh! The fellow only merits contempt," I said.

"There are fifteen Irishmen in the corps, and they're all raging about him. They say he ought to be hung for a traitor. He doesn't deserve to be shot."

"But there isn't an Irishman in the corps would put it to the proof," I said.

"Humph! Well," said Denham, "I suppose not, for he is a prisoner after all. Officer and a gentleman—eh? One who must have left his country for his country's good."

Chapter Thirty One
Denham's bad luck

The men of the corps were in high glee during the following days, the Boers making two or three attempts to cut off our grazing horses and oxen, but smarting terribly for being so venturesome. In each case they were sent to the right-about, while our cattle were driven back into safety without the loss of a man.

The enemy still surrounded us, occupying precisely the same lines; and, thoroughly dissatisfied with a style of fighting which meant taking them into the open to attack our stronghold, they laagered and strengthened their position, waiting for us to attack them. This could only be done at the risk of terrible loss and disaster, for the Boers were so numerous that any attempt to cut through them might only result in our small force being surrounded and overwhelmed by sheer weight of numbers. Therefore our Colonel decided not to make an attack.

"The Colonel says they're ten to one, Val; and as we've plenty of water and provisions, he will leave all 'acting on the aggressive' to the Doppies."

This remark was made by my companion Denham when we had been in possession of the old fortress for nearly a fortnight.

At first, while still suffering a little from the injuries I had received, the confinement was depressing; but as I gradually recovered from my wrenches and bruises, and as there was so much to do, and we were so often called upon to be ready for the enemy, the days and nights passed not unpleasantly. Discipline was strictly enforced, and everything was carried out in the most orderly way. Horses and cattle were watered and sent out to graze in charge of escorts, and a troop was drawn up beyond the walls, ready to dash out should the Boers attempt to cut them off; guard was regularly mounted; and the men were set to build stone walls and roofs in parts of the old place, to give protection from the cold nights and the rain that might fall at any time.

As for the men, they were as jolly as the proverbial sandboys; and at night the walls echoed with song and chorus. Then games were contrived, some played by the light of the fires and others outside the walls. Bats, balls, and stumps were made for cricket; of course very roughly fashioned, but they afforded as much amusement as if they had come straight from one of the best English makers.

There was, however, a monotony about our food-supply, and the officers more than once banteringly asked me when I was going to cut out another half-dozen wagons.

"Bring more variety next time," they said merrily. "Pick out one loaded with tea, coffee, sugar, and butter."

"Yes," cried Denham, laughing; "and when you are about it, bring us some pots and kettles and potatoes. We can eat the big ones; and, as we seem to be settled here for the rest of our days, we're going to start a garden and plant the little 'taters in that."

"To be sure," said another officer; "and I say, young fellow, mind and choose one of the next teams with some milch-cows in it. I feel as if I should like to milk."

I laughed too, but I felt as if I should not much like to undertake such another expedition as the last, and that it would be pleasanter to remain content with the roast beef and very decent bread our men contrived to make in the old furnace after it had been a bit modified, or with the "cookies" that were readily made on an iron plate over a fire of glowing embers. Oh no! I don't mean damper, that stodgy cake of flour and water fried in a pan; they were the very eatable cakes one of our corporals turned out by mixing plenty of good beef-dripping with the flour, and kneading all up together. They were excellent—or, as Denham said, would have been if we had possessed some salt.

One of our greatest difficulties was the want of fuel, for it was scarce around the old stronghold when we had cut down all the trees and bushes growing out of the ledges and cracks about the kopje; and the question had been mooted whether we should not be obliged to blast out some of the roots wedged in amongst the stones by ramming in cartridges. But while there was any possibility of making adventurous raids in all directions where patches of trees existed, and the men could gallop out, halt, and each man, armed with sword and a piece of rein, cut his faggot, bind it up, and gallop back, gunpowder was too valuable to be used for blasting roots. This was now, however, becoming a terribly difficult problem, for the enemy—eagerly seizing upon the chance to make reprisals when these were attended by no great risk to themselves—had more than once chased and nearly captured our foraging parties.

Consequently all thoughts of fires for warmth during the cold nights, when they would have been most welcome, were abandoned; while the men eagerly volunteered for cooks' assistants; and the officers were not above gathering in the old furnace-place of a night, after the cooking was over, for the benefit of the warmth still emitted by the impromptu oven.

Meanwhile every economy possible was practised, and the fuel store jealously guarded. The said fuel store consisted of every bone of the slaughtered animals that could be saved, and even the hides; these, though malodorous, giving out a fine heat when helped by the green faggots, which were in turn started ablaze by chips of the gradually broken-up wagons.

Then, too, the veldt was laid under contribution, men going out mounted, and furnished with sacks, which they generally brought back full of the scattered bones of game which had at one time swarmed in the neighbourhood, but had been ruthlessly slaughtered by the Boers.

So the days glided on, with not the slightest prospect, apparently, of our escape.

"Every one's getting precious impatient, Val," said Denham one day when we were idling up on the walls with his field-glass, after lying listlessly chatting about the old place and wondering what sort of people they were who built it, and whether they did originally come gold-hunting from Tyre and Sidon. "Yes," he added, "we are impatient in the extreme."

"It doesn't seem like it," I replied; "the men are contented enough."

"Pooh! They're nobody. I mean the officers. The chief's leg's pretty nearly right again, and he was saying at mess only yesterday that it was a most unnatural state of affairs for British officers to be forced by a set of low-bred Dutch Boers, no better than farm-labourers, to eat their beef without either mustard, horse-radish, or salt."

"Horrible state of destitution," I said quietly.

"None of your sneers, Farmer Val," he cried. "He's right, and I'm getting sick of it myself. He says it is such an ignoble position for a mounted corps to suffer themselves to be shut up here, and not to make another dash for freedom."

"Well, I shall be glad if we make another attempt to get through their lines," I said thoughtfully.

"That's what the Major said, when, hang me! if the chief didn't turn suddenly round like a weathercock, and say that what we were doing was quite right, because we held this great force of Boers occupied so that the General might carry out his plans without being harassed by so large a body of men."

"That's right enough," I said.

"Don't you get blowing hot and cold," cried Denham, with impatience. "Then some one else sided with the Colonel. It was the doctor, I think. He said the General must know when, where, and how we were situated, and that sooner or later he would attack the Boers, rout them, and set us at liberty."

"That sounds wise," I hazarded.

"No, it doesn't," said my companion; "because we shouldn't want setting at liberty then. Do you suppose that if we heard the General's guns, and found that he was attacking the enemy, we should sit still here and look on?"

"Well, it wouldn't be right," I replied.

"Right? Of course not. As soon as the attack was made we should file out and begin to hover on the enemy's flank or rear, or somewhere else, waiting our time, and then go at them like a wedge and scatter them. Oh, how I do long to begin!"

"It seems to me," I said thoughtfully, "that the General ought to have sent some one to find us and bring us a despatch ordering the Colonel what to do."

"I dare say he has—half-a-dozen by now—and the Boers have captured them; but it doesn't matter."

"Doesn't matter?" I said wonderingly.

"No; because, depend upon it, he'd have ordered us to sit fast till he came."

"Well, but oughtn't the Colonel to have sent out a despatch or two telling the General how we are fixed?"

"Yes—no—I don't know," said Denham sourly. "I'm only a subaltern—a bit of machinery that is wound up sometimes by my superior officers, and then I turn round till I'm stopped. Subalterns are not expected to have any brains, or to think for themselves."

"Now you are exaggerating," I said.

"Not a bit of it, my little man. But I know what I should have done if I had been chief."

"What's that?"

"Sent out a smart fellow who could track and ride."

"With a despatch for the General?"

"No; a message that couldn't fall into the enemy's hands. I'd have gone like a shot."

"You couldn't send yourself," I said dryly.

"Eh? What do you mean?"

"You were telling me what you would have done if you had been chief."

"Bah! Yah! Don't you pretend to be so sharp. That's what the old man ought to do, though—send out a messenger, and if he didn't find the General he'd find out how things are going. I believe the Boers are licking our regular troops."

"Oh, nonsense!" I said, looking startled. "Impossible."

"Nothing's impossible in war, my boy. I'm getting uncomfortable. You'd go with a message if you were ordered?"

"Of course," I said.

"Of course you would. That's what the chief ought to do, and I've a good mind to tell him so. But I say," he added, in alarm, "don't you go and tell any one what I've been talking about."

I looked him in the face and laughed.

"Of course you will not," said Denham confidently. "Hullo! Going?"

"Yes; I want to go and see how the great Irish captain is," I replied.

"What do you want to go and see him for?" said my companion angrily.

"I hardly know," I replied. "I like to see that he's getting better."

"Well, you are a rum chap," cried Denham. "I should have thought you would like to go and sit upon the bragging brute. Why, last time, when I went with you, he talked to both of us as if we were two privates in his Boer corps."

"Yes, he's a self-satisfied, inflated sort of fellow; but he's wounded and a prisoner."

"What of that? It's only what he ought to be. I want to know what's to be done with him."

"The Colonel won't send him to the Boer lines when he's well enough to move, I hope."

"Not he. I expect he'll be kept till he can be handed over to the General. Here, I'll come with you."

I was quite willing, and we descended to the hospital, as the shut-off part of one of the passages was called; and there sat the only patient and prisoner, with an armed sentry close at hand to prevent any attempt at escape.

The Captain turned his head sharply on hearing our footsteps, and gave us both a haughty stare, which amused Denham, making him look to me and smile.

"Oh, you've come at last," said the patient. "I've been wanting you."

"What is it?" I said. "Water?"

"Bah!" he replied, his upper lip curling. "I want you to bring your chief officer here."

"I dare say you do, my fine fellow," cried Denham. "Pretty good for a prisoner! You don't suppose he'll come—do you? Here, what do you want? Tell me, and I'll carry your message to the chief."

Moriarty gave the young officer a contemptuous glance, and then turned to me.

"Go and tell the Colonel, or whatever he is, that I am greatly surprised at his inattention to my former message."

"Did you send a message?" I asked, surprised by his words.

"Of course I did, two days ago, by the surgeon. It's not gentlemanly of your Colonel. Go and tell him that I feel well enough to move now, and that I desire him to send me with a proper escort, and under a white flag, to make an exchange of prisoners."

"Well, I'll take your message," I said; "but—"

"Yes, go at once," said Moriarty, "and bring me back an answer, for I'm sick of this place."

He turned away, and, without so much as a glance at Denham, lay back, staring up at the sky.

"Well," said Denham when we were out of hearing, "of all the arrogance and cheek I ever witnessed, that fellow possesses the most. Here, what are you going to do?"

"Take the message to the Colonel," I replied.

"Going to do what?" cried Denham. "Nothing of the kind."

"But I promised him."

"I know you did; but you must have a fit of delirium coming on. It's being too much up in the sun."

"Nonsense," I said. "I've no time for joking."

"Joking, my dear boy? Nothing of the kind. I'm going to take you to the doctor; he'll nip your complaint in the bud."

"Absurd," I cried. "Come with me to the Colonel."

"What! To deliver the message?"

"Of course."

"No, Val, my boy. I like you too well to let you go to the old man. Do you know what he'd do?"

"Send me back to our friend there with a message as sharp as a sword. Of course I know he will not send him across to the Boers."

"My dear Val," said Denham solemnly, "let me inform your ignorance exactly what would happen. I know the chief from old experience. He'll sit back and listen to you with one of those pleasant smiles he puts on when he's working himself up into a rage. He'll completely disarm you—as he did me once—and all the time, as he hears you patiently to the end, he'll think nothing about my lord Paddy there, but associate you, my poor boy, with what he will consider about the most outrageous piece of impudence he ever had addressed to him. Then suddenly he'll spring up and say— No, I will not spoil the purity of the atmosphere this beautiful evening by repeating a favourite expletive of his—he'll say something you will not at all like, and then almost kick you out of his quarters."

"I don't believe it," I said.

"That's giving me the lie, Val, my boy. He'll be in such a rage that he'll forget himself; for, though he's a splendid soldier, and as brave a man as ever crossed a charger, he is one of the—"

"What, Mr Denham?" said the gentleman of whom he spoke, suddenly standing before us. "Pray speak out; I like to hear what my officers think of me."

Chapter Thirty Two
Denham Shivers

I wanted to dash off—not from fear, but to indulge in a hearty roar of laughter—for Denham's countenance at that moment wore the drollest expression I have ever seen upon the face of man.

"I—I—I beg your pardon, Colonel," he stammered at last.

"For backbiting me, sir," said the Colonel shortly. "I could not help hearing your last sentence, for you raised your voice and forced it upon me. Now, if you please, I am one of the—what?"

"I was—I was only telling Moray here, sir, that you were—er—er—very passionate, and that if—"

"Passionate, am I?"

"Yes, sir," stammered Denham. "No, no; I beg your pardon, sir. I didn't mean to say that."

"I presume you are saying what you consider to be the truth, Mr Denham," said the Colonel coldly. "Now, pray go on: and that if—"

"If he came to you with—with a message, sir, that he has just received, you would kick him out of your presence."

"Humph!" said the Colonel sternly. "Just this minute, sir, you said of me what you believed to be the truth; but now you have been saying what you must know to be false.—Pray, what was the message Moray?" he added, turning to me.

There was only one thing to do, and I did it, giving Moriarty's message to the end.

"The insolent, conceited idiot!" said the Colonel scornfully. "You need not go back to him with my answer; but if you come across him again and he asks what I said, you can tell him this: that at the first opportunity I shall hand him over to my superior officers, as one of Her Majesty's subjects found with arms in his hand fighting against the British force after taking service with her enemies, and doing his best to impress Englishmen to serve in the same ranks.—Mr Denham, I should like a few words with you in the morning."

He turned upon his heel and strode heavily away, with his spurs clinking loudly and the guard at the end of his scabbard giving a sharp *chink* every now and then, as, field-glass in hand, he climbed to the top of the wall to take a look round at the positions of the enemy before the evening closed in.

"Well," said Denham at last, looking the while as if all the military starch had been taken out of him, "you've done it now."

I could keep back my laughter no longer.

"Somebody has," I cried merrily.

"Yes," he said dolefully; "somebody has. Oh, I say, Val, you oughtn't to have told tales like that."

"What?" I cried. "How could I help it?"

"Well, I suppose you couldn't," said my companion. "But there never was such an unlucky beggar as I am. What did he want to come upon us just at that moment for? Oh dear! oh dear! and I got to face him to-morrow morning! I say, can't we do something to put it off—something to make him forget it?"

"Impossible," I said.

"Oh, I don't know; try and think of a good dodge—a sortie, or doing something to make the Boers come on to-night. If we had a jolly good light he'd forget all about it, and I shouldn't hear any more about the miserable business. Here, what can we do to make the Boers come on? I might get killed in the set-to, and then I should escape this awful wigging."

"Who ought to go and see the doctor now?" I said. "Who's going mad?"

"I am, I believe, old fellow; and enough to make me. It's enough to make a fellow desert. Here, I know; I'll do something. It's all the fault of that miserable renegade. I'll go in and half-kill him—an insolent, insulting brute!"

Just then Denham, who was as fearless as any man in the ranks when out with the corps, started violently in his alarm; for a hail came from high up on the wall in the Colonel's familiar voice; and upon looking up, there he was, glass in hand, looking down at us.

"Denham," cried the Colonel, "run to the Major. Tell him to come here to me at once, and bring his glass."

"Yes, sir," cried my companion.—"Come with me, Val. My word! He gave me such a turn, as the old women say; I thought he'd heard me again. Hurrah, old fellow! there's something up, and no mistake. I shan't get that tongue-flogging after all."

Chapter Thirty Three
Denham Proves to be Right

In a few minutes the Major had joined the Colonel, and soon every officer and man in the old fortification was waiting breathlessly for information as to what intelligence regarding the movements of the enemy the two stern-looking men up on the wall were gathering into their brains through their glasses—intelligence far beyond the ken of the sentries, whose duty it was to keep strict watch upon the great circle which was formed by the Boer lines.

There was no hurry or bustle; but our trumpeter had buckled his sword-belt and taken down his instrument from where it hung, and then stationed himself upon one of the blocks of stone in the great courtyard, watching his chiefs, and holding his instrument ready, while his eyes seemed about to start out of his head in his excitement. Everywhere it was the same. Men glided about here and there, after a glance at the ranges of rifles against the wall, with their well-filled bandoliers, and only paused at last where each could dart to his horse, ready to saddle and bridle the tethered beast. The officers were also silently preparing—buckling on their swords, taking revolvers from their belt-holsters, and filling the chambers from their cartridge-pouches, quite mechanically, without taking their eyes off the watchers on the wall. But in spite of all these preparations no sounds were heard save those made by the horses—an impatient stamp or pawing at the stones, followed by a snort or a whinnying neigh.

I did as the rest had done. Meeting Denham after his return from the sheltered spot occupied by the officers, we stood together, looking up at the wall.

"What a long time they are taking!" whispered Denham impatiently. "The Doppies can't be coming on, or they'd have been seen before now."

Almost as he spoke the two officers strode to one end of the rampart and began to inspect the veldt again. The next minute they were making for the opposite side of the great building, to examine the country in that direction; and here they stood for a long time.

"Oh dear!" groaned Denham at last. "What's-its-name deferred makes the heart sink into your boots. It's a false alarm."

"Not it," I said, "for there has been no alarm."

"Well, you know what I mean. It's all over. I did hope the chief would be so busy that he'd forget all about what I said. There never was such a miserably unlucky beggar born as I am. Now we shall—"

Just then the Major left the Colonel's side, came to the edge of the wall, and looked down into the court, gave a nod of satisfaction, and made a sign to the trumpeter, whose bugle went with a flip to his lips, and there was a sound as if the pent-up breath of some four hundred men had been suddenly allowed to escape. Then the walls were echoing to the call "Boot and Saddle," and every man sprang to his hung-up saddle and then to his horse, the willing beasts seeming all of a tremor with an excitement as great as that of their riders. Long practice had made us quick; and in an incredibly short time I was standing like the rest with my rifle slung across my back, holding Sandho's bridle ready to lead him out through the gateway, military fashion, though he would have walked at my side like a dog.

"We're only going for a bit of a reconnaissance," said Sergeant Briggs gruffly as, after a sharp, non-com glance at his men, he settled down close to my side.

"How do you know?" I asked, speaking as if to a friend, and not to a superior officer on parade.

"No orders for water-bottles and rations, my lad. I was in hopes that we were going to make a dash through them and get out of this prison of a place."

"What! and leave all that splendid beef, Briggs?" said Denham, who came up in time to hear the Sergeant's words.

"Yes; and the gold-mine too, sir. We could come back and take possession of that."

"But the bullocks?"

"They'd find their way out and get their living on the veldt. Needn't trouble about them, sir. Look out."

We were looking out, for our two chief officers had now descended from the walls and crossed to where their servants were holding their chargers.

Directly after a note was sounded, followed by a sharp order or two, and horse and man, troop after troop, filed out into position and stood ready to mount.

The order was not long in coming, and we sprang into our saddles, all in profound ignorance of what was before us, save that we were soon to return. About fifty men had been left as garrison.

Then an order was given, and we divided into two bodies. One detachment, under the Major, moved off, to pass round by the kopje; the other, in which I served, taking the opposite direction, but turning after passing round the stronghold, and meeting the other detachment about half a mile to the east. There we sat, obtaining in the clear evening light a full view of the enemy's proceedings.

We had no sooner halted than the officers' glasses were focussed, and all waited anxiously for an explanation of the movements which the non-commissioned officers and privates could see somewhat indistinctly with the naked eye.

Denham was close to me; and, like the good fellow he was, he took care to let me know what he made out, speaking so that his words were plainly heard by Sergeant Briggs and the others near.

"It seems to be a general advance of the enemy," he said, with his eyes close to his glass. "They're coming steadily on at a walk. Yes; wagons and all."

"That doesn't mean an attack, sir," said the Sergeant.

"I don't know what it means," said Denham. "Yes, I think I do. They've got some notion into their heads that we mean to break through the ring, and they are going to close up, to make it more solid."

"They think we're getting tired of it, sir, and that when we see them loaded with plenty of good things we shall surrender."

"Perhaps it's out of kindness, Briggs," said Denham, laughing. "They want to tempt us into making another raid because the distance will be shorter for us to go."

"Then I'm afraid they'll be disappointed, sir, for the Colonel isn't likely to risk losing any of his men while we've got all those bullocks to eat."

"I don't know what to make of it," said Denham; then, thoughtfully: "It looks to me like some bit of cunning—a sort of ruse to get within rifle-shot. Look how steadily they're coming on."

That was plain enough to us all, line after line of horsemen advancing as regularly as if they had been well-drilled cavalry; and for my part, inexperienced as I was in such matters, I could not help thinking that the wagons were being pushed forward on purpose to afford cover for their best marksmen, and that in a short time the bullets would begin to be pinging and buzzing about our ears.

I can't say what the Colonel thought; but almost directly the trumpet rang out, and we were cantered back, to file steadily into the great courtyard again, with the men grumbling and muttering among themselves at having been made what they called fools of.

"I tell you what it is, Val," said Denham as soon as he had another chance to speak; "I believe I've got it."

"What—the Boers' plan?"

"Yes; don't you see? They'll come right in so as to be within easy shot of our grazing grounds."

"Oh!" I exclaimed, "I never thought of that. Of course; and if the horses and cattle are driven out, they'll be able to shoot them down till we haven't a beast left."

"Nor a bit of beef. It's to force us to surrender—a regular siege."

It was rapidly getting dark then; and we soon learned that our ideas of the Boers' ruse were the same as those entertained by our chiefs.

Upon the strength of the closer approach the sentries were doubled, and by means of the wagons the entrance to our stronghold was barricaded in a more effectual way; but we were not to be allowed to rest with a feeling of security that night. In about a couple of hours after our return a shot was fired by one of the sentries, then another, and another; and the men stood to their arms, on foot, ready for an attack by the enemy. In a few minutes, however, the news ran round that the sentries had fired at a dark figure creeping along under the wall inside the courtyard after repeated challenges; and, later, the news spread that the sentry on guard over the prisoner was lying insensible and bleeding from a great cut on the back of his head, and that Captain Moriarty was nowhere to be found.

Chapter Thirty Four
An Ambuscade In Stone

"The chief's in an awful rage, Val," said Denham, when he came to me after a thorough search had seemed to prove that the prisoner had eluded the vigilance of the sentries. "He swears that some one must have been acting in collusion with the pompous blackguard, and that he means to have the whole of our Irish boys before him and cross-examine the lot."

"I hope he will not," I said.

"So do I; for I don't believe one of them would have lent him a hand, and it would offend them all."

"Yes," I said; "they're all as hot-headed and peppery as can be."

"Spoiling for a fight," put in Denham.

"Yes; and so full of that queer feeling which makes them think a set is made against them because they are Irish."

"Exactly," cried my companion; "and it's such a mistake on their part, because we always like them for their high spirits and love of a bit of fun."

"They're the wittiest and cleverest fellows in the corps."

"And if I wanted a dozen chaps to back me up in some dangerous business, I'd sooner depend on them for standing to me to the last than any one I know."

"Oh! it would be a pity," I said warmly. "I hope the Colonel will think better of it."

Denham winked at me as we sat in shelter by the light of a newly-invented lamp, made of a bully-beef tin cut down shallow and with a couple of dints in the side; it was full of melted fat, across which a strip out of the leg of an old cotton stocking had been laid so that the two ends projected an inch beyond the two spout-like dints.

"What does that mean?" I asked.

"The chief," said Denham, "good old boy, kicks up a shindy, and swears he'll do this or that, and then he thinks better of it. I've got off my wigging."

"How do you know?" I said.

"Met the old boy after I had been having a regular hunt everywhere with half-a-dozen men, and he nodded to me in quite a friendly way. 'Thank you, Denham,' he said. 'Tell your men that they were very smart.'"

"I'm glad of that," I said.

"Same here, dear boy. It's his way, bless him! He likes a red rag to go at, the old John Bull that he is; but if another begins to flutter somewhere else, he forgets number one and goes in for number two."

"Yes, I've noticed that," I said. "But it's a great pity that fellow got away. I believe he has been shamming a bit lately."

"No doubt about it. The nuisance of it is, that the brute will go and put the Boers up to everything as to our strength, supplies, ammunition, and goodness knows what else. But, look here, I'm going on now to see how Sam Wren is."

"Sam Wren?" I cried wonderingly. "What's the matter with him?"

"Matter? Why, he was the sentry Moriarty knocked down."

"Oh, poor fellow! I am sorry," I said, for the private in question was one of the smartest and best-tempered men in our troop.

"So's everybody," replied Denham. "I say: it was contusion in his case, not collusion."

"Where is he?" I said.

"In hospital. Duncombe's a bit uneasy about him. I'm going on again to see him. Will you come?"

"Of course," I said eagerly.

"Come along, then. We'll take the lamp, or some sentry may be popping at us."

"The wind will puff it out in that narrow passage."

"Not as I shall carry it," replied my companion; and he led off, with his broad-brimmed felt held over the flickering wick, in and out among the fallen stones between the walls, nearly to the other side of the court. Here another covered-in patch had been turned into a fairly snug hospital by hanging up two wagon-tilts twenty feet apart, after clearing away the loose stones; and a certain number of fairly comfortable beds had been made of the captured corn-sacks.

On reaching the first great curtain Denham called upon me to hold it aside, as his hands were full; and as I did so I caught sight, on the right-hand side, of our doctor down on one knee and bending over his patient, whose face could be seen by the light of a lantern placed upon a stone, while his voice sounded plainly, as if he were replying to something the surgeon had said.

"Only me, Duncombe," said Denham. "Just come to see how Wren is."

"Better, thank goodness," said the doctor. "He seemed to come-to about five minutes ago."

"I am glad, Wren," said Denham, setting down the lamp beside the lantern.

"Thank ye, sir," said the poor fellow, smiling. "Moray's come with me to look you up." The wounded man looked pleased to see me, and then his face puckered up as he turned his eyes again to the doctor and said:

"I don't mind the crack on the head, sir, a bit. Soldiers deal in hard knocks, and they must expect to get some back in return. I know I've given plenty. It's being such a soft worries me."

"Well, don't let it worry you. Help me by taking it all coolly, and I'll soon get you well again."

"That you will, sir. I know that," said the man gently. "But I feel as if I should like to tell the Colonel that I was trying to do my duty."

"He doesn't want telling that, Sam," said Denham. "Of course you were."

"But I oughtn't to have been such a fool, sir—such a soft Tommy of a fellow. I knew he was a humbug; but he looked so bad, and pulled such a long face, that I didn't like to be hard. 'Here, sentry,' he says, as he sat up with his back to the wall, just after you'd gone, 'this right leg's gone all dead again. It's strained and wrenched through the horse lying upon it all those hours. Just come and double up one of those sacks and lay it underneath for a cushion. The pain keeps me from going to sleep.'"

"Oh, that's how it happened—was it?" said the doctor, while we two listened eagerly.

"I'm coming to it directly, sir," said the man querulously. "Well, sir, seeing as I felt that, as I was sentry over the hospital, I was in charge of a wounded man as well, I just rested my rifle against the wall, picked up one of the sacks, and doubled it in four. Then, just as innocent as a babby, I kneels down, lifts up his leg softly, bending over him like, and was just shoving the bit of a cushion-like thing under his knee, when it seemed as if one of the big stones up there had fallen flat on the back of my head, and I heard some one say, 'Take that, you ugly Sassenach beast! and see how you like lying in hospital.' Then it was all black, sir, till I opened my eyes and saw you holding that stuff to my lips."

"Yes, my man," said the doctor; "now don't talk any more, but lie still."

"Tell me about that crack on the head again, sir, please. It wasn't one of the stones fell down, then?"

"No; the prisoner must have got hold of this piece somehow, then kept it ready by the side of his bed, and struck you down."

"And a nasty, dirty, cowardly blow, too," said the poor fellow feebly. "Beg pardon, sir; you'll pull me round as quickly as you can—won't you?"

"Of course," said the doctor, smiling.

"Thank ye, sir. I want to have an interview with that gentleman again."

"I suppose so," said Denham; "and so do about four hundred of the corps. He'd have been stood up with his back to one of the walls and shot by this time, but the brute has got away."

"We shall run against him again, though, sir," said the wounded man confidently, "and we shan't mistake him for any one else.—Beg pardon, though, sir; you're quite sure my skull isn't broken?"

"Quite," said the doctor. "Now be quiet."

"Certainly, sir; but is it cracked?"

"No, nor yet cracked," said the doctor, smiling. "You're suffering from concussion of the brain."

"And I'll concuss his brain, sir, if I can only get a chance; but I will do it fair and— Yes, sir, I've done, and I'm going to sleep."

He smiled at us both, and then closed his eyes; while, after a few words with the doctor, Denham picked up the lamp, and we went gently to the other rough curtain.

"It's just as near to go back this way," said Denham as I lowered the canvas again, and we passed on, to be confronted directly after by a sentry, who challenged with his levelled bayonet pointed at our breasts; but after giving the word we passed on.

"Seems queer for poor Sam Wren," said my companion, "changing places like that. Sentry one moment; patient the next. Bah! it is a nuisance that the prisoner should have been able to get away."

"And go back to the Boers, full of all he has seen here," I said.

"Well, it will make us all the more careful," said Denham, still shading the lamp with his hat as we went on, till we had passed where we could hear the movement of the horses tethered to the long lines, with none too much room to stir, poor beasts! Commenting on the condition of our mounts, I remarked that, as the Boers had come in so close, the horses would have but little opportunity for stretching their legs.

"Oh, don't you be afraid about that; the chief isn't the man to let the Doppies come close like this without having something to say on his side. You may depend upon it that the moment he feels that the horses are going the wrong way, there'll be such a dash made as will astonish our friends outside."

"Well, I shall not be sorry," I said, "for I don't like being shut up as we are. Look up. I say, what a lovely starlight night!"

"No, thank you," replied Denham. "I like fine nights, but I like to take care of my shins; and if I get star-gazing the lamp will be blown out, and we shall be going down one of those holes into the old gold-mine. There is one just in front—isn't there?"

"Two," I said; "but there are great stones laid across now."

"Across the middle; but there's plenty of room to go down on one side. Look! Here we are."

He stopped and held the lamp down, its feeble rays showing that he was upon a broad stone laid across one of the old mine-shafts, one of those close by the ancient furnace we had discovered on our first visit. On this he now halted for a moment, partly from curiosity, partly to draw my attention to the danger.

"I should like to tie some of the horses' reins together and have a decent lantern, so as to be let down to explore these places."

"You couldn't," I said. "Don't you remember when we threw a stone down this one it fell some distance and then went splash into the water?"

"It was the one farther on, not this one," said Denham, bending lower.

"Well, you may depend upon it that there'd be no going far before coming to water."

"Val!" cried my companion suddenly.

"What's the matter?"

"That's what some of our chaps have been doing."

"What! going down to the water?"

"No; exploring to find gold. Look here; they've been doing exactly what I said. Here's a rein tied round this stone with the end going right down, and—"

Crash!

"Ah! Val!"

There was the sound of a couple of strokes, one falling upon the lamp, which seemed to leap down into the shaft at our feet, the other stroke falling on Denham's head; and as I sprang to his assistance I was conscious of receiving a tremendous thrust which sent me headlong downward, as if I were making a dive from the stone I tried to cross. The next minute my head came in contact with stones, strange scintillations of light flashed before my eyes, there was a roar as of thunder in my ears, and then all was blank.

Chapter Thirty Five
In Doleful Dumps

Mine was a strange awakening to what appeared like a confused dream. There was a terrible pain in my head, and a sensation as of something warm and wet trickling down the side of my face, accompanied by a peculiar smarting which made me involuntarily raise my hand and quickly draw it away again, for I had only increased the pain. Then I lay quite still, trying to puzzle out what was the matter.

At first I could only realise the fact that the darkness was intense. After a time the idea occurred that I must have been out with my troop attacking the Boers, and that a bullet had struck me diagonally on the forehead and glanced off after making the cut, which kept bleeding; but I was so stunned that a kind of veil seemed to be raised between the present and the past.

"I shall think all about it soon," I mused. "It's of no use to worry after a fall."

Then I wondered about Sandho, and how the poor beast had fared, a pang of mental agony shooting through me as I listened.

I could not hear a sound.

"He's killed," was my next thought; "for if he had been alive he would have stopped directly I fell from his back, and waited for me to remount."

I began to feel about with my hands; but instead of touching soft earth or bush I felt rough stones, wet and slimy as if coated with fine moss, and it had lately been raining. A faint musical drip, as of falling water, strengthened this notion; but I did not try to follow it out, for my head throbbed severely. So I lay still trying to rest, and gazing upward expecting to see the stars. All above, however, was black with a solid intensity that was awe-inspiring. I could see nothing; but I could feel, and became aware of another fact: I was lying among rocks in a most uncomfortable and painful position, with my head and shoulders in a niche between two pieces of stone, and my feet high above me.

"At the foot of some kopje," I remember fancying. Then my mind grew clearer—so much clearer that I felt for my handkerchief, got it out of my breast, doubled it, and bound it round my forehead to stop the bleeding. This took me some time; but the movement, painful though it was, seemed to give me more power of thinking, and I began to do more. After an effort, I managed to get my back and shoulders out of the crevice in the rocks where they were wedged. Then my legs slipped down of their own weight, and I felt myself gliding down a sharp incline. I spread out my hands to stop myself, and succeeded, bringing up against some loose stones.

"Sandho's somewhere at the bottom of this slope," I thought, and I called him by name; but I was horrified to hear my words go reverberating from me with strange, whispering echoes which died slowly away.

"How strange!" I muttered, as the intense darkness made my feeling of confusion return. "Where am I? What place is this?"

I knew I was saying these words aloud; and what followed came like an answer to my question, for from somewhere close at hand there was a deep moaning sigh. I started violently and tried to creep away; but my head began to swim with terrible giddiness on attempting to move. As this subsided a little I thrust out my hand cautiously and began to feel about, touching at the end of a few seconds something which brought back my memory with a rush. My fingers had come in contact with the tin contrivance we had used for a lamp; and, naturally enough, the touch recalled to me who had borne it, and the accident that had befallen us. Accident? No; it must have been an attack.

However, my head was clearing rapidly, and the sense of horror and pain was passing off like mist; and now I began again to feel cautiously about, but without avail, till I turned upon my hands and knees and crawled a yard or two, slipped, and clung to the rugged surface to check my descent. Then my feet went down to the full extent before they were stopped by something soft, and a thrill of satisfaction ran through me, for a well-known voice said peevishly:

"Don't—don't!—What is it?"

"Val," I cried, and my voice was caught up, and died away in whispers.

Then there was a pause, and I lay listening till, from below, came the words:

"Did any one speak?"

"Yes, yes, I did," I cried. "Where are you?"

"I—I don't know. Think I must have had a fall."

I was about to lower myself to the speaker, when a sudden thought made me turn a little over on my left side. The next moment I was clinging hard with both hands, for a stone I had touched gave way, and there was a rushing sound, silence, and then a horrible echoing splash which set my heart beating fast. In imagination I saw the loosened stone slide down to an edge below me, and bound off, to fall into the water, which I could hear lapping, sucking, and gliding about the sides of the chasm, strangely suggestive of live creatures which had been disturbed and had made a rush at the falling stone in the belief it was something they might tear and devour.

Recovering from my momentary panic, I set one hand free to search for and get out my little tin match-box. It was no easy task, under the circumstances, to get it open and strike one of the tiny tapers.

"Val, is that you?" came from just below.

"Yes; wait a moment. Hold tight," I said in a choking voice, as I rubbed the match on the bottom of the box, making a phosphorescent line of light, then another, and another, before impatiently throwing the match from me and seeing its dim light die away in the darkness.

I knew the reason why I had not got the match to light. As I opened the box again to get another, I did not insert finger and thumb till they got a good rub on my jacket to free them from the dampness caused by holding on to the wet stones. Now, as I struck, there was a sharp crackling noise, and the light flashed out, caught on, and the match burned bravely, giving me light enough to look for the tin lamp I had touched before. There it was, some little distance above me, on a terribly steep, wet slope.

No time was to be lost; so, mastering my hesitation as I thought of what was before me if I slipped, I began to climb; but, before I had drawn myself up a yard, Denham's voice rose to me, its tones full of agony and despair:

"Don't leave me, Val, old fellow!"

"Not going to," I shouted. "I'm getting the lamp."

"Ah!" came from below.

Almost before the exclamation had died away I was within reach of the fallen lamp; but just then I dislodged another loose stone, which went rolling down and plunged into the water below.

The match had burned out.

"All right," I shouted. "I'll get another."

The same business had to be gone through again. Untaught by experience, I moistened the top of the first match I took out, my fingers trembling the while with nervous dread that I would drop the box or spill the matches, when the result might be death to one, if not to both. I tried the damp match three times before throwing it away; then, taking out two together and striking them, my spirits rose as I got a light, which was passed into my left hand, and with the other I secured the lamp, which lay bottom up.

"The tallow and wick will have fallen out," I thought. No; the hard fat was in its place. Again I took out a match, shivering as I saw how rapidly it burned away. The very next moment I had laid it against the bent-down wick, which had been flattened by the fall; and it sputtered and refused to burn. All I could do till my fingers began to burn was to melt out some of the tallow and partially dry the wick. Then all was darkness again.

"Cheer up!" I cried hoarsely; "third time never fails." There was no response. I turned cold as I fumbled at the box once more; my fingers needed no moisture from the slippery stones now to make them wet, for the perspiration seemed to be oozing out of every pore.

I was again successful when I struck a match, and it burned up brightly. My heart now beat more hopefully, as one tiny strand of the cotton caught and ceased sputtering, giving forth a feeble blue flame, which I was able to coax by letting the fat it melted drain away till more and more of the wick caught and began to burn.

I dared not wait to light the second wick, but looked for a safe place to set the lamp; this I found directly, within reach of my hand. My hurried glance showed that we were in a rough tunnel or shoot, sloping down rapidly into darkness—a darkness too horrible to contemplate; and, to my despair, I could not see Denham. Then, as the sight of the light revived him, I could hear his shivering sigh.

"Where are you?" I said, trying to speak firmly.

"Just below you," came faintly.

I felt my teeth were clenched together as I asked the next question, knowing only too well what must be the answer:

"Can you see to climb up to me?"

"No," came back after a pause of a moment or two. "I'm hurt and sick. I feel as if I shall faint."

"Can you hold on till I get down to you?"

"I—I think so, old fellow," he said faintly. "I'm on a sort of shelf. But don't try—you can't do it—you'll send the loose stones down upon me. That last one grazed my head."

"But I must," I said harshly, and I remember fancying that my voice sounded savage and brutal. "I can't leave you like this."

"Climb up out of this horrible hole yourself, old fellow, and leave me."

"I won't," I shouted, so that my voice went echoing away; but as I looked up past the light it seemed to me that I could not, even if willing.

"You must," said Denham more firmly. "Climb up and call for help."

At that moment, sounding faint and distant, there was the report of a rifle; then another, and another, followed by four or five in a volley.

"The Boers are attacking," I cried. My heart sank as something seemed to say to me, "Well, if they are, what does it matter to you?"

The firing went on, and just then the wick of the lamp, of which a good deal must have been loosened by the fall, began to blaze up famously. I looked around to ascertain if I could get down to help Denham; but it seemed impossible. I saw, however, that I might lower myself a couple of feet farther, and get my heels in a transverse crack in the rock, where I could check myself and perhaps afford some help to a climber.

"Look here, Denham," I shouted out as if I had been running, "I can help you if you can climb up here. You must pluck up and try."

He muttered, with a low groan:

"Don't talk like that, old chap. I've got the pluck, but feel as if I haven't got the power. If I stir I shall go down into that awful pool, and then— Oh dear, it's very horrible to die like a rat in a flooded hole!"

"Hold your tongue, you idiot!" I shouted, in a rage. "Who's going to die? Look here; I can't get down to you, so I must climb out and fetch help. I'll go if you'll swear you'll sit fast and be patient, even if the light goes out."

There was no answer.

"Denham, old fellow, do you hear me?" I cried, with a thrill of horror running through me as I imagined he had fainted, and that the next moment I should hear a sullen splash.

"Yes, I hear you," he said. "I'll try. It's all right. But why don't you shout?"

"No one could hear me, even if that firing was not going on," I said. Looking upwards, I felt that the only chance was to try; but I was almost certain that I should slip, fall, and most likely carry my poor friend with me. The flickering light made the rocks above appear as if in motion; and, as I stared up wildly, the various projections looked as if a touch would send them rushing down. Then I uttered a gasp and tried to shout, but my voice failed. Was I deceiving myself? Almost within reach was a rope hanging down, close to the wall of the shaft on my right. Then I could speak again.

"Hurrah!" I shouted. "Here's help, Denham. Hold on; some one's letting down a rope. Ahoy, there! swing it more into the middle."

Echoes were the only answer. Almost in despair, I crept sideways, and made a frantic dash just as I felt I was slipping, and a stone gave way beneath my feet. There I hung, flat upon the rock, listening to a couple of heavy splashes, but with the rope tight in my grasp as if my fingers had suddenly become of steel. I could not speak again for a few minutes; but at last, as the echoes of the splashes died out, the words came:

"All right, Denham?" A horrible pause followed; then, with a gasp:

"Yes—all right—yes—I thought it was all over then."

Chapter Thirty Six
The Use of Muscles

Some one wrote, "Circumstances alter cases." Everybody knows how true that is, and how often we have illustrations in our own lives. Here is one: to catch hold of a rope after jumping to it is wonderfully easy, and in our young days the sensation of swinging to and fro in a sort of bird-like flight through the air is delightful—that is to say, if the ground is so near that we can drop on our feet at any moment; there is no thought of danger as we feel perfect confidence in our power to hold on. It is a gymnastic exercise. But change the scene: be hanging at the end of the same rope, with the knowledge that a friend and comrade is in deadly peril, and that, though resting against a rocky slope which gives you foothold and relieves the strain on your muscles, there is beneath you a horrible chasm full of black water, hidden by the darkness, but lapping and whispering as if waiting to receive the unfortunate. It is then that the nerves weaken and begin to communicate with and paralyse the muscles, unless there is sufficient strength of mind to counteract the horror, setting fear at defiance.

The best thing under these circumstances is to get the body to work, and make brain take the second place. In other words, act and don't think.

I must confess that my endeavours during those perilous moments were quite involuntary; for it was in a kind of desperation that I got my toes upon a solid piece of the slippery rock and pressed myself against the steep slope for a few moments, listening to the firing, some of which sounded close, some more distant. Then, shouting to Denham to hold on, I glanced at the lamp, which was flaring bravely and giving a good light, but only at the expense of the rapidly melting fat. The next minute I was climbing as quickly as I could by the rope, and shuddering as I heard stone after stone go down, any one of which I knew might crash full upon Denham.

There was no time to think—I was too hard at work; and, to my surprise, I found myself just beneath the long bridge-like piece of stone which had been laid across the opening to the shaft; while, by holding on to the rope with one hand and, reaching up the other to grasp the stone, I could see by the light which rose from below—reflected from the glistening wall, for the lamp was out of sight—that the rope was one of the strong tethering-reins, fastened round the stone as if for the purpose of lowering a bucket.

The next minute I was seated on the stone, with my feet resting on the side of the shaft-hole, and drawing up the raw-hide rope hand over hand. After pulling up some feet of it I came upon a knot which felt secure, and I then hauled again till I came upon another, also well made. With the rope gathering in rings about my knees and behind me, I kept hauling till I came to knot after knot, all quite firm. I found that the rope was dripping with water, and knew that it had been just drawn out of the pool below. The end of the rope came to hand directly; and, with trembling fingers, my first act was to tie a knot a few inches up before doubling the strong raw-hide plait and tying it again in a loop, which I tested, and found I could easily slip it over my head and pass my arras through so as to get it beneath the armpits.

I had the rope off again in a few seconds, held it ready, and shouted down to Denham, who had been perfectly still.

"Now then," I cried; "can you hear what I say?"

"Yes," came in a strange, hollow tone.

"Look out! I'm going to lower you a rope with a loop all ready tied. Slip it over your head and under your arms."

"Ah!" he said softly; and, as I rapidly lowered down the rope, though the tone seemed only like an expiration of the breath, it yet sounded firmer than that "Yes" of a few moments before.

"I can't see, old fellow," I cried, when I had paid out what I thought must be enough; "but this ought to be near you now. Can you see it?"

"Yes; but it is a dozen feet too high," he replied. "It won't reach me."

"Yes, it will," I roared, for there was a despairing tone in those last words. "Plenty more. Look out!"

I lowered away, and then shouted again:

"That enough?"

"Yes," he said, with a little more spirit in his tone; "it's long enough, but quite out of my reach—a couple of yards away, and I dare not move."

"I'll swing it to and fro till it comes close. Look out! Here goes."

I began to swing the rope; and as it went to and fro it sent small stones rattling down and then splashing into the water, making me shiver. But they evidently fell clear of Denham, who sent a thrill of encouragement through me when he now spoke more cheerily.

"That's right," he said, and his words were repeated by the echoes. "A little more—a little more. No. Harder. It keeps catching among the stones. Give a good swing."

I did as he told me, and then nearly let go, for he uttered a wild cry, almost a shriek. The next moment there was a peculiar rattling sound; the lamp flashed out brilliantly and lighted up the shaft; there was a sharp hiss, followed by a splash, and then all was in darkness.

"Denham!" I yelled, and I let the rest of the rope run through my hands till it could hang taut, meaning to slide down it and go to his assistance, for I was sure that all depended upon me now. I was already changing my position, when—my sinking heart, which seemed to suggest that I was about to descend to certain death, giving a sudden bound, and I felt choking—Denham spoke again.

"I couldn't stop the lamp," he said; "the rope caught it and knocked it off the ledge; but I've got hold."

"Hurrah!"

I suppose I shouted that word, but it came out involuntarily. Then I listened, my heart beating painfully, for I could hear the poor fellow moving now, but, as it seemed, sending stone after stone rolling and splashing into the water.

However, nerved into action again, I did as he bade me, all the time fearing it was too late, for he shouted hoarsely:

"Pull up, Val—pull! I'm going down."

My hands darted one over the other, the slack seeming endless as I heard a low rushing sound mingled with the splashing of falling stones. Then there was a sharp jerk at my wrists, and the rope began to glide through my hands till I let one leg drop from where my foot rested against the edge of the shaft-mouth, and quick as thought flung it round the rope so that my foot and ankle formed a check; with the result that I was nearly jerked off my seat before the rope was stopped.

"Ah!" came from below, and I heard no falling of stones now; but there was a splashing and dripping sound which for the moment I did not understand. Once more I thought all was over, for the rope seemed to slacken; but hope came again.

"Pull up steadily," came in firmer tones; and, though I could not see, I supposed that Denham had drawn his feet from the water and was trying to climb up the rope. I knew it was so directly, for he spoke.

"I've got the rope well under my arms," he panted out, "and if you keep hauling gently, I think perhaps I can climb up the side; but you must be ready for a slip. Can you pass it round anything?"

"Yes," I said; and as the rope was eased I got both legs back into their position again, thus hindering my power of hauling dreadfully, but guarding against the rope being dragged down again rapidly by passing it over my right leg and under the left.

"Are you sure you can hold on if I slip?" said Denham now.

"Yes, if you come slowly. The rope's strong enough, and I'll get it up a yard at a time, so that's all the distance you can pull."

"Ah!" he cried; "then I can use both hands, and climb with more confidence. Now then, I'm coming up."

"Ready!" I shouted; and I toiled on with the perspiration moistening my hands as I steadily hauled with my right and left alternately, gaining a foot with one and making it secure over and under my legs with the other. All the while I could hear him painfully climbing as if gaining confidence with every yard he came nearer the surface.

"Now rest," he said, and I could hear him breathing hard.

Stones had fallen again and again as he climbed; but I was getting accustomed to their rattle and sullen plunge, for so long as the rope proved true they were robbed of their terrible meaning. Just, however, as my poor comrade said he meant to take a rest, there was another sharp jerk which told that his foothold had given way, and for a moment or two I was wondering whether I could hold on, as I listened to the falling of many stones. Once more he gained a good footing, and from where he half-hung, half-lay, he began to talk slowly about his position.

"It's like climbing up the side of a house built of loose stones," he said in a low tone; "but I mean to do it now if you can keep hold of the rope firmly."

"I can," I said.

"Ah! It's a horrible place, Val; but you give me confidence. Now then, I'm rested. Can you haul up more quickly? I want to get it done?"

"No," I said quietly; "I can only just make the rope safe."

"Very well. Go on as you like. There, I'm going to begin."

"Go on," I said; and once more the painful climb went on, with the stones falling and splashing, and the sound of Denham's breath at times coming to my ears in sobs which seemed terribly loud. It did not last many minutes; but no more agony could have been condensed into hours, and no hours could have seemed longer than the interval during which I strove to save my companion from death.

However, all things come to an end; and at last, when I was nervously on the *qui vive* for another slip, and just when Denham seemed to be creeping painfully up, though still many feet below, I suddenly felt one of his hands touch my ankle, and the other get a good grip of the rope where it lay cutting into my leg. Then I heard his feet grating and scraping against the side, and my heart leaped as he threw himself on his side away from the mouth of the hole, and lay perfectly still.

"Ah!" I cried; "at last!" and, freeing my legs from the rope, I moved painfully after him; but at the first attempt I felt as if the darkness was lighting up, flashes played about my eyes, there was a horrible swinging round of everything in my head, and I sank down, crawled aside a little way instinctively to get from the shaft-mouth, and then for a few moments all was blank. Not more than a few moments, however, for Denham roused me by speaking.

"Is anything the matter?" he said.

"Matter?" I replied, as the absurdity of his question seemed to surprise me. "Oh no, nothing at all the matter, only that my head feels as if it had been crushed by a stone, and we had just saved ourselves from the most terrible death that could have come to two poor wretches who want to live. It's very comic altogether—isn't it?"

Denham sat in silence, and we could hear the firing still going on. At last he spoke with a low, subdued voice.

"Yes," he said, "we have escaped from a horrible death. Val, old fellow, I shall never forget this. But don't let us talk about it. Let us talk about who did it. Some one must have struck at us and knocked us down that hole."

"Yes," I said; "and there's only one 'some one' who could have done it."

"That renegade Irishman?"

"Yes," I replied. "It seems like this: he couldn't have got away, but must have been in hiding here. He couldn't escape the watchfulness of the sentries, I suppose."

"No; and he must have managed to get that rope to let himself down from the walls."

"To let himself down into a place where he could hide, I think," was my reply.

"For both purposes. But what a place to hide in!" said Denham, with a shudder. "He could not have known what he was doing, or he would not have gone down."

"I believe he went down and was afraid to stay. Of course he was hiding somewhere here when we came along with the light."

"And then struck us down. Are you much hurt?"

"I don't know," I replied. "I forgot all about it for the time in the excitement of trying to escape. How are you?"

"My head hurts me badly now. I believe I was struck with a heavy stone."

"Of course. That was the wretch's trick, and how he served poor Sam Wren. Here, let's go to the hospital. I feel as if I want to see the doctor."

"Yes," said Denham faintly. "I hope he has no more wounded after all this firing."

Denham rose to his knees in the darkness, and I did the same, bringing on the giddy feeling once more, so that I was glad to lean against the wall of the great passage.

"What is the matter?" said my companion.

"Not much; only a bit dizzy," I replied; "and my legs feel so awfully stiff and strained that I can hardly stand."

"My head swims too," said Denham. "I am glad to lean against the wall. Ah! Look! here is some one coming with a light."

I uttered a sigh of relief, and then, taking a good deep breath, I gave a hail which brought half-a-dozen men to us, headed by Sergeant Briggs, who uttered an ejaculation of surprise as he held up the wagon lantern he carried and let the light fall on our faces.

"Why, you gents haven't run up against that savage sham Paddy, have you?" he cried.

"Yes, Sergeant," said Denham, speaking faintly; "and he got the better of us."

"He has, sir, and no mistake."

"Have you caught him, Briggs?" I asked anxiously.

"No, my lad; I only wish we had. I never saw such shots as our men are! Wasted no end of cartridges, and not one of 'em hit. Did nothing but draw the enemy's fire, and they have been answering in the dark. All waste."

"But Moriarty?" asked Denham.

"Moriarty!" said the Sergeant scornfully. "I'm Morihearty well sick of him, sir. It's all easy enough to see now. Instead of getting away, as we thought, after hammering poor Sam Wren with a stone, my gentleman's been in hiding."

"Yes," I said.

"Yes it is, my lad. Then he's been sneaking about in the dark, going about among the men like a sarpent, and then among the horses, helping himself to the reins with his knife."

"To join together and make a rope to let himself down from the wall," I said.

"That's right, my lad—right as right; and all our chaps asleep, I suppose—bless 'em! They ought to be ashamed of theirselves. There was quite a dozen nice noo reins missing, and half of 'em gone for ever."

"Not quite, Sergeant," said Denham; "take your light and look carefully down yonder."

The Sergeant stared, but did as he was told, holding the lantern low down by the crossing-stone.

"Well, I am blessed!" he cried. "Here, one of you, come and loosen this knot and coil the ropes up carefully.—But, I say, Mr Denham, how did they come there?"

Denham told him briefly of our adventure, and of what we surmised.

He whistled softly, and then said, "Why, I wonder you're both alive. You do both look half-dead, gentlemen; and no wonder. This accounts for one lot, though. The others were tied together and one end made fast to a big stone—a loose one atop of the wall. He must have slid down there and got away. I never saw such sentries as we've got. All those cartridges fired away, and not one to hit. Why, they ought to have pumped him so full of lead that he couldn't run. Run? No; so that he couldn't walk. But you two must come to the Colonel and let him know."

"No, no! Take us to Dr Duncombe," said Denham.

"Afterwards, sir."

"Then you must carry me," said Denham, with a groan.

"Right, sir.—Here, two of you, sling your rifles and dandy-chair your officer to the Colonel's quarters. Two more of you serve young Moray same way."

"No," I said, making an effort. "One man give me his arm, and I'll try to walk."

"So will I," said Denham, making an effort. "That's right, Val; we won't go into hospital, only let the doctor stick a bit or two of plaster about our heads for ornament. Now then, give me an arm."

The result was that we mastered our suffering, and were led by the Sergeant's patrol to the officers' rough quarters. The first thing the Colonel did was to summon the doctor, who saw to our injuries, while Denham unburdened himself of our adventures, my head throbbing so that I could not have given a connected narrative had I tried.

Denham protested stoutly afterwards that there was no need for the doctor's proposal that we should be sent to the hospital to be carried into effect, and appealed to the Colonel.

"Look at us both, sir," he said. "Don't you think that after a good night's sleep we shall both be fit for duty in the morning?"

"Well, Mr Denham, to speak candidly," was the reply, "you both look as dilapidated as you can possibly be; so you had better obey the doctor's orders. I give you both up for the present."

Denham groaned, and I felt very glad when a couple of the Sergeant's guard clasped wrists to make, me a seat; and as soon as I had passed my arms over their shoulders their officer gave the word, and we were both marched off to the sheltered hospital, where I was soon after plunged in a heavy stupor, full of dreams about falling down black pits, swinging spider-like, at the end of ropes which I somehow spun by drawing long threads of my brains out of a hole in the back of my head, something after the fashion of a silkworm making a cocoon.

Then complete insensibility came on, and I don't remember anything. But on the day following Denham and I lay pretty close together, talking, and looking up at the sky just above, one of the wagon-tilt curtains being thrown back.

Chapter Thirty Seven
A Hospital Visitor

"Hang being in hospital!" Denham said over and over again. "I seem to be always in hospital. There never was such an unlucky beggar."

I sighed deeply.

"It is miserable work," I said.

"Yes; and it seems so absurd," said Denham. "There's something wrong about it."

"Of course," I said; "we're wounded, and suffering from the shock of what we've gone through."

"Gammon!" said Denham. "That wouldn't knock us up as it has. We both got awful toppers on the skull; but that wouldn't have made us so groggy on the legs that we couldn't stand."

"Oh, that's the weakness," I replied.

"My grandmother! It's your weakness to say so. We're made of too good stuff for that. Why, you were as bad as I was when the hospital orderly washed us. Bah! How I do hate being washed by a man!"

"Better than nothing," I said. "We can't have women-nurses."

"No," said Denham. "But what was I saying when you interrupted so rudely? Really, Val Moray, I shall report your behaviour to the Colonel. You're not respectful to your officer. You're always forgetting that you are a private."

"Always," I replied, with what was, I fear, a very pitiful smile, for my companion looked at me very sympathetically and shook his head.

"Poor old chap!" he said; "I am sorry for you. There, he shall be disrespectful to his officer when he isn't on duty. I say, old chap, I wish you and I were far away on the veldt shooting lions again. It's far better fun than fighting wild Boers."

"What a poor old joke!" I said.

"Best I can do under these untoward circumstances, dear boy," he said. "Yes, it's a 'wusser.' I wish I could say something good that would make you laugh. But to 'return to our muttons,' as the French say. About being so weak. You and I have no business to shut up like a couple of rickety two-foot rules when we are set up on end. It's disgusting, and I'm sure it's old Duncombe's fault."

"No, you're not," I said.

"Well, I say I am, just by way of argument. It's all wrong, and I've been lying here and thinking out the reason. I've got it."

"I got it without any thinking out at all," I said.

"Don't talk so, private. Listen. Now, look here, it's all Duncombe's fault."

"That we're alive?" I said.

"Pooh! Nonsense! It's that anti-febrile tonic, as he calls it. It's my firm belief that he hadn't the right sort of medicine with him, and he has fudged up something to make shift with."

"What nonsense!" I said.

"It's a fact, sir, and I'll prove it. Now then, where are we hurt?"

"Our heads principally, of course."

"That's right, my boy. Then oughtn't he to have given us something that would have gone straight to our heads?"

"I don't know," I said wearily.

"Yes, you do, stupid; I'm telling you. He ought to have given us something that affected our heads, instead of which he has given us physic that has gone to our legs. Now, don't deny it, for I watched you only this morning, and yours doubled up as badly as mine did. You looked just like a young nipper learning to walk."

I laughed slightly.

"No, no, don't do that," cried my companion in misfortune.

"You were wishing just now that you could make me laugh," I said, by way of protest.

"Yes, old chap; but I didn't know then what the consequences would be. It makes you look awful. I say, don't do it again, or I shall grow horribly low-spirited. You did get knocked about. I say, though, do I look as bad as you do?"

"I believe you look ten times worse," I said, trying to be cheerful and to do something in the way of retort.

"No, no; but seriously, do I look very bad?"

"Awfully!" I said.

"Oh, I say! Come, now, how do I look?"

"Well, there's all the skin off your nose, where you scratched against the rock."

"Ye–es," he said, patting his nose tenderly; "but it's scaling over nicely. I say, what a good job I didn't break the bridge!"

"It was indeed," I said.

"Well, what else?"

"Your eyes look as if you'd been having a big fight with the bully of the school."

"Are they still so very much swollen up?"

"More than ever," I said, in comforting tones.

"But they're not black?"

"No; only purple and yellow and green."

"Val," he cried passionately, "if you go on like that I'll sit up and punch your head."

"You can't," I replied.

"No, you coward! Oh, if I only could! It's taking a mean advantage of a fellow. But never mind; I'm going to hear it all. What else?"

"I won't tell you any more," I replied.

"You shall. Tell me at once."

"You don't want to know about that place on the top of your head, just above your forehead, where you are so fond of parting your hair?"

"Yes, I do. I say, does it look so very bad?"

"Shocking. He has crossed the strips of sticking-plaster over and over, and across and across, till it looks just like a white star."

"Oh dear," he groaned, "how horrid! I say, though, has he cut the hair in front very short?"

"Well, not so short as he could have done it with a razor."

"Val!" he shouted. "It's too bad."

"Yes," I said; "it looks dreadful."

"No, I mean of you; and if you go on like that again we shall quarrel."

"Let's change the conversation, then," I said. "I say, oughtn't old Briggs to have been here by now?"

"I don't know; but you oughtn't to give a poor weak fellow such a slanging as that."

"I say," I said, "you wished we were up the veldt shooting lions."

"So I do," replied Denham. "Don't you?"

"No. I wish you and I were at my home, with old Aunt Jenny to nurse and feed us up with beef-tea and jelly, and eggs beaten up in new milk, and plenty of tea and cream and—"

"Val! Val, old chap! don't—don't," cried Denham; "it's maddening. Why, we should have feather-beds and beautiful clean sheets."

"That we should," I said, with a sigh; "and— Ah! here's old Briggs."

"Morning, gents," said the Sergeant, pulling back the tilt curtain after entering. "Hope you're both better."

"Yes, ever so much, Sergeant," cried Denham. "Here, come and sit down. Light your pipe and smoke."

"What about the doctor, sir?" said Briggs dubiously.

"Won't be here for an hour. I'll give you leave. Fill and light up."

The Sergeant obeyed orders willingly.

"Now then," said Denham, "talk away. I want to know exactly how matters stand since yesterday."

"All right, sir," said the Sergeant, carefully crushing out the match he had struck, as he smoked away.

"Well, go on," said Denham impatiently. "You said yesterday that things were as bad as they could possibly be."

"I did, sir."

"Well, how are they now?"

"Worse. Ever so much worse."

"What do you mean, you jolly old muddler?" cried Denham, rousing up and looking brighter than he had been since he came under the doctor's hands.

"What I say, sir," replied the Sergeant, staring. "Things are ever so much worse."

"Val," cried Denham, turning to me, "poor old Briggs has had so much to do with that scoundrel Moriarty that he has caught his complaint."

"I beg pardon, sir," growled the Sergeant stiffly; "I've always been faithful to Her Majesty the Queen."

"Of course you have, Sergeant."

"Beg pardon, sir. You said I'd caught his complaint, meaning I was turning renegade."

"Nothing of the kind; but you have caught his national complaint, for there you go again—blundering. Can't you see?"

"No, sir," said the Sergeant, drawing himself up stiffer than ever.

"Then you ought to. Blundering—making bulls. If the state of affairs was as bad as it could be yesterday, how can it be worse to-day?"

The Sergeant scratched his head, and his countenance relaxed.

"Oh!" he said thoughtfully, "of course. I didn't see that at first, gentlemen."

"Never mind, so long as you see it now. But go ahead, Briggs. You can't think what it is to be lying here in hospital, with fighting going on all round, and only able to get scraps of news now and then."

The Sergeant chuckled.

"Here, I don't see anything to laugh at in that," cried Denham, frowning. "Do you find it funny?"

"I just do, sir. Think of you talking like that to me? Why, twice over when I was in the Dragoons I was bowled over and had to go into hospital, up north there, in Egypt. Thirsty, gentlemen? I was thirsty, double thirsty, in the nasty sandy country—thirsty for want of water, and twice as thirsty to get to know how things were going on. That's why I always come, when I'm off duty, to tell you gentlemen all I can."

"There, Val," cried Denham, beaming. "Didn't I always say that old Briggs was a brick?"

"I don't remember," I replied.

"Well, I always meant to.—Now then, Sergeant, go ahead."

"Nay! I don't want to damp your spirits, sir, seeing how bad you are."

"I'm not bad, Sergeant; neither is Moray. We're getting better fast, and news spurs us on to get better as fast as we can. Now then, don't make us worse by keeping us in suspense. Tell us the worst news at once."

"That's soon done, sir. These Doppies, as they call 'em—these Boers—shoot horribly well."

"Yes," sighed Denham; "they've had so much practice at game."

"They've got so close in now, with their wagons to hide behind, that I'm blessed if it's safe for a sentry to show his head anywhere."

"But our fellows have got stone walls to keep behind, and they ought by now to shoot as well as the Boers," I said.

"That's quite right, Mr Moray," cried the Sergeant, angrily puffing at his pipe; "they ought to, but they don't—not by a long way. Every time they use a cartridge there ought to be one Doppie disabled and sent to the rear. I keep on telling them this fort isn't Purfleet Magazine nor Woolwich Arsenal; but it's no good."

"But, Sergeant," cried Denham anxiously, "you don't mean to say that we're running out of cartridges?"

"But I do mean to say it, sir; and the time isn't so very far off when we shall either have to hang out the white flag—"

"What!" cried Denham, dragging himself up into a sitting position. "Never!"

"Or," continued the Sergeant emphatically, "make a sortie and give the beggars cold steel."

"Ah! that sounds better," cried Denham, dropping back upon his rough pillow. "That's what we shall have to do."

"Right, sir," cried the Sergeant. "Cold steel's the thing. I've always been a cavalry man, and I've seen a bit of service before I came into the Light Horse as drill-sergeant and general trainer. I've been through a good deal, and learned a good deal; and I tell you two young men that many a time in a fight I've felt wild sitting on horseback here, and trotting off there, dismounting to rest our horses; finding ourselves under fire again, and cantering off somewhere else—into a valley, behind a hill, or to the shelter of a wood, because our time hadn't come—and the infantry working away all the while. I'm not going to run down the cavalry; they're splendid in war when they can get their chance to come to close quarters. You see, we haven't done much with our swords, for the Doppies won't stand a charge.

Where we've had them has been dismounted, as riflemen, and that's what our trouble is now. We can't get at the enemy; what we want is a regiment of foot with the bayonet. Just a steady advance under such cover as they could find, and then a sharp run in with a good old British cheer, and the Doppies would begin to run. Then we ought to be loosed at them, and every blessed Boer among them would make up his mind that it was quite time he went home to see how his crops are getting on."

"Yes, Sergeant," said Denham gravely; "that's exactly the way to do it, and that's what people at home are saying. But we're shut up here, ammunition is failing, and we have no regiment of foot to give the brutes the cold steel and make them run; so what's the best thing to do under the circumstances?"

Chapter Thirty Eight
The Sergeant's Notion

"Ah!" said the Sergeant, tapping the ashes out of his pipe and refilling it; "that's a bit of a puzzle, sir."

"Hang out the white flag?" cried Denham bitterly.

"No, sir," cried the Sergeant fiercely.

"What then?" I said.

"What then, sir?" said Briggs fiercely. "We've got plenty of pluck and lots of fight in the boys."

"Yes," said Denham, with his eyes flashing. "Plenty of prime beef and good fresh water, Briggs; but scarcely any cartridges."

"That's right, sir; and so I took the liberty, when I got a chance, of saying a word to the Colonel."

"What about?"

"The Doppies' ammunition-wagons, sir."

"Ah!" cried Denham, rising to his elbow. "I ventured to say, sir, that the young officer as brought in our supply of provisions would have laid himself flat down on the top o' the wall and watched with his glass till he had made out where the best spot was, and then after dark he'd have gone out and made a try to capture one of the ammunition-wagons, and brought it in."

"Impossible, Sergeant," said Denham.

"Bah! That word isn't in a soldier's dictionary, sir. You'd have done it if you'd been well enough."

"But the cartridges mightn't fit our rifles, Sergeant."

"Mightn't, sir; but they might. Then, if the first lot didn't, you'd have gone again and again till you had got the right sort. If none of 'em was the right sort, why, you'd ha' said, 'There's more ways of killing a cat than hanging it,' and gone on another plan."

"What other plan?" I said sharply. "There is no other plan."

"Isn't there?" said the Sergeant, grinning. "They've got one wagon that I can swear to, having made it out through the glass Mr Denham lent me, full of spare rifles of the men put out of action."

"Of course, of course," cried Denham. "Oh dear! oh dear!" he groaned, falling back again with a pitiful look in his eyes. "I'm lying here, completely done for. Why can't that doctor put us right?"

The Sergeant smoked on for a few minutes, looking fiercer than ever.

"Where's Sam Wren, sir?" he said suddenly.

"He was fretting so much last night at being kept in hospital," I replied, "that the doctor said he might rejoin his troop."

"Glad of that. He's one of our best shots. But what's gone of your blacky, Mr Moray?"

"Joeboy? I don't know," I said. "Isn't he with the horses? Oh, of course he'd be looking after mine."

"He ain't, then," said the Sergeant.

"What!" I cried excitedly; "then what about my horse? I've been lying here thinking of nothing but myself. I ought to have seen to him."

"Couldn't," said the Sergeant dryly. "But he's all right."

"Are you sure?" I cried.

The Sergeant nodded. "I saw to him myself. I like that horse."

"Oh Sergeant!" I said, with a feeling of relief. "But what about Joeboy? I did wonder once why he had not been to see me."

"I didn't look after him, sir," said the Sergeant. "He's a sort of free-lancer, and not under orders."

"But when did you see him last?" I asked.

"Well, I'm a bit puzzled about that. I say, hear that?"

"Hear them? Yes, of course," said Denham angrily. "The brutes! The cowards! Oh, if I were only well!"

"Oh, let 'em alone, sir," said the Sergeant coolly as, beginning with a few scattered shots, the firing outside had rapidly increased. "They're doing no harm. Do you know what it is?"

"Our poor fellows exposing themselves thoughtlessly, I suppose," said Denham bitterly.

"Only their hats, sir. It's about the only pleasure the poor lads have. It's a game they have for pennies. Some one invented it yesterday. Six of 'em play, and put on a penny each. Each game lasts five minutes, and the players put their hats upon the top of a stone. Then the man who has most bullets through his hat takes the pool."

"What folly!" said Denham fretfully.

"Well, as I told them, sir, it isn't good for their hats; but, as they said, it wastes the Doppies' cartridges, and pleases the lads to make fools of 'em. You can hear them cheer sometimes when a hat is suddenly pulled down. They think they've killed a man—bless 'em! They're very nice people."

"But, Sergeant, you were telling me about Joeboy," I said. "Can't you think when you saw him last?"

"Not exactly. I've been trying to think it out, because I expected you'd be asking about him. It strikes me that the last I saw of him was the night I was going the rounds after the search for that Irish prisoner. Perhaps he's tired of being shut up?"

"No," I said emphatically.

"Those blacks are men who are very fond of running wild."

"Joeboy wouldn't forsake me, Sergeant," I said impressively.

"Perhaps you're right. He always did seem very fond of you—never happy unless he was at your heels; but he hasn't been hanging about the hospital, you see. It looks like as if that Irishman had given him a crack on the head too, and pitched him down one of the mine-holes."

"Oh no; horrible!" I said.

"Glad you take it that way," said Briggs grimly, "because it would be bad for the water. Well, there's only two other things I can think of just now. One's that he might have been shot by the enemy when driving in the cattle."

"Is it possible?" I said, in alarm.

"Well, yes, it's possible," said the Sergeant; "but I didn't hear any one hint at such a thing happening."

"Oh, surely the poor fellow hasn't come to his end like that! Here, what was your other idea?"

"I thought that, being a keen, watchful sort of fellow, perhaps he might have caught sight of our prisoner escaping."

"Ah!" I ejaculated.

"Yes; and knowing what I do of my gentleman, it seemed likely that he might have followed him just to see that he didn't get into more mischief, particularly if he saw him upset you two."

"No, no; he couldn't. We saw no sign of him," I said excitedly.—"Did you, Denham?"

"Who could see a fellow like that in the dark?" cried Denham peevishly.

"It is possible that, knowing what he did of Moriarty's treatment of me, he may have felt that he had a kind of feud with him, and watched him."

"For a chance to say something to him with one of those spears he carried," said Denham, suddenly growing interested in our remarks.

"Oh no. I don't think he would use his assagai except in an emergency."

"That would be an emergency," said the Sergeant. "I've thought it out over my pipe, and this is what I make of it: he has followed Master Moriarty, and I expect that we shall never hear of him again."

"What! Joeboy?" I cried.

"No; Master Moriarty."

"But that would be murder—assassination," I cried.

"You can use what fine words you like over it," said the Sergeant gruffly; "but I call it, at a time like this, war; and when Mr Joe Black comes back—as I expect he will, soon—and you ask him, he'll say he was only fighting for his master; and that's you."

I was silenced for the moment, though my ideas were quite opposed to the Sergeant's theory.

But Denham spoke out at once.

"That's all very well, Sergeant," he said, "but Mr Moray's black boy is about as savage over his ideas of justice as he is over his ideas of decency in dress. He looks upon this man as an enemy, and his master's enemy; and if he overtakes Moriarty he won't have a bit of scruple about sticking his spear through him."

"And serve him jolly well right, sir."

"No, no; that won't do," said Denham.

"Not at all," I cried, recovering my balance a little.

"But isn't he a renegade, sir?" said the Sergeant.

"We call him so," replied Denham.

"And didn't he attack you two and try to murder you, sir, just as he did poor Sam Wren?"

"Yes, I grant all that, Sergeant; but we're not savages. Now, suppose you had gone in chase of this man, and say you had caught him. Would you have put your revolver to his head and blown out his brains?"

"That ain't a fair question, sir," said the Sergeant gruffly; "and all I've got to say is, that I'm very glad, knowing what I do, that I wasn't in pursuit of him, sword in hand."

"You mean to say that you would have cut him down?" I cried.

"I don't mean to say anything at all, Mr Private Moray, only that I've got my feelings as a soldier towards cowards. There, I won't say another word."

"Then I'll speak for you," said Denham. "You wouldn't have cut the scoundrel down, nor shot him, but you'd have done your duty as trained soldiers do. You'd have taken him prisoner, and brought him in to the Colonel."

"And he'd have had him put up against the nearest wall before a dozen rifles and shot for a murderous traitor, sir."

"But not without a court-martial first, Briggs," said Denham sternly.

"I suppose you're right, sir; but I don't see what comfort a trial by court-martial can be to a man who knows that he's sure to be found guilty and shot."

"But not till he has been justly condemned," I put in.

"Like to know any more about what's going on round about the fort, sir?" said the Sergeant, after giving me a queer look.

"Yes, of course," cried Denham.

"Well, not much, sir. Colonel's always going round about to see that the men don't expose themselves, and I expect that at any time there'll be orders given that neither the horses nor the bullocks are to be driven out to graze."

"Then they are all driven out?" I said.

"Of course, sir. We couldn't keep the bullocks alive without."

"I wonder the Boers don't shoot them," I said.

"Don't like shooting their own property," said the Sergeant, with a grin. "They're always hoping they'll get 'em back; but they'll have to look sharp if they do, for if they're much longer we shall have eaten the lot."

"Take some time to do that, Sergeant," said Denham, laughing.

"Not such a very long time, sir. You see, the men have nothing but water to drink; tobacco's getting scarce; there's no bread, no coffee, no vegetables; and the men have very little to do but rub down their horses to keep 'em clear of ticks: the consequence is that they try to make up for it all by keeping on eating beef, and then sleeping as hard as ever they can."

"I don't know what we can do unless we cut our way through the enemy," said Denham sadly. "I go on thinking the matter over and over, and always come back to the same idea."

"No wonder," said the Sergeant. "That is the only way; so the sooner you two get fit to mount the better, for I don't see that anything can be done till then."

"Are there any more—cripples?" said Denham bitterly.

"Oh, there's a few who'd be off duty if things were right," said the Sergeant cheerfully; "but they make shift. The Colonel limps a bit, and uses his sword like a walking-stick; six have got arms in slings, and four or five bullet-scratches and doctor's patches about 'em; but there isn't a man who doesn't show on parade and isn't ready to ride in a charge."

"But riding," I said, with the eagerness of one who is helpless—"what about the horses?"

"All in fine condition, gentlemen," said the Sergeant emphatically, "but a bit too fine, and they look thin. The Colonel's having 'em kept down so that they shan't get too larky from having no work to do."

"But they're not sent out to graze now?" I said.

"Oh yes, regularly."

"Then why don't the Boers shoot them, so as to make them helpless?"

The Sergeant chuckled.

"Colonel's too smart for them," he said. "The bullocks are sent out in the day with a strong guard on foot to keep behind the oxen, but the horses go out as soon as it's dark, every one with his man to lead him, and all ready for an attack. Ah! but it's miserable work, and I shall be very glad when you two gentlemen are ready to mount again, so that we can go."

"You'll have to go without us, Briggs," said Denham sadly. "I don't suppose the Boers will shoot us if we're taken prisoners."

"That's just what the Colonel's likely to do, sir. It's his regular way with his men. I must be off now, though. Time's up. You'll like to see this, though, Mr Denham?"

The Sergeant began to fumble in his pouch, bringing out several cartridges before he found what he wanted—a dirty-looking piece of milky quartz.

"What have you got there?" we asked in a breath.

"Stuff the men are finding in a hole at the back of the cook's fireplace."

"Why, it's gold ore," I said eagerly.

"Nonsense! What do you know about it?" said Denham, turning the lump over in his hand.

"I know because pieces like that are in the kopje near my home. Joeboy could find plenty like that. He took some to my father once, and father said it was gold."

"Then you've got a mine on your farm?"

"I suppose so; but father said we'd better get rich by increasing the flocks and herds. Look there," I said; "all those are veins of gold, and those others are crystals and scales."

"There, catch, Sergeant," said Denham bitterly. "We don't want gold; we want health, and a way out of this prison."

"That's right, sir; and if you like I'll try and come and tell you how things are going to-night."

"Yes, do," cried Denham. Then the Sergeant thrust his piece of gold ore and quartz back into his pouch, and marched away.

"Val, old chap," said Denham as soon as we were alone, "that fellow seemed to cheer me up a bit while he was here."

"Yes," I said; "he roused me up too."

"But now he's gone I'm down again lower and lower than ever I was before. I begin to wish I were dead. Oh dear! who'd be a wounded man who feels as helpless as a child?"

I was silent.

"Is that doctor ever coming to see us again?"

"Yes," said a sharp, clear voice. "Now then, most impatient of all patients, how are you getting on?"

"Getting ready for the firing-party to waste a few cartridges over, doctor. Can't you see?"

"Humph!" said our visitor, feeling the poor fellow's head and then his pulse. "Here, drink a little of this."

"More physic?" groaned Denham despondently.

"Yes, Nature's," replied the doctor, holding out a folding cup which he had refilled. "Fresh water; a bucket just brought to the screen there by the orderly."

As he spoke he raised the poor fellow up with one arm and held the cup to his lips.

Denham took a few drops unwillingly, then a little more, and finally finished the cupful with avidity, while the sight of my companion drinking seemed to produce a strange, feverish sensation in my throat.

The next minute the doctor had let Denham sink down, and refilled the cup and handed it to me. It was delicious, and I drained the little vessel all too soon. Then I was gently lowered, and the doctor repeated the dose with us both.

"That's better," he said quietly. "You two fellows have been talking too much; now shut your eyes and have a good long sleep."

"What! in the middle of the day?" protested Denham.

"Yes. Nature wants all your time now for healing your damaged places. No more talking. I'll come again by-and-by."

"How absurd!" said Denham as soon as the tilt had fallen back to its place. "I can't sleep now. Can you?"

"Impossible," I said, and I lay looking up at the long slit of blue sky over the wagon-tilt. Then I was looking at something black as ink, and beyond it the slit of blue sky was fiery orange.

"Joeboy?" I said wonderingly.

"Um? Yes, Boss," was the reply.

"How long have you been here?"

"Um? Long, long time. Boss Val been very fass asleep."

"Hist! Is Mr Denham asleep?" I whispered.

"Um? Very fass; not move once."

I was silent for a few moments, struggling mentally to say something, I could not tell what.

"Boss Val like drink o' water?" said the black just then.

"Yes—no. Ah, I remember now," I cried eagerly, for it all came back. "Where have you been all this time?"

The black smiled.

"Um? Been to see Boss and Aunt Jenny."

"You have?" I cried eagerly. "But stop a moment. You went after that Irish captain?"

The black nodded, and, to my horror, his face contracted and his lips drew away from his white teeth, but not in a grin.

I lay back looking at him wildly, and as I gazed in his eyes the appearance of his countenance made me shudder just then, lit up by the fiery glow of the sunset which flooded the place through the openings above the tilt. It seemed to me horrible, and for a long time I could not speak. At last the words came:

"Did you know that he struck down Mr Denham, and nearly killed us both?"

"Um? Yes. Soldiers tell Joeboy."

"And you followed him?"

"Um? Yes," came, accompanied by a nod.

"And you've killed him with your assagai?" I said, with a shudder, as I glanced at where three of the deadly weapons lay at the side of my rough couch, across his shield.

"Um? No. Nearly kill Joeboy."

"Ah!" I cried, with a curious feeling of relief.

"Joeboy run after him all away among the Doppies; when they shoot, Joeboy lie down, and then follow um till he see um. Then he shoot, and — look here."

Joeboy held up his left arm, smiling, and I saw that it was roughly tied up with a piece of coarse homespun.

"He wounded you?"

"Um? Yes. Shot pistol, and make hole here."

"And he got away unhurt?"

"Um? Yes; this time," said the black. "Next time Joeboy make hole froo um somewhere. Hate um."

"But your wound?" I said. "Is it bad?"

"Um? Only little hole. Soon grow up again."

"Now tell me, how are all the people at home — my father, my aunt, and Bob?"

Joeboy shook his head.

"What do you mean?" I said. "Haven't you seen them?"

"Um? No; all gone right away. Doppies been and burnt all up. All gone."

"What's that?" said Denham, who had been awakened by our talking — "the Boers have been and burnt up that jolly old farm?"

"Um? Yes, Boss. All gone."

"The brutes!"

Chapter Thirty Nine
The Doctor's Dose

"Look here, Denham," said the doctor; "you're an ill-tempered, ungrateful, soured, discontented young beggar. You deserve to surfer.— And as for you, sir," he continued, turning to me, "you're not much better."

That was when we were what the doctor called convalescent—that is to say, it was about a fortnight after our terrible experience in the old mine-shaft, and undoubtedly fast approaching the time when we might return to duty.

"Anything else, sir?" said Denham sharply.

I said nothing, but I winced.

"I dare say I could find a few more adjectives to illustrate your character, sir," said the doctor rather pompously; "but I think that will do."

"So do I, sir," said Denham; "but let me tell you that you don't allow for our having to lie helpless here fretting our very hearts out because we can't join the ranks."

"There you go again, sir," cried the doctor. "Always grumbling. Look at you both; wounds healing up."

"Ugh!" cried Denham. "Mine are horrid." I winced again.

"Your muscles are recovering their tone."

"I can hardly move without pain," groaned Denham. I screwed up my face in sympathy.

"Your bruises dying out."

"Doctor!" shouted Denham, "do you think I haven't looked at myself? I'm horrible."

This time I groaned.

"How do you know? You haven't got a looking-glass, surely?"

"No; but I've seen my wretched face in a bucket of water," cried Denham.

"Bah! Conceited young puppy! And compared notes, too, both of you, I'll be bound."

"Of course we have, lying about here with nothing to do but suffer and fret. You don't seem to do us a bit of good."

"What!" cried the doctor. "Why, if it hadn't been for me you'd have had no faces at all worth looking at. Most likely— There, there, there! I won't get into a temper with you both, and tell you what might have happened."

"Both would have died, and a good job too," cried Denham bitterly.

"Come, come!" said the doctor gently; "don't talk like that. I know, I know. It has been very hard to bear, and you both have been rather slow at getting strong again. But be reasonable. This hasn't been a proper hospital, and it isn't now a convalescent home, where I could coax you both back into health and strength. I've no appliances or medicines worth speaking about, and I must confess that the diet upon which I am trying to feed you up is not perfect."

"Perfect, Val!" cried Denham. "Just listen to him. Everything is horrible."

"Quite right, my dear boy," said the doctor; "it is."

"The bread— Ugh! It always tastes of burnt bones and skin and grease."

"Yes," said the doctor, with a sigh; "but that's all the fuel we have for heating the oven now the wagons are burned."

"Then the soup, or beef-tea, or whatever you call it. I don't know which is worst—that which is boiled up in a pannikin or the nauseous mess made by soaking raw beef in a bucket of water."

"But it is warmed afterwards, my dear boy," said the doctor, "and it is extremely nutritious."

"Ugh!" shuddered Denham. "What stuff for a poor fellow recovering from wounds! I can't and I won't take any more of it."

The doctor smiled, and looked hard at the grumbler.

"Won't you, Denham?" he said. "Oh yes, you will; and you're going to have bits of steak to-day, frizzled on ramrods."

"Over a bone fire!" cried Denham. "I'm sick of it all."

"Come, come, come! you're getting ever so much stronger, both of you."

"But are we really, doctor?" I said; "or are you saying this to cheer us up?"

"Ask yourselves, boys. You know as well as I do that you are. Climb up on the wall this morning and sit in the sunshine; but mind you keep well in shelter. I don't want one of the Boers to undo in a moment what has taken me so long to do."

"Oh, I don't know," said Denham dismally. "We're poor sort of machines—always getting out of order."

"Have you two been falling out?" said the doctor, turning to me.

"No," I said; "we haven't had a word. Denham's in rather a bad temper this morning."

"Why, you impudent beggar!" he cried, "for two pins I'd punch your head."

"Bravo!" cried the doctor. "Here, I'll give 'em to you. Humph! No; only got one. Stop a minute; I'll give you a needle out of my case instead. Will that do?"

"Look here, doctor," cried Denham; "I can't stand chaff now."

"Chaff, my dear boy? I'm in earnest. That's right; go at him. Have a really good fight. It will do you good."

"Bah!" cried Denham, as he saw me laughing. "Here, come along up to the wall, Val. I don't want to fall out with the doctor any more."

"That you don't," said that gentleman, offering his hand. "There, good-morning, patients. I know. But cheer up. I like that bit of spirit Denham showed just now. It was a splendid sign. You'll eat the grill when it comes?"

He did not wait for an answer, but bustled away, Denham looking after him till he was out of hearing.

"I wish I hadn't been so snappish with him," he said rather remorsefully. "He has done a lot for us."

"Heaps," I said.

"And we must seem very ungrateful."

"He knows how fretful weak people can be," I said. "Come, let's get up into the sunshine."

For I was having hard work with poor Denham in those days. His sufferings had affected him in a curious way. He was completely soured, and a word or two, however well meant, often sent him into a towering rage. Even then I had to temporise, for he turned impatiently away.

"Hang the sunshine!" he said.

"But it will do you good," I said.

"I don't want to get any good. It only makes me worse. I shall stop down here in the shade."

"I'm sorry," I said, "for I wanted to be up in the fresh air this morning."

"Oh, well, if you want to go I'll come with you."

"Yes, do," I said; and we went out into the great court, where the horses were fidgeting, and biting and kicking at one another, and being shouted at by the men, who were brushing away at their coats to get them into as high a state of perfection as possible. There were the bullocks too, sadly reduced in numbers, and suggesting famine if some new efforts were not made.

"Don't stop looking about," said Denham peevishly. "How worn and shabby the men look! It gives me the horrors."

I followed him, but after his remark I gave a sharp look at the groups of men we passed, especially one long double line going through the sword exercise and pursuing-practice under the instructions of Sergeant Briggs; and as, at every barked-out order, the men made their sabre-blades flash in the sunshine, I felt a thrill as of returning strength run through me; but I noticed how thin, though still active and strong, the fellows looked.

We climbed up the rugged stones, which had gradually been arranged till the way was pretty easy, and reached the top of the wall, now protected by a good breastwork high enough to enable our sentries to keep well under cover.

It was very bright and breezy up there; but Denham did not seem disposed to sit down quietly and rest in the sun, for he stepped up at once to where he could gaze over the breastwork, resting his elbows on the stones and his chin upon his hands.

"Hi, Denham! don't do that," I said. "It's not safe."

"Bah! I want to look out for those ammunition-wagons old Briggs was talking about."

"But—" I began, and then I was silent, for Joeboy had followed us up, and seeing Denham's perilous position, he stepped up behind him, put his hands to his waist, and lifted him down as if he had been a child.

"How dare— Oh, it's you, Blackie," he said, laughing.

It was a strange laugh, and I could see that the poor fellow had a peculiar look in his eyes. For as Joeboy snatched more than lifted him down, *ping*, *whiz*, the humming of two bullets went so close to his head on either side that he winced twice—to right and to left; and *crack, crack* came the reports of the rifles fired from the Boer lines opposite.

"Doppie want to shoot Boss Denham," said Joeboy coolly. "Shoot straight."

"Yes, they shoot straight," said Denham; "but I didn't think— I don't know, though; perhaps I did think. I say, Val," he added in a strange, inconsequent way, as if rather ashamed of his recklessness, "that was rather near—wasn't it?"

"Why do you act like that?" I said reproachfully.

"I suppose it was out of bravado," he replied, seeming to return to his old manner again. "I wanted to show the brutes the contempt I feel for them."

"You only made them laugh to see how quickly your head disappeared when they fired."

"How do you know?" he said sharply.

"Because that's exactly what they would do," I replied.

Denham frowned, and turned to Joeboy.

"Here," he said, "put up that big stone on the edge there."

The black obeyed, and then Denham pointed to another.

"Put that one beside it, and leave just room between them for me to peer out. I want to see whether it's possible to do as you did, Val, and bring out a wagon of cartridge-boxes."

Joeboy raised first one and then another great stone upon the edge as he was told, and Denham stepped up directly to look between them, but bobbed his head and stepped down again directly, for *spat, spat, spat,* three rifle-bullets struck the stones and fell rattling down.

Denham looked sharply towards me, frowning angrily; but I met his eyes without shrinking.

"I wish I wasn't so nervous," he said, by way of apology. "It's from being weak, I suppose."

"It's enough to make a strong man shrink," I said. "Don't look again. The next bullet may come between the stones and hit you."

"But I must look," he said angrily. "It's quite time you and I did something to help."

"If you are hit it will do every one else harm instead of good."

He turned upon me fiercely, but calmed down directly.

"Yes," he said; "I suppose you're right. Oh, here's the Sergeant coming up. He has done drilling, I suppose."

The Sergeant announced that this was so directly after joining us.

"The boys are getting splendid with the sword now," he said, seating himself upon a block of stone and wiping his moist brow; "but it's dreary work not being able to get them to work."

"Tell the Colonel to get them all out, then, and make a charge. We ought to be able to scatter this mob."

"So we could, sir," said the Sergeant gruffly, "but they won't give us a chance. If they'd make a mob of themselves we'd soon scatter them, numerous as they are; but it's of no use to talk; we can't charge wagons and rifle-pits. It wouldn't be fair to the lads. Why, they'd empty half our saddles before we got up to them, and then it would be horrible work to get through. No, it can't be done, Mr Denham, and you know it as well as I do."

"No, I don't," said my companion stubbornly. "It ought to be done. Once we were all through, the enemy would take to flight."

"Once we were all through," said the Sergeant, with a grim chuckle; "but that's it. How many would get through? Now, just put it another way, sir. Say there's only six or seven of them out there, and there's one on our side. That's about how it stands as to numbers. Very well; say you lead that charger of yours out. The Boers see what's going to happen directly, and the minute you're up in the saddle they begin to fire at you—the whole seven."

"You said six," cried Denham.

"Six or seven, sir. Well, let it be six. Don't you think it very likely that one out of the six Doppies would manage to hit you?"

Denham frowned and remained silent, while Joeboy sat all of a heap, his arms round his knees, watching the Sergeant, and I saw his ears twitch as if he were trying hard to grasp the whole of the non-com's theory.

"You think not, sir?" continued Briggs. "Well, I don't agree with you. They'd hit you perhaps before you got far; they'd hit you for certain, you or your horse, before you got close up; and let me tell you that the chances would be ever so much worse if we were galloping up to them in line."

"Yes, you're right, Sergeant," said Denham slowly. "It would be murder, and the chief couldn't, in justice to the men, call upon them to charge. But they'd follow us," he added excitedly.

"Follow their officers, sir? Of course they would, and some of 'em would get through."

"Gloriously," cried Denham.

"Well, I suppose some of those fine writers who make history would call it glorious; but I should call it horrible waste of good stuff. It wouldn't do, sir—it wouldn't do, for there'd be nothing to gain by it. If we could make an opening in the enemy's lines and put 'em a bit into disorder, so as to give a chance for another regiment to slip in and rout 'em, it would be splendid; but to do it your way would be just chucking good men's lives away."

"Yes, yes, Sergeant; you're right, and the Colonel's right, and I'm all wrong. I know better; but my head got so knocked about by that renegade Irishman and my fall down that hole that it doesn't work right yet."

"I know, sir," said the Sergeant, nodding his head. "When you talk in that bitter way I know it isn't my brave, clever young officer speaking; and I say to myself, 'Wait a bit, old man; he'll soon come round.'"

"Thank you, Sergeant; thank you," said Denham, holding out his hand, which Briggs grasped, shook warmly, then turned to me to go through the same business; he did so hotly, for my hand felt crushed, and I vainly tried to respond as heartily, while the tears of pain rose in my eyes, but did not dim them so much that I could not see my torturer's eyes were also moist.

"Well, what are you looking at?" he growled. "I say, don't squeeze a man's hand like that. Why, you've made my eyes water, lad. Look, they're quite wet. Phew! You did squeeze."

"It's because he has so much vice in him, Briggs," said Denham, smiling.

"That's it, Mr Denham. Well, we must wait, for there's nothing to be done but send one or two smart fellows to creep through the enemy's ranks in the night, on foot. You can't get horsemen through."

"You mean, send for help from the nearest British force?" said Denham.

"That's it, sir—some one to tell the officer in command that we shall soon be on our last legs here; but if he'll como on and attack them in the rear, we'll be out and at 'em as soon as we hear the shooting; and if we didn't polish off the Doppies then, why, we should deserve to lose."

"Briggs," said Denham warmly, "of course that's the plan. You ought to have been in command of the corps yourself."

"Ah! now your head's getting a bit the better of you again, sir," replied the Sergeant, "or you wouldn't talk like that. What I say's only second-hand. That's the chief's plan."

"Then why doesn't he carry it out?" I said indignantly.

"You hold your tongue," growled the Sergeant. "You're only a recruit yet, and your head's getting the better of you too.—Yes, Mr Denham, that's the Colonel's own plan, and he's tried it every night for the last twelve nights."

"What!" I cried.

"Yes, my lad; called quietly for volunteers, and sent out twelve of our lads; but so far there don't seem to be one that has got through, and the game gets expensive. There, I must go down again now and get to duty. I saw you two coming up while I was going through the exercise, and I'm very glad to see you both looking so much better.—Well, Joe Black," he said as he turned away, "how's Mr Moray's horse?"

"Um? Coat shine beautiful," said Joeboy.

"And enough to make it, my lad, seeing the way you rub him down."

"Denham," I said that night as we lay wakefully gazing up at the stars, "do you feel any stronger yet?"

"I don't know. I seem to fancy I do. Why?"

"I thought you did because you've been so quiet ever since we had that talk with the Sergeant. I feel stronger."

"Why do you ask?" he said.

"Because I've been thinking that I ought to do that job, and you ought to be on the lookout again, to come to my help if I succeed."

"No," he said quickly; "it's a job for two. I'd go with you."

"But I should take Joeboy."

"Then it's a job for three, Val; we can take our time, and the slower we go perhaps the better. If we get stopped by the Boers, we're wounded and getting away from the fighting."

"Yes, that might do. We do look bad."

"Horribly bad, Val. You look a miserable wreck of a fellow."

"And you, I won't say what," I retorted, a little irritably.

"So much the better. When shall we go—to-night?"

"No. Let's have a good sleep to-night, and talk to Joeboy about it in the morning. To-morrow night as soon as it's dark we'll be off," I said.

"The Colonel won't let us go if we volunteer."

"Of course not. Let's go without leave; but that will look like deserting."

"I don't care what it looks like so long as we can get through and bring help."

"The same here."

"But we ought to steal away to-night," said Denham.

"No; let's have Joeboy. Ha!" I said, with a sigh of relief. "I seem to see my way now, and I shall sleep like a top."

"I'm so relieved, Val, old chap, that I'm half-asleep now. Quite a restful feeling has come over me. Good-night."

"Good-night," I replied; and I have some faint recollection of the rays of a lantern beating down and looking red through my eyelids, and then of feeling a soft hand upon my temples. But the next thing I fully realised was that it was a bright, sunny morning, and that Denham was sitting up in his sack-bed.

"How do you feel?" he cried eagerly.

"Like going off as soon as it's dark."

"So do I," he said. "I'm a deal better now. What's the first thing to do — smuggle some meal to take with us?"

"I don't know," I replied. "Yes, perhaps we'd better take some; and, I say, we must have bandages on our heads as well as the sticking-plaster."

"Of course. Then, I say, as soon as ever we've had breakfast we'll talk to Joeboy."

"Exactly," I replied. "He'll be half-mad to go, and when we've said all we want to him we'll come back and lie down again."

"Oh! What for?"

"So as to rest and sleep all we possibly can, for if all goes well we shan't have a wink to-night."

"Perhaps you're right," said Denham.

"There's one more thing to think about."

"What's that?"

"Our going off without leave," I said—"you an officer, I a private."

"Oh! I say, don't get raising up obstacles."

"I don't want to," I said; "but this is serious."

"Very, for us to run such risks; and of course it isn't according to rule. But it's an exception. Let's argue it out, for it does look ugly."

"Go on," I said, "for I want my conscience cleared."

"Look here, then; what are we going to do?"

"Try and get help, of course."

"Then I consider that sufficient excuse for anything—in a corps of irregulars. Old Briggs would say it was mutinous in the regular army. To go on: if we asked leave, the Colonel or Major would say we were mad, and that we are not fit. Then— Oh, look here, I'm not going to argue, Val. I confess it's all wrong, only there's one thing to be said: we're not going to desert our ranks, for we're both on the sick-list; and, come what may, I mean to go and bring help somehow. You're not shirking the job after sleeping on it?"

"No," I said emphatically. "Now for breakfast, and then we'll have a talk with Joeboy."

Chapter Forty
Joeboy is Missing Again

"What a breakfast!" groaned Denham half-an-hour later.

"Never mind," I said; "we'll get something better, perhaps, to-morrow."

"That we will, even if we commando it at the point of the sword, which is another way of saying we shall steal it. I say, though, the thought of all this is sending new life into me."

"I feel the same," I said; then we sat back waiting till the doctor visited us, examined our injuries, and expressed himself satisfied.

"Another week," he said, "and then I shall dismiss you both. Nature and care will do the rest."

The doctor then left us; and, watching for an opportunity, we called to one of the men passing the hospital, and told him to find the black. However, ten minutes later we found that this might have been saved, for the Sergeant paid us a morning call, and on leaving promised to go round by the horses and send Joeboy to us.

"What news of the messengers?" we asked. The Sergeant shook his head sadly, and replied, "Don't ask me, gentlemen. It looks bad — very bad. The Boers ain't soldiers, but they're keeping their lines wonderfully tight."

"That's our fault," said Denham. "We gave them such lessons by our night attack and the capture of the six wagons and teams."

"I say," said the Sergeant, and he looked from one to the other.

"Well, what do you say?" cried Denham.

"Doctor been changing your physic?"

"Why?" I said.

"Because you both look fifty pounds better than you did yesterday."

"It's the hope that has come, Briggs," cried Denham, his face lighting up.

"Haven't got a bit to spare, have you, sir?" said the Sergeant; "because I should like to try how it would agree with my case, for I'm horribly down in the mouth at present. I don't like the look of things at all."

"What do you mean?" asked Denham.

"I had a look round at the horses, sir, last night."

"Not got the horse-sickness, Briggs?"

"No, sir, not so bad as that; but, speaking as an old cavalry man, I say that they mustn't be kept shut up much longer. But there, I shall be spoiling your looks and knocking your hope over. Good-morning, gentlemen—I mean, lieutenant and private. Glad to see you both look so well. I'll tell Joe Black you want him."

"Yes, he'd upset our hopefulness altogether, Val, if it wasn't for one thing—eh?" said Denham as the wagon-tilt swung to after the Sergeant. "But, I say, that fellow of yours ought to be here by now."

"Yes," I said. But we waited anxiously for quite an hour before the man we had sent came back.

"Can't find the black, sir," he said.

"Did you go to the horses?"

"Yes, sir, and everywhere else."

"You didn't go to the butcher's?" I asked.

"Yes, I did; but he hadn't been there."

"Perhaps he's gone out with the bullock drove."

"No," said the man; "the oxen are being kept in this morning because the Boers have come a hundred yards nearer during the night. They're well in opposite the gateway, and the Colonel's having our works there strengthened."

"The Sergeant didn't say a word about that," Denham said to me.

I shook my head, and turned to the messenger.

"Is he asleep somewhere about the walls?" I asked.

"No; I looked there," was the reply. "He always snoozes up on the inner wall, just above the water-hole. There's a place where a big stone has fallen out and no bullets can get at him. I looked there twice."

"Hasn't fallen down one of the holes, has he?" said Denham.

"Not he, sir," replied the man, laughing. "He'd go about anywhere in the dark, looking like a bit o' nothing, only you couldn't see it in the darkness, and never knock against a thing. It's his feet, I think; they always seem to know where to put theirselves. He wouldn't tumble down any holes."

"Keep a sharp lookout for him, and when you see him send him to me directly."

"Yes, sir," replied the man. "I dessay he'll turn up in the course o' the morning. He's always hiding himself and coming again when you don't expect it."

"I say, Val," cried Denham as soon as we were alone, "we didn't reckon on this. Why, if he doesn't turn up our plan's done."

"Not at all," I said.

"Eh? What do you mean? We couldn't go without him."

"Indeed, but we could; and what's more, we will," I said firmly. "I would rather have had him with us; but we're going to-night—if we can."

Denham seized my hand and wrung it warmly.

"I like that," he said; "but you shouldn't have put in that 'if we can.'"

"Obliged to," I replied. "We may be stopped."

"Oh, but I shall give the password."

"We may find even that will not be enough. The orders are very strict now. Besides, if we did not come back the guard would report us missing, and then there'd be great excitement at once."

"What would you do, then?" he asked.

"Take a lesson out of that Irishman's book."

"Knock two or three sentries on the head with a stone?"

"No, no," I cried, laughing. "Get a couple of reins, tie them together, and then slide down from the wall."

"Good!" exclaimed Denham; and, after a pause: "Better! Yes, that will do. Start from the far corner?"

"No, from just up here where Joeboy arranged the stones. We can tie up to one of those big ones that you stand on to look over. You feel strong enough to slide down?—it isn't far."

"Oh yes."

"Then, once on the ground, we can crawl away. That's how I mean to go all along."

"What about the tethering-ropes?"

"We'll go and have a look at our horses towards evening, slip the coils over our shoulders, and bring them away. No one will interfere."

"Val," he cried, "you ought to be a commissioned officer."

"I don't want to be," I said, laughing. "I want the war to be over, and to be able to find my people, and settle down again in peace. This fighting goes against the grain with me."

"But you always seem to like it, and fight like a fury when we're in for it."

"I suppose it's my nature," I said; "but I don't like it any the better."

We said no more, but waited anxiously in the hope that Joeboy would return, and waited in vain, the time gliding by, some hours being passed in sleep, till we were suddenly aroused by firing. There were two or three fits of excitement in the course of the afternoon, and a smart exchange of shots which at one time threatened to develop into a regular attempt to assault the fort; but it died out at last, direct attack of entrenchments not being in accord with the Boers' ideas of fighting. It is too dangerous for men who like to be safely in hiding and to bring down their enemies as if they were wild beasts of the veldt.

No Joeboy appeared, and in the dusk of evening we went across the yard, had a good look at our horses, stopped patting and caressing them for some time, then went back to the hospital unquestioned and, I believe, unseen, with the coils of raw-hide rope. From that time everything seemed to me so delightfully easy that it prognosticated certain success.

The doctor came at dusk and had a chat; then the Sergeant looked us up to tell us that he had seen nothing of Joeboy, but that the butcher told him he had missed some strips of beef hung up in the sun to make biltong, and that he believed the black had taken them.

"Why?" I asked sharply.

"Because he was so fond of eating; and he said the black would be found curled up amongst the stones somewhere in the kopje among the baboons, sleeping off his feed."

"It isn't true," I said warmly. "Joeboy wouldn't steal unless he knew we were starving, and then it would be to bring it to his master and his master's friend."

"That's what I like in you, Val," said Denham as soon as the Sergeant had left us. "You always stick up for a friend when any one attacks him behind his back."

"Of course," I replied angrily.

"Don't be cross, old man," he cried. "I didn't mean to insult you by calling a black fellow your friend."

"That wouldn't insult me. Joeboy is a humble friend, who would give his life to save mine."

"I wish he was with us, then, so as to make a present of it to somebody if we should be in very awkward quarters."

"I can't understand it," I said; "but we mustn't worry about that now. What about arms?"

"Revolvers under our jackets, out of sight, and a few cartridges in our pouches along with the cake and beef we saved."

"No rifle, bandolier, or sword?" I said thoughtfully.

"Neither one nor the other, my lad. We're going to get through the lines as sick men tired of it all, and whose fighting is done."

"Perhaps to be taken as spies," I said.

"Ugh! Don't talk about it," cried Denham. "We're invalids, and no one can doubt that who looks at your battered head."

"Or yours," I replied. "But look here, Denham; we must give up all idea of capturing wagons. What we have to do is to fetch help."

"Yes, I think so too—get through the Boer lines and find the General's quarters. The other idea was too mad."

We sat in silence for a while, till we felt that the time had come; then we passed our coils of rope over our chests like bandoliers, and strolled out into the dark court, to saunter here and there for a few minutes, listening to the lowing of the oxen or the fidgety stamp of a horse annoyed by a fly. Here Denham exchanged a few words with some of the men. Finally, after a glance at the officers' quarters, from which a light gleamed dimly, Denham led the way to the rough ascent, and with beating heart I followed right up on to the wall. So intense was the darkness that we had to go carefully, not seeing the first sentry till he challenged us and brought us up.

Denham gave the word, and stood talking to the man, who lowered his rifle and rested the butt on the stones.

"How are they to-night?" said Denham. "Quiet?"

"No, sir; they seem to have been having a good eat and drink. More wagons came up from their rear; so the man I relieved told me. It's been a sort of feast, I think. Wouldn't be a bad time for a good attack on the beggars, sir. The boys are, as one of them said, spoiling for a fight."

"Let them wait a bit," said Denham shortly. "It will come."

"The sooner the better, sir," said the sentry; and we went on as far as the next sentry, passing the stones where we had sat to sun ourselves. We talked with this second man about the Boers, received a similar account of the proceedings of the enemy, said "Good-night," and then strolled back to the stones, to sit down for a few minutes, my heart beating harder than ever.

"Now," said Denham at last, in a low tone of voice; "off with your rope, and give me one end. I'll make your line fast to mine, while you secure the other end to that big stone. Tight, mind; I don't want to fall sixty feet and break my neck."

"Nor I," was my reply. "Be sure of your knot, too."

"Right."

Then, in the silence, we each did our part of the task, ending by Denham letting the strong thin rope glide over the edge of the great stones which formed the breastwork. The next minute we stood listening to the sounds from the court, and narrowly watched for our sentries. Far out in the darkness a feeble light or two showed where a lantern burned in the Boer lines. Everything seemed to favour our design, even to the end, and I was breathing hard with excitement, waiting to begin. Just then a hand touched my arm and glided down over my wrist. I knew what it meant, and grasped Denham's hand.

"Good luck to us!" he whispered. "I'll go first and test the rope—hush! I will. As soon as I'm down I shall lie flat and hold on. Ready?"

"Yes."

"Off!"

Chapter Forty One
Our Wild Attempt

Denham's words sounded so loud that, as I dropped on one knee to hold the knot of the rope round the stone to prevent it from slipping, I felt sure that the sentries to right and left must have heard him speak. But it was only due to my excited way of looking at things. For the next minute, after a preliminary rustling, I felt a peculiar thrill run along the hide rope. This went on while I wondered if my companion had made the joining of the two ropes secure, my imagination working so rapidly that I seemed to see the knot stretching and yielding till one of the ends slipped through the loop of the knot, and—

The thrilling sensation had ceased; and the rope, which felt in my hands like some living, vibrating thing, hung loose. The next moment a kink ran up it and dissolved in my hands. It was Denham's way of saying "All right," and I knew my turn had come.

The starting was the difficulty—that creeping over the breastwork, just at a time when my strength was far from at its best; but I tackled the business at once, stepped up on to a stone, seated myself on the top of the breastwork, took tight hold of the rope, raised my legs so that I could lie down, turned upon my face, and then softly swung my legs round so that I could twist my feet about the rope and reduce the weight on my arms. The next minute I was hanging at full length, holding the rope with one hand, the edge of the breastwork with the other, and afraid to move; for, to my horror, *tramp, tramp* came the sound of the approaching sentry to my loft. The perspiration began to ooze out on my face and temples now, and I prepared for a rapid descent, fully expecting the man would see the rope, stop, and, under the impression that I was one of the Boers trying to get into the fort by escalade, would strike me from my hold with the butt of his rifle.

I might have spared myself the horror of those few moments of anxiety; for even when he came nearer I could not see him, and with my head beneath the level of the rough parapet he could not see me, but passed on.

I counted the steps, and at the sixth began to let the hide rope glide slowly through my moist hands.

Soon I felt the knot over my boots stop my progress, and had to slacken the rope off my feet, gliding down till my hands touched the knot. This was, I thought, so very loose that I had either to tighten it or slide quickly down. I chose the latter, and went on so swiftly that my hands were hot with the friction when my feet touched Denham's hands, as he held the rope, and then the ground. I dropped to my knees at once, then lay, panting as if I had run a mile.

Denham placed his lips close to my ear and whispered, "I was afraid the sentry would see you. Here, give me your knife."

I answered by taking it out and placing it in his hands, listening, and wondering then what he was about to do, for he rose to his feet, and I heard a peculiar sound as of cutting something and Denham breathing hard.

He was down by me when the noise ceased, and once more his lips were at my ear.

"Get up and join hands," he whispered. "There's a light straight ahead, and another about a quarter of a mile to the right. We'll make for this last one. Mind, not a sound."

The order was not needed. We rose silently. There, as he had stated, right in front and away to the right, were two of the tiniest sparks of light; they were almost invisible, the nearest being fully a thousand yards off.

Then, hand in hand and step by step, we went on through the pitchy darkness straight for the light on our right. We moved very cautiously, for our first fear was that we might be heard from the walls; and, setting aside the extreme doubtfulness of receiving a bullet in the back from a friend, there was the danger of one shot bringing many, as the sentries carried on the alarm, with the result that every Boer in front would be on the *qui vive* and our venture rendered impossible. But all was perfectly still, while the darkness overhead seemed to press down upon us.

In about ten minutes Denham whispered, "Don't take any notice."

When he had spoken there was a faint, rustling sound, and I knew he had thrown something from him, to fall with a dull sound upon the ground.

"Bother!" he whispered. "I didn't think it would make such a row."

"What was it?" I asked.

"About a dozen feet of hide rope. I cut it off as high as I could reach; but, my word, wasn't it hard!"

"Why did you cut it?"

"So that no Boer, exploring, should run against it and take it into his head to climb up. How do you feel?"

"Rather hot."

"So do I. We're precious weak yet. Now, look here; we'll keep on walking as long as we dare; then we must go down on hands and knees; last of all, we must creep on our chests, helping ourselves along with our elbows."

"It will be very slow work," I said.

"Yes, but it's the only way. We shall do it, for it's gloriously dark. If we come suddenly upon a sentry we must drop on our faces and lie still till I see the way to circumvent him."

"I understand," I said.

"Not all yet. If we get close up you'll have to take the lead; and the thing to do is to get close up among the sleeping Boers. That means safety, for if any one wakes up and speaks you must answer in Dutch, with your face close to the ground."

"It seems very risky," I said.

"So did your going to cut out six wagons with their teams; but you did it. Now, don't talk; come on."

We moved forward again very slowly in what seemed to be a tedious journey, though I knew perfectly well that, taken diagonally, it could not be more than twelve hundred yards, it having been reckoned that the Boers' advance-parties were about a thousand yards from the walls of the fort. But we were getting nearer, for the lights seemed to grow, not brighter, but less dim, and during the last few minutes we had noticed a third light away to the right. I wanted to say that we were getting pretty near to the enemy at last; but talking was now out of the question, and I had to telegraph to my companion, by a pressure of the hand, that we must be on the alert.

Then, with a suddenness that startled my composure, I heard an impatient stamp close by on my left, followed by the sound of reins jerked, and an angry adjuration growled out in Dutch between the teeth by a mounted sentry. He was invisible; and, taking advantage of the startled movements of the horse consequent upon the punishment it had received, Denham dragged heavily upon my right hand with his left, when, as I yielded, he bore off to his right, walking very slowly, till we had left the sentry some distance behind.

Directly after that incident Denham seemed to alter our course again, and once more we were walking straight for the dim lantern. This went on for a short time, and then we had another check, for the sound of tramping feet arose to our right—not the regular beat, beat of well-drilled military, but a rough, heavy, anyhow walk of about a dozen men. They were very near, and the chances were that, whether we stood still, went back, or hurried forward, they might come right upon us. But my companion did not hesitate. He chose to advance, hurrying me forward half-a-dozen steps, and then lay down upon his face. For a few moments I thought we were discovered, and that our attempt was a failure; but the men just missed us, going on twenty or thirty yards, and then a gruff Boer called "Halt!"

From what followed we knew that guard was being changed.

Everything was still succeeding, for, instead of walking right upon a dismounted sentry, we had passed him to our left, and learned not only where the new one was placed, but that we had succeeded in passing the outer line of mounted men and an inner one of foot.

As if telling me of the delight he felt, Denham's pressure on my hand was like the working of some military code; and I responded the best way I could, as we lay listening to the resumed tramp of the guard.

Just as Denham signalled me to rise, there was a sharp crack, a flash of light, and we dropped down again, to look in the direction of the flash, and saw a pair of big hands lighted up as they were held lantern fashion; and, directly after we had glimpses of the lower part of a bearded face, at first seen distinctly, then it grew darker, and again seen plainer as its owner puffed at the big pipe he was lighting. Then all was in darkness once more, and the pungent smoke of coarse tobacco floated to our nostrils.

We started again, crawling on all-fours side by side, and pressing close like sheep so as to keep in touch; but always forward now towards the lantern, which seemed suddenly to be very near.

Denham's lips were close to my ear directly, and he whispered, "We must keep more away from the light. Now you take the lead, crawling very slowly. I shall keep up by touching your heel regularly. If I leave off, stop till I begin again."

I nodded, though it occurred to me directly afterwards that he could not see the nod; but I showed him that I fully understood by bearing off to the left, crawling steadily and softly, and feeling Denham's hand come *tap, tap* regularly upon my heel. All the time I had a presentiment that the Boers must be lying around by the hundred.

In another minute I knew we must be close to oxen, for I could hear them ruminating; and, convinced that a wagon would be before us, with perhaps a dozen men underneath, I bore still more to my left, with Denham following close, till I stopped once more, knowing that horses must be just in front.

I made a short pause now, longing to ask my comrade's advice; but I dared not whisper. So, feeling that probably there would only be about fifty yards of perilous ground to pass over before we had cleared the Boer lines, I did what I imagined was best—bore off a little to the right as I advanced— my idea being to get back towards the oxen and pass softly by the side of the wagon which I believed must be close at hand.

"They'll be asleep," I thought, "and I may get past."

It was all a chance, I knew; but we had been lucky so far, and I hoped that fortune would still favour us. In this spirit I still kept on, crawling now very slowly, till suddenly I let myself subside, for my hand had come in contact with the butt of a rifle lying on the ground.

Denham too must have taken the alarm, for I felt him drawing steadily at my heel, which I read to mean retreat. But I felt there was no retreat, knowing that we had crept right in among a number of sleeping men. So I let myself slowly subside, lying on my chest; and in the effort to cross my arms and let them rest beneath my chin my left elbow struck sharply against a sleeper's face, making him start so violently that he kicked his neighbour, and in an instant there was a furious burst of Boer Dutch oaths and imprecations.

"Quiet!" said a deep, severe voice in Dutch. "There, you've roused the patrol."

My heart sank, for there was the hurried tramp of footsteps approaching, and, worse than all, the gleaming of a lantern, which lit up the heavy body of a man lying right across the way I sought to go, while right and left, and within a foot of me, were two more burly figures. They were all in motion now, and as the lantern was borne closer it was thrown open, and, in what one of my neighbours would have called an *augenblick*, I saw in the background on one side the tilt of a wagon, and on the other the dim forms of horses.

My agony, in spite of feeling Denham's hand pressing firmly on my heel, seemed to have culminated; but the worst was to come, and I shivered, for a high-pitched voice cried in Dutch:

"Hwhat's all this? Didn't I tell ye to loy still and slape till it was time to start? Why, ye blundering, thick-headed idiots, you have made enough noise to rouse the Englanders."

Denham pressed my heel now so that it was painful; but I did not stir, only listened to the grumbling apology of the two men.

"Don't go to sleep again," said the abusing voice. "We start in an hour, if you haven't put the enemy on the alert."

Just then the light was softened, for the door of the lantern was closed and the fastening clicked.

Then I felt that all was over, for the man on my left suddenly started up and seized me by the arm.

"Open that lantern again, Captain Moriarty," he cried. "I want to see who this is we've got here."

"Yes," said another voice; "two of them. I'll swear they weren't here when we lay down."

Chapter Forty Two
In the Trap

If either Denham or I had felt the slightest disposition to run, it was checked by the brotherly feeling that one could not escape without the other; but even if we had made the attempt it would have been impossible, for the words uttered by the big Boer at my side acted like the application of a spark to a keg of gunpowder. In an instant there was an explosion. Men leaped to their feet, rifle in hand; there was a roar of voices; yells and shouts were mingled with bursts of talking which rose into a hurricane of gabble, out of which, mingled with oaths and curses delivered in the vilest Dutch, I made out, "Spies—shoot—hang them;" and it seemed that after thrusting ourselves into the hornets' nest we were to be stung to death.

The noise was deafening, and as we were held men plucked and tore at us, while the roar of voices seemed to run to right and left all along the line, alarm spreading; with the result that those outside the narrow space where the facts were known took it to be a sudden attack from the rear, and began firing at random in the darkness. In spite of the despair that came over me, I even then could not help feeling a kind of exultation—satisfaction—call it what you will—at the surprise we had given the blundering Boers, and thinking that if the Colonel had been prepared with our men to charge into them at once, the whole line of the enemy for far enough to right and left would have turned and fled, after an ineffectual fire which must have done far more harm to their friends than to their foes, and then scattered before our fellows like dead leaves before a gale.

However, we were not to be torn to pieces just then by the infuriated Boers, for we were each held firmly by two burly fellows, while Moriarty, yelling at the excited crowd in his highly-pitched voice, opened and held the lantern on high, so as to get a good look at our disfigured faces. The light fell upon his own as well, and I saw him start and shrink, as if for the moment he fancied that we had returned from the dead. But his dismay was only momentary. Then a malevolent grin of exultation came over his countenance, his eyes scintillated in the lantern light, and he yelled orders to those around till he obtained comparative silence.

"Pass the word all along the line," he shouted. "False alarm. Only spies, and we have got them. Cease firing."

His words had but little effect for a few minutes; but by degrees the tumult was stilled and the firing ceased. The men about us readily obeyed the Irish captain's orders.

"They're old fr'inds of mine," he said, with a peculiar grin—"dear fr'inds who have come after me to join our ranks; and I'm going to make them take the oaths properly."

There was a groan of dissent at this, but Moriarty paid no heed; he only showed his teeth at us in a savage grin like that of some wild beast about to spring.

"Yes," he continued, "they're old fr'inds of mine—dear fr'inds. That one"—he pointed to me—"is a deserter from our forces, and the other miserable brute is an officer who has been fighting against us and helping his companion. Be cool and calm, dear boys, and as soon as it is light you shall have the pleasure of shooting the young scoundrels. For we're all soldiers now, and we must behave like military min, unless you would like to set a Kaffir to hang them both from a tripod of dissel-booms at the two ends of a rein."

"Shoot them! Shoot them!" came in a burst of voices.

"Very well, we'll shoot them; but we must do it properly. We'll have a court-martial upon them, and teach the spies to crawl into our camp like snakes."

"It's a lie!" I shouted. "We are no spies."

"Ah! you understand the beautiful language of my fr'inds," cried Moriarty. "You are not spies, then?"

"No, neither of us," I said in Dutch.

"Indade?" said Moriarty. "And perhaps you are not a deserter from our troops?"

Amidst hootings, groans, and yells, I managed to make myself heard.

"No," I said, "I am not a deserter. I am English, and I refused to fight against my own countrymen."

A savage yell greeted my plain words; but Moriarty held up his hand.

"Let him condemn himself out of his own lips, brethren," he cried.— Then, to me, "You preferred to fight against and shoot down the people among whom you dwelt?" he cried.

"I joined my own people," I replied; "and this gentleman with me is no spy."

"What is he, then?" said Moriarty, holding up his hand in the light of the lantern he kept aloft, so as to secure silence.

"An officer and a gentleman of the Light Horse."

"Indade!" said Moriarty sneeringly. "Then you have both had enough of the British forces, and have deserted to ours?"

"No," I said coolly. "We have both been badly wounded, as you can see, and we wanted to break through the lines and get away."

"What for?" said Moriarty fiercely. "What for?"

"We are too weak to fight," I said.

"Bah!" roared Moriarty, "you are both spies; and do you hear? You shall both be shot by-and-by."

A yell of triumph, which sounded like a chorus of savage beasts in anticipation of blood, rose from all around.

"Get reins and tie their arms behind them, my brothers. They're English, and can spake nothing but lies."

As some of the men hurried away to fetch the necessary cords, I turned to one of the big Boers who held me.

"Is it a lie," I said, "that my friend has been badly wounded? Is it a lie that I have been hurt?"

There was a low growl for reply from one, and the other—the man who had first discovered my presence—only said, "But you are spies."

"What are they all saying, Val?" said Denham coolly. "I don't seem to get on at all in this game."

"They say we're spies," I replied.

"Let 'em. A set of thick-headed pigs. Don't be downhearted over it all, old chap. We played our game well, and we've lost. We're prisoners; that's all. They daren't shoot us."

I looked him fixedly in the eyes, but made no reply.

"Well," said Denham hurriedly, "it's murder if they do. But I don't believe they will. Whatever they do, we won't show the white feather, Val. I say, shall we give 'em the National Anthem?"

"Hush!" I said. "You're a gentleman; don't do anything to insult them; we're in their power."

"Yes; but I want them to see that we're ready to die game. I say, Val, we've made a mess of it this time, and we might have been lying comfortably asleep over yonder."

"No," I said; "we should have lain awake thinking of how to get help for our friends."

"True, O Calif! so we should.—Ugh! You ugly brutes. Tie our hands behind our backs, would you?—Here, Mr Irishman, there's no need for this. We didn't serve you so."

"Oh yes," said Moriarty. "Spies like to get all the news they can, and then to run away with their load."

"After treacherously trying to murder the sentry on duty, and then treacherously striking down two people in the dark."

"Hwhat!" cried Moriarty fiercely.

"I mean you, you cowardly hound!—you disgrace to the name of Irishman!"

There was the sound of a smart blow, and Denham staggered back against the men who were binding his wrists.

A cheer rose from some of the fierce men around us, a murmur of disapprobation from others, as Denham recovered himself and stood upright, with his chest expanded and a look of scorn and contempt in his eyes.

"Yes," he said quietly, "you are a disgrace to a great name. I am a prisoner, and my hands are tied."

"Silence, spy!" cried Moriarty fiercely, and a dead silence fell.

"I'll not be silent," said Denham. "Val, if we die for it, repeat my words in Dutch. But if I live I'll kill that man, or he shall kill me.—Moriarty, you're a treacherous coward and a cur, to strike a helpless, wounded man."

"A treacherous coward and a cur, to strike a helpless, wounded man," I said aloud in the Boer tongue, the words seeming to come from something within me over which I had no power whatever.

Moriarty, white with fury, turned upon me, but one of the two men who held me interfered, saying bluntly, "Let him talk, Captain; his tongue will soon be still."

"Yes, yes," said Moriarty, with a forced laugh; "his tongue will soon be still. Putt them in the impty wagon, and bind their legs too. Then put four men over them as guards. You'll answer for them, Cornet."

The grim looks of the two speakers and the horrible nature of their words, which meant a horrible death, ought to have sent a chill through me; but just then I was so excited, so hot with rage against the cowardly wretch who had struck my friend, that I did not feel the slightest fear as to my fate;

and, obeying the order to march, I walked beside Denham with my head as erect as his, till we were by the tail of a great empty wagon, into which two of the Boers scrambled so as to seize us by the pinioned arms, causing great pain, as they stooped, and then dragged us in as if we had been sacks of corn, and then let us down.

"Look here," said my captor, speaking from the tail-end of the wagon, "there are four men on duty with rifles, and their orders are to shoot you both through the head if you try to escape. Now you know."

While he was speaking one of the men who had dragged us in reached out his hand for a lantern, which he took and hung from a hook in the middle of the tilt.

Then he and his companion dropped down from the end of the dimly-lit wagon, and we were alone for a few moments. But the two men who had left us returned directly with two more reins and set to work binding our ankles together as tightly as they could.

"There," said one of them, in Dutch, as soon as they had finished, "we can see you well from outside, and you know what will come if you try to get away."

Then we were alone again, and as the curtain of stout canvas at the end ceased to vibrate, Denham as he lay back began to laugh merrily.

"Denham!" I cried.

"I can't help it, old chap," he said. "It's very horrible, but there's a comic side to it. Blows hit terribly hard."

"Yes, the coward!" I cried passionately, "to strike you like that!"

"I wasn't thinking of that, old chap," he replied. "Yes, that was as nasty a thing as the savage could do; but I was thinking of how hard you can hit a sensitive man with your tongue."

"What do you mean?" I said.

"Moriarty! Why, I spoke quite quietly, but if I had given him a cut across the face from the left shoulder with my sabre, which cuts like a razor, it wouldn't have hurt the brute half as much."

"Don't—don't talk about the business," I said bitterly.

"Why not? I'm just in the condition that makes my tongue run. But I say, old chap, we've made a pretty mess of our scheme. Never told a soul what we were going to do, so we can't get any help."

"And left a hanging rope to show our people that we have run away and deserted them in their terrible strait."

"Yes; that's about the worst of the whole business, my lad. Well, we meant well, and it's of no use to cry over spilt milk. I don't think it will be spilt blood; but it may, and if it does I'm going to die like a soldier with his face to the enemy, and so are you."

"I'm going to try," I said simply.

"Then you'll do it, like a true-born Englishman," he said cheerily. "How does that song go? I forget. There, never mind. I won't act like a sham, even if I am where there's so much Dutch courage. Now, look here, Val."

"Yes?" I said gravely.

"We're weak from our long sickness, and done up with the exertion of what we've gone through."

"Yes," I said; "I feel as weak as a rat."

"Then we're going to sleep, so as to be ready to face them in the morning."

"What!" I said. "Can you sleep at a time like this?"

"My dear old Val, as you said about facing the muzzles of the Dutch rifles, I'm going to try."

Chapter Forty Three
In the Dark Watches

"I can't sleep," I said to myself, feeling that history was repeating itself, as I lay on my side in the lit-up wagon, with my wrists tied behind my back and my torture increased by having my legs served in the same way just above the ankles and again above the knees. "No one could sleep in such a position," I thought to myself; but I did not speak to my companion in misery. I was too weary and heart-sore, thinking that I should never see father, brother, aunt, or home again. "Poor old home is gone for ever," I remember, was the thought that occurred to me. Next I fell to wondering what had become of my people, and whether they had fled to Natal. Then my thoughts turned quickly to something else: to the heavy, regular breathing of Denham, who was fast asleep and suffering from a bad dream, for he began muttering angrily. Then he was silent, but only to begin again. I believed I knew the subject of his dream, for he suddenly exclaimed, "Coward—coward blow!" Then he was silent for a few minutes, breathing hard and fast as if his growing excitement had worked up to fierce passion, for he was going over the scene of an hour ago, ending with "I'll kill you—or you shall kill me." He was suffering as if from a nightmare; and, unable to lie there listening, I managed to work myself along over the rough, cage-like bottom of the wagon till I could get my face close to his, just as he was panting and sobbing as if in a desperate encounter in which his strength was rapidly ebbing away.

"Denham!" I whispered. "Denham!"

"Ha!" he sighed softly, and ceased to struggle; while, as I lowered my head from the painful position into which I had strained it, I felt relieved to know that the poor, overwrought companion of my adventure could forget his sorrows for the time in sleep.

"I wish I could sleep, and never wake again; for when the time comes I shall be a coward"—such was the train of my thoughts. "Yes, I am sure to be a coward. One doesn't think of the bullets when one is fighting and they *ping* and *whiz* by one's head; but to stand up and face a row of rifles, waiting for the order to fire—I'm afraid I shall be a coward then."

I shivered now; and a minute later, as I listened to Denham's breathing, I shivered again. Perhaps it was from fear, perhaps it was from being cold, for the night wind, not far removed from freezing, blew up through the openings in the bottom of the wagon. I told myself it was from dread, and a peculiar feeling of shame and despair attacked me as the thought of what would occur on the coming morning rose up so vivid and clear that I strained my eyes round a little so as to look up at the hanging lantern, but lowered them again with a shudder, for I seemed to see a row of rifle-muzzles with the orifices directed down at me.

A noise occurred at the end of the wagon almost immediately, and upon looking back there was in reality the barrel of a rifle forcing back the canvas curtain, and then a second barrel appeared; but the owners only used their weapons to hold back the curtain while their big-bearded faces peered in to see if the prisoners were safe. They disappeared directly, and I could hear muttering, and could smell the fumes of their strong tobacco.

I was thinking with something like envy of the Boers' lot as compared with mine, and the envy had to do with Denham, who was sleeping soundly; and then something happened—the something which I had thought impossible; but it was quite true. I was staring painfully up at the lantern which shed its yellowish glow all around, and then it seemed to have gone out, and I was fast asleep, with the restful sensation which comes of utter exhaustion. I dreamed, and it was of home and the beautiful orchard I had helped to plant, of driving in the cattle, of chasing the ostriches over the veldt; and then it was of having Bob and Denham with me in a wagon, for we were after lions. It was night, and the moon shone in through the front of the wagon with a yellowish light like that of a lantern hanging from the top of the tilt. The wind was blowing up icily through the bottom, and I had just been awakened by the distant deep barking roar of one of the great sand-coloured brutes. His roar had startled our oxen and made them low uneasily, as if they knew what the fate of one of them would be unless a flash of fire came from beneath the wagon-tilt just as the lion had crawled up and gathered himself together for a spring. The night was very cold, and somehow the thought occurred to me that it would be a good thing if that lion made a bound right on to the wagon-box, and then jumped in to seize me and carry me off as a cat does a rat; and when its roar sounded again, nearer, all dread and pain died out, for it seemed as if it would be far better to be killed by a lion than to stand up before the muzzles of a dozen rifles and be shot as a spy, while Moriarty stood smiling malignantly at my fate. It was all very vivid as the oxen bellowed softly now, and Bob whispered into my ear, his breath feeling quite hot after the chilling iciness of the night wind. "Cheer up, old Val," he said; "they won't dare to shoot you. I shall be there, and if they attempt it, and that Irishman gives the order—you know how true I can aim? I'll send a bullet right through his head, if father isn't first."

I started violently and made an effort to rise; but I only succeeded in making a noise, as I looked up, to see the yellow lantern sending down its feeble light; but a lion was barking faintly in the distance, and some oxen close at hand were lowing uneasily. There was another sound, too, at the back of the wagon—that of some one climbing up—and in a wild fit of anxiety I listened for Bob's voice again. But it was only that of the Boer who had first seized me, and he spoke in a gruff but not unkindly way, as he said in his own tongue:

"Hullo! What's the matter? Lion scare you?"

"I've—I've been dreaming," I faltered heavily, my heart beating all the time with big, regular thumps.

"Oh!—He's dreaming too. You're two brave boys to sleep like that the night before you're both to be shot for spies."

"Ah!" I sighed as he dropped back heavily from the back of the wagon, "and it was all a dream. Ugh!" I shuddered. I lay still again, my mind going over the fantasy of the night, which came back so vividly, yet was so strangely mixed and absurd; but all the time Denham slept on, breathing heavily, dead to all the sorrows and horror of our unlucky situation.

The night was cold—bitterly cold—and I was dreadfully wide awake, wishing now that I could sleep again, but wishing in vain. I lay and listened to the sound of talking outside, two of the Boers engaging in a conversation in which I heard the word "cold." Then there came the sound of the drawing aside of the back curtains, and a big, soft bundle was pitched in, then another. Directly afterwards two of our guard climbed in, opened one of the bundles, and spread it out on the floor beyond us. It was a great skin *karosse*, or rug, such as the Kaffirs make up of the hides of the big game.

"It's a cold night," said the man who had spoken before; and, one at my head and the other at my feet, they lifted me between them on the big rug.

"Now, sleepy," he said, "rouse up."

But Denham was perfectly insensible in his deep sleep of exhaustion, and unconscious of what was going on as he was laid beside me. Then the second bundle was opened and thrown over us.

"There," said the big Boer; "we don't want you to be too cold to stand up like men in the morning. Can you go to sleep now?"

"Yes; thank you," I said hoarsely, and I lay and listened as they got out of the wagon.

"Can I sleep?" I thought. "No. But if I could, and dream all that again! Poor old Bob!" I murmured to myself as a peculiar sensation of warmth began to creep through my numbed limbs, and once more I lay thinking about that strangely confused and realistic dream of which fragments began to flit before me, and for a time made me more wakeful, but not for long. Then the morning, the thoughts of my coming fate, the recollection of the night-alarm which seemed to have put an end to what must have been intended for a night-attack, even the sense of pain—all these died away, and I was soundly asleep once more; this time without a dream.

Chapter Forty Four
In the Queer Prison

I was roused up by the great skin-rug being jerked off me. I tried to rise, but sank back, just able to repress a groan, and stared wildly at the four bearded faces looking down at me. The curtains at front and rear had been thrown back, and the sun was shining in from the front, the horizontal rays striking right through the wagon. For a few moments I was so much confused and stupefied by sleep that I could not grasp the meaning of the scene. Then like a flash it all came. These four Boers were going to lead us out to execution—to be shot—the fate of spies!

I set my teeth, and felt as if getting hardened now. My eyes turned to Denham, who was seeking mine. He did not speak, but nodded and smiled faintly, the look giving encouragement. Clenching my teeth, together, I mentally vowed I would not let him be ashamed of me.

Just then my attention was diverted by one of our morning visitors, who differed in appearance from the others. He was better dressed, wore his hair short, and his moustache and beard were clipped into points. His hands, which he laid upon my shoulders, were white. To my surprise, this man examined my head, with its bandages and traces of injuries. Then he looked hard in my eyes, and turned me a little over to examine my tightly-bound wrists and ankles. Next he examined Denham in the same way, my comrade gazing straight away, with his brow knit and lips tightened into a thin red line, but he never once glanced at the examiner.

"Well," said the latter, rising from one knee, "even if they are spies, you need not treat them as if they were wild beasts."

"Captain Moriarty's orders," said the Boer, whom I recognised as my captor of the previous night.

"Bah!" growled the other angrily. "You are soldiers now; act like them."

I was listening with a feeling of gratitude that this man spoke differently from the others, and he saw my eyes fixed upon him.

"Do you speak German?" he asked sharply.

"No," I replied; "but I understood you just now."

He nodded, and then turned to the others to speak in a low tone. The result of this was that two of the men knelt down and set our arms free, placing them before us, for they were perfectly numb and dead. Mine looked as if the thongs had cut almost to the bone, the muscle having swollen greatly.

The party then went out at the back; but my captor, who was last, turned back and said:

"There are two sentries with loaded rifles at each end, and they have orders to fire."

"What did he say, Val?" asked Denham as soon as we were alone.

I told him, and he laughed softly.

"What is it?" I said wonderingly.

"I was only thinking," he replied. Then quickly, "Will they bind our hands again—at the last?"

"I don't know," I said in a low, husky voice. "Perhaps not."

"Let's hope not; and we must rub some feeling into them first."

"What are you thinking about?" I asked.

"Don't you know, old fellow? Guess."

I shook my head.

"Well, it is hard work; but look here: they didn't search us last night, only tied us hand and foot. We've got our revolvers inside our shirts. Let's have one shot each at Moriarty before we die."

I looked at him wonderingly, for the vivid dream of the night came back, and my brother's words seemed to be thrilling hotly in my ear once more.

Denham looked at me curiously.

"Well," he said, "wouldn't you like to shoot the wretch?"

"No," I said; "not now. If we are to die I don't want to try to kill any more."

Denham frowned, and sat gently rubbing his wrists. I followed his example during nearly an hour. While thus employed we could hear a good deal of bustle and noise going on in the neighbourhood of the wagon, and sundry odours which floated in suggested that the Boers in camp did not starve themselves. Meanwhile we were very silent and thoughtful, expecting that at any moment we might be summoned to meet our fate.

At last there was the sound of approaching steps, and I drew my breath hard as an order was given to halt, followed by the rattle of rifles being grounded.

I was unable to speak then, but held out my hand quickly to Denham, who seized it in both of his, and his lips parted as if to say good-bye, yet no words were uttered. The next moment he let my hand drop and turned his eyes away, for the big Boer who had become so familiar now climbed into the wagon, glanced at us, and then reached down outside for two large pannikins of hot coffee, which he carefully lifted inside.

"Here," he said gruffly; "help to keep up your spirits."

He set the tins beside us, then went to the back of the wagon and reached down again for a couple of large, newly-baked cakes, which he handed to us.

"The Irish captain didn't give any orders," he said; "but we don't starve our prisoners to death."

With that he scowled at us in turn, and left the wagon.

"Toll me what he said, Val," whispered Denham in a tone of voice which sounded very strange.

With difficulty I repeated in English what the man had said; I felt as if choking.

"I wish they hadn't done this, Val," said Denham after a minute's interval. "It seems like a mockery."

I nodded, then remarked, "That man seems to have some feeling in him."

"Yes; but we can't eat and drink now."

"No," I replied. "I feel as if food would choke me."

Denham nodded, and sat gazing out at the bright sunshine.

"Think it would give us a little Dutch courage if we had some breakfast?"

"I don't want any," I said desperately. "I want them to put us out of our misery before that wretch Moriarty comes back."

"But we want to face them like men," said Denham suddenly. "We're so weak and faint now that we shall be ready to drop. Let's eat and drink, and we will show the Boers that English soldiers are ready to lace anything."

"I can't," I replied desperately.

"You must," cried Denham. "Como on." He took up his pannikin, raised it to his lips, and took a long deep draught before setting the vessel down and taking up the cake.

"Come, Val," he said firmly, "if you leave yours the Boers will think you are too much frightened to eat."

"So I am," I said gravely, "It is very awful to face death like this."

"Yes; but it would be more awful if we stood before the enemy trembling and ready to drop."

I nodded now. Then catching up the tin in desperation, I raised it to my lips and held it there till it was half-empty. Setting the pannikin down, I took up the cake, broke a piece off, and began to eat. The animal faculties act independently of the mental, I suppose; so, as I sat there thinking of our home and our approaching fate, I went on eating slowly, without once glancing at my companion, till the big cake was finished; then I raised and drained the pannikin.

It was while I was swallowing the last mouthful or two that Denham spoke in a low tone. Looking in his direction, I noticed that he had also finished the rough breakfast.

"They're watching us, Val," he said softly.

I glanced round to back and front, and saw that the big Boer and four others were looking in, the sight making the blood flush to my face.

Directly after the big fellow climbed in, to stand by us with a grim smile.

"Have some more?" he asked.

"No, thank you," I replied.

"Hungry—weren't you?" was his next question.

I bowed my head.

"Well, it'll put some courage into you."

He picked up the two pannikins, and stepped out again.

"I'm glad we took it," said Denham. "It's better than looking ready to show the white feather."

"I don't think we should have faltered even without the food," I replied.

We both relapsed into silence now, for talking seemed to be impossible. We had to think of the past and of the future. One minute I felt in despair, and the next I was filled with a strange kind of hope that was inexplicable.

It was during one of these oft-recurring intervals, as the time wore on, that Denham turned to me suddenly and said, just as if in answer to something I had said, for his thoughts were very much the same as mine:

"There, I can't make anything else of it, Val: we were doing our duty, and trying to save the lives of our friends."

"Yes," I said quietly; then, both shrinking from speaking again, we sat listening to the sounds outside. From time to time one or other of the men on guard looked in to see that we were safe, though for the matter of that we had hardly thought of stirring, as escape seemed to be quite impossible.

It was about midday, after a very long silence, when Denham suddenly remarked, "It went against the grain at first, Val; but I won't attempt to fire at that brute. He'll get his deserts one of these days. You're right; we don't want to go out like that. I want us to be able to stand up before the enemy quite calm and steady. We must show them what Englishmen can do."

I could not speak, but I gave him a long and steadfast look.

The sound of footsteps was again heard, and I was not surprised this time when our friendly Boer brought us two good rations of freshly-roasted mutton and two cakes. These he put down before us without a word, together with a tin of water, and then left us.

Denham looked at me, and I looked at him, as—each feeling something akin to shame—we ate the food almost ravenously. Then the afternoon was passed in listening to the busy movements of the Boers; but we never once tried to look out of our strange prison.

At sunset, as I looked at the glorious orange colour of the sky, a curious feeling of sadness came over me, for I realised it was the last time I should behold the sun go down. There was such a look of calm beauty everywhere that I could hardly realise the fact that we were surrounded by troop upon troop of armed men ready to deal out fire and destruction at a word; but once more my musing was interrupted by the big Boer. He brought us coffee again, and this time cake and butter.

"There," he remarked as he placed all before us, "make much of it, boys, for I shan't see you again."

A chill ran through me; but I don't think my countenance changed.

"I'm going away with our men to the other side yonder, and the Irish captain's coming back. Good-bye, lads," he said after a pause. "I'm sorry for you both, for I've got two boys just such fellows as you. I'm sorry I caught you, for you're brave fellows even if you are spies."

"We are not spies," I replied quietly. I was determined to speak now; I wanted that Boer to look on us as honest and manly.

He shook his head. I repeated the words passionately.

"Look here," I said; "we have been wounded, and were on the sick-list. We could do no good, so we said we'd try and got through your lines and fetch help."

"Ah!" cried the Boer slowly and thoughtfully. "Yes, I see. But you were caught, and I can do nothing, boys. Moriarty will have you shot in the morning when he comes back, and begin to rage because it is not done. Well, life's very short, and we must all die. I'm going to fight to-night, and perhaps I shall start on the long journey too, for your men fight well. God knows best, lads; and there is no fighting yonder—all is peace."

He bowed his head down and went out of the wagon without a word. When Denham asked me a few minutes later what the Boer had said, my voice in reply sounded hoarse and strange, quite unlike my usual tones.

We were now in darkness. The coffee was cold; the cakes lay untouched. We were both sunk in a deep interval of musing; but Denham broke the silence at last.

"Then we have another night of life, Val," he remarked.

"Yes," I replied; "and then the end."

"Look here," he said thoughtfully, after he had taken up the coffee-tin and drunk; "that Boer said that he was going over yonder to-night to fight, and that perhaps he would be where we were."

"Yes—dead," was my reply.

"Perhaps, Val. What do the doctors say?—'While there's life there's hope.'"

"I see no hope for us," I said gloomily.

"I do," Denham whispered in a low, earnest tone. "We've been too ready to give up hope."

I smiled sadly, stretching out my swollen legs.

"Yes, I know," said Denham; "but my hands are not powerless now, and I have still a knife in my pocket—the one with which I cut the reins—and it will cut these."

His words sent a thrill through me, and I glanced at the two openings in the wagon.

"Be careful," I whispered.

"All right; but the Boers don't understand English. Look here, Val; if the big friendly fellow is going to fight to-night, what does it mean?"

"Of course," I replied excitedly, "an attack upon the fort. They're going to get in when it's dark; and if they do there'll not be half of our poor fellows left by morning."

"Couldn't we slip off as soon as it's dark, and warn them? Once we were outside the lines we might run."

"Might run?" I said bitterly. "I don't believe we could even stand."

"Ah! I forgot that," he muttered, with a groan. "Well, nothing venture, nothing have. It'll be dark enough in a few minutes, and then I shall slip the knife under your ankles and set your legs free. When that's done you can do the same for me."

"Suppose the Boers come and examine us?"

"We must risk that. Perhaps they'll just come and look at the cords with a lantern. We must sit quite still until they come."

"No," I said eagerly; "don't let's cut the rope till they've been. I dare say they'll come for the pannikins, and perhaps that Boer has told them to bring us those rugs again."

Chapter Forty Five
A Damper For Our Plans

I had hardly ceased speaking when a couple of our guards appeared at the back of the wagon, and climbed in after they had tossed in the two big rugs they had taken away when the German doctor came to examine us.

Though anxious to dart a quick glance at Denham, I dared not, for at the first glance I saw that each man was provided with a rein. Taking our tins and passing them to two men whose rifle-barrels appeared above the back of the wagon, they returned to where we sat up and carefully examined our bonds, one of them giving a grunt and speaking to his companion as he pointed to them. They next dragged our arms roughly behind us, slipping our hands through running nooses, which they drew tight before winding the thongs round and round, securing them as firmly as ever.

"You needn't have done that," I said angrily to the man who, while tying me up, had roused my resentment by his brutality.

"We'll take them off in the morning, when the Captain comes," he replied. The other man laughed. They had finished their task deftly enough.

"That's the way we tie up a Kaffir," said the first one.

"Yes," replied the other; "and it does just as well for a spy. There, you may thank the field-cornet, Piet Zouter, for the skin-rugs. You wouldn't have got them from us."

"Then we won't thank you," I said bitterly.

"And look here; we've six men with loaded rifles about the wagon, and they've orders to shoot if you try to get away."

I nodded my head. One of the Boers lifted down the lantern, passed it out, and received a fresh one from a comrade. After this the men retired; and we were alone, listening to their talk, with the sentries placed over us. When the conversation ceased I whispered to Denham an interpretation of all that had passed.

"The brutes!" he muttered. "Lucky we hadn't cut our ropes; they would have found us out. Now, what's to be done? We must get away."

"How?" I asked sadly.

"Let's draw the rugs over us, lie down, and keep on trying till we can wriggle out of the thongs."

"How are we to get the rugs over us?"

"As a bird makes a nest—with the beak."

I laughed bitterly. Then we each tried in turn, but vainly, and afterwards lay back panting and in great pain.

"I know," I said. I called aloud to the sentries.

There was a rush, and a man appeared at once, his rifle rattling against the back of the wagon. I told him what we wanted, and in a grumbling way he climbed in and did as requested, spreading one *karosse* and drawing the other as a cover up to our chins.

"Now loosen the reins about our wrists," I said; "they hurt dreadfully."

The man laughed.

"It isn't for long," he answered brutally. "Do you want to try to escape, so as to be shot before morning?"

With this parting sally, he climbed out of the wagon, leaving us alone. We lay still for about half-an-hour, when the sentries looked in from front and back to see us lying as if asleep; but as soon as they had gone we began a hard struggle to get our wrists free. In this attempt we only gave ourselves excruciating pain, and found, to our despair, that the knots of the Boers were far too well tied to be loosened. At last, with a groan, Denham gave up the attempt. I desisted then, having only waited for him to set the example.

"What does that sound mean?" asked Denham after a time.

"Moving horses," I replied.

"Yes; they're going to take advantage of the darkness for an advance against the fort. Oh dear! We shall have to lie here and listen to the firing soon. Val, I don't think I'd mind being shot in the morning if I could only warn the Colonel. Do you think you could gnaw through my rein?"

"I'll try," I said; and Denham was about to turn his back to me when we heard a sound behind us—that is to say, at the front of the wagon—which we knew to be caused by one of the sentries looking in. It soon ceased; but just as I was going to fix my teeth in the thong which bound my companion's wrists there came another noise at the foot, and then again there was silence. But not so at a short distance, for we could hear whispered orders plainly enough as we lay still, followed by the tramp of horses' feet, and now and then the clink of bit or buckle, which gave ample intimation that the Boers were slowly making an advance, not to invest the fort more closely in a contracted ring, but, as far as we could make out, in our direction.

"They're marching in troops, I believe," whispered Denham, "and they must be making for the gateway. Then they'll dismount and deliver an attack. They mean to take the place by assault."

"And we are to go through the agony of lying here and listening all the while, perfectly helpless. Oh Denham, they'll never carry the place—will they?"

"Not unless it's quite a surprise," he replied. "Oh no," he added more confidently; "our lads will be too smart for that."

"They'll try hard," I said, "and fail, losing a great number of men, and they'll come back at daybreak mad with rage."

"And shoot us," said Denham coolly. "That's it."

"Let me try at your knots now."

"No. Listen; the sentries are coming in again."

He was right; for, as if suspicious, the sentries climbed in, four strong, two standing with rifles at the ready, while the others stripped down the top rug and carefully examined our wrists and ankles, then spread the *karosse* over us once more, uttering grunts of satisfaction as they did so.

Alone again, we lay listening for the movements of the Boer troops: but the sounds had nearly died out.

Then the sentries began to talk together earnestly, and it seemed as if the man on duty in front of the wagon had joined those at the back, with the result that the conversation was becoming excited.

"They're on the lookout after the advance," whispered Denham. "It seems to be very dark outside. I believe it will not be long before we hear the attack begin."

"No; they'll wait till our men are asleep."

"Perhaps," said Denham; "but it must be getting late. Our fellows may be asleep now."

"Yes," I replied, with a sigh; and then irritably, "Why did you do that? You can whisper."

"What do you mean?" he asked after a pause.

"Hitting me on the hands like that. You hurt me dreadfully."

"I didn't—" he began; but I stopped him with an excited "Hush!" and lay perfectly still, the perspiration starting out all over me.

"What is it?" whispered Denham, after waiting for some time. "What's that gnawing and tearing sound?"

"Something under the wagon," I replied very softly.

"A lion?" he whispered.

"No; some one as brave as a lion. He has been cutting a long slit in the *karosse*, and now he has hold of my wrists with one hand, and he's sawing with a knife through the thong with the other."

"Val!" panted the poor fellow wildly.

The hot perspiration on my face turned icily cold at this cry, for I heard a quick movement among the sentries, and two of them sprang up on the wagon to look at us lying there upon our backs beneath the upper *karosse*, under the yellow light of the lantern. I thought now all was over; the new hope had faded out into darkness; but a measure of confidence returned when Denham, feigning sleep, muttered, and uttered a sob which ended in a low, uneasy groan.

My eyes not being quite shut, I could dimly see through the narrow slit the faces of two of the Boers, one showing his teeth in a grin as they drew back and returned to their companions, when the talking began again. As this went on I felt the sawing movement of the knife being resumed, the two active hands which had been passed between the slits in the wagon-bottom working more rapidly. Then there was a pause, and I felt terrible pain as something thin and hard was passed under one of the bands before the sawing recommenced. I could hardly repress a cry of pain; but silence meant perhaps liberty and life. I knew, too, that it was a piece of iron that had been thrust in for the knife to cut down upon and save my wrist from a wound.

Just then Denham whispered, "I couldn't help it, old chap; but I cheated them afterwards. Is he still cutting?"

"Yes; he has gone through the reins on my wrists, and has begun at my ankles."

"Val," whispered Denham again, with his face below the great rug, "it's that big black angel of a fellow, Joeboy."

"No," I said softly, though I could hardly utter my thoughts, my voice panting with emotion. "It's not Joeboy: the hands are too small. It's my brother come to our help."

I knew now that my previous night's experience was not a dream, and that Bob really was in the Boer camp with my father, and had crept under the wagon and whispered hope.

"Are there two Val Morays in the world?" murmured poor Denham, with something which sounded very much like a sob.

Lying perfectly still, I made no answer. I knew that the knife had set my ankles free; but they were still tethered, not by raw-hide rope but with insensibility, as if perfectly dead.

"They will come right in time," I thought, my heart meanwhile beating fast. "Bob will tell us what to do. Will it be to make our escape when the attention of the Boer sentries is taken off us by the coming attack upon the fort?"

Then I was listening to a low tearing sound as of the knife passing once more through the skin-rug, and directly after I heard Denham begin to breathe hard. I understood what that meant. Making a slight effort, as I lay covered up, I brought my arms out from beneath me, numbed and aching but not powerless, and thrust my left hand inside my flannel shirt, my fingers coming in contact with the butt of my revolver.

"My hands are free, Val," Denham whispered faintly.

"Feel for your revolver," I whispered back. "Hist! Careful" — for I could plainly hear the Boer sentries coming towards the wagon again, and the faint cutting noise ceased as the talking stopped.

One of the men placed his hand on the back of the great vehicle, and was in the act of climbing in, doubtless to examine our fastenings again. My left hand now clutched my revolver tightly, though I knew that we could do nothing, in our helpless state, to save ourselves.

"Oh, how hard!" I thought; "just when there was a chance of life!"

Then my breath seemed to stop short, for the sound of a shot came to us from out of the distance where the Boer advance must be. This checked the climbing Boer. Then another shot, and another. He had dropped back to join his companions, who were doubtless gazing towards the fort, where the firing was rapidly increasing into a perfect storm.

I heard no more of the cutting; but Denham whispered that his feet were free, and almost at the same moment a hand felt for my face and then seized my ear as if to pull it down to the owner of that hand.

Understanding what was wanted, I turned over on my right side and laid my ear against the opening, listening.

"Don't try to get up," buzzed into it, and seemed to set my brain whirling. "The Boers are making a great attack on the fort, and you two must try and creep out while the sentries are listening to the firing. Can you both run?"

"We could not stand up to save our lives," I whispered. "Our legs are quite numb and dead."

"Then I must carry you to where father is waiting," was whispered.

I uttered a low sigh of misery, for I knew that was impossible. The Boers must hear the movements, even if so young a lad as my brother had possessed sufficient strength.

"Lie still, and sham sleep," was the advice from below. "Your legs will get better. The Boers won't be back for hours yet. Hark!"

There was no need to speak, for the firing grew louder and louder, as if echoing from the walls of the fort, not much more than half a mile from where we lay; and I was thinking that a terrible assault might be made, when my brother whispered again:

"The Boers mean to take the place to-night. Now, do as I say. Pretend to sleep. I'm going to fetch father."

He had hardly ceased speaking when there was a rush of feet, and one of our guards scrambled up at the back, rifle in hand; but he contented himself with looking in when he saw us lying apparently unmoved beneath the rug.

"Hear that?" he said loudly.

"Yes," I replied as calmly as I could.

"There'll be hundreds more prisoners to shoot in the morning. Lie still, you two, for if you try to move we'll serve you like jackals on the veldt."

At that moment he turned sharply to listen, and I listened too. As the Boer suddenly leaped down, uttering a warning cry, I sat up, and Denham followed my example; for there was a rushing sound in the darkness from the side opposite that fronting the fort, and the tramp of many feet, followed by the ringing notes of a bugle, taken up by another and another, succeeded by so close a volley that the wagon lantern looked dim in the flashes from the rifles. Then came a ringing cheer, bugle-notes sounding the charge; and in the darkness, with cheers that thrilled us through and through, a couple of regiments rushed the Boer lines from the rear with the bayonet.

Chapter Forty Six
How we were saved

"Hurrah!"

"Hurrah!"

We yelled together with all our might; but our cheers sounded like whispers amidst the noises of firing in front and the rush of men from the rear. The Boer sentries, however, were true to their duty even in the midst of the terrible confusion in their lines; and four of them made at once, rifle in hand, for the wagon. But we were mad with excitement now, and *crack, crack,* our revolvers began to speak. Our shots and the rapid advance of the soldiers made them turn and flee.

Then came the crash: the cheering and bayonet-work of the charge, as our men dashed through the Boer lines, scattering them, horse and man, across the veldt, panic-stricken.

"Denham," I cried excitedly; "my friends!" He said nothing for a moment; then, unable to give me comfort, he said, "Oh, if the Colonel could only bring our fellows out now and charge!"

Just then bugles rang out the recall, and in the midst of the many sounds Bob's voice rose from the front of the wagon: "In here, father—quick!"

The pair had only just clambered in when we heard the shouting of an order and tramping of feet, and half a company of foot with fixed bayonets dashed up to the wagon, the light within having attracted attention. At the moment it looked like escaping from one great peril to plunge into another; but, frantic with excitement, Denham saved us by his shout: "Hurrah! Prisoners; help!"

A young officer sprang into the wagon, sword in hand, followed by half-a-dozen of his men with bayonets levelled at us; but the officer halted the men.

"Prisoners," he cried excitedly, "or a ruse?"

"Get out!" shouted Denham. "Do you take me for a Dutchman? Look at our hands and feet."

A sergeant sprang forward and took the swinging lantern from the hook, opened its door, and, as he held it down, they saw our horribly swollen and useless limbs, with the hide-thongs just freshly cut through.

"Who did that?" asked the young officer.

"My young brother here," I said quickly; "we were just going to try and escape."

"Ah!" cried the young man sharply, as an angry murmur ran round the group. "You couldn't escape with feet like that. I mean, who tied you up in that brutal way?"

"The Boers!" cried Denham passionately, for his face was convulsed, and he looked hysterical and weak now.

The soldiers uttered a fierce yell, and as others crowded to back and front I heard a burst of excited ejaculations, oaths, and threats.

"'Tention!" shouted the officer.

"Now then," he cried, "who are you? Oh, I see you both belong to the Light Horse."

"Yes," I said, for Denham was speechless. "They took us last night as we were trying to creep through their lines to come to you for help."

"Ah!" cried the officer.

"They said we were spies, and we were to be shot at daybreak."

"We've come and shot them instead," said the officer. His men inside and out burst into a wild cheer. "But who are these? Boers?"

"No," I cried quickly. "My father and brother, who came to help us to escape."

"That's right," cried the officer, and the firing and cheering went on near at hand. Then he added hastily, "Sergeant and four men stop and help these gentlemen to the rear. Now, my lads, forward!"

He sprang out into the darkness, followed by his men, and we were left together, with my father down upon his knees holding me to his breast, and his lips close by my ear murmuring softly two words again and again— "Thank God! Thank God!" while Bob held on to one of my hands, jerking it spasmodically; and then I heard him cry out to one of the soldiers, "Don't stare at me like that! I can't help it. You'd be as bad if you were as young."

"What!" cried a rough voice. "Why, I'm 'most as bad, and I'm six-and-thirty; and here's big George wiping one eye on his cuff."

"Sweat, Sergeant, sweat," growled a rough voice, and there was a laugh from other three men.

"That was a lie, George," said the Sergeant. "Why don't you own up like a man?"

"Well, 'nuff to make any one turn soft when he's cooling down after a fight like this. Look at them two poor fellows here."

"Ah!" came in chorus, as the men standing around bent down in sympathy.

"'Tention!" cried the Sergeant. "Here. Files one and three mount guard front and rear of this dropsical timber-wagon. Two and four get some water. First aid here. Stop a minute. No; kneel down and just rub their legs gently as if you were trying to take out those furrows made by the ropes.—Why, your legs and feet are like stone, sir."

"Are they?" said Denham, quietly now, as he reached forward to shake the Sergeant's hand. "I didn't know—I don't feel as if I had any legs at all. There," he added excitedly, "I want to shake hands with you all round. It's so much better than being shot in the morning."

"Ay—ay!" cried the men eagerly.

"Oh, never mind our hurts."

"But we must, sir. I didn't know you were an orfficer at first," said the Sergeant. "I say, look at your head."

"I can't," said Denham, with a faint attempt at mirth which was very pitiful.

"Well, I can, sir, and you can look at your comrade's. Did the Boers do that too?"

"No," cried Denham fiercely; "it was a brute of a renegade Irishman serving with the Boers."

"Is he out yonder now, sir?" said the Sergeant, giving his head a side jerk in the direction from which, in the darkness, came the sound of cheering and scattered shots.

"Yes, I believe so," said Denham.

"Then I'm sorry for him, that's all," said the Sergeant dryly.

"Ah! Do you think your men are whipping them?"

"Think!" cried the Sergeant scornfully. "Think, sir? Why, we've got at 'em at last with the bay'net. They've been playing at shooting behind a stone and firing at a target—targets being us—till we've been sick of it, and then up on horse and gallop away; but we've got at 'em at last with the bay'net, and there's no need to think."

"But," I cried excitedly, as I strained my ears to listen, "they're coming back."

"Eh?" cried the Sergeant. "Here, files two and four support one and three. Hold your fire till they're close in, and then receive 'em on your bay'nets."

The two men who were chafing our deadened ankles sprang to their places, while my brother reached out of the side of the wagon and dragged in two rifles, evidently their own, and Denham and I cocked the revolvers we had thrust back into our breasts.

"That's good business, gentlemen," said the Sergeant grimly. "I like to see reinforcements when one's in a tight place."

He patted Bob on the shoulder as my brother took his place beside the two soldiers at the front of the wagon, my father going to the back.

"You can shoot, then, my lad?"

"Oh yes," said Bob quietly. "My father taught me five years ago."

"That's right," said the Sergeant, and he set the lantern on one side and covered it closely with one of the rugs. "Now, silence. We don't want to invite attack. Here they come! They're mounted men, and they may sweep past. Hear that bugle?" he said to me.

"Yes," I replied, almost below my breath.

"Officers hear them coming. Prepare for cavalry. Here they come. They've rallied, and— No, no. Hark! Hark! Hurrah! No, no; don't cheer, my lads. They're racing for their lives, and there's a line of cavalry after them."

"Hurrah, Val!" shouted Denham wildly. "Our Light Horse out and at 'em at last!"

"Oh," I groaned, "and we not with them now!"

"But they're sweeping after them in full charge, and sabring right and left. Look—look! I can see it all. No, no," he groaned; "it's as dark as pitch.— But they're scattering them, Sergeant?"

"Like chaff, sir, and— Hark at that!"

Crack! crack! Two volleys rang out.

"I hope that has not gone through to friends," growled the Sergeant. "Ah, all right, gentlemen; there goes the 'Cease firing.' They know your Light Horse have been let loose. The Boers won't stand after this, so we may sing 'God save the Queen!' 'Rule Britannia!' and the rest of it. This fight's won, boys. Silence in the ranks!"

He was just in time to stop a cheer, after which we listened to the sounds of the engagement or pursuit, now growing more distant, and I asked a question or two of my father, who now returned to my side.

"Your aunt, my boy? She is safe in Pietermaritzburg. The farmhouse was burned to the ground, all the sheep and cattle commandeered, and your brother and I forced into the Boer ranks."

I could ask no more questions for a few moments; but Denham was not restrained by his feelings, and I heard him ask the Sergeant:

"But how was it you came to the help of the Light Horse, Sergeant? Did you know we were shut up?"

"Not till yesterday morning or this morning at daybreak, sir. The General knew your corps was missing, and that there was a strong force of Boers camped out this way; but we were precious badly shut up ourselves, and could get no proper communications for want of cavalry. Our officers did nothing but swear about your corps for keeping away when they would have been so useful."

"But how did you get to know at last?"

"Through a big nigger dressed up in two white ostrich-feathers, a bit of skin, and an assagai and shield for walking-stick and cloak. He brought the news, and as soon as the General had proved him a bit, two foot-regiments, ours and 'Yellow Terror Tories,' were sent off to make a forced march. That black—Joeboy he called himself—brought us up within striking distance, and then he went off to warn them in that old ruin that we were coming, so that they might be ready to copyrate with us."

"But didn't they suspect that the black might be going to lead you into a trap?"

"At first, sir; but when he took our young lieutenant and some of our fellows as scouts, with orders to shoot him on the slightest sign of treachery, and he showed us where the Boers lay in the plain, and where we could take possession of a kopje on to which our men could march and act quite unseen, and where we could have defended ourselves against ten times our number, we knew it was all right."

"And you got there unseen?" said Denham.

"That's right, sir; and then the Colonel in command of both lots let this Crystal Minstrel go to warn the cavalry."

"He has done his work cleverly, Sergeant, or our corps could not have worked with you so well."

"That's right again, sir. I quite took to that chap, Joeboy, as he called himself; but it's a pity he's so jolly black."

I had been listening quietly while all this talk went on; but, with a heavy and fast-increasing feeling of depression, I could restrain myself no longer, and exclaimed, "Oh Denham, suppose the poor fellow's killed!"

"What, sir!" cried the Sergeant cheerily. "Killed? Who's to kill a chap like that on a dark night? Nobody could see where to hit. Besides, he goes through grass and bushes and rocks like a short, thick boa-constructor. He'll turn up all right. Hurrah! Hear that?"

We could hear, distinctly enough, repeated bugle-calls and the frantic cheering of our men. Our little forces had gained a complete victory, scattering the enemy in all directions, the morning light showing the terrible destruction caused by our onslaught.

Chapter Forty Seven
A Clear Sky

The rising sun showed that the enemy had disappeared; but ample stores had been secured for those who had so long suffered severe privations.

"Val," said Denham, "we must ride with our troop this week."

"Of course," I said cheerfully; but I had my doubts. Some time later, after we had met our comrades again, we had a long visit from the Colonel.

"Look here, young fellows," he said; "you're both invalids and cripples, so I'll wait till you're well before I have an inquiry into your conduct in leaving the fort without leave. I'm too busy now, and you are both too weak; but it will wait a bit. This matter must be thoroughly investigated."

"He'll never say another word about it, Val," prophesied Denham.

He never did.

Immediately after our interview with our Colonel, Denham and I lay in our wagon—ours by right of conquest—with the doctor looking at our injuries in evident perplexity.

"I never saw such a pair of scamps," he said. "Why, if every man behaved in the same way the life of a regimental surgeon wouldn't be worth living. Just as if I hadn't enough to attend to. Always in trouble."

"Don't bully us, doctor," said Denham, "we're both in such pain."

"Of course you are, my dear boys; so I'm going to have this wagon made into a sick-room for you."

"Into a what?" cried Denham. "Nonsense; we want to join the ranks again to-morrow."

"I suppose so," said the doctor fiercely; "but—you—will—not. Your wrists are bad enough, but look at your legs."

"Bah! Hideous!" cried Denham. "Who wants to look at them?"

"Then your head's not healed. Now, my dear boys, experience has told me that in this country very slight injuries develop into terrible ulcers and other blood-poisoning troubles. That renegade beast you tell me about is to answer for your limbs being in a very bad condition, and it will take all I know to set them right."

"But, doctor, I wouldn't have cared if they were good honest wounds."

"All wounds are wounds, sir, and injuries are injuries, to a surgeon. Frankly, neither of you must put a foot to the ground for weeks."

"Oh doctor!" we exclaimed together.

"My dear boys, trust me," he said. "I want to see you stout men, not cripples on crutches, and— How dare you, you black-looking scoundrel!"

"Joeboy!" we shouted together excitedly. "Jump in. Hurrah!"

As the doctor had spoken we noticed Joeboy's black face, with gleaming eyes and grinning mouth, rising above the big box at the end of the wagon. He wanted no further orders, but swung himself in lightly.

"Um?" he exclaimed. "Boss Val, Boss Denham right?"

"Yes," I cried, holding out my hand, which he took. "Joeboy, you frightened me; I thought you were killed."

"Um? Joeboy killed? What for? Been look all among the dead ones and broken ones; um dead quite."

"Who's dead?" I cried.

"Um? Ugly white boss captain, Irish boss Boer. Joeboy meant to kill um, but um run away too."

"That will do," said the doctor. "Just listen to my orders before I go off to the poor fellows waiting for me. You two are not to set foot to the ground. Promise me. I'll let you keep that black fellow to lift you about. He will do so, I suppose?" he added, turning to me.

"He will. He'd be only too glad."

The doctor rose, nodded, and went away; and soon after we had visits from the colonels of both the regiments, and from the young captain who had saved us from the zeal of his men, all these visitors congratulating us warmly upon our escape, and praising Joeboy for his bravery.

That afternoon we were on the march in what Denham called our peripatetic hospital; but he was not happy. Pain and disappointment seemed always uppermost in spite of the friendly attentions we received from his brother-officers.

"Yes, it's all very good of you," he said sadly; "but fancy being laid aside now, after the Boers have been thrashed and there's nothing to do but give them the finishing-cuts to make them behave better in the future."

As days glided by, Denham, to his surprise, learned that there was no more fighting to do.

First of all, our little forces of the Light Horse and the infantry were depressed by the news that the General, with the main body, had met with a terrible reverse from the Boers, whose peculiar way of fighting had stood them in good stead and made up for the qualities they lacked.

Thus the making of history rolled on; and, to the rage and indignation of the fighting-men, the order went forth that there was to be peace; that the troops were to be withdrawn, volunteers disbanded, and everything settled by diplomacy and treaty. I need not go into that matter; my father only shook his head and said that such an arrangement could never mean lasting peace.

"I'm glad the fighting is over, my boys," father said to Denham, who was sharing our new temporary home.

"Oh, Mr Moray," he replied, "how can you talk like that?"

"Because I am a man of the ploughshare and not of the sword. I want to get back to my quiet farming life again, and that is impossible while war devastates the land."

"But you'll never start a home again in the old place?"

"Never," said my father—"never."

"No," I said; "the Boers ruined you. They ought to be made to pay."

"Not ruined, Val," said my father, "though the burning and destruction meant a serious loss; but I had not been idle all the years I was there, and I dare say we can soon raise a home in Natal, where we can be at peace. Nature is very kind out here in this sunny, fruitful land; and I dare say when Mr Denham comes to see us, as I hope he will often do in the future, we can make him as comfortable as in the past days when the farm was younger, and perhaps find him a little hunting and shooting within reach."

"You'll come, Denham?" I said.

"Come? Too much, I'm afraid. I'm to have no more soldiering, I hear. I've been corresponding with my people, and asking my father if it is possible for me to get into the regulars. He wrote back 'No,' with three lines underneath, and said I must go back to stock-raising till my country wants me again to unsheath the sword."

"Well," said my father, smiling, "what do you say to that?"

"Nothing at all, sir," replied Denham, with a smile. "Somehow I always do what I'm told."

"That's what makes him such a good soldier, father," I said, laughing.

"Do you hear that, Bob?" said Denham. "You ought to take example from me. But, I say, can't we have the horses out for a run?"

"Of course," said my father, "if you feel strong enough."

"Oh, I'm strong enough now," replied Denham. "Nothing whatever's the matter, except that one leg gives way sometimes. Here, let's go and rouse up Joeboy. Will you come with us, Bob?"

That question was unnecessary; and soon Joeboy the faithful and true had brought round Sandho, Denham's horse, and a fine young cob the black had captured on the night of the fight and given to my brother.

The horses were all fresh and sprightly from want of work; and when the three were brought to the veranda of the farm which my father had leased for a time, Aunt Jenny—who had rejoined us, and was looking as if nothing had occurred—warned us to be careful, for the horses looked very fresh.

We promised to be careful, and were off cantering towards the veldt, the horses soon making the dust fly beneath their hoofs in a wild gallop.

"Oh Val," cried Denham, with flashing eyes, "isn't this glorious?"

"Delightful," I replied.

"Doesn't it make you think of being in the troop once more?"

"No," I said bluntly; "and I hope we shall never again ride knee to knee to cut down men."

"But if the need should arise," he shouted, "you would volunteer again—yes, and you too, Bob?"

"Of course," cried my brother, flushing; "and so would Val."

"You hear that, Val?" said Denham. "Don't say you wouldn't come and help?"

"How can I?" was my reply. "This is sandy Africa, with savages who might rise at any time; but I am English born, with a touch of Scottish blood, I believe."

"I've got a dash of Irish in mine," said Denham. "I say, shall we ever see Moriarty again?"

"I hope not," I answered, turning red up to my hair.

"I don't want to see him now," Denham said. "But answer my question, Val. Will you volunteer again if a bad time comes!"

"So long as you mount a horse, and want me," I answered.

It was very stupid and boyish; but we were excited, I suppose, with the motion of our horses and the elasticity of the morning air. Just then Bob rose in his stirrups in answer to a sign from Denham, clapped his fist to his mouth, and brought forth a capital imitation of a trumpet's blast, which made the horses stretch out and tear away close together over the open veldt as if in answer to the cry which thrilled me with recollections. For Denham, too, had risen in his stirrups, thrown his hand above his head, and shouted, "Charge!"